DISGUISED
with the
Millionaire

Romancing With Danger Series

Debra Andrews

ELUSIVE STAR PRESS

DISGUISED WITH THE MILLIONAIRE

ISBN: 978-0-9881805-3-6

This is a work of fiction. Names, characters, places and incidents are either the product of the author's imagination or are used fictitiously, and any resemblance to actual persons, living or dead, business establishments, events or locals is entirely coincidental.

Editor, Patricia Thomas

Photos for cover from:
bigstockphoto.com
RomanceNovelCovers.com

Printed in the U.S.A.

DEDICATION

This one is for my sisters and my mom.
You are the best.

ACKNOWLEDGMENTS

I'd like to thank all those who helped me with this story, my incredibly patient sisters, my critique partners over the years, and other writer friends who have helped with this book.

I'd like to give a final thanks to my fabulous editor Patricia Thomas.

****

OTHER BOOKS AVAILABLE BY DEBRA ANDREWS

ROMANCING WITH DANGER SERIES

WEEKEND WEDDING DECEPTION

DANGEROUS PARADISE

HIS WYOMING LAIR
(Coming soon!)

CHAPTER ONE

Kate Meyers rushed through the glass doors leading into the hospital's emergency waiting room. "I'm here to see Matt Jackson," she said breathlessly as she reached the main desk. "He was brought in by ambulance a few hours ago."

The receptionist glanced over wire-rimmed glasses. "Next of kin?"

Kate blinked back tears. "Yes, I'm his stepsister. Is he going to be all right?"

"Miss, I'll notify the doctor that you're here. Now, please, take a seat."

"Kate." She turned at the familiar voice of Matt's good friend and co-worker.

"What happened, Bobby?" she asked.

Dressed in a t-shirt, jeans and scuffed construction boots, he ran his fingers through his brown hair. "Matt was working on the fifth floor. His harness broke and for a few minutes he dangled from the line. Then his tether snapped. I'm sorry, Kate."

She gasped. "You mean he fell five floors?"

"A tree broke his fall, and he's alive. We've got to hold on to that."

Kate collapsed onto a couch and dropped her tear-stained face into her hands. "Last week, he told me he'd discovered a piece of equipment he'd used was nearly worn out, and some of the materials seemed sub-standard. He promised me he'd be careful when he worked at those heights."

She shuddered and went on, "Something was going on there, Bobby. Matt told me that when he asked about the condition of some of the supplies, his supervisor said Trent Farrington must be trying to save money and he was told to keep his nose out of it if he wanted a paycheck." Sniffling, she pressed a tissue to her nose. "I pleaded with Matt to leave such a dangerous and corrupt outfit."

"Kate, in my department, I've never seen the Farringtons run anything but a reputable company," Bobby said.

"Ms. Meyers." The receptionist waved Kate over to the desk. "They moved him to ICU. You can go back to be with him now."

When she reached Matt's door, a doctor in green scrubs stepped out. "He's stabilized, but in critical condition. We'll know more, if he makes it through the night."

If he makes it through the night. Kate's knees nearly buckled. "Is he awake?" she asked in a shaky voice.

"He's been in and out, but he hasn't fully regained consciousness."

When she stepped into the room, her stomach clenched at the bruises marring her brother's face. Swathed in bandages, he lay on the bed, hooked to an IV and numerous monitors.

Tears blurred her vision as she walked on shaky legs to his side. "Matt, it's me—Kate."

His eyes flickered open.

Relief rushed through her. Swiping away the wetness from her cheeks with the back of her hand, she leaned closer. "I love you."

Through each labored breath, he rasped out the words, "The supplies...grandson... Trent...tell...found..."

She rested her palm over his cold hand and choked back a sob. "Matt, please, don't talk. Save your strength."

"Jeopardizes...integrity...building..." He groaned and panted between his words.

He closed his eyes and drifted away from her. Only the hum of the machines broke the silence as the minutes passed.

Breathing in the strong medicinal odors, she laid her face against the cool white sheets on the edge of the bed. He had to be okay. Everything in their lives was getting better. She'd been on her way to tell him the newspaper had hired her to take over her late Aunt Kate's local advice column. However, none of that mattered now.

"Supplies..." he murmured. Kate raised her head and leaned over him. His icy fingers rubbed hers, as if desperate for her to understand something. "Farrington...*Trent*..."

She sucked in her breath. He was the owner's grandson and vice president of Farrington Construction—Matt's employer. "Is Trent Farrington responsible for your accident?" she demanded.

"Tell…police…" Matt closed his eyes. Suddenly, an alarm went off on one of the monitors.

"Matt, no," Kate cried. "Please don't leave me." Her stepbrother had been her rock in this life and had protected her from her stepfather and other evils of the world more times than she could count.

Within seconds, a team of nurses and doctors entered with a crash cart and surrounded her brother.

A doctor yelled, "He's flatlining! Get this lady out of here."

A nurse propelled Kate into the corridor.

Fifteen minutes later, a hospital staffer stepped into the hallway and put an arm around Kate's shoulders. "I'm sorry, dear. We couldn't revive him."

"But I—"

"There's nothing you can do. He's gone."

In the waiting area, Kate collapsed on a couch beside his friend, Bobby. She buried her face in her hands and let the tears flow. "He's never going to get married, or have children, or do any of those things he dreamed of doing. I just can't believe he's gone. He was my hero and meant the world to me."

There was nothing she could do…

* * *

Six months later, Kate entered the plush executive offices of Farrington Construction in downtown Fort Lauderdale. Still shaky after her horrific ride in the glass elevator, she took a seat in the reception area, glad to have a moment to calm herself. She hated heights.

She had arrived thirty minutes early for her appointment, hoping to get a glimpse of the competition for the Human Resources Manager position in the company that had employed her stepbrother. *Could she really go through with this?*

With a trembling hand, she reached into her briefcase and extracted the envelope containing the four-month-old newspaper article. She held it and reminded herself why she had to get this job, why *she* had to find the person responsible for Matt's death. After months of nothing from the Occupational Safety and Health Administration, and the police, she had finally decided it was up to her to find justice for Matt. She'd been unable to forget Matt's last words, or to let it go. She was determined that the company, and whoever was responsible or negligent, wouldn't get away with it.

It's all up to me to get irrefutable evidence. I'm going to find out who is responsible, Matt. Pushing her glasses further up on her nose, she reread the devastating news again:

> **Tropical News** – **Fort Lauderdale** – Police have cleared Farrington Construction of any wrongdoing in the death of employee Matthew Jackson who failed to take proper safety precautions. Trenton Farrington, spokesperson for the company, said he was satisfied with the results of the investigation, having complied with the Occupational Safety and Health Administration's regulations (OSHA) and the highest of safety standards…

Kate put the article away. *The highest of safety standards!* The pain of her brother's death returned like a reopened wound. *Yeah, she knew in her gut that someone in this company was responsible.*

Even so, OSHA and the police had cleared the company. Afterwards, Farrington, a handsome man with dark hair and dark eyes, had been on every local news channel where he'd put on a grave face. He called Matt's death an 'unfortunate tragedy which had taken a promising young man from his family.' However, Kate didn't think Farrington felt anything close to what he described.

Farrington had gone on to say Matt had violated long-standing safety measures by not checking his harness. To Kate, he'd made it sound as if Matt had been a careless hothead who'd gotten exactly what he deserved. She had wanted to throw something at the television to obliterate the man's strikingly handsome face.

To calm herself, Kate took in several cleansing breaths. She wasn't about to blow her cover, or change her plan now. She glanced around the lavish office with its costly furniture and expensive oriental rugs on highly polished hardwood floors. Obviously, the company was prosperous.

A woman with an upswept hairdo, and wearing an expensive suit, sat beside her in the waiting area. "Are you here for the interview, too?"

Her palms were perspiring as Kate nodded and clutched the briefcase on her lap. In comparison to this sophisticated woman, Kate had arranged her blond hair into a tight, plain bun. Her simple suit was anything but stylish. However, she hoped she appeared older than her twenty-six years.

"I'm sure they want experience, honey. I have a master's degree and over twenty years with several well-known large corporations." She pushed her sharp nose closer. "And your credentials?"

Kate lifted her chin. "*I have* some experience."

"Probably not enough." The woman turned her attention back to the business magazine on her lap.

Kate shrugged. The truth was she'd worked at the Children's Crisis Center and hired the occasional worker. While she had majored in psychology, she had minored in human resources in college. It was nothing in comparison, but she wasn't going to divulge anything to her.

Thankfully, after she'd made the appointment for the interview, she'd gotten the idea of embellishing her own credentials with that of her late great-aunt Katherine, who'd been a psychologist. She was the last of Kate's blood relatives and had always been called Kate, too. Aunt Kate had died three years ago, so Kate didn't think her charade could hurt anyone. The name was close—except Kate's full name was Katelyn.

Kate would prefer to use her own credentials completely, but she didn't think she would stand a chance to get the job.

Another professional-looking applicant in a dark suit exited the office where the interviews being held. "Thank you, Mr. Farrington." The applicant shook the hand of an elderly man who, despite his age, had a full head of wavy gray hair and was dressed in a navy suit that oozed wealth and power.

James Farrington. Kate gulped. When she did her research, she'd seen his picture. He was the patriarch of the company and probably knee-deep and in cahoots with his grandson—the man who was probably taking risks with employee safety so he could skim money off the top.

"Mr. Clark, you'll be hearing from us," James Farrington said. "We have several more applicants to interview before we make our final decision." He returned to his office.

Can I really go through with this? All she had to do was walk out the door and this charade would end, but she sat frozen in her chair.

Mr. James Farrington's secretary ushered in the snarky woman who'd quizzed Kate earlier. Fifteen minutes later, the woman exited the office. "Good luck, honey," she said with a confident smile as she strode by Kate on her way out.

Kate winced. It was obvious the woman was confident of her success and didn't think Kate stood a chance to get the job.

Mr. Farrington strode into the waiting area. When his gaze roamed over Kate, a smile tugged at his lips. "Come on in, my dear," he said and waved her inside. "I'm James Farrington, President of Farrington Construction and Farrington Enterprises. Can I get you anything? Coffee? Water?" he asked politely.

"No, thank you."

"Then let's get started." He waved his hand toward a chair and sat across from her behind his desk. She sat down primly. "We're looking for an immediate replacement for our Human Resources Manager who was forced to retire because of ill health." While he scanned her resume, her stomach knotted. "I see you're a psychologist?" He gazed at her over the rim of his reading glasses.

"Yes, sir." She hated to lie. One day it would be the truth if her studies paid off, and she justified her lie because she needed to get into the company to get evidence against James Farrington's grandson.

"Why, your being a psychologist might be handy around here with…" He cocked a shaggy, gray eyebrow. "The name *Dr. Kate Meyers* does sound familiar."

She could be in serious trouble if he remembered her aunt. "So you've heard of my reputation?"

"I believe I have." He said nothing more, but gave her a shrewd look. "So, you're not engaged? Married? Have any children or anything?"

Why was he asking her these questions? "No," she said, puzzled.

He smiled brightly. "*Good.*"

Kate locked her gaze on his and frowned. Surely, he wasn't hitting on her at his age. He must know those were illegal questions to ask an employee in this day and age, too.

As if he read her mind, he shrugged and returned an almost boyish grin, his baby-blue eyes twinkling. "I'm asking because if you take the job you need to be aware that on occasion there might be long hours here at the office." He studied her for a moment. "Do you have any experience hiring construction personnel?"

She shook her head. "No, but I am a quick learner."

He asked her more questions about her background in human resources. She told him the truth about the Children's Crisis Center.

"All right, Dr. Meyers. I'm hiring you on the spot. I like you. I think you'll be good for the company." Shock spread through her when she realized she'd landed the position. "Now don't worry about not having a construction company background. I have just the person to help you—my grandson, Trent Farrington. He likes to have his hands in all aspects of the business."

Kate's back grew rigid. "I'm sure he does," she muttered.

"Trent is our vice president. He's not in the office today or I would introduce you to him." He leaned toward her. "He's second in command and runs the company's day-to-day operations. Nothing goes on around here that Trent isn't aware of. I can't tell you how proud I am of him. Under his watchful eye our profits have soared."

"I'm sure they have." She gritted her teeth. *Cheating, liar—Trent Farrington!* Her stepbrother had lost his life because of that man. Any guilt she felt over lying to get the job, evaporated. "And thank you so much, Mr. Farrington. I look forward to working here."

Her research told her that for forty-seven years, James Farrington had run a reputable company, but something had changed recently—and not in a good way. Her instincts told her where to firmly place the blame and now she was sure she'd been right. This elderly gentleman probably had no idea those high profits came at the expense of quality and on-site safety and that his grandson was probably skimming money from the company.

Mr. Farrington strode to the door. "Allow me." He ushered her into the reception area. "You can start on Monday. Your first duty will be to hire someone to work as your assistant. Do you have anyone in mind that could fill the position?"

She thought about that for a moment. Her best friend, Darcy, needed a job. While she didn't want Darcy involved with her investigation into the company, it would be nice to have her in the office for support.

Kate nodded. "I do know someone."

"I hope she's as pretty as you are."

Kate narrowed her eyes. She didn't think she had dressed attractively at all. In fact, she thought she'd succeeded to look downright plain.

He chuckled. "I mean qualified as well, dear. Don't mind me. Please don't think I'm a dirty old man or a chauvinist, but I have to admit that most of my loyal staff is aging alongside me. We need some younger blood around here."

Kate relaxed her shoulders. "Yes, Mr. Farrington, she is pretty."

At his age, he had to be harmless. She could forgive him because he was from a different era. She'd ask Darcy if she'd like to work at the company between jobs.

As she walked out of Mr. Farrington's office, she thought she heard him whistling "Here Comes the Bride."

Seriously? Confusing, to say the least.

Inhaling a deep breath, Kate stepped down the outside steps and into the Florida sunshine. She had succeeded in landing the job. She'd have access to the records at the company and would be able to prove the truth—that they were cheating. *So, Trent Farrington's hands were in all aspects of the business?* If she could prove he traded the safety of his employees and the integrity of his projects to beef up his profits, she'd nail him to a wall.

Matt deserved justice. She owed it to her brother for all the beatings he'd taken in her place. If it was the last thing she did, she would see that Trent Farrington rotted in prison.

* * *

The following Monday, Kate marched down the sidewalk of Las Olas Boulevard like a general going to battle, her co-conspirator, Darcy King, at her heels. When they neared Farrington Towers, they paused. The building soared skyward, resplendent in dark green marble and framed against a blue, cloudless sky.

A chill ran up Kate's spine. She was about to play the masquerade of her life, and it all seemed too real now. How had she ever thought she could take on the rich and powerful Farringtons? It was one thing if she were caught in this crazy scheme to get evidence to convict Trent Farrington, but she didn't want her friend Darcy implicated or hurt.

As if she'd read her thoughts, her friend asked, "Do you really think we can get away with this?"

With her cute upturned nose, smattering of freckles on her pale face, and her bubbly personality, Darcy appeared so innocent. No one would suspect her of anything underhanded.

Kate sighed. "I have to. If you have any second thoughts, don't worry. I can do this by myself."

Flipping a short, carrot-red curl behind her ear, Darcy—originally from Georgia—said in her slight southern accent, "You need my help, plus I owe you. Anyway, I find this exciting. I feel like Darcy King, Secret Agent, reporting for duty."

Kate gave her a tentative smile. "This is serious, remember? If we're caught, we might be in trouble, or at least I could be for lying about my credentials to get the job."

"You know I have your back, but I really just want to see you happy and carefree...with all of this behind you."

"Carefree is something I've never been able to be, Darcy."

"You can be, Kate. Matt's dad can't hurt you anymore."

"I'll smile again when I have the evidence," Kate said, wanting to wipe that concerned look from Darcy's freckled face.

Darcy's red curls blew in the breeze as they continued down the sidewalk. "They must be rich enough if they own all of this. Maybe they bought someone off?"

"I don't know. And now we're risking coming here...and I'm putting my education on hold to do the job the police investigators should have done."

Just the thought of letting this big corporation get away with Matt's death seared her soul and ruined her concentration. To resolve this was worth putting her psychology master's program on hold, and so much more.

They climbed the entry stairs. Squaring her shoulders, Kate swung open the door, allowing her friend to go in first.

In the magnificent lobby, cream-colored marble adorned the walls and floors. Water cascaded from a three-tiered fountain. They passed an oil painting of the company's founding father, Joshua Farrington, dating back to the late 1800s. Kate noted again, as she had on the day of her interview, he had been a good-looking man with thick brown hair and midnight-blue eyes. Good looks must run in the family.

After signing in with the main desk and getting a key to her new office, Kate spotted the elevators across the crowded lobby. A sinking feeling lodged in her stomach. "I hate glass elevators. Last time I was here, I thought I'd faint."

Darcy clasped Kate's elbow. "Maybe you should close your eyes while we ride."

Kate winced. "And how professional would that look? If I want this to work, I have to get over my fear of heights." She inhaled a deep breath as she and Darcy joined the growing group of people waiting to board.

A tall, gangly man, with light brown hair spun around, his blue eyes shining behind wire-framed glasses. He smiled as he shook his head. "State-of-the-art building, with two million dollars in Italian marble and granite floors, home to eight large corporations, several prestigious law firms and more, and only one out of eight elevators work. Go figure."

Kate glanced toward the doors of the stairwell. She shuddered at the long climb to the offices of Farrington Construction which occupied the top four floors of the forty-five story structure. Stairs weren't her thing either. The second step of a ladder was higher than she liked to be.

She frowned at the clock on the wall. "Do you know how much longer before they're all running?"

"No. Last week it took several hours. Nervous? First day on the job?"

Were her sweaty palms that obvious? She forced a smile. "Yes. I don't want to be late."

"Welcome to the building. I'm Greg Dalton, head computer programmer at Farrington Construction. Which company in the building do you work for?"

"I'm with…" She turned to gather Darcy into the introduction, but her friend stared, as if mesmerized, at a man striding through the lobby.

Kate pushed her glasses farther up her nose for a closer glimpse. *Trent Farrington.* Tall, dark and handsome, he was even better looking in the flesh than he appeared on TV.

He wore a gray suit, which didn't hide his muscular physique and the tailoring only emphasized the width of his shoulders. He moved across the lobby with casual masculine grace. Kate balled her fists. *An orange prison jumpsuit would be more appropriate for him.*

He might look like a Greek god, or a movie star with his nearly black hair and his muscled body, but she knew that on the inside he was an ugly crook.

However, when he stopped nearby to wait in line, Kate couldn't deny that on the surface, he was one of the most attractive men she'd ever seen. While he was nearly an exact likeness of his ancestor in the portrait near the entrance, Trent Farrington had darker hair and eyes. The man had a sensuous mouth and eyes that could seduce a woman without even trying. Women probably threw themselves at him.

Anger sizzled inside Kate. She clenched her teeth and angled away from his direction.

"Excuse me for a moment, I see my boss," Greg said. "I'll be right back. Save my place?"

"Sure," Kate murmured, only half listening. She hadn't expected to see Farrington so soon.

The *boss* Greg walked over to was Trent Farrington—the *devil incarnate* himself.

Kate gulped and glanced toward her friend who gawked as if she'd never seen a man before. "Stop it... Please." Darcy had a weakness for good-looking men and that was one of the major reasons her heart had been broken numerous times. Kate knew because she had been there to mop up Darcy's tears on several occasions.

"That's Trent Farrington?" Darcy whispered. "Whoa. You didn't tell me he was so freakin' hot."

Kate shrugged and said in the same low tone, "My stepfather was all looks with no soul, too, so just remember who we're dealing with. Not only is Farrington crooked, but he also has a reputation for breaking hearts. He's a player."

"But now I know why he was written up in that magazine as 'Bachelor of the Year.'"

In the photo on the cover, Kate remembered he had leaned against a Porsche with a group of women surrounding him. She didn't confess to Darcy she'd saved the article to remind her of the lavish lifestyle he led with the money he'd stolen from the company, the money that should have gone toward safety of his employees before feathering his nest. Farrington had better enjoy his playboy life now, for it would soon end.

She glanced at him again and gritted her teeth. It was ironic. An evil person shouldn't be so handsome. He looked like he owned the world in every way. Being rich and handsome probably helped him get away with whatever he wanted—illegal or otherwise.

Livid tears burned Kate's eyes. He had everything and could have contributed in good ways to the world, but he chose to cheat. *Didn't he care who was hurt in the process?*

Her eyes welled up as she whirled to face the crowd in front of her. This man had taken the last person in her family away from her––but she couldn't break down on her first day at work no matter how badly she felt. And she had to accept that no matter what she did to this man, nothing would bring Matt back.

Darcy tapped her shoulder. "Are you all right?"

Kate nodded and dabbed at her eyes with her fingers. "I just thought of Matt again. I'll be fine in a moment."

After another group boarded the only working elevator, Kate shuffled forward in the line with the rest of the crowd that still waited. Just knowing Trent Farrington stood nearby caused the skin on the back of her neck to prickle. She hoped they boarded soon, but knew that was unlikely. There were at least forty people in front of them.

"Trent," Greg said over Kate's shoulder, "allow me to introduce you to…" He turned to Kate and Darcy. "By the way, what *are* your names?" he asked.

Kate's spine stiffened and panic swept through her. Could she face an introduction to him *now*? However, she had no choice and composed herself quickly. She took a deep breath and pivoted to face them. She found Farrington right there, with no one and no space between them.

Trent Farrington's gorgeous body and his black heart now stood too close for comfort—jolting her senses. He flicked his gaze over her, frowned and gave her a brief nod, then turned to Darcy.

Kate raised her chin a notch. She wasn't surprised his interest diverted so quickly. Her friend dressed for attention in her quirky clothes. Today, Darcy wore a multicolored dress with high-heeled boots. Kate was aware how dowdy she must appear next to her friend because she'd dressed in her conservative, brown suit and black-framed glasses. She wore her blond hair in a tight bun, severe compared to Darcy's riot of short, red curls.

Darcy dated often. Kate never did, but that suited Kate just fine. She'd found out the hard way she couldn't trust most men, especially handsome, charming ones. The way she dressed kept those shallow men away. *Perfect.*

When Darcy beamed an enraptured, toothy grin at Farrington, Kate clenched her teeth. Well, at least Darcy knew Farrington was corrupt so she shouldn't fall for him. For her, not being of interest to a man like him would make her task of finding evidence all that much easier.

Kate rolled her eyes. She thought with some satisfaction that with his good looks he might have a tough time in prison.

His gaze flicked back to Kate. Before she could register what that look meant, or before they could be introduced, a pretty brunette with shiny, shoulder-length hair strode across the marble floor. "Trent, *love*," she cooed when she neared him, "are you hiding from me? When did you return?"

"Yesterday," he answered.

The woman flung herself at Farrington. "I missed you. I'm so glad you're home."

In response, he stepped aside and bumped into Kate. As if seared by Satan, Kate jerked away—but a little too quickly. She lost her balance and flailed backwards. One of his hands skimmed the side of her breast just before his strong arms caught her around the waist. A whiff of his cologne wafted to her nose and disoriented her.

"My apologies," Trent Farrington said, so close that his breath warmed her ear.

Shock rushed through her, while the touch of his hands caused a flush of awareness that tingled to her toes. She tried to jerk away, but he didn't release her. Was he apologizing for touching her breast or for almost knocking her down? Why wasn't he more careful? He'd probably spent his life trampling over everyone in his path.

"Take your hands off me," she demanded. "*You…*"

He reared his head back in surprise but didn't let go.

The lobby grew quiet and people stared at them. Kate winced. So much for being discreet on her first day on the job.

In a deep voice, as smooth as satin, he said in her ear, "Calm down, sweetheart. It wasn't intentional. Just coming to your rescue."

Sweetheart? Leaning back in his arms, she glanced up at him. Their gazes locked. For a moment, despite her intention to give him a scathing look, she was transfixed. From close up, she could tell his eyes were as nearly black as his hair, but there were gold flecks that shot through them like sparks.

"Nice of you to help her, Trent." The pretty brunette's voice snapped Kate out of her trance. "But she seems fine to me."

Trent set Kate on her feet, but kept a steadying hand on the small of her back. She barely managed to stand on her wobbly legs.

The woman grasped Farrington's free arm in a possessive grip, while she swept a dismissive glance over Kate as if Kate couldn't possibly be a rival.

Trent removed his hand from Kate's back. "Greg?"

"Right here," Greg replied cheerfully. "Glad to take her off your hands," he teased, with a wink at Kate.

"I'm fine now, thank you," Kate murmured.

Greg stepped closer to her. "I still didn't get your name."

Before she could respond, the elevator doors opened. From the front of the line, a gray-haired man, in a sharp blue suit and with an air of authority gestured for Trent and Greg to come over. "Gentlemen," he said.

Greg smiled and shrugged. "It'll have to be another time. Business calls."

Along with Greg and the pretty brunette, Trent brushed past people who had waited twice as long. He explained to the waiting crowd, "I need to find out why the rest of the elevators aren't working."

Nobody seemed to mind missing the elevator and being late for work. Their voices and laughter filled the lobby.

Looking out from the elevator car, Kate caught Trent's gaze again. His brow furrowed and his eyes narrowed.

Heat flared on her cheeks. To her chagrin, she found that every inch of her body tingled as if it remembered his touch.

He dipped his head, giving her a brief, curious nod. Finally, the doors closed.

Kate's stomach plummeted to her toes and her heart pounded. Why had he looked at her in that manner? Had he recognized her from the police investigation? No, that was impossible. Their paths had never crossed. And as stepbrother and stepsister, she and Matt hadn't looked anything alike, or even had the same last name.

Trent Farrington had not been at the funeral either. She'd been too filled with grief to notice all who had attended from the company, but surely she wouldn't have missed *him*.

* * *

By the time the elevator neared the top floors of Farrington Towers, almost everyone had disembarked, except for Trent, Greg and Cecilia. Trent gazed down at the dark-haired woman. Cecilia worked in Purchasing and was the latest employee hired by his grandfather as Trent's potential bride.

"Why don't we do lunch?" she asked with her sexiest smile, as if he would fall for her attempts to ensnare him.

Trent raised an eyebrow. "I don't have the time."

She brushed her fingers along the lapel of his jacket. "I could always bring you something. How about lunch in your office?"

"But then I wouldn't get any work done," he said dryly.

Cecilia stood on her tiptoes. "I don't mind. Who needs *food*?" She blew her warm breath into his ear. Because her family and his were longtime friends, she might think she could get away with this public familiarity, but he needed to remind her they were at work.

Trent smiled and clasped her shoulders. She shut her eyes as if she expected him to kiss her. He wasn't sorry to disappoint her. "Don't you have some purchase orders to get out?" he asked. When the elevator doors opened on her floor, he turned her toward the door and gave her a gentle push.

She stepped out and glanced over her shoulder with a pout.

After the doors closed, Trent sighed in relief and ignored Greg's Cheshire Cat grin. He had to give Cecilia credit for her persistence these past couple of months. With respect to her looks, she was attractive enough to tempt any man. However, his mother had been in on the hiring of Cecilia to entice him, and he wasn't taking the bait. His early appointments easily took priority over her.

After they exited on the top floor, Greg said, "Cecilia's got it bad for you."

"Did you ever think it might be my *money* she has it bad for, Greg?"

"How do you get that? Her family's loaded. American blue bloods and all."

"Their fortune crashed in the real estate market. Cecilia lied and told me they were doing well. If there's one thing I despise, Greg— *it's a liar*. Cecilia needs a rich husband to bail them out of their bad investments. She probably thinks I'm their meal ticket."

When they entered his office, he stopped at his secretary's desk. The poor woman looked exhausted. Her thin, gray hair hung in wisps and wasn't done up in her usual style.

He frowned. He knew she'd been worried about her husband's health. "Good morning, Mrs. Nash. How's Norm today?"

She handed him his mail and said in her usual raspy voice, "As cantankerous as ever now that he's home from the hospital. Doesn't seem to think a mild heart attack is enough reason for retirement. Which means, Trent, you can look forward to a few more years of my services here."

Trent snorted. "Ah, wedded bliss."

"It is, most of the time." The obvious intent in her raised, gray eyebrows wasn't lost on him. Even his secretary pushed marriage on him.

"You're wasting your time trying to convince me, Mrs. Nash. Put in a call to Western and get Jack Prichard on the line for me. I need to find out what's going on with the elevators again."

"Yes, *Trent*," she said sweetly.

He grinned. "*Mr. Farrington* will do."

Mrs. Nash smirked. "Never called you that and never will. I've known you since you were a toddler. I even babysat you from time to time when your mother was rushing off on one of her European trips."

"Don't remind me," he said dryly.

"By the way, good morning, *Mr. Dalton*," she said with a wink toward Greg.

Trent chuckled. "If you need to leave early to check on Mr. Nash, one of the other secretaries can fill in for you."

"Thank you. Your mother called and said she is extending her vacation and hoped you wouldn't mind handling a few matters for her." His secretary handed him a long list that belied it was only a few small matters.

"That's just great. All I need is to have to handle the Ice Queen's responsibilities too." He strode into his office and sat down at his desk, putting the pile of paperwork in the center.

Greg plopped down on the sofa. "Hey, don't be so hard on her."

"Greg, she hates you. She calls you 'the geek.' Why defend her?"

His friend shrugged. "She's getting older."

"If only age would soften my mother. Not sure if anything can..."

"You know, Cecilia might be interested in you for other reasons," Greg said, picking up their previous conversation.

"You're dead set on a discussion about women, aren't you, while I've got a building with seven elevators not working?" Trent smiled grimly and leaned back in his chair. "All right. You saw the woman downstairs, the plain blonde with the ugly glasses? She didn't know who I was, and she wasn't impressed in the least. I could have been a bug on the floor that she'd like to squash, but if she heard the name *Farrington* associated with me..."

"She will. She works in the building, but I didn't get her name."

Frowning, Trent gave him a sideways glance. *Was Greg interested in the blonde?*

Greg shrugged. "Today was her first day, but I didn't find out which company in the building she works for. However, I did find her reaction to you amusing. It's true. Most women throw themselves at you. But this one, she fell into your arms, and then practically bit your head off. If looks could kill, buddy… Now there's a glitch if I ever saw one." Greg's shoulders shook with suppressed laughter.

"What's so funny?" Trent asked.

"In fact, I think she'd have preferred falling right to the floor. I like the woman already."

Trent opened a file and flipped through the papers. "Laugh at my expense," he remarked dryly. "She had a bite to her, but she hasn't had much acquaintance with the Farrington name." Trent glanced at Greg. "Money has a way of changing people. Sometimes, I wish I hadn't been born into such a wealthy and prominent family. Then, instead of taking on an established company, I'd have had to prove myself and make my own way."

"You are making your own way. You've taken this company to a new level, and you're going to win the State's award for the Karger building's design…and their contract." If that were true, Trent's building design would come to the attention of various builders across Florida.

"We *will* be the top construction company, if Frank Blake doesn't beat us. He'll do anything to overtake our position in the State. Even cheat."

Despite what he'd said about starting his own company, Farrington Construction was in his blood. His familial duty was to continue what his great-great-grandfather had started. Working hard labor after arriving from Ireland penniless, his forefather, Joshua Farrington had built this company for his family, from the ground up.

Trent sighed. He had achieved a measure of success these past two years and was close to putting his personal mark on the company's future, except for one terrible tragedy. This year, he'd lost a man on the job.

Now, his entire focus had to be mainly on the Karger project— keeping his crews safe and bringing the building to completion.

Still, his thoughts returned to the blonde in the lobby. With those thick glasses, he had barely noticed her at first. However when she'd fallen into his arms he had found quite a surprise hidden under the shapeless outfit, enough to stir his body to react. He'd embarrassed her, so he pretended he didn't notice that his hand had brushed her full breast as he caught her in his arms. What was curious was that, even before the incident, she seemed to dislike him for some reason. He wasn't used to that.

"What did you think of the redhead?" Greg asked, jarring Trent from contemplating the blonde. Before Trent could respond, Greg added, "I thought bright hair, dress too short. She probably hasn't a brain in her giggly head. Which makes her more *your type*."

"*Mine*? What makes you think I don't go for women with brains?" Trent placed his hand over his heart, pretending to be wounded, although what Greg said was pretty much true. Trent had not been looking for anything more serious than a good time. Meaningless, but satisfying sex was what he wanted, with no strings attached. That had been his mantra for years.

Greg rose from the couch. "By her expression, it was obvious the redhead was impressed. She seems to have it bad for you and she doesn't know who you are."

Trent swept his hand over the stacks of paper on his desk. "I've got bigger issues to worry about so I'll have to forgo women for now. These days, I'm living and breathing the construction business."

That preoccupation with business over the last several months had meant he did not have much time for anything other than his work. He'd been running the other way every time Cecilia or anyone else came on to him, so he hadn't been with a woman in two months. That was probably the reason he'd been strangely aroused by the slightest brushing of the uptight blonde's body.

"In forty minutes," Trent said, flipping on his computer, "I have a meeting with my grandfather. Last night, another accident happened at the Karger site."

"Anyone hurt?"

"Yeah, Mac burned his hands. But luckily, he corrected the problem before someone was electrocuted."

However, that wasn't the only thing that bothered him. Minor accidents occasionally happened but even a single minor one was one too many. He had been at the Karger site just before the accident, but had been called away for a problem in Homestead.

Greg stood. "Good thing. Off to work. Good luck with your grandfather."

"I need it. He won't retire, even though the business is killing him."

After Greg left, Trent sighed. The old man was getting more demanding and didn't want to lose an inch of control over the family business. Trent had gradually assumed more responsibilities, trying to lighten the load for his seventy-eight-year-old grandfather. The man needed to retire. It wouldn't be easy to manage the family's holdings without him, but Trent had to get him to slow down.

Mrs. Nash buzzed. "Mr. Prichard from Western is on line one."

Trent picked up the phone. "Jack, it's the third time this week that the elevators have malfunctioned. I need you here right away. You need to get to the bottom of this and fix the problem."

Trent hung up and then checked his watch. He had a few calls to make, and then he'd head off to face his grandfather. After the company's latest near-fatal accident, Trent expected to hear a round of accusations—and deservedly so. Since he planned to take over the company, the buck now stopped with him. Everything that went wrong weighed on his shoulders and lately too many things had gone wrong.

They were either becoming accident-prone or having a hell of an unlucky streak.

CHAPTER TWO

After nearly ten more minutes of waiting, Kate and Darcy boarded an elevator and soared upward to the forty-fourth floor. Once the doors opened, Kate stepped off, relieved, her heart thumping in a panicked rhythm.

What a way to start the first day on the job? How could she have lost her temper with Trent Farrington? She—who was always so calm and in control... Why hadn't she simply allowed him to help her and played the part of the grateful lady? In one swift movement, he had saved her from a fall on the hard marble floor. Normally she'd have thanked someone so gallant, but had she...? No. She'd nearly bitten his head off. And he was her new boss...

Was this masquerade going to work? Everything she hoped to accomplish hinged on her being civil. In control. *Could she do it?*

And would *he* forget brushing against her in the lobby? Her breasts tingled at the thought. He had touched her, held her in his arms. Although she tried to curb it, another wave of sizzling heat swept through her.

Disgusted by her reaction to him, she mentally shook herself and turned the key in the lock to her new office. She flashed Darcy a meaningful look, and then swung the door open. Kate's gaze shot straight through to the expansive windows and her heart lurched.

Darcy entered the office first. "Wow, what a great working space." She placed her purse on the secretarial desk in the outer office and then ambled into Kate's.

Kate cringed at the height. She watched nervously as Darcy made her way to the desk in front of a huge window. Kate followed, reluctantly inching forward on shaky legs. The City of Fort Lauderdale sprawled below with Farrington Towers dwarfing the surrounding buildings.

"Forty-four floors up, huh?" Kate asked with a gulp. "The people on the street look like ants."

Darcy gasped. "Hey, you're so pale. Are you going to be okay with this?"

Kate returned a weak smile. "Sure. I'll be all right, but this incredible height will take some getting used to."

Darcy pulled the curtains partially closed. "I can't believe you got us jobs here."

Kate sighed. "Yeah, James Farrington believed me, but for how long, I don't know. We need to gather our evidence and get out of here quickly."

"But while we're here, get a load of this luxury," Darcy exclaimed.

Kate whirled to study the spacious office with its sleek desk and a seating area consisting of a gray chenille sofa and matching chairs. If all this was hers, she thought with grim sarcasm, how was the *prince and heir's* office decorated? "I suppose I can handle working here for a while. It'll be different from the dining room table in my little bungalow, don't you think?"

"How do you plan to handle this job and still have time for the paper's advice column?"

"I'll write in the evenings. I just hope the Farringtons don't mind if their employees moonlight," Kate quipped dryly.

Darcy shut the door and leaned against its sturdy, polished mahogany. "He's so handsome."

"Who is?" Kate whispered, half-afraid of the answer.

"Trent Farrington, of course. He was the only Greek god I saw downstairs. And he held you awfully close," Darcy said wistfully.

"For one second...and I almost fell." Kate wasn't going to mention that she'd made the same comparison, or that his hand had brushed against her breast. "Do you really care how handsome he is—when we both know he's a crook?" she asked.

"Too bad he's the person you suspect. What did you think about the other guy? What's his name?" Darcy snapped her fingers and plopped down on the chenille sofa. "He was not bad, if you like the computer-geek type."

Kate rolled her eyes. Darcy wouldn't remember any truly eligible man's name, but would take in every detail and trail after the impossible—an unobtainable player like Farrington who was corrupt to boot. "Put that way, you make Greg Dalton sound *so* appealing."

Darcy dismissed Kate's sarcasm and grinned. "He's perfect for you, Kate. Your biggest problem with meeting men right now is that pair of glasses you wear."

"That's nice," Kate said dryly. "I couldn't see a thing without them."

"Come on. There's always corrective surgery or contacts. Or even those thinner lenses…"

"I have contacts, and I prefer these glasses." Kate sat at the desk and opened the drawers. Inside, she found the it stocked with pens, file folders and the standard office supplies.

"Why don't you let me do something with your hair, Kate? I think Greg Dillon likes you. Let's go on a shopping spree, too. You need some fashionable clothes for work."

Kate laughed and put up her hand to curb Darcy's ramblings. "Stop. And his name is Greg *Dalton*. In addition, there's nothing wrong with this suit. I think it makes me look older and I need to be taken seriously in this job."

Darcy crossed her arms over her chest. "Kate, I know why you dress that way. Not all men are creeps like your stepfather, or those shady men he used to bring around your house. I remember when you went to college… You weren't trying to hide yourself then."

The blood drained from Kate's face.

Darcy blew out an exasperated breath. "Gosh, Kate. Whatever your stepfather did to you that put that look on your face—please forget I said anything. I'm sorry I brought it up. "

Wincing, Kate nodded. "He's not my favorite subject." She preferred to keep her past with Bill Jackson bottled up with a tight lid, as a kind of protection for her sense of self-worth and wellbeing.

"And you had a stupid fiancé, too," Darcy added.

Her college boyfriend had pursued her for a year. They had been friends first. She had grown to trust him, after years of not trusting anyone. Then he dumped her. "Jeff just wasn't strong enough to stand up to his mother when she found out about my stepfather's prison record."

Her stepfather, Bill Jackson, was a notorious conman. When she was eighteen, he had used her name for his cover in one of his schemes. She'd been arrested and spent a night in jail, thanks to him.

Kate shrugged. "And I really can't blame Jeff's mother. It sure didn't look good that I'd been arrested."

"But you were exonerated—weren't even charged when they found out it was your stepfather."

"But do people really believe my innocence? I don't think so. And my education plans to become a psychologist were nearly ruined by that jerk—"

"Okay, Kate, but not everyone is going to judge you by your creep of a stepfather. And I'll drop it for now about the clothes, but the shoes—the shoes are great."

Kate swiveled her chair away from the desk and stuck out her foot, admiring the simple, black pumps with slim, high heels. "Do you like them? They're my plainest."

"I love the shoes. I'd take them off your feet in a minute, *but darn it*," Darcy said, putting her hands on her hips, as if pretending to be disgruntled, "they're two sizes too small."

Kate ignored that comment. "I do have a weakness for pretty shoes."

"Okay, but the rest? Come on, you might not look half-bad and hook a boyfriend if you wore maybe a shorter skirt... You have great legs—"

"*Darcy*, please. Let's get one thing straight. I'm not here for romance...or to meet anyone. I have to do this first."

"All right." Sighing, Darcy leaned back on the sofa. "It's funny, but Trent Farrington doesn't look like a criminal to me. Damn, all I can say is it's just *too* bad for us single women."

"I don't think it would matter. Didn't you see the woman draping herself all over him in the lobby? It looks like he's already taken."

"Kate, why would he steal and cheat when he has everything going for him?"

"Look," Kate said bluntly, "Farrington probably didn't intend for Matt to die—I'm not saying he did—but he runs a crooked, unsafe operation, and my brother was killed because of it. Who knows what Farrington's covering up? Rich people have ways of getting around the law. Not everyone in this world is good."

"And not everyone is *bad* either, Kate."

"I don't think they are either, but you can't tell a book by its cover. What's on the inside is what should count. Farrington is dishonest. So let's get to work, but just remember why we came here, all right? I need evidence that he's buying inferior products to save a buck, then I'll turn it over to the police. We won't get into this any deeper than that."

"All right, whatever you say...but are you sure *he's* the one?"

Sighing, Kate leaned her elbows on the desk and put her hands under her chin. "Yeah, I know I'm right. So today, we set up the office. Tomorrow I'll see if I can get into the records and see how Farrington was cheating. I think a few invoices showing he was buying products below the required code and causing a hazardous situation by doing so, should be enough."

"I'll see if I can get his computer password."

"No, Darcy! Just keep me posted on what gossip you hear from the other employees. I hope we have enough evidence within a few days so we can leave the company.

After Darcy went into the outer office, Kate glanced around at her surroundings and blew out a deep breath at the magnitude of her accomplishment. She'd landed a managerial position at Farrington Construction.

Then apprehension gnawed at her confidence. Would the police even consider concrete evidence from her over the Farringtons' denials? Especially when they found out she'd misrepresented herself to get the position.

When she'd issued her theory about faulty and under-code equipment to the police, they promised to investigate thoroughly. Then she'd overheard one detective say, 'Kate Meyers' stepfather is a career criminal. The acorn doesn't fall far from the tree.' They went on to say she was probably trying to bilk the Farringtons out of millions.

Kate winced at the memory. The police had refused to consider her accusations seriously and had lumped her in with the likes of her stepfather. However, all of her life she and her brother had been walked all over. She'd learned a person had to stand up for what they believed was right. Matt's life was worth something. He deserved justice and she was determined to convict the culprit who was responsible.

* * *

Trent strode into the massive office his grandfather refused to relinquish and eyed the elderly man with concern.

His grandfather's flushed face indicated his blood pressure hovered in the high range. "Where were you yesterday afternoon?

This is the second accident in five months…and in your department. If you can't handle your responsibilities now, how can I expect you to take care of the business?"

"If you're referring to yesterday, I was called away for a problem in Homestead—"

"Spare me. I know very well what you have been up to, and I know all about your womanizing. Following further in your father's footsteps?"

Trent's jaw hardened. "I haven't been "womanizing" as you call it, at least not lately."

His grandfather ignored his comment. "Next, you'll be as bad as your blasted cousin. It amazes me that both of you are still alive with the carousing and partying kind of lifestyles you lead. I won't have it. Do you hear me? Womanizing killed your father. I won't let it kill you, too. If he hadn't been out cheating on his wife, he would never have gotten into that car accident."

Trent tensed at the memory of that painful day and the following months of grief. He straightened his shoulders and wiped that away. "What's the problem? I've been working hard. Why all these accusations?"

His grandfather opened a drawer and pulled out a pair of red lace panties. He waved them in the air. "I found this bit of lace when I went into your office looking for you yesterday."

"Well, they're certainly not mine," Trent said dryly.

His grandfather's face colored almost as red as the sexy thing dangling from his fingertips.

Fearing the elderly man could have a stroke at any moment, Trent held out his hands. "Calm down. Someone placed it there as a practical joke. I had nothing to do with it."

"*Sure,*" his grandfather said, sarcastically. He rocked back in the leather chair, his hands clasped tightly before him. "I can't help but be upset with Mac burning his hands. Thank God he'll be okay but OSHA will be at the site again."

"I expect that. They'll search for anything they can, but we have gone by the letter of the law. You don't need to worry."

"Damn it, we don't need any more delays for the Karger project. I'm beginning to doubt my judgment, trusting you with such a large project. We've taken considerable loans out to build the damned thing. It's given us nothing but problems. And that young man getting killed…" His grandfather ran his hand down his weathered face.

"Don't blame yourself. If anyone is to blame, it's me," Trent said because a day didn't go by in which he didn't think about Matt Jackson, and relive the guilt.

His grandfather's steely gaze leveled on Trent. "I've been expecting you to uphold your end, damn it. You were to be in charge of that site."

"I was called away—"

"Save it. I've already spoken with the men involved in the accident. One man claims he placed a Lockout-tagout on the switch. The other claims there wasn't one when he turned on the power. Now which one is telling the truth?"

"I have everything under control. I visited the site this morning."

James Farrington wagged his gray eyebrows. "No, Trent, until I retire, I'm the one in control here. I suppose it's my fault for not instilling in you your duty. I spoiled you when you lost your father. As for your mother, that's a different story, but this company's not under your control until I say so. And damn Roland… Yesterday, he showed up after lunch, three sheets to the wind." His grandfather banged his fist on the desk again. "I'm no fool. Roland is a lost cause."

At thirty-seven, Trent's only cousin, Roland, spent most of his time at the casinos or the track. The last time Trent had seen the man, two attractive women had been clinging to his arms even though his cousin had grown paunchy and at the time was beyond drunk. Women tended to overlook those things with an heir to a fortune.

"Trent, there isn't a day that goes by that I don't miss your father. Thank God, I have my grandsons… But I need them to be able to carry on our legacy."

"I know it looks bad that both accidents on the site were under my watch. There won't be any more, even if I have to stand guard over the job site myself. But all that aside, you need to think of retiring."

His grandfather raised a gray eyebrow. "You want to control the company?"

Trent blew out a deep breath. "I don't want the business to kill you."

His grandfather coughed and put a hand over his heart. "My doctor says I need to take it easy, that stress could take a toll. My heart isn't what it used to be—"

"Then you *need* to retire. You'll still have your hands in Farrington Enterprises, but turn over the construction company to me."

"I'd consider retiring and letting you step in as president, but the deal...*your marriage.*"

"You're going too far by forcing that on me."

The older man pierced Trent with his blue eyes and closely examined him as if he were a bug under a microscope. "You seem determined not to marry, but I need to know the family line will continue. Just because your parents had an unhappy marriage doesn't mean you will," he said perceptively.

Trent's shoulder muscles bunched as he strode to the window. He braced his hands on the sill and stared over the city without seeing it. "Yes, they were not particularly happy."

His parents had fought a lot and often the fights were about him.

Then his father had died when Trent was nine. After that, his mother either grew bored with motherhood, or she found it too painful to be around him. Maybe he reminded her too much of his father.

Never affectionate, his mother's parties and social life had always trumped any needs he had as a child. His mother had grown up pampered, with plenty of money from her own wealthy parents. After his father died, as a rich widow, she decided to travel the world. She dumped Trent at a boarding school in England. Before she left, she had pinched his cheek and asked him to forgive her. She said she had to go away to heal, but even at the time he didn't believe she'd really come back for him.

When his grandfather had heard she'd exiled him so far away from home, he'd immediately brought Trent home to live in his house permanently and he'd personally overseen Trent's upbringing and education. Trent was much happier with his grandfather and grandmother than living in boarding schools.

"A good marriage will give your life stability," his grandfather said.

Trent returned to the chair across from his grandfather's desk. "Is there really such a thing as a *good* marriage?" He didn't know if he was cut out for marriage because perhaps there was a wild streak running in his genes, just like his father's.

His grandfather picked up the gold-framed picture of his wife that he always kept on his desk. His coloring had returned to a more normal hue. "Your grandmother was the love of my life. Sometimes love comes by only once… Twice if you're lucky." There weren't too many soft sides to his grandfather, but talking about Trent's grandmother always brought out one of them.

"I miss her, too, but life's not that simple anymore," Trent reminded him.

"Marriage made me happy. It will make you happy, too."

"One day, I might find the right woman," Trent agreed, but hell, he didn't really believe such a thing would happen. But he'd humor the old man if it encouraged him to retire because that could save his life.

"I'll tell you what your problem is, Trent. You're not going to find 'the right one' with the type of women you see." His grandfather had a point as Trent definitely avoided marriage-minded women.

However, he wasn't going to have his life decided for him. "Sorry, but marriage I won't do. Not until I'm ready. Besides, I haven't met anyone I'd want to marry."

"You're the last to carry the Farrington name. You want to inherit control of this company, don't you? Those days of your carrying on with women, even in your office, and under my nose," he said, slapping the flat of his hand on his desk, "are over."

"I haven't done that in years."

His grandfather snorted in disbelief and dangled the red lace panties. "Crotch-less," he said before dropping them in the waste can.

Trent had no idea how the panties had gotten into his office, but he could guess who had planted them—*Cecilia*. "You've got one month to give me an answer about my deal, or I'll consider selling the company. This company is important to me and I won't let my undeserving grandsons cause the family's work to come tumbling down."

Trent's jaw tightened, but he held his simmering anger in check. He didn't think for one moment that the old man would sell. However, he didn't want to push his grandfather into his grave either. For as hard as the man could be over any problems concerning the business, Trent loved him dearly. He owed his grandfather everything, for the home he'd given Trent and for being the family Trent needed when he lost both a father and a mother.

His grandfather laid his hand over his chest and gasped twice as if out of breath.

"Are you going to be okay?"

His grandfather waved Trent away with his hand and nodded. "The doctor said no stress… I'll be okay if I get some rest."

"Then I'd better leave, but I'll consider what you've said." Trent stalked toward the door.

"I have something else to say."

Trent turned and folded his arms over his chest. "Yes, what is it?"

"I've hired someone I want you to meet," his grandfather said in a voice considerably calmer. "Dr. Kate Meyers will be our new Human Resources Manager." He extended his hand. "Her resume."

Trent strode back to the desk and scanned the resume. "She's a *psychologist?*" he asked, cocking an eyebrow.

"Yes. And I want you to consider discussing some of the problems you have with women, with her."

"I don't *have* any *problems* with *women*," Trent ground out.

His grandfather snorted. "I might even send Roland to her. Maybe she can figure out what the hell is wrong with my grandsons."

It would be a cold day in hell before Trent talked to a psychologist about his life. They'd tried to pull that stunt on him after his father died. He had refused to say one word about his family and they'd finally given up. There was nothing wrong with his mind, and he was perfectly content with his life. He didn't need a shrink to figure him out, and he didn't want a faithless wife.

The intercom buzzed. "Dr. Meyers is here, Mr. Farrington."

A moment later, the cool tempered woman Trent had met earlier in the lobby walked into the office, wearing her frumpy suit and her golden hair in that tight bun—like something his older secretary, Mrs. Nash, would wear.

So they were to be introduced.

Was the haughty plain Jane to be their new Human Resources Manager and also hired to help him work out what his grandfather thought were his personal problems? The only real problem he had, other than the business, was an old man trying to run his life.

His grandfather rose from his desk. "Dr. Meyers, this is my grandson, Trent Farrington."

Looking down his nose, Trent studied her, then he rechecked her application. He frowned. *Thirty-four years old?* She certainly held her age well—she didn't look a day over twenty-four. What he could see of her skin looked as fresh as a newly bloomed rose. His gaze focused on her perfect little shell of an ear with the pearl earring. He narrowed his eyes. Something didn't ring true about her.

"It's nice to meet you, *Mr. Farrington*," she said in a cool voice.

Trent gave her a lazy nod and watched closely. His name hadn't produced the effect he'd come to expect. Instead of dollar signs lighting up in her eyes, she gave him a disdainful look.

It was hard to be certain with those thick glasses. However, she had gray eyes—like the morning mist—and clearly, contempt for him now flashed in those eyes. *Why?*

At his intent perusal, her full lips compressed into a grim line.

He'd been right for she couldn't be any less intrigued by him. He almost laughed out loud. His grandfather's latest ploy to throw another potential bride at him had backfired. *You hired the wrong one this time, Grandpa.*

Forcing a smile, Trent extended his hand. She seemed reluctant to place hers in his for the usual business handshake, but she did anyway. How dainty and fine-boned her hand seemed against his large, tanned one.

"It's a pleasure to meet you again, *Dr. Meyers*," Trent said in a mocking voice, making it evident he thought otherwise. He released her hand.

She didn't appear rattled by his cold greeting. "Thank you. I'm looking forward to working here," she returned in a voice as cool as his.

However, when her lips curved in a warm, dazzling smile that she bestowed on his grandfather, Trent's breath caught in his throat. Mesmerized by her mouth, he had to mentally shake himself and consider the fact: She was perfectly congenial to his grandfather, but not to him.

"Take a few moments to get acquainted," his grandfather said, excusing himself. "I'll be back."

Trent's shoulders stiffened. "Take a seat, *Dr. Meyers*." He swept his hand toward the leather couch and two chairs. She chose a chair, but instead of relaxing, her delicate figure sat ramrod straight in front of him.

His grandfather's scheming to get them alone did not amuse Trent either. In fact, he was already sick to death of the women hired to work at the company—rather, to be his potential wife. It was time to let Dr. Meyers know that he wouldn't be led around by a ring in his nose, not by anyone.

Trent strode to her and put one hand on the arm of the chair and the other on the back of it. However, when he breathed in her fresh scent, he almost forgot what he'd intended—to be somewhat intimidating.

He thrust his face close to hers and said in his most biting tone, "So, my grandfather tells me that you're a *shrink*."

CHAPTER THREE

When Trent Farrington leaned over her, Kate inhaled the scent of his cologne that mingled with the smell of the new leather chair in his grandfather's office. Her heartbeat quickened. Was he deliberately trying to intimidate her? Kate swallowed her nerves and lifted her chin. Surely he couldn't suspect her of anything—at least not yet.

He studied her, his dark eyes glittering. Clearly, the man didn't like therapists. She longed for a glass of cold water for her parched throat.

Kate returned his direct stare and ignored his rude statement. "Yes, *I am* a psychologist." She hated to lie, but she'd gotten herself into this situation and needed him to buy into her story.

Abruptly, Farrington straightened and stepped back from her. He glanced over her resume again and then his gaze met hers. "Dr. Meyers, you look barely old enough to have finished college."

"Looks can be deceiving," she pointed out. Wasn't that the situation with him, she thought dryly—handsome on the outside, ugly on the inside?

He moved away and dropped down on the sofa, then his dark gaze locked on her. A muscle in his jaw twitched. When he turned his attention back to her resume, Kate sighed and relaxed her shoulders. The seconds ticked by. Only the hum of the computer and the ringing of a distant telephone broke the silence.

He stabbed her with his gaze. "If part of your job description is to *psychoanalyze me*, you can be assured it won't happen."

"But your grandfather didn't mention psychoanalyzing *you*," she blurted out. Then she bit her lip. "I don't know what you're thinking, but I'm here to hire personnel and nothing more." The man was arrogant and offensive. With her hatred for him, would she be able to pull off being so close to him and keep her anger to herself? "Being a *psychologist* wasn't a requirement, but your grandfather thought my background would provide helpful insights into anyone hired to work at the company."

"I see." Trent Farrington's arched eyebrow indicated he didn't believe her. Once again, he lowered his gaze to her resume. Farrington continued to read, his dark head bent over the papers.

He shifted and leaned back on the leather sofa. He was extremely masculine, and held an air of casual elegance. Although impeccably dressed in a suit, with his athletic build he seemed the kind she'd expect to run into on the construction site, not working in the offices. He exuded a dangerous sensual quality that no doubt appealed to women.

When he loosened his tie and unbuttoned the top button of his shirt with a negligent hand, Kate's breath caught in her throat. Despite her nervousness and knowing what he was, heat spread through her and she felt the disconcerting force of his attraction. She frowned. The last thing she wanted was to find this man attractive.

He glanced at her again with his shrewd dark eyes, as if he knew she had been studying him. Kate forced herself to continue a direct gaze.

"How many years did you work for the Institute for Human Behavior in San Diego?" he asked.

"Three," she answered, without flinching.

"My grandfather might be lax about it, but I may check that out."

She nodded. "Please do." If he did, by the time he received the feedback, she hoped to be long gone.

While reading the resume, occasionally he'd look up and glance at her. She hoped she hadn't made an enemy of him—at least not yet. There would be plenty of time for that when he was behind bars.

"What made you decide to take a job here instead of going into private practice?" he asked.

She couldn't tell the truth: that she wanted him to rot in jail for the rest of his life. "I've always had a desire to work in the corporate world." She hoped he bought that because she wanted the lying part over. She hated to lie, which reminded her of her conman stepfather.

His gaze swept over her. Did he see through her disguise?

Good Lord, she had to be brave. He was intimidating.

Something lurked in the back of his eyes. "And Mr. Connor, our last Human Resources Manager, what happened to him?" Trent asked.

Irked by his question, she tensed. If Trent Farrington cared about his family business, he should know that.

"He retired," she answered flatly.

"I see. It must have been sudden," he ground out, "because I wasn't notified for any input on who was to take his place. And now, my grandfather has replaced him with a *woman?*"

Kate straightened in her chair, remembering he had called her 'sweetheart' in the lobby. Not only was Trent Farrington a despicable person, he was also a male chauvinist. She remembered the meeting with his grandfather... *Did it run in the family?*

"Something wrong with me being a woman?" she asked in her coolest tone.

"No need to take offense, Miss Meyers. Or...is it *Mrs.* Meyers? You didn't indicate your status on your resume."

"It's *Dr. Meyers.*"

He scowled. "So which is it? Are you *married* or *not?*"

This was outrageous. The man couldn't be flirting with her, could he? His tone was accusatory if anything. "I'm not married."

"I knew it!" He bounded out of his seat and stepped toward her. The suddenness reminded her of a leopard pouncing.

She shrank back in her chair, her heart pounding. "What do you know?" she whispered.

Farrington slapped his hand down on her chair again and leaned over her, his breath warm against her ear. "What was that *little show* in the lobby? Thought I might fall for you if you fell into my arms, is that it?"

Her eyes widened. "I don't know what you're talking about. *You* bumped into *me.*"

He moved away from her and straightened. "Right," he said with dry sarcasm. "How convenient, and certainly not a coincidence that I got a feel of your *assets?*" His eyes gleamed with a mocking light.

The blood drained from Kate's face. "That was an accident, and *you* caused it." She curled her hand into a fist. If she didn't need this job to send him to jail, she'd punch him and tell him where to shove it. "Mr. Farrington," she said as calmly as she could. "As your new HR Manager, I must inform you that such comments are *inappropriate* and *unacceptable* in the workplace."

Dismissing her statement, he let out a dry chuckle. "My dear old grandfather is at it again. Trying to fix me up with yet another *qualified* woman."

"*Qualified?* Qualified for what?" she choked out.

"My question exactly." His brow furrowed. "He really didn't tell you? He's looking for a *wife* for me, and he's very active about it. Check the employment records. In the past two years, he's hired at least ten single, attractive women to work here. He's thrown them at me. Fortunately, most of them are all now married—to someone else. The man just won't give up."

"But you have me all wrong. I—"

"You'll see. He'll make up some excuse for us to work together. *Closely.* I'm sure of it."

The blood rushed to her face. She rose from her chair. "Listen, Mr. Farrington, I'm not interested in marriage…"

Trent snorted in disbelief.

Kate choked out a laugh at the absurdity. "Come on. You can't believe I'm scheming with your grandfather to marry…you?"

"I must admit he should know you're not my type. However, he could be taking a different tack…and must be hoping I have *librarian fantasies.*"

She gaped at his rudeness. *Conceited pig.* She swallowed the words rushing to her lips. If she wasn't so worried about being fired, she'd have said them.

Kate inhaled a deep breath to calm her rising temper. "*Marry you?*" she asked dryly. "Why I'd sooner push you off the roof of this building."

He reared back in shock.

She enjoyed the taken-aback expression on his face. Was that because her comment made him think of her brother Matt, who fell to his death on the job, or had she chipped away at his ego?

Since she couldn't risk losing her job on the first day, she gave him a faint smile before softening her words. "You see, I'm not marriage material either, just like you. I have no desire to marry anyone. I want to be left alone to do my job."

At that moment, James Farrington sauntered through the doorway, wearing a smile. "How's everything? Are you two getting along?"

No way, Kate thought. Not in a million years. She'd just found out Trent Farrington thought she was out to marry him. Of all the idiotic things for him to come up with.

"Everything is fine," Trent said. It was an obvious lie because he glared at her, even now.

James Farrington beamed at them both, totally missing his grandson's sarcasm. "We had a long discussion on the day I hired her. She will be an asset to our staff."

"Oh, I am sure she has *some assets*," Trent drawled.

He flicked his gaze over her as if to say that while he might think she had something going for her in the boob department, *he* wasn't succumbing to her charms.

Kate lifted her chin. Did he really think his grandfather had only hired her just because he wanted to throw another single woman in his path? She frowned and studied the older man.

James Farrington fumbled through the papers at his desk with a satisfied smirk on his lips.

Frowning again, Kate glanced back at Trent. His eyes lazily contemplated her. She shifted uneasily in the leather chair. Let him worry about his grandfather's matchmaking. The only thing she didn't like about it was that Trent Farrington was now on guard against her. That wasn't a good thing if she wanted to gain enough trust for her to investigate and gather the information she needed.

She caught Trent's gaze.

Pointing a finger at herself, she shook her head to indicate she wasn't in on any of his grandfather's schemes, but Trent lifted a sardonic eyebrow and crossed his arms over his chest.

He didn't believe her.

James Farrington stood and held out his hand, signaling an end to their meeting. "Dr. Meyers, welcome on board. If you need any help hiring employees for the job sites, contact Trent. I want him involved, and he has final approval over all new employees. I'm sure he'll be glad to help you with anything you need."

After thanking the older man for the opportunity to work at the company, she gave his grandson a curt nod and left the office. She hoped this would be one of the few meetings between them. Trying to loosen the stiffness in her shoulders, she walked back to her office. She wouldn't ask for his help, even if it was to save the planet from an asteroid. If she had questions, she'd ask someone else at the company. Good grief, he thought she and his grandfather conspired to marry him off—to *her*.

With his good looks, she imagined Trent Farrington had to fight off many women his grandfather threw his way. Poor man… *Yeah, right*. She hoped he'd turn tail and run anytime she came close to him. That would make her job of investigating him so much easier.

On her way back to her office, she muttered to herself about how wrong they were about her… Imagine. *Her*, of all people, wanting to marry Trent Farrington. She wanted to scratch his eyes out or use his guts for garters…but marry him? *No way*. She was sorry to disappoint the grandfather, but the only honeymoon his grandson was going to enjoy was one alone—and in a five-by-eight jail cell.

Now, she had to get down to work and find the evidence to convict him, then get the hell out of this company before they discovered her ruse.

The old man had smiled at her…as if he knew something she didn't.

And yes. There'd been sparks, but not the kind Trent's grandfather hoped for.

* * *

After Doctor Meyers left, Trent scrutinized the older man's face, and didn't he have a sheepish grin. Trent clenched his teeth and inwardly groaned.

After closing the office door of his grandfather's office for privacy, he faced the older man. "All right. Out with it. Why did you hire her? I'm not falling for your innocent look. You're too shrewd."

"We needed a HR Manager. So, what did you think of Dr. Meyers?"

"Depends on what you mean? Are you trying to set us up?"

"Not a bad idea. I like her. Why?" His grandfather smiled blandly. "Are you interested?"

"*Miss* Meyers is not my type." Trent scowled.

His grandfather chuckled. "She isn't, is she? Too bad you're only interested in women with empty heads and trumped-up sexy looks. Have you thought that a nice, intelligent woman could pass on better genes to my great-grandchildren? Besides, she's pretty no matter what she's wearing."

"Damn, I'm not thinking about your great-grandchildren."

Dr. Meyers and her sour glances glared at him in his mind. If his grandfather's intentions weren't so serious, he'd burst out laughing. She obviously disliked him.

'Marry you? I'd sooner push you off the roof of this building.' *Had she really said that?* Her attitude was a refreshing change from the women who threw themselves at him all the time.

The sudden thought of how he and the doctor would get those children sent an unwelcome surge of heat through him. First, he'd ditch the awful glasses, then pull the pins from her hair and caress the long silkiness falling over her shoulders. He suspected she hid a good figure and he remembered her full breasts. Images of her lying naked in his bed flashed before him.

"Since you're not thinking of reproducing any Farringtons as yet," his grandfather muttered, "someone must consider these issues for you."

Trent's gaze shot toward the elderly man, who was still talking about great-grandchildren, while Trent had been lost in his own thoughts of the strangely appealing Dr. Meyers—and how he'd bed her. He suspected his self-imposed celibacy these past couple of months for the sake of the company had to be responsible for this ridiculous attraction he felt for the dowdy psychologist.

"Trent, at least discuss your problems with Dr. Meyers."

"I don't *have* any problems," Trent grumbled.

"Then allow your mother to make the arrangements and you can marry Cecilia. Granted she's not the sharpest tool in the shed, but I can't wait forever. Your mother is fond of her. The Farrington brains will just have to make up for her shortcomings. I want great-grandchildren to bounce on my knee before I die."

Trent folded his arms over his chest. "I thought arranged marriages went out with the invention of the light bulb."

"I've told you where I stand on this issue. I warned you two years ago to find a wife. It's your duty. You have one month to produce a fiancée, or I'm changing my will."

"I don't really care what you do with your money, but I do care about the company."

Trent hated arguing with his grandfather because of his age. He could walk away and start over, but Farrington Construction was part of him, his birthright. He'd been groomed for Farrington Construction and had been brought to his grandfather's office for his indoctrination before he was even a teen.

For years, what was expected of him and Roland had been drilled into them. Finally, Trent rebelled when he'd gone away to Princeton. Wild parties and wilder women—and Roland had blazed the same path before him.

His grandfather leaned toward Trent. "Is the legacy of this family not important to you?"

Trent narrowed his eyes. "Of course it is. Have you given this pitch to Roland? He's older than I am."

The old man's face reddened. "You've got the right last name and the Farrington side of the genes. Roland's a carbon-copy of his knuckle-headed father whom I detest."

Trent knew the story of Aunt Vera's marriage against his grandfather's wishes and the subsequent divorce. Her ex-husband had then absconded with half of her fortune. James Farrington had never forgiven the man or let her forget it.

Trent had reasons and might dislike his cousin these days, but fair was fair. "You can't blame Roland for his father."

"There's more to it than that. I won't be around forever. I want to know this family isn't going to die out. I want to know that your parents' failed marriage didn't ruin you or influence your relationship with women. Or your mother's…" His grandfather placed a hand over his heart and coughed. "Did her coolness effect you?"

For the first time, Trent thought the old man looked weak. His grandfather had saved him from despair as a child and had never asked him for anything. Was it possible that his parents' failed relationship and his unhappy early childhood *had* affected his ability to have meaningful relationships with women—as well as his opinion about marriage?

Trent shoved a hand through his hair. He owed the man so much. "I won't talk to your new shrink, but I'll think over what you've said."

* * *

On her second day at Farrington Construction, Kate entered her office after an evening working at the Children in Crisis Center, where she'd read a story to a little girl who'd reminded her of herself at six. Not only was Annie petite and blond, and all arms and legs, but seeing her bruised face deeply touched Kate's soul. She would do everything she could to protect children like Annie from abusive parents.

Not all children had wonderful lives, and most weren't born with silver spoons in their mouths. Her thoughts turned to Trent Farrington—the rich, spoiled playboy. He probably had a great family life, too, but he'd chosen to cheat and risk lives.

Not wanting to dwell on what his private life was like, she shoved him from her mind.

She crossed the floor to the windows. *Did people really get used to looking down from this height?* She didn't think she ever would, and she partially closed the drapes to avoid the dizzying view.

With a satisfied sigh, she returned to her desk, ready for work. Last evening, she had piled folders of potential construction workers on her desk because while she investigated she also had a job to do. Before she got engrossed in actual work, she picked up Matt's supervisor's file, which Darcy had retrieved for her.

Perhaps his boss could tell her a little of his conversation with Matt before he died, as well as what happened afterwards. Kate bit her lip. She'd just have to think of an excuse to go to the construction site to question Stephen Carr about products that might be below code. Would he even confide in her? Matt had told her before he died that when he had challenged his supervisor about some of the condition of products that the man had told Matt to keep his nose out of it, that Trent Farrington must be trying to save money, and to back off if he wanted a paycheck.

Probably not. He hadn't told the police or OSHA.

She flipped through his records and found a resignation letter. *Oh, no, Carr had left the company!* A note in the file stated a final employment check had been mailed to him two months earlier.

Now she might never get the chance to talk to the man. Disappointed, she glanced through the rest of the file to find a home address, but those papers had been removed. Perhaps she could get an actual address from Accounting and now that Stephen Carr didn't work for the company, perhaps he'd be more likely to tell her the truth.

She scooped up the file and strode toward the entrance to Darcy's office area. Kate stopped before entering when she heard Trent Farrington's voice on the other side. She frowned and listened.

"A week from this Friday," he said in his deep, rich tone, "the company will be hosting a benefit in the ballroom. If you'd like to attend, here are two tickets."

"Thanks, Mr. Farrington," Darcy said.

"Call me Trent. We're not formal around here."

"All right, *Trent*. I'll ask Kate if she'd like to go, too."

He chuckled. "Dr. Meyers? I can't imagine she knows how to have a good time."

His comment stung, but Kate wasn't sure why she cared. She clutched the files closer to her chest. Well, he could laugh about her all he wanted. She didn't care what he thought of her because she *hated* him.

"Not at all like you, is she?" he asked in a smooth voice.

"No, but Kate can be a lot of fun if you give her a chance."

Kate clenched her teeth. She imagined his dark gaze roving over Darcy, who had worn a tight-fitting green dress with matching high heels today.

Did Trent prefer women who dressed like Darcy? Of course, he did. What man wouldn't? Besides, who cared what type of *woman* he liked? In jail, he wouldn't have any of them.

"Is the party formal?" Darcy asked. "What should I wear?"

"Since the benefit is close to Halloween, it's a tradition for my grandfather to host a masquerade. Unfortunately, costumes are required to get in."

Humph, Kate thought ironically, if she were picking out Trent's costume, he'd wear a black-and-white-striped prison outfit with a ball and chain around his ankle.

Remembering how cute Darcy had looked sitting at her secretary's desk, Kate gritted her teeth. She could just imagine Trent sitting on the edge of her friend's desk, flirting with Darcy. Didn't the spoiled playboy have better things to do than chat it up with her assistant and deliver invitations to parties? No wonder people under his employ were being killed or hurt.

Tired of eavesdropping, Kate strode through into the smaller front office only to find that Trent wasn't sitting on the edge of Darcy's desk, as she'd imagined, but stood several feet away. Today, again, he was impeccably dressed and handsome in his dark suit with a crisp white shirt and burgundy tie. He looked tall, fit, and lean. Once again, his amazing good looks sent an electrical shock to her senses and her pulse leaped.

Kate winced. *Oh, Darcy, watch out for him. He's oozes sexual appeal—he's dangerous.*

However, if the awed expression on Darcy's face indicated anything, she might already be under his spell. And if Trent's grandfather has his way, Darcy might also be a candidate for an upcoming wedding.

When Farrington glanced toward Kate, his smile faded abruptly. With narrowed eyes, he stepped toward Kate until he was so close she had to tilt her head to see his face.

His power ploy to make her feel small wasn't going to work. "Good morning, *Mr. Farrington*," she said coolly.

He gave her a curt nod. "Dr. Meyers."

So there wasn't going to be a 'call me Trent' for her? Kate straightened her shoulders and decided she wasn't going to let him get to her today. She was determined to remain her usual calm self.

Since this meeting appeared to be between him and Darcy—and Darcy had been forewarned about Trent's womanizing and that he was a crook—Kate started to walk past him.

He stuck out his hand with two tickets, stopping her. "Here."

Her gaze flew up to his. So he'd invite her too, but without any cajoling, or explanation of what the tickets were for. No, of course not. A man seeking physical beauty wouldn't want to personally invite someone like her to his party. He probably felt obligated to pass on the tickets because she worked there. Fine. She had no intention of going to a benefit sponsored by his corrupt company. He probably stole the funds collected for the charity.

She glanced at the tickets in his hand and her resolve grew. The benefit was a week and a half away and she planned to be long gone from the company by then—with damning information in hand, to prosecute him.

Still, she couldn't refuse the tickets he held in his extended hand. To be civil, she took them. "Thank you. Aren't you going to tell me what the tickets are for?" she asked sweetly, unable to resist looking up into his dark eyes.

He crossed his arms over his chest. "A masquerade…benefit ball. Next Saturday. You should come," he said in a clipped tone.

"All right." Frowning, she tried to pass him again.

He nodded toward her office. "I'm here to talk to you." He strode through the door as if he owned the place. Her shoulders sagged—because *he did*. Own the place.

Reluctantly, she turned and followed him, her stomach knotting. Once she was inside, he closed the door and looked down at her.

"Will this be brief?" she asked, exasperated by his commanding ways.

"Not that brief."

Her shoulders tensed. She was fairly sure she officially worked for his grandfather and not him. "I'm very busy at the moment. I was just stepping out of the office. Would you mind setting up an appointment with Darcy?" she said, doing her best to keep the irritation out of her voice. "She'll know my schedule." She sidestepped him to get to the door.

Trent was not to be put off and stepped into her path. His body effectively blocked her exit. "Unless it's a *bathroom break*, the time for our talk is now."

Was he purposely trying to make her angry? Because it was working.

"I was on my way to Accounting," she said through tight lips.

"Please…have a seat. This is not easy for me to say." At his insistent tone, her stomach fell. *Had he found out something about her?*

Since he was the boss and she was his employee, Kate nodded and went to her desk to take on the power position. She reluctantly sat and folded her hands on her desk and gave him direct eye contact. Her heart was beating wildly yet she focused on presenting a calm facade. "Yes, now what can I do for you?"

He blew out a deep breath and took the chair across from her. "I'm here to…apologize."

She gaped at him. Only moments ago, he had put her down in front of her assistant.

"Listen." He picked up a paperweight, toyed with it, then placed it back on the desk. "We started out wrong. Why don't we clear the air? I admit I have somewhat of a temper. I shouldn't have accused you of being in on any scheme my grandfather had in the works."

Now he was making sense. "You've got that right."

"I've told you I have my reasons for my suspicions, but I was rude, and you didn't deserve it." By his voice and expression, he sounded sincere. "Let's begin again. My grandfather thought you might need help in HR and I'd already intended to take a closer look at who's hired at the company. I'd also like to check the personnel records of our existing employees. It's not something I normally concern myself with, but unfortunately, I must at this time. You and I will be working closely together—"

"*We will?*" she blurted out. Why was he interested in *this* department all of a sudden? "I mean, of course, if that is your wish."

"Yes, so I thought it would be better if we began again, on a more civil footing."

She sank back in her chair and contemplated his sincere expression. "I'd like that, too." A halt to their open hostility would help her remain cool during her investigation, make her work easier. "Really, I don't think your grandfather had any tricks in mind when he hired me."

His dark eyes evaluated her again and he shrugged. "Both he and my mother can be deceitful about trying to marry me off."

The seriousness in his expression made her smile. For a second, she forgot she hated him. "Why? Won't your grandfather get his wish soon enough? I thought the woman I met in the lobby on my first day was a contender."

"Cecilia Sheffield?" His lips twisted cynically. "No. She's not."

"Well, I'm sorry, but it's amusing that you thought I could be one of those women your grandfather is trying to set you up with." She pointed to her outfit, then up to her hair and glasses.

He cocked his head. "You might have a certain appeal."

"*Me?*" Her eyes widened at his flattery, but then she realized a player like him might find something to like in every woman, or tell them he did. She shook her head. "And you have no reason to worry as marriage is the last thing I want." At the gleam in his dark eyes, she added, "I meant at the moment… Maybe someday." She picked up a file from her desk and thumbed through it, hoping he wouldn't notice the heat spreading on her cheeks.

"You'll need to hire a temporary replacement for Mac." He was the man she'd heard had burned his hands on the job site the day before she had arrived at the company. "Plus, we'll need more crew. Did you get the memo describing exactly what hires we need?"

She tapped her finger on a stack of folders. "Yes, and I've looked into several applicants for those positions. Do you want to look at the files?"

"I'd like to, but weren't you off to Accounting?"

"It can wait." Going to Accounting could wait because working with him might reveal something.

Kate picked up the stack of files and moved them to the large table where it would be easier to work. Trent rolled his chair close to hers and she caught a whiff of his tantalizing aftershave. Kate tried to ignore the rapid beating of her heart as he reached across her for the top file. She told herself the reaction was only because she had to gather evidence to convict him—and this definitely could be an opportunity.

After discussing several applicants, Kate's uneasiness waned. Deciding she could let her guard down a bit while she investigated him, she relaxed in his company. "Only two more." She handed him the second-to-last file.

His fingers brushed hers as he accepted the papers. Startled by the contact and the warmth of his bare skin, she dropped the file. The papers scattered onto the floor.

"Oh, my fault." Kate rolled back her chair.

Trent knelt down. "I'll get them. Read the last file to me."

She scanned the application. "The name is Michael Peterson. He used to work for Blake Building and Construct—"

"*Frank Blake?* For how long?" Trent's voice was muffled under the table.

"Five years. Who is Frank Blake?" He seemed to have a more than casual interest in that person.

"Only our biggest competitor. He runs a slime-ball operation. Put that one aside."

Could it be any slimier than the one Trent Farrington ran?

Trent straightened up. The intensity in his eyes made her wary. "I'll take Peterson's file with me."

"What's wrong?" she whispered. His body language and tone indicated something had changed.

He stood. "Nothing. I think that's enough for one day. And *do not* hire anyone with a connection to Frank Blake. I don't trust him or anyone that has worked for him. Please send me any records of employees at our company who previously had a job at his company. I also want you to check the files of anyone you consider hiring."

He gave her a curt nod and headed for the door. Then he paused and turned. "I hope I didn't hold you up too long."

"No, I'll head over to Accounting now. *Wait!*" She jumped to her feet. She couldn't let him get away without asking him one more question. "Since a worker was killed on the site four months ago, I wanted to ask you what I should say to any potential employees who might inquire about our safety record."

"Tell them the man's death was a regrettable accident," he said, his voice turning cool. "The man didn't take the proper precautions or check his equipment before use."

His words kicked her in the chest, forcing the air from her lungs.

He tipped his head. "Have a good day, Dr. Meyers."

Fortunately for Trent Farrington, he'd left her office before she could pummel him with her fists. If she didn't have to bite her tongue to keep her job, she'd have accused him of jeopardizing his workers' lives to save a dollar.

CHAPTER FOUR

After returning to his office, Trent dropped down in the chair at his desk and scanned the file on Michael Peterson. The connection to one name stood out like a rusty nail—*Frank Blake*. Blake would profit if Farrington Construction didn't get the Karger Building built on time. Trent shoved his hand through his hair. He was suspicious because of that poor kid who was killed, and recently, because of the incident where Mac burned his hands.

And to have his grandfather, whose health seemed to be rapidly deteriorating, breathing down his neck, trying to force him to marry, added too much pressure.

As well, he now had to face the enigma of his grandfather's latest addition to their staff, Dr. Kate Meyers.

While he retrieved the papers from under the table, his eyes had focused on her slender ankles. His gaze had traveled up to her exquisite calves. Hell, he'd gotten turned on just by looking at her legs in those sleek, high heels, which, by the way, didn't fit at all with the unattractive clothing she wore.

What was it about her that got to him? Did she wear a perfume, formulated to intoxicate males? Was there such a thing? He scoffed. No, because if there were, his grandfather would have purchased it long ago for one of his other hires.

But even her scent didn't explain why *he* enjoyed their sparring. He must be experiencing some sort of a chemical attraction to her. Another thing was her lack of interest in him. He'd never made less of an impression on a woman and that intrigued him.

For the sake of his sanity, he should find one discrete woman for a bedmate, but images of Dr. Meyers flashed before him whenever he thought of a woman in his bed. Did her lips taste as sweet as they looked? He groaned. *Forget it*. She was definitely not interested in him.

Then who?

Certainly not Cecilia. Everyone in the building would know the next day and his family would have him married and chained to the Sheffields before he could shout no. Thankfully, he wasn't the least bit interested or tempted by her.

Another available woman was Darcy King, who he could probably seduce without trying, but it wasn't Darcy who attracted him... It was her boss...

In spite of himself, his thoughts returned to Dr. Meyers. Now, having a brief no-strings-attached liaison with her would be an interesting switch. He was used to flamboyant women who flaunted their looks. She might not be interested in him now, but what if he turned on the charm? She said she wasn't interested in marriage—*and neither was he*... So perhaps...?

What the hell was he thinking to even consider making a move on Dr. Meyers? In spite of what she thought, his grandfather had definitely hired her with marriage in mind. Besides, she seemed about as uptight as any woman could be. Damn it. Why did that make him want to loosen her up and bring that incandescent smile to her lips—for him?

He groaned. If he wasn't careful, he'd fall into his grandfather's trap and Dr. Meyers would be psychoanalyzing him too. In spite of what his grandfather thought, he didn't have a problem with a commitment. He just didn't want a wife. Period.

Since he couldn't trust his family's motives, and he couldn't trust himself around her, he realized he had to stay as far away as possible. He could still maintain a good working relationship—by phone and email instead of face to face.

He had to prove that as a single man, he was committed to the business. And for now, his focus had to be on keeping his crew safe while completing the building and winning the award and bid. He had to convince his aging grandfather to turn over control of the company.

The last thing he needed now was to be distracted by Dr. Meyers.

So, first things first. How could he fix this outrageous, blatant, escalating desire he was developing for her?

He reached into his pocket for his wallet, pulled out the few condoms he carried and shoved them into the back of a drawer. There—he had just curtailed his sex life. After a bitter paternity suit several years ago, he always used his own birth control. Thank God for DNA tests, which had proven he wasn't the father of the baby.

He leaned back in his chair, satisfied. While his sexual drive was strong, he was the master of his body. He could handle a few more months of celibacy to keep the company his main focus.

Taking a deep breath, he scooped up a stack of correspondence. With his jaw set firmly, he resolved to stop thinking of Dr. Kate Meyers…though he admitted he was intrigued. Besides, something did not ring true about the woman.

He settled down, planning to work until well past eight p.m., and counted on exhaustion to keep his mind off sex and his growing fascination with their latest employee.

* * *

A man with a hat pulled low over his forehead drove a rental car along NE 3rd Street.

He surveyed the empty streets. Blanketed under darkness, the city held an edge of calm he liked when he handled this kind of business. He parked near the construction site of the towering office building—all concrete and open steel girders at this stage.

The clock on the dashboard read four a.m. Not much more time before daylight and this place would be crawling with workers.

He took the last sip of convenience store coffee. Soon, no cheap coffee for him. After this job was finished, he'd collect big— with enough to retire if he wanted to and then he'd live the life. While a price had been agreed upon, with some money delivered to him before he started and the rest promised after the job's completion, there were ways of squeezing more money once the job was done. Especially when his clients freaked out that he might leak the name of who hired him to the police. He knew the value of his work and wanted a bigger stake in the prize.

He pitched the empty cup into the back seat. Not wanting to leave fingerprints at the construction site, he slipped on heavy gloves.

He strode to the entrance of the chain-link fence surrounding the work site and stuck the key into the lock. The gate swung open with a clang. However, he wasn't particularly concerned about the noise as the place was empty, and he'd dressed to blend in with the rest of the workers, should their paths unexpectedly cross.

After grabbing a hard hat, he headed up one of two construction elevators that hugged the outside of the building. The wind blew harder as he traveled higher in the open-cage car. He rode to the thirteenth floor. *Someone's lucky number.*

He exited the elevator and moved around the outside of the building. He pulled out a few pins from the scaffolding and replaced each with a half, sawed-off one. The scaffold would hold for a while, until weight caused the pins to snap and then, *kapoowweee.*

He chuckled under his breath. A few *good deeds* for the company before he left. Then he went to several more floors and did the same thing. If he hurried, he had enough time to remove a bolt here and there and spill some acid on a few cables. Little, unnoticeable tweaks that would cause devastation later.

At the moment, no one would know when another 'accident' was about to happen—not even him. That's why he planned to stay the hell away from this section of the building when he visited the site again. Otherwise he too might be a goner.

He looked over the edge to the concrete slab far, far below. Anyone underneath this thing when it fell would be history. After the next *accident*, he wanted the praise that he truly deserved from the boss. And he wanted an appropriate payoff.

He crossed some girders and rode the elevator on the other side of the building to the ground.

On his way out, he paused and glanced up at the soaring structure. A thrill surged through him at having such power over the lives of so many other human beings. It wasn't fair he should get this much pleasure from his work, since it was the high pay that had originally suckered him into the business—and he didn't mind killing, hadn't since he was a teen.

He grinned. What would it feel like to fall? If you knew it was your last day, would you have eaten a different breakfast, one high in sugar and cholesterol? Too bad he couldn't ask Matt Jackson. Stupid kid had poked his nose into one too many holes.

There were only a few subtle details to take care of and he'd leave the site. Soon, one carefully orchestrated calamity would be the *coup de grâce* for Farrington—just as the boss wanted. And if he did a good job, he'd get the 'big bonus' he'd been promised. The extra money would come in handy.

He chuckled and murmured under his breath, "Jingle bells, Jingle bells...just in time for Christmas."

CHAPTER FIVE

On the second floor of Farrington Towers, the hostess at the Green Tree Restaurant seated Kate and Darcy at a table beside a cluster of potted palms. The trees reached upward toward two-story high greenhouse windows. Tropical plants, saltwater aquariums, and a cascading waterfall gave the large eatery a lush outdoor ambiance.

"Darcy," Kate whispered, not wanting to be heard over the bubbling of the nearby aquarium. "We're through our first week and we've gotten nowhere. I don't know how much longer we can get away with this."

"I mailed the letter to Matt's old supervisor as you asked."

"Well, let's just hope Carr calls me since I couldn't find a phone number for him." Kate frowned and worried her bottom lip with her teeth.

"You still think Trent is responsible?"

At Darcy's hopeful expression, Kate winced. "Yes, I do."

"Maybe Matt falling and the man burning his hand were just two separate accidents. Maybe you're all wrong about the Farringtons."

"But how many accidents can one company have?" Kate pointed out. "They'd have to be extremely careless. I just don't see any evidence of that." She sighed. "I've got to get into Trent's office soon."

Darcy frowned. "Well, be careful."

"I will." Kate shuddered at the prospect of snooping around his lair. She'd found no damning evidence so far, and even gaining access had taken longer than she'd anticipated. "And I haven't been able to get into Purchasing's online records as my job description doesn't allow me access. Luckily, Mr. James Farrington, being old school, requires paper backups of everything. But every time I tried to get into Purchasing's file room, Cecilia was sitting at her desk—

and that woman *does not* like me. I don't know how I'm going to get in there."

After the waiter delivered their food, Kate chewed a bite of seared tuna and lettuce and contemplated the entire mess she'd taken on.

Darcy stared over Kate's shoulder and her fork paused midair. "Oh, My God. Don't look... *He's* here."

Even though Kate faced the opposite direction, she knew Darcy meant Trent by the excitement in her voice. Kate was annoyed too that her own heartbeat accelerated with anticipation.

"Not so loud," Kate whispered.

"Okay, but there really ought to be a law against someone looking like *him*."

At her friend's awestruck face, Kate drawled, "You mean don't hate him because he's *beautiful*?"

Darcy nodded. "And Greg's with him. Gossip says they've been friends since high school."

"Really?" Kate asked, frowning. "Interesting that corrupt Farrington should have such a nice friend."

She hadn't seen Trent since he'd come to her office two days before. How strange it was when he abruptly left that day, however, not before he'd made the comment blaming Matt for not taking proper safety precautions, being negligent, and causing his own death.

Beneath the folds of the tropical-print tablecloth, Kate clenched her hands in her lap. "Darcy, be careful around him. If he finds out we're trying to get information on him... Well, we just don't know what lengths he'll go to protect his precious money and his company."

"All right, but you're being awfully cryptic." Darcy took a bite of her sandwich, swallowed, and then gave Kate a pointed stare. "Don't you at least find him compelling?"

"No," Kate lied and pierced a piece of tuna with her fork. "But I agree he does seem to have everything going for him, so why would he steal?"

"Yeah, he certainly does have it all," Darcy quipped.

"You know what I mean." The other day, after he apologized, he had seemed nice, but a friendly facade was probably how he got away with his criminal activity, and how he got to know the women in the company.

Resolved to remember why she came to Farrington Construction, Kate said, "He's a crook who caused Matt's death. I have every reason to hate him, you know."

"And you have every reason to distrust men, but in this instance, you might have the wrong person."

"I think you're swayed by his handsome face."

Darcy giggled. "And don't forget that *gorgeous* body, but I won't forget to be cautious, Kate… At least until you find out you're wrong."

"I don't see how I can be wrong." *Could she be?*

"Uh, oh. The hostess is leading them in our direction."

"Act like you don't notice them. Maybe they'll pass us by." Kate ducked her head and hoped the potted plants hid them.

"Hello, Kate, Darcy," Greg bellowed. She glanced up as he swayed back and forth to get a view of them through the palm trees. "Mind if we join you?"

Kate sighed in dismay. "Oh, we were just about to leave."

Darcy smiled and nodded enthusiastically. "Yes, come on. Please, join us. We can stay a little longer, can't we, Kate?" Kate narrowed her eyes at Darcy's deliberate ploy to keep them there.

Greg's friendly smile contrasted with Trent's somber nod toward her. Although his reluctance seemed to match her own, he sat in the chair next to hers.

His nearness caused Kate's heart to pound in an erratic rhythm. Irked by her reaction, she told herself it had to be because she planned to search his office soon.

The glass doors to the restaurant opened. Cecilia, the woman who had flung herself at Trent in the lobby on Kate's first day at Farrington Construction, strode toward them. Her tasteful cream-colored suit flattered her svelte figure. Gossip ran rampant around the building that Cecilia was hot for Trent.

When Cecilia reached the table, she ignored everyone else. "Hello, Trent. I was hoping to catch you for lunch."

At Cecilia's unintentional pun, Kate caught how Greg's lip curved into a slight smile. He sent his friend a sideways glance. Trent raised a sardonic eyebrow in return.

When Cecilia turned to Kate, the skin on the back of Kate's neck prickled.

"May I join you all?" the brunette asked coolly.

Kate nodded. "Sure." How could she or Darcy refuse? Cecilia's expression told Kate she could be gunned down on the spot if they declined.

Although both men stood, it was Greg who strode to a nearby table and grabbed an extra chair for Cecilia.

"Next to Trent," Cecilia instructed. Once seated, she scooted her chair even closer. Her dark eyes gleamed as she leaned toward him. Her shirt was unbuttoned to reveal just a hint of cleavage and her lacy bra. Her fragrance, light and elegant, carried across the table.

Losing her appetite, Kate tossed down her napkin and stood. "I need to get back to work."

Greg pleaded, "Don't go, Kate. You haven't finished your lunch. And we'd like to get to know you better."

We?

Reluctantly Kate sat down again, not knowing how to refuse such a nice request, but she didn't think for one moment Trent felt the same. After their last meeting, where he'd abruptly left her office, he had limited his contact with her by communicating through their assistants and emails. She hadn't seen him—which was perfect for her. She unclenched her teeth and took a sip of water. She'd just have to endure a few more minutes in Farrington's presence.

The waiter took the rest of the food order and left.

Trent turned to Kate. "Have you met Cecilia Sheffield?"

When she looked into his eyes her stomach fluttered. Kate hated herself for being so weak just because he was so physically appealing. "No, not officially."

Wrenching her gaze from his, she smiled at Cecilia, but the woman's narrow-eyed gaze was scrutinizing Kate as if she were competition.

"Of course, I remember *her*," the brunette said. "She's the woman who nearly fell in the lobby."

Trent introduced them. "Dr. Meyers, Cecilia works in Purchasing."

Cecilia gaped at Kate. "*You* are a *doctor?*"

Kate smiled. "Yes." Difficult as it was, she resisted tweaking the woman's jealousy further. She might need to befriend Cecilia to get into the Purchasing department.

Not returning the smile, Cecilia gave Kate a thorough going-over. "I received the memo that we had a new Human Resources

Manager, but I didn't imagine *you* were the one. She doesn't look like a *psychologist*, does she Trent?"

He lifted an eyebrow. "What's a psychologist supposed to look like? *Sigmund Freud?*"

"That would be a good start," Cecilia retorted.

Greg smiled at Kate. "No. She doesn't look anything like *him* to me."

"Not quite, but give her a beard and she could." Cecilia dimpled and turned a perfect little grin to Trent. "When I was told the company had hired two new women... Well, I'm just glad it's someone like you, Dr. Meyers."

The woman didn't realize that competing for Trent Farrington was the last thing on Kate's mind. It was more important for Kate to make friends with Cecilia to access Purchasing, than to have a catfight with one of Trent's potential girlfriends. One day, she wanted him to eat his words that her brother had been responsible for the condition of his shoddy harness and for his own death.

Kate kept her face serene. "I'm glad to meet you, Cecilia. I hope we'll have a great working relationship. Perhaps we can go to lunch together soon."

Cecilia's forehead creased as if she hadn't expected a friendly response after her statement. She turned toward Trent and patted his arm. "How is your mother? Have you spoken to her?"

Trent shook his head. "No, not since she left for Europe three months ago. However, I don't keep tabs on her. Call the house. They'll fill you in." He sipped his water, but Kate noticed his expression had soured and his shoulders hunched when he spoke about his mother.

Cecilia smiled. "I know she wouldn't miss you getting accolades for your building. She's so proud of you—like we all are. I'm sure she'll return in time for the awards ceremony next month."

Trent shrugged. "One never knows with her and it's too early to say I've won."

Cecilia touched his arm again. "I need to speak to you this afternoon...about some matters... I'll come to your office—"

He gave her a sharp look. "No. I'm leaving for the Karger site. I won't be back today."

"Tomorrow then?"

"I'll let you know. You can run anything for me through Mrs. Nash."

Too excited to think, Kate didn't listen to what else they said because this was her chance. *He would be out of the building.*

The rest of lunch was served. While Cecilia held his attention with her constant chatter, and Darcy and Greg discussed the upcoming party, Kate considered her next move. This afternoon, when Trent was out, she would find a way to sneak into his office.

* * *

While Cecilia rattled on about things that didn't interest him, Trent watched Dr. Meyers out of the corner of his eye. She'd not been happy to see him. Her first cool glance told him that. He thought she'd gotten past his accusation that she was in on his grandfather's schemes. When he sat next to her, her full lips pressed into a grim line. Despite that, she laughed enthusiastically at something Greg said.

Trent sucked in his breath. From her smile, he had to speculate she was interested in his friend—he himself seemed to be the only one she despised. Today, she was dressed as drably as the previous two days. However, instead of making her seem pale, the plain, light gray, shapeless suit gave her skin a creamy glow. He didn't think she wore any makeup. He wondered why she didn't go for contacts or for glasses that were more attractive.

Greg smiled warmly at her, too. No doubt, his friend had taken a liking to their new HR Manager.

Greg threw Trent a wink as if he knew what he was thinking and then glanced at Dr. Meyers and her assistant. "I have several tickets. Either of you like the Dolphins?" he asked.

Darcy chimed in, "I love football."

"Do you, Dr. Meyers?" Greg asked, more pointedly.

Trent didn't get the chance to hear her response because Cecilia gripped his arm and said something in his ear. He turned and said, "Sure," too distracted by Dr. Meyers' voice and her pleasing laughter to know what Cecilia had said.

"I didn't think you would ever say yes," Cecilia purred near his ear.

Frowning, he stared at her. "*What?*"

She beamed. "I bought tickets for the musical, hoping you'd agree to go out with me. You can pick me up on Saturday at six." She leaned in closer, her hot breath fanning his cheek. "We can have dinner before the show."

Trent frowned. *How would he get out of it now?*

Lunch was over and Dr. Meyers did not meet his gaze again.

On the way out of restaurant, Cecilia clutched his arm as if they were a couple. "It's about time we went out together. When I heard two more women would be working here, I admit I was jealous, Trent. Can you imagine yourself with a woman like the doctor, with those horrible glasses and suit, or the other woman with her garish red hair and freckles?"

He didn't dignify her comment with an answer. He'd had no problems fantasizing being with one of Farrington's newest employees. In fact, he'd dreamed about Dr. Meyers the night before—a dream so hot, he would scorch Kate Meyers' dainty little ears if he were to tell her about it.

And despite his conviction that she was not potential for a seduction, he found himself more and more concerned with why she disliked him. And he had to question himself: Why did *he* want to change her mind?

* * *

With a sinking heart, Kate strolled past Trent's office for the fifth time that afternoon. With him out of the building, she could explore his office if she could get in. She checked her watch. After five p.m., and his secretary was still at her desk. Although she knew Trent's whereabouts, she'd just have to find out if the elderly lady was going to remain firmly ensconced at her secretarial chair all night.

Kate smiled and stepped into Trent's assistant's office. "Hello, Mrs. Nash. You're still here. Is Mr. Farrington in?"

"He's at a meeting. I don't expect him back today, but the '*Ice Queen*' called—she's in town. Oops, sorry. Perhaps I shouldn't have said that since Mrs. Farrington is one of the executives." The older woman rolled her eyes. "But that's one of Trent's endearing names for his mother." She added under her breath, "And frankly it fits."

Kate recalled his hunched shoulders and his cool reaction at the mention of his mother at lunch. "That's okay," she said softly.

Mrs. Nash stood. "I was just finishing up a letter, dear, because I might be in late tomorrow. My husband's ill. Thankfully, Trent is very understanding—unlike his mother. He's a fine man and deserves..." She sighed. "Oh, dear, do forgive me. I'm saying too much. Comes with the territory. We're like family around here, so many of us have been with the company for years."

Kate smiled. "I understand." But she wondered how such a nice older woman could work for and respect such a louse...

Trent's secretary straightened her desk, readying for the next day. "I'm just so anxious. Norm's cold has gotten worse. Thankfully, it's not his heart this time, but I'm going to run him to the Urgent Care Center as a precaution."

Mrs. Nash was a sweet lady and Kate had to admit she liked the employees she'd met so far. Sighing, Kate made a pretense of checking her watch. "I'm sorry to hear he's not feeling well. Well, if it looks like Mr. Farrington isn't returning, and it's nearing five-thirty, I'll talk to him some other time." Kate walked Mrs. Nash to the elevator. "I hope your husband feels better."

"Thank you, sweetie. He worries me half to death sometimes." She pushed the call button and soon a *ding* announced the elevator had arrived.

"Oh, I just realized I left something in my office." Kate hated to lie to the kind woman, but she had no choice. "Goodnight, Mrs. Nash."

Once the elevator doors closed with a whoosh, Kate blew out a deep breath. She whirled and hurried down the hallway to Trent's office.

Her stomach clenched into knots as she turned the knob on his door. *Locked.* No way would she get in tonight.

Relief swept through her that now she wouldn't have to go through with this, but then she groaned in frustration. She *had* to search his office, as she was getting nowhere. She swiped her hand along her perspiring forehead. She didn't want to contemplate how close she would have to get to him to get his keys.

Very close. She dreaded the thought.

Her gaze flew to Mrs. Nash's forgotten jacket hanging on a coat tree. *Was it possible?* Kate crossed the floor, shoved her fingers into the pocket and felt a cool metal key ring. *Bingo. This might be it.* With shaking hands, she unlocked the office.

She paused before the darkened room, guilt washing over her. She had always respected a person's privacy and here she was ready to go through a man's office. Once she crossed that threshold there would be no turning back.

What had made her think she could do this? She was not like Bill Jackson—her stepfather had never had a conscience. Instead, she agonized over what she planned to do. She blew out a deep breath.

She *had* to find some evidence and her time at the company couldn't last forever. Any day,they could find out she'd falsified her resume.

She wouldn't feel guilty because she'd promised herself she'd find the evidence and truth. It was obvious to her that in spite of his outward appearance and manners, Trent Farrington was a ruthless man with no morals. He deserved to be punished and stopped before others were hurt. Straightening her shoulders, she flipped on the lights. Her gaze swept over Trent's office, even larger than hers— one fitting a man who was second in command.

One table held various completed models of the company's projects over the years. On another table was a large model of the works in progress.

The office had a seating area. Above the credenza, behind his desk, an arrangement of frames graced the wall. She drew closer. Both from Princeton University, one diploma was an engineering diploma, the other an architecture degree.

The next was an award given on the behalf of the City of Fort Lauderdale, for outstanding community service. That had to be a lie.

Beneath was another award for his work, along with a picture of him smiling, this time surrounded by a group of underprivileged children—not the bevy of beauties she'd seen around him in the magazine. Quickly scanning the walls, she surveyed the numerous awards he'd received. Apparently, he was actively involved in the community.

"No!" She shuffled back a step. "Can't be? He's a cheat." How could he receive so much praise? How could Mrs. Nash say he was a *fine* man?

Stunned, she moved to his desk and dropped into his black leather chair. After turning on the lamp, she took Mrs. Nash's keys, unlocked the center drawer and rapidly scanned the contents. Everything was arranged in an orderly fashion. This was not the desk of a negligent person who did sloppy work. If he did something wrong, he knew exactly what he'd done.

She picked up a small book and read the spine to find it was a book of poetry. Was Trent, with his apparently analytical mind, a romantic, too?

The thought twisted her gut. Could she have been all wrong about him? Had Darcy's instincts been right? *Was someone else in the company skimming from the supplies?*

Kate gritted her teeth. Not likely. No one else had the power Trent had. And if he wasn't a part of it, then he was in a position to know who was. She couldn't soften on him until she had evidence otherwise. His good deeds may have been done to cover up his criminal activity. And perhaps one of his many girlfriends left the poetry book.

Scowling, Kate could imagine Cecilia reading poetry to him as she sat seductively on the top of his desk. "Oh, Trent, let me count the ways I love you?" Kate mimicked.

And he had *lied* to Kate, too. At lunch, she'd overheard them making a date, which proved he liked Cecilia.

Kate slid open a side drawer. From the back, she pulled out an assortment of small foil packages. *What's this?* She read the label and dropped the packages, her cheeks growing warm.

The rumors Darcy heard must be true. He probably did it right here in his office, at this desk, or on the comfortable couch.

"Now, that is more like the irresponsible, immoral man I know he is," Kate muttered. *Poor Trent Farrington. Doesn't want to marry any of the women his grandfather hires, but he just can't keep his hands off them…can't keep his sex life away from the business.*

An unwanted image of her sitting on his desk and him standing between her thighs flooded her mind, sending a surge of heat through her.

Enough of that. She snapped the drawer shut. She had to get out of here.

Next, she opened the large side drawer and pulled out a file labeled the Karger Building. The completion date on the building was five months away. She quickly sifted through the papers. Taking a sheet of paper, she jotted down the names of construction suppliers. She would still have to get into Purchasing and find out what he had ordered, and if those products were up to code.

Next, she pulled out a file marked: Personal Correspondence. She skimmed what appeared to be a stack of letters of congratulations. She returned the files and closed the drawer.

Mystified, she blew out a deep breath and slumped in his chair. "Too many congratulations for work well done." She worried her bottom lip with her teeth. Aside from the condoms, was it possible she had been wrong about him? Matt had implied substandard supplies were being used… But could it be someone else in the company…another high-ranking employee ordering them to siphon off money? She'd have to make a list of potential suspects if Trent didn't pan out.

She didn't have time to dwell on that now and didn't want to analyze why hope sprang inside her that it wasn't Trent. She really should get out of here.

The doorknob turned. A soft gasp escaped Kate's lips. She jumped to her feet and grabbed a folder from the top of the desk.

A tall, older blond-haired woman, in a stylish blue suit, strode into the room.

Kate's knees nearly buckled, but a wave of relief swept over her. *It wasn't Trent.*

The woman put one hand on her hip. "Am I interrupting something?" she asked in a chilling, sarcastic voice.

A shiver ran up Kate's spine. "W-who are you?"

The striking woman, probably in her late fifties, narrowed her pale blue eyes. "No. The question is who are you? And why are *you* here in this office?"

Kate swiped her sweaty palms on her skirt, wondering when the lady would call Security. "I'm Kate Meyers—"

"You'll never have him," she hissed. "*I swear it.*"

Kate stiffened. She'd been prepared for thievery or espionage as an accusation, but she hadn't expected this. "What?" she asked, confused.

"I don't care if his grandfather told you that you had a chance," the woman snapped. "I'd never allow any of the bimbos he's hired to marry Trent. So, if you're here to screw him and think it will lead to more, you're wasting your time."

Calming her shattered nerves with a deep breath, Kate pulled herself together. "I'm sorry. I don't know what you're talking about." She held out her hand and forced a smile. "Please allow me to introduce myself. I'm Dr. Kate Meyers, the new Human Resources Manager here at Farrington Construction."

Remembering her planned excuse, if caught, she pointed to the several files on Trent's desk. "I'm looking for an employee file Mr. Farrington had the other day."

The woman's cheeks reddened. "Oh, I assumed...because you were in his office after hours... Never mind what *I* assumed." She stepped closer. Her pale, blue eyes penetrated Kate. "Did you say, *doctor?*"

"Yes, I'm a psychologist. And you are?"

"Why, I'm Eden Grayson *Farrington*."

Trent's mother! Panic ripped through Kate. She didn't think she could be faulted for not knowing because she didn't see any resemblance. The woman was as fair as he was dark. *He must have taken after his Farrington side.*

His mother would surely tell him that Dr. Meyers had been in his office. At least she'd given a fairly good reason for being here, but she'd probably have to face him tomorrow about this.

The woman folded her arms over her chest. "Go ahead and look for the file. I'll wait."

Kate flipped through the stack of files on his credenza and picked out an employee file. "Here, I've got it."

"Then shall we go?"

After they swept through the exit, Trent's mother pushed the button on the lock, then closed the door behind them. "Dr. Meyers, my assistant will arrange for a private meeting with you so we can get to know each other better. As one of the executives, I like to thoroughly know all our upper staff. Also, I'm interested in everything Trent does."

"Yes, I understand, ma'am. If you'll excuse me, I need to go put this file in my office and lock up."

"I'm sure we'll meet again soon, Dr. Meyers." She flicked her gaze over Kate, then stepped onto the elevator. The doors whooshed closed for the second time that night, leaving Kate alone in the hallway.

Kate's breath caught in her throat. She had left the list of construction suppliers on Trent's desk—and Mrs. Farrington had locked the door. The keys. Had she left them on the desk, too?

Her heart was racing as she fumbled in her jacket pocket. When she touched the keys, she exhaled a deep breath. She hurried back to Trent's office and thrust the list into Mrs. Nash's pocket, still wondering how much time she'd have before Security arrived if his mother hadn't believed her story. She locked his desk and took a moment to straighten the files.

When the lock clicked and the door opened, her head jerked up. *Was Mrs. Farrington back? What excuse could she use now?* Her heart pounded.

Kate's gaze flew to Trent. Tall, dark, and handsome, he filled the doorway. "Mr. Farrington!" she gasped.

His looks were not what hit her today, but his expression. His face looked shocked as he propped a shoulder against the doorframe.

She thought she'd have more time before his mother alerted him or Security. She must have called him the instant she was on the elevator, and he had to have been in the building.

His dark gaze glinted like black granite, but with surprise more than anger in his eyes. "Why are you here?" he asked in a puzzled voice.

Feeling faint, Kate licked her dry lips as she struggled to compose her thoughts.

In a few strides, he reached her. "Not going to answer me?"

His nearness overpowered her and she stepped back from the desk. "I thought you might have an employee file," she said in a rush. "And your door was unlocked—I didn't think there would be a problem if I checked for it."

His expression held disbelief. "I see," he ground out. "And that's why you're here in my office after hours?"

"Yes." She nodded emphatically. "That is correct."

He tugged on the center drawer of his desk. Relief spread through every cell in her body that she had locked his desk.

Trent threw her a cautious glance, but seemed satisfied. However, at his concern, she wondered, if she'd overlooked something?

He stepped closer to her, his height and nearness forcing her to take a step backward. "I'll speak to Mrs. Nash about why my door wasn't locked."

"Oh, please, don't blame Mrs. Nash," Kate said, not wanting to get the kind secretary into trouble. "Her husband wasn't feeling well. She had to leave quickly to take him to the doctor."

He frowned. "*Norm*? Is he all right?"

Kate winced, sorry to have worried him. Based on his expression, he cared for the Nashes, but she needed to use the excuse. "He's okay, but she wasn't taking any chances and wanted the doctor to look at him."

"All right." He seemed visibly relieved by the news that Mr. Nash was not in serious danger, but then he crossed his arms over his chest. "But what is it about you, Dr. Meyers? Here it is late into the evening, and you're creeping around my office. I thought you might be out on a date…or off making plans with *Greg* for the game on Sunday."

She should ask him the same thing, why wasn't he out with Cecilia. "I didn't have *plans* for tonight."

"If you're not in on any scheme with my grandfather, what is it you want from me? You obviously don't like me, but I have this feeling you want something from me. I just don't know what it is yet."

"I do want something from you," she said sweetly, raising her face to his.

He raised an eyebrow. "Care to enlighten me?"

"This." She lifted the file in her hand. "I assumed since the door wasn't locked, you wouldn't mind if I retrieved a file." She gave him a piercing glance. "You don't have anything to hide, do you?"

He glared. "Of course, I don't. But I do need to lock my door or *anyone* could come in here."

"Mr. Farrington, I'm only trying to do the job your grandfather hired me for. Being new, it might take me a little longer to accomplish certain duties, so I was working late."

He snorted at her statement and stepped forward, so close she couldn't help but breathe in the scent of him.

"I admire your dedication, but I do believe he hired you to do a different job. And you don't even know what it is yourself." The silkiness of his voice made her insides warm and liquefy. She stepped back from him, but found herself backed against the credenza.

Holding his gaze, she groped for something to say. "I hope you're only referring to your grandfather's suggestions that I speak to you as a *psychologist*—and nothing more?"

Though there was a gleam in his eyes, he didn't answer and moved toward her. "That's not what I'm thinking at all."

She moistened her lips. "I know what you're getting at, but—"

"You do? Because *I'm* not sure." Frowning, he traced his finger down her face in a caress. Then he ran his thumb across her cheek. "Something is going on here."

Her thighs pressed more tightly against the credenza. She breathed in his essence, while his gaze fell to her lips. She felt the warmth of his hand on the nape of her neck as he pulled her to him. A wild heat swept through her. When he lowered his mouth, she raised her lips and closed her eyes. He was going to kiss her, and strangely, she wanted him to—which was total insanity.

"Kate," he whispered. She flung her eyes open. He stared at her, his mouth only inches away from hers. Then he dropped his hands to his sides and took a step back. "Don't look so hopeful."

Heat flooded her cheeks. *What had come over her?* "Is that what you think?"

Trent had the bleakest look in his eyes. "A warning, doc. I'm not playing into my family's scheme. I'm available for warming your bed if you want, but I don't plan to marry anyone—especially someone my family has handpicked for me."

Her knees were knocking together and she wanted to slap his face. Had he deliberately tried to humiliate her and to test her to see how she would respond? "Mr. Farrington, sleeping with you will never be a possibility. And I restate this for clarity: I'm not in on any marriage plot with your grandfather, so be careful you don't step over the boundaries of polite business into *harassing* me."

"Your point is taken."

"I don't know why you keep asking me my motives."

"Hell, it's the only reason he would have hired you. Do you have a construction background?"

She straightened her shoulders. "No. This is my first job of this nature."

"So my grandfather hires an inexperienced HR Manager. Do you think I'm stupid?" he ground out. "His eyesight must be failing, because you don't even look old enough to be the age on your resume—"

"I've taken good care of my skin, and he liked my credentials," she pointed out.

He snorted. "Listen, Dr. Meyers, I have no illusions your interest would be in me—for me, personally—but you could be interested because of the company or my family's money. So I'll reiterate that I'm not after some gold-digging wife."

Didn't he think a woman would like him for himself?

Kate held a steady gaze. "Have I ever done anything or come onto you in any way? I can promise you that I would never, *ever*, be interested in you."

After a moment, he gave her a curt nod. "All right, Dr. Meyers, whatever you say, but the next time you have a reason to be here, you're to ask my permission—*personally*."

"I will," she said, grateful not to be fired on the spot.

He escorted her to the door, but blocked it, effectively letting her know he'd allow her to leave only when he was ready. "Security is being tightened. Anyone working after hours is to clear it through the guard at the front desk. *Comprehend?*"

"Why? Is there a problem at the company?"

"I have my reasons." Apparently, he wasn't going to divulge any information to her. "If you assure me you have no ulterior motive for being here, I'll give you the benefit of the doubt…*this time.*"

"I was here for the reason I said and was just leaving. Goodnight, Mr. Farrington."

Their gazes locked until he must have assured himself she told the truth.

"Goodnight, Dr. Meyers." He stepped aside and allowed her to pass.

* * *

A few minutes later, her hands trembled on the wheel as Kate drove her car the short distance to her home in Victoria Park. After Trent had closed the door to his office, she had quickly dropped the keys into Mrs. Nash's jacket.

However, now that she had time to think…she knew being caught in his office wasn't the thing that bothered her the most. What really worried her was her response to him. She had stood there waiting and wanting him to kiss her, as if she'd lost her mind.

Thankfully, she'd recovered enough composure to tell him she'd never be interested in him. That should keep him away.

Kate pulled her car into her driveway and turned off the engine. She rested her forehead against the steering wheel. A few nice letters and awards didn't mean Trent Farrington was in the clear, although now she felt she needed to widen her net for other possible suspects. Something shady was going on, yet she couldn't deny she was drawn to the good things about him. When she had decided to do her own investigation, she hadn't thought about how involved she would be with the people who worked at the company. Nothing was black or white.

She entered her little bungalow, her sanctuary, the house she had slowly and lovingly renovated to create the happy home environment she'd never had. A cold knot formed in her stomach and an unbidden thought from the past rushed to her mind. What would Bill Jackson have done to her if she'd been caught in one of his sleazy schemes—like the time she refused to take money out of someone's desk for him? He'd backhanded her when she had refused... She'd hit her head against the wall so hard...

But she couldn't think of him now; she had other concerns.

She flipped on the lights in her office and sat at her desk. She needed a reminder of who Trent Farrington was. From a file, she took out a magazine. "Bachelor of the Year" was printed and beneath a picture of Trent Farrington. He grinned and leaned against a black Porsche, surrounded by bathing beauties.

But all the evidence she'd seen tonight, except for the condoms, showed him to be a caring person whom people liked.

Just who was Trent Farrington?

CHAPTER SIX

Standing outside the chain-link fence surrounding the Karger building, Kate tensed as jackhammers slammed concrete and blasted their deafening sounds. The smell of oil and diesel fumes wafted in the air all around the construction site, making Kate's stomach roil. Resolved to do this, she trudged on shaky legs through the entrance gate, determined to find and photograph some samples of the inferior products the company used.

Over the weekend, she had called Matt's friend, Bobby, wanting to have him meet her at the site, but he still hadn't answered the phone or returned her call.

She strode toward the nearest construction worker who stood beside a white work van. His back was to her and he wore a hard hat. A white t-shirt accentuated his broad shoulders and strong back, which tapered into a V toward a narrow waist. Tight blue jeans encased muscular, long legs and a sculpted backside.

Wow! If his rugged appearance was any indication of the workers on the site, she'd better keep this to herself or Darcy would make a beeline over here to check out the guys.

"Excuse me, sir," Kate called out. "I need to ask you something."

Apparently, the man didn't hear her because he disappeared behind the open doors of the van.

Kate followed him. "Could you please tell me if Bobby Owens is working today...?" she asked as she rounded the corner, only to find the man had stripped off his t-shirt, revealing a muscular, toned back. He turned to answer her.

Trent Farrington! She gasped and stepped back.

He stood before her bare-chested with his grimy t-shirt bunched in his hands. His muscles gleamed in the sunlight. Every thought in her mind evaporated. She couldn't take her eyes off his chest, the smattering of dark hair there...

"Dr. Meyers?" he asked, surprise in his voice. "I'm changing my shirt. What the hell are you doing here?"

Cringing that she'd have to come up with some excuse, she raised her gaze to his face. She hadn't seen him since the time he'd discovered her in his office. That day, there had been no doubt that a fiery attraction burned between them—unwanted on both sides.

Afterwards, whenever he had needed an employee's records, he'd sent Mrs. Nash. In turn, Kate had Darcy return the files to him.

Now, here he was, stripped practically naked before her eyes. It wasn't the first time the words 'Greek god' rushed to her mind. Even with a sheen of perspiration coating him, he was incredibly sexy.

"Oh, Mr. Farrington, excuse me," she said, snapping to her senses.

Trent ran the shirt over his sweaty face and torso, all the while watching her face intently. "Did you say Bobby Owens? What is your concern with him?"

She grasped for a logical explanation. "Ah, just a question about his home number not being on his records. It's no big deal."

Cleaning his safety glasses with his t-shirt, Trent's eyes gleamed with ire. "Kind of a lame excuse. He's not a potential date, huh, doc? One would think someone like you would go for the English Professor types, not someone who gets sweaty and greasy for a living. Of course, then there is…*Greg.*"

"*Greg who?*" she asked in a hoarse whisper. Why did he bring up Greg when Greg was the furthest thing from her mind? Her gaze raked down over Trent's muscular shoulders and biceps, his chest, and the taut muscles of his abdomen. A sprinkling of dark hair disappeared into the snug blue jeans slung low on his hips…and toward a bulge that left little to the imagination. Heat curled around her insides and settled in her lower region.

He frowned. "Something wrong? Or have you never seen a man without a shirt before?"

Her cheeks warmed. "None like you," she muttered truthfully. "Sorry, I mean, I'm used to seeing you in business attire." She whirled to face the tall building. "Is it particularly hot today for October or what?"

"And growing hotter, Dr. Meyers? One would think seeing me shirtless unsettles you."

"Not at all." She raised her chin and turned to face him.

The gaze he flicked over her held simmering heat. "Are you sure?"

Remembering what he had said about only being available for warming her bed, she flushed from head to toe. She nodded. "I'm sure. It's only a warm day."

Trent chuckled. "Right." He pulled a clean t-shirt over his head and tucked it into his jeans. "If I see Bobby, I'll tell him to call you."

Panic swept through her. The last thing she wanted was for Trent to mention her name to Bobby, who might in turn tell him she was Matt's sister and not a doctor at all. "That won't be necessary, Mr. Farrington. I'll get in touch with him." She turned to leave.

"Wait. You are coming for a tour, aren't you?" Trent strode into her path. "I don't believe you've been to the site. However, you must get a hard hat whenever you go through those gates—and safety glasses."

He replaced his own. Then he strode over to the entry gate and picked up the items from a stack for her. He stepped in front of her and unceremoniously placed the hard hat on her head, then adjusted it. "Come on. I'll take you up in the elevator. You can see the entire city."

Kate wrinkled her brow at this personal assistance from him. "I think I have something to do back at the office."

"What's wrong?" he asked as they strode onto the site and toward an elevator. "Are you afraid of heights…or of *me*?"

Feeling a little too ill to lie completely, she nodded. "Heights bother me. *You* don't in the least. But I don't know about this…especially those open-cage elevators. I feel a little queasy just thinking about it."

"You'll do fine. It's perfectly safe. I'll be right beside you. After all, this is what we do here. You know," he teased, "we build buildings. This is our largest project to date."

"Does it sound silly to you, my fear of heights?" she asked, her voice quivering.

"Not at all. We're all afraid of something." His ironic gaze swept over her.

Was he afraid of commitment? Was that why his family pushed him so hard toward marriage?

Trent headed toward the place where Matt had fallen. Pain and sadness hit her as she followed him. As they neared the spot, panic swept through her. Unable to face the spot at this moment, she backed away. "I'm sorry. Please excuse me. I remember something I have to do at the office. I-I'll tour the building and go up in the elevator some other day."

Kate hurried on shaky legs toward the entrance, dropping the hard hat and safety glasses on the stacks. She fled through the gates.

* * *

On Saturday, the sun set low on what promised to be a gorgeous fall Florida evening for the benefit ball.

Trent slid out of his Porsche and rang the doorbell at his grandfather's mansion. Every member in the family, no matter where else they lived, had their own bedroom suite at the house. His mother resided here part time, while his Aunt Vera lived here all the time.

Trent had been at his condo dressing, when he'd received a call from his mother. His grandfather wanted them at the house for a family meeting before the party. He didn't look forward to these gatherings, but would attend for the sake of his grandfather.

Trent stepped up the bricked steps and rang the doorbell.

The butler opened the mammoth front door. The diminutive Beasley, his hair in white wisps over his balding head, craned his neck upward. "Mr. Trent, what a pleasure it is to see you," he said in his British accent. "A man in black. Your costume this year is…?"

"Zorro."

"The ladies will be impressed."

Every time he saw their short English butler, Trent was reminded of a television comedian in a bad skit. He suppressed his laughter into a warm smile. "Hey, Beasley, anyone tell you that you look like an actor?"

"Oh, no, Mr. Trent. I don't think anyone would mistake me for a star. If you're looking for your grandfather, he's been in his library all day. He said he's relaxing."

"Relaxing my ass," Trent ground out under his breath.

He shook his head in disgust as he strode down the hall, his leather boots echoing on the black-and-white checked marble floor. Without knocking, Trent thrust the door open and entered his grandfather's two-story library with its gleaming mahogany-paneled walls, vintage leather furniture, and towering bookshelves.

The old man should have been resting, but he sat at his desk with pen to paper. His face reddened when he saw his grandson. "Trent."

"Caught in the act." Trent strode across the floor. "Eden said the doctor told you to take it easy. Why are you working?"

"You know I dislike it when you call your mother by her first name—and I can't take it easy. I'm bored stiff." He started to haul himself out of the chair, but the effort seemed too much. He sat back in his seat.

Trent moved around the desk. "Damn it, you're going to kill yourself. No more work today." He helped his grandfather over to the leather sofa, then propped a pillow behind his back and slid an ottoman under the elderly man's feet. "While you look as healthy as a horse, if the doctor says you're to rest because of a weak heart, you're to rest."

Eden traipsed into the room with Beasley following. "Let's hope so," she said.

Dressed like a queen with a diamond tiara on her head, she brushed by Trent. Her wide evening gown rustled against his legs. "Now, give your mother a kiss, since I haven't seen you in ages."

Her appearance of warmth was the usual lie. She didn't approve of Trent. Never had. To her, his looks and his playboy lifestyle was a constant reminder of his father who must have broken her heart, and Trent had always borne the brunt of her anger after his father's death. He had tried so hard when he was young to make her happy, but he no longer cared.

"You look lovely as usual, *Mother*." He touched his lips to her cheek—a gimmick to keep the elderly man satisfied that all was right between them.

While his mother sat on the sofa, she patted a space beside her, signaling her son to sit next to her. "Trent…dear."

He nodded and sat down.

"Beasley, drinks for everyone," his grandfather ordered.

"Except for *you*," Trent quipped. "You're going to follow doctor's orders."

After the butler served Eden a martini and Trent a beer, his grandfather said, "Now, where the hell is Roland?"

Trent straightened the cuff on his shirt and shrugged. "Is he even in town?" Trent wasn't his cousin's keeper and hadn't seen him in a month. They both avoided each other's company unless business or holidays forced them together. Not since Trent had been eighteen and Roland twenty-four had they been close. And that closeness ended abruptly for good reason. His cousin had betrayed him with a woman that Trent had at one time thought he loved.

"Well, I can't wait all day for him to decide to show," his grandfather said. "I could be on my deathbed, and he would be late."

Strolling into the library, Roland showed signs the good life had assaulted his waning looks. Dark circles revealed how much he partied, while his blond hair curled in wisps over his forehead. "Discussing me with great affection I hope?"

"*What* are *you* wearing?" Eden asked, sarcasm lacing every word.

Roland patted his portly stomach. "When I'm finished dressing, I'll be Batman." He stalked to the bar and poured a drink. "Trying to make me look bad again, cuz?"

Trent met his cousin's pale blue gaze. "No one has to do that for you. You do an adequate job yourself."

Roland raised his beverage in salute. "At least, I don't have employees dying—"

"Stop, please," his grandfather interrupted. "I don't want your squabbling in front of me. I expect the two of you to put aside your differences now. I have something important to say." He sighed and leaned back on the sofa.

"Take it easy," Trent said. "Don't upset yourself."

His grandfather's gaze studied his. "My doctor ordered me to rest. I'm leaving you at the helm, Trent. You'll assume my duties and make all the major decisions. Roland, you are second in command and will be his right-hand man."

"What the hell? I'm older. Why choose him and not me?" Roland asked.

"Trent's been my vice president this past year. When you prove yourself responsible, then we'll talk again. Now, both of you need to show me over the next couple of weeks that I can rely on you to run the business."

Trent wasn't surprised when Roland cast a threatening glance in his direction.

Eden waved her hand. "Your grandfather is right. Now, Roland, stop being such a baby. And, Trent, why don't you and your cousin apologize to each other for whatever it has been that has been bothering you two for the past decade."

Did she really think years of animosity could be solved in a single sentence? And why should he be the one to apologize? Trent rose and strode to the bar.

His grandfather shook his fist. "You'd better settle your differences. Farrington Construction is your heritage. I'm depending on you both. Roland, I'm giving you a second chance to step into the VP role, but leave now. I need to discuss some other issues with Trent."

Roland raised his hand in mock salute. "Of course. He's the *favored* grandson. I'll say good night." On his way out, he walked past the bar where Trent leaned. "Watch your back, cuz, because you might find a knife in it."

Then Roland strode out.

Sighing, Trent returned to his chair. He wished his grandfather wouldn't always pit them against each other.

"I don't understand why you two can't get along?" Eden said.

Trent shrugged and shook his head. Too much water under the bridge now, as the saying goes.

"It was the same with my brother," his grandfather muttered. "Only one of us could be in charge. Luckily, *I* was the one." He leveled his gaze on Trent's mother. "Eden, I expect you to support Trent while I'm off work and at home."

His mother raised an eyebrow. "Of course, James, but frankly, you should have made me Trent's right-hand woman. Haven't I always done everything you've asked?"

His grandfather gave her a curt nod. "You've been a good daughter-in-law."

Trent sighed and ran a hand through his hair. "*Mother*, please... Don't worry about anything at the company and you'll have my gratitude."

"What is that supposed to mean?" Eden's mouth curved downward. "No, darling, I'll be happy to help you. I will not let you or James down."

Now what did that veiled statement mean?

Trent groaned under his breath. That was all he needed. A few years ago, when his mother—Miss Socialite—had insisted on a position of power in the company, his grandfather had placated her and invented the title of Executive Vice President of Affairs. No surprise to Trent, she had proven herself unreliable in even the lightest of duties. She had never been dependable—anytime or with anything in his life.

His mother and his cousin had become headaches to be tolerated, even more than his grandfather would ever know. Other than the three of them, there was Roland's mother. Though a member of the family, Aunt Vera never had any interest in the business.

His grandfather leaned toward him. "Tonight, at the party, you're to take over my duties as host. Your mother will assist you.

"Fine," Trent said inclining his head. Eden was her best at social functions.

"Now, Trent, the last thing I need to discuss with you, before you and your mother take off, is about your settling down. I would retire if you proved yourself capable to run the company...*and* if you would marry."

Trent blew out a deep breath. "You're not going to let up, are you? I can tell you, you'll have to do better in your scheming than throwing Dr. Meyers at me. She is not in the least interested in me...at all."

After he'd seen her at the construction site, he ran into her and Greg in the hallway. Both of them seemed happy. She smiled at Greg like she never had at him, and it had been a sucker punch of reality. Greg had winked as if giving Trent a signal that things were going well with her. Trent had backed off on any pursuit, for his friend's sake, even though he had considered ramping things up with the little psychologist.

His grandfather snorted. "I didn't throw her at you."

Trent raised a cynical eyebrow.

"All right, fault me," he grumbled. "If I hire a pretty girl once in awhile, it's only because I want to do what's best for you and this family." His grandfather laid a hand against his heart and slumped back on the sofa.

"Are you all right?" Trent rose to his feet.

"It's nothing... Growing tired, but let me finish what I have to say. For some reason, Farringtons don't reproduce easily... My brother died without any children. Now, our entire future rests on you."

"*And Roland*," Trent stated flatly. "He's your grandson, too."

Eden rose from her chair. "Trent, let's go, and leave James to rest."

* * *

A few minutes later, Trent stepped outside with his mother and onto the front porch of the mansion, with its tall white columns and red brick bathed in moonlight.

Eden gave him a sideways glance. "Please…ride with me to the ball."

Trent surveyed her cool demeanor. Although riding with her was against his better judgment, he nodded in agreement. From his car, he gathered up the hat, sword, and mask that went with his costume.

Her chauffeur opened the limousine door. "Thank you, Marc." Eden patted the man's lapel and slid into the car.

Trent wondered as he climbed in, what the Ice Queen's relationship was with her burly driver and all-around assistant?

Once they were seated, Trent shut the glass between them and the driver.

"Marc makes me feel safe and not a target for muggers," she said, as if she could read his mind. Her fingers stroked a diamond earring dangling from her earlobe. A diamond bracelet adorned her wrist. "What's the point of having lovely things, if one can't take pleasure in them? And I admit I enjoy being taken around town by a handsome man."

Trent shrugged. "What you do is your business."

His curt remark had little effect on her. "I must say thank you for riding with me to the party."

Trent raised an eyebrow. It wasn't like his mother to want to be alone with him.

The black limousine rolled down the long brick driveway and through the wrought iron gates toward downtown. Silence fell between them as they passed shops and restaurants lining Las Olas Boulevard. He waited for an explanation.

Finally, she pulled an envelope from her purse. "This is the speech your grandfather was to give."

Trent scanned the material and put the paper in his inside jacket pocket. "I'm sure you've done another fine job of putting the benefit together."

She clasped her hands in her lap. "Thank you. One of your duties tonight will be to make the Granthams feel welcome. I know they make you crazy, but they're major benefactors to the charities. I'm sure you can handle the rest of the responsibilities."

He inclined his head. "I'll do my best." He'd never cared for the Granthams because Eden sucked up to them all the time.

"I know you will, and that's why James is leaning heavily on you. Will you also think about what your grandfather is proposing?"

Trent raised an eyebrow. "You mean, find a wife?"

"Yes. Why not Cecilia? Along with the Granthams, Cecilia's parents will be here. Both Mr. and Mrs. Sheffield agree with me that their daughter would make you an excellent wife."

"I'm sure they think so," he muttered. "But don't you feel that's a bit strange since she's related to us?" *And they need my money because of their bad investments*, he thought dryly, but didn't add that.

"Gracious me. Where do you come up with these things? With the Sheffields distantly related to my side of the family before the Civil War, and generations away, that hardly counts as some sort of incest."

He shifted uneasily in his seat. They were driving him crazy with their constant chatter about marriage. Was that the plan, to wear him down so he'd marry just anyone?

Anger simmered in him. "So, marriage to Cecilia is what you want?"

"I think you couldn't find anyone more suitable. She's not some slut who will marry you for your money and divorce you later."

"As *you* have reminded me so many times before: My money is all a woman would want from me."

"In our position, we must be careful." She reached out and brushed her hand briefly across his. He flinched. "The Sheffields are an old family of distinction. Cecilia's uncle is a senator, and might even be president one day."

He folded his arms over his chest. "And *I'm* aware that her family is having financial difficulties. Do you want me to trade my money for someone with political prestige?"

"It's done often enough, even today."

"If I ever marry, *Eden*, it won't be because I've checked the woman's pedigree or what she can bring to our family."

He knew he'd struck a blow by reminding her of her own marriage to his father—that her family had brought money to the table.

Eden pursed her lips. "I didn't expect you would ever give Cecilia a chance, especially since it's something *I* want." She turned her back on him and gazed out the window. "I think she's a delightful girl."

Last Saturday night, he *had* taken Cecilia out to dinner and a musical, but he wasn't telling Eden. During the show, he had endured Cecilia brushing her hand against his cheek, then *accidentally* his groin. He dropped her off promptly after the show. Cecilia had thrown her arms around him, rubbed her breasts against him and invited him in for the night. She told him graphically what she wanted them to do.

Not interested, he'd left her pouting in her hall.

Eden turned and glared. "No. You'd never consider Cecilia because she's someone I'd be proud to say is my daughter-in-law."

He shrugged, acknowledging there was some truth in her statement. Just knowing his mother pushed Cecilia on him doubly turned him off.

"You're as selfish as your father was—he couldn't be faithful. And you've never tried to do what I want you to do, to make me happy. That's why we've never gotten along, Trent."

His jaw tightened. He was her son. When had she ever cared to make *him* happy? He remembered being really sick when he was three or four, but it was his grandmother who had taken care of him. His mother had not been there for him either when he was six and had crashed his bicycle and broken his arm. She'd already planned a luncheon engagement so she arranged for Mrs. Nash to sit with him in the hospital emergency room. It was Mrs. Nash who sat with her arm around him while he cried. He still remembered his mother telling him that boys were hurt all the time by their stupid actions— grubby things that they were—and for him to let the pain be a reminder he shouldn't be so careless.

Nor, was she there for him after his father died.

He looked down his nose at her now. "Then I think we're even," he snapped. "You want me to marry someone to increase your status in the social world? Isn't your circle lofty enough?" He could barely hold his anger in check. "Do you want me to be miserable just because you and my father were? Your father and my grandfather all but arranged your marriage to benefit their families and you wanted my father. Is that what you want for me?"

Eden's face reddened. "You ungrateful bast…" She raised her palm as if to strike him and then lowered her hand and braced the seat.

"No, at least you've never hit me. You're too much in control."

"Sometimes I think you purposely try to upset me," she said more calmly. "Perhaps James is right. You can't handle the responsibilities that come with being a true Farrington."

"I *am* a true Farrington and my responsibility is to myself—*first*. I learned that from you, Eden. The last thing I'll do is marry someone pushed on me, *so back off.* I'll decide when and if someone will be my *wife*."

"It would serve you right if your grandfather sold everything or turned the business over to Roland. You're going to fall in love with one of those sluts you see. You've already had Dr. Meyers up to your office, after hours."

He frowned. How did she have that information? "You're really way off base if you think Dr. Meyers and I—"

"*Really?*" she said dryly. "I'm not at all surprised at what goes on in your office. Why don't you *marry* Cecilia and make us all happy? You could still have your cheap whores behind her back, just as your father did to me. Then *I* would have someone presentable for my friends." She turned her back on him again and her shoulders shook as if she cried.

His shoulders bunched. He hated to see a woman in tears and Eden never cried. No matter how bad their relationship was, she was his mother. "Don't cry."

She shook her head, and mumbled over her shoulder, "I'm fine. I didn't mean to get so angry with you. It's not your fault your father cheated on me…although you remind me so much of him, in looks and in your lifestyle. Despite what you think…I want you to be happy." While she still kept her back to him, she reached out and patted his arm. "You spoke the truth about my marriage," she choked out. "Then you came a long… Even so, Porter still lived his whoring lifestyle as if he were single. I think he only came home to me because of…*because of you*."

Trent's stomach tensed in a knot of guilt for upsetting her so.

She exhaled a deep breath and turned to face him. "The company is riding on your shoulders now. I want to be there for you, to make amends."

"Too late, *Eden*."

"It's never too late as long as we're alive. If I could take back everything and be a better mother to you… I'm so sorry. Please, at least let me be your friend now."

The boy inside him wanted her love, but not the man. He didn't need her anymore.

"I don't think there's a chance in hell of that ever happening."

"I won't give up." She turned her head toward the window again. "I may not be the perfect mother, but I want you to know how proud I am of your latest achievements. I look forward to the award's ceremony. And James, he is also proud of you." She didn't glance at Trent, although her icy fingers groped for his hand. "Please…"

A long time ago, he would have done anything for her approval or affection. He shook off her hand. "Don't try. Now, let's carry on the remainder of the evening civilly."

They rode the rest of the way to the benefit ball in silence. As they pulled in front of the main doors of Farrington Towers, he couldn't help but wonder about her strange behavior tonight. Was something wrong with her? Was she ill? Was that why she wanted to make amends—*now*?

* * *

Jazz music floated from the stereo in the living room and into the bathroom of Kate's small bungalow in Victoria Park. She and Darcy dressed for the benefit ball. Glancing into the big bathroom mirror, Kate tugged at the silver-blue, eighteenth-century ball gown, trying to get the neckline to cover more. The wide skirt made her waist seem tiny. She ran her fingers through the creamy lace hanging from the three-quarter length sleeves, then turned sideways.

She frowned at how her breasts swelled over the tight bodice. "Darcy, I knew I should have gone with you to pick out my costume. I swear I can't wear this. It's too revealing."

In a similar pink ball gown, Darcy preened in the mirror. A hairpiece of rich red curls flowed down her back. She took a brush and dusted a rosy blush over her cheekbones. "Oh, come on, Kate. Showing your bosom was all the rage back then, and now you look the part."

A final misting of hair spray to Darcy's hair threatened to choke Kate in the small bathroom.

Darcy plumped up the curls of the fall. "I'd love thick hair like this—like yours."

"You look pretty. How I envy the fiery color of your hair."

Darcy clamped her hands on her hips and glanced down at her own small breasts. "And I wish I had your problem there, too."

Kate stared at the mirror in dismay. "Thanks, but I think I'll catch a cold," she said noticing the irony.

"It's South Florida and seventy-five degrees outside. You're not showing that much. You're just not used to it."

"You know there's such a thing as air-conditioning."

"I should have the problem of freezing mine off," Darcy said, stuffing tissues in the bodice of her dress. "Guess I should have bought a padded bra."

Kate turned back to the mirror and frowned again. "I suppose there's nothing I can do about this costume, but live with it."

"Now, for your makeup and hair. Did you bring the contacts?"

"Yes. Right here."

"Okay. Put them in. I'll be right back with our wine after I change the music."

Darcy had insisted she put on Kate's makeup so Kate settled onto the barstool she'd brought into the bathroom. She supposed makeup would add to her disguise tonight. The starchy satin of the gown rustled and felt foreign against her skin.

Kate muttered under her breath, "Perhaps I should have dressed as 'Cat Woman' and worn a black cat suit for stealth."

What costume would Trent wear tonight? She inwardly groaned, stopping her thoughts. What could it matter? Even though she now suspected the villain could be someone else, she had not officially cleared Trent—and she was at the company on false pretenses. Besides, she wasn't planning to go into the ballroom, just the offices. This evening presented a perfect opportunity to snoop.

Since seeing him at the construction site, she'd only run into him one other time during the week, and it had been in the hallway at work. She'd been talking to Greg and had laughed at something he'd said just as Trent rounded a corner. Trent's gaze had briefly met hers before traveling over to Greg, then her employer gave them both a brief nod and walked on.

Darcy changed the music in the living room and a classical song filled the air.

Kate leaned toward her reflection and popped in the contacts she'd ordered last week. Tonight, it was a necessity to be in disguise and unrecognizable.

She hadn't worn contacts in years, but for a few days, she'd been trying them out in the evenings to accustom herself to wearing lenses again. For a few seconds her eyes teared at the intrusion. She blinked and opened them to find deep, dark, forest-green eyes staring back at her.

Darcy returned to the bathroom and thrust a glass of Chardonnay into Kate's hand. "I put on Beethoven. We need some mood music to get us into character. Now, turn away from the mirror. No peeking, until I'm finished with your hair and makeup."

While Darcy applied makeup, Kate took an occasional sip of wine, trying to calm her ever-tightening nerves. Kate couldn't believe she was actually going to search in some of the Farrington offices tonight.

Darcy arranged Kate's long hair on top of her head, securing her blond tresses with pins.

Finally, Darcy brushed a finishing coat of powder and pressed something onto Kate's cheek. "You need a beauty mark. Now close those eyes."

After another choking mist of hairspray, Darcy held a feathered fan to Kate's face and swiveled the barstool around toward the mirror. "All right, get ready for the unveiling." She theatrically lowered the fan.

Staring into the mirror, Kate's eyes widened. Long, blond curls cascaded over her left shoulder and emphasized the small heart-shaped birthmark she had on her collarbone. The lipstick accentuated her full lips.

Darcy put her hands on her hips. "I always knew you were pretty, but now, you're *drop-dead gorgeous.*"

Kate's mouth turned down.

"I must be your fairy godmother. Who would have believed?" Darcy asked.

Anxiety gnawed at Kate, but Darcy shook her head. "Don't worry, girl. No one will recognize you with this transformation. *I* wouldn't recognize you. You're usually so drab." A blush spread on Darcy's cheeks. She put her hand to her mouth and coughed. "Sorry."

Kate gulped her wine to relieve her dry throat. Even she was amazed at the change, since a few years had passed since she'd tried to look pretty.

Panic revolted in her stomach. She didn't like this at all. It reminded her of her stepfather's seedy friends ogling her, and how her fiancé, Jeff, had paraded her about to his friends in college. She realized later that her fiancé had cared more about her looks than about *her*—and he couldn't get beyond her stepfather's criminal past.

After they broke up, she had decided her *brains* were going to take her places—not her outward appearance.

Kate grabbed the powdered wig that went with the costume. "I'm wearing this."

"No way. I worked so hard on your hair. Trust me, no one is going to recognize you."

"I can't chance it, Darcy." Kate pulled the wig over her blond curls.

"Doesn't matter," her friend said, shaking her finger at her. "You still look beyond beautiful. I don't know why you've been hiding your looks all of these years, girl." Darcy exhaled a deep breath. "Forget that statement. I can guess why—your fiancé and your stepfather both did a number on you."

CHAPTER SEVEN

The elevator bell dinged as Kate and Darcy reached the forty-second floor of Farrington Towers. Kate released her clammy grip on the railing and blew out a deep breath. No matter how many times she rode these high-tech elevators, she still trembled as if it were the first time.

Once they stepped onto the floor, she pulled her friend aside and allowed their fellow passengers to pass by. A medium-sized gladiator strode by and winked at them. He gave Kate a long going-over and a low whistle.

His date, dressed as a slave girl, tugged on his arm and yanked him along and down the hallway. "You're no Russell Crowe. So unless you want me to feed *you* to the lions, keep your eyes on *me*."

In the next group was a wimpy-looking Dracula. Behind him, a bulky Frankenstein shuffled down the hall. His bride wore a towering beehive hairdo and her tittering laughter filled the air as they drifted toward the doorman taking tickets. Each time the doors opened and someone entered, rock music vibrated from the ballroom.

"This should be fun," Darcy whispered, after everyone had passed.

Kate placed her hand on Darcy's arm. "Listen, I meant it. I'm not going inside. This disguise was just to get me into the building."

Darcy sighed. "Why can't we enjoy tonight? We can always return to our *covert ways* on Monday."

"Funny; but tonight is for Matt. And it's the perfect opportunity for me to get into those offices."

Darcy's shoulders drooped. "Do you want my help?"

"No. Of course not. You go and have fun, just let me know later what gossip you hear." She gave her friend a bland smile that belied her nervousness. "Besides, tonight is your night. You look radiant. I'm sure some lucky guy is going to fall madly in love with you."

The next load of people streamed out of the elevator and blocked the doorman's view of the stairwell. This was her chance.

"Darcy, wish me luck. I'm going up. If nothing comes of tonight's investigation to implicate Trent or someone else, I might just leave the company." She also didn't like that she was so attracted to him, especially now that she thought he might be innocent.

"Why can't we stay anyway? You're doing a good job."

"You can stay, but there is no way I can. Eventually they'll figure out I falsified the psychologist part—they might even find out that I'm Matt's stepsister and figure out why I came here."

She waved Darcy on and opened the door to the stairwell. It was vacant, faintly lit, and too dark for her taste tonight. Goose bumps prickled up Kate's arms.

The heavy door closed behind her. Glad her slippers were quiet on the metal steps, she climbed up the stairs toward the executive offices.

At the sound of quick footsteps hitting the stairs and coming down toward her, Kate's heartbeat quickened. She backed against the wall and sucked in her breath. A tall, dark figure rounded the corner and nearly bumped into her. She gasped.

"Excuse me. I didn't see you," said a man in a familiar voice.

Trent! Her heart skipped a beat.

Although he wore a black hat and a mask, she would recognize him anywhere. Of all the people to run into, on her way to breaking into the offices… How could she explain her presence up here?

"Are you all right?" he asked.

She lifted her hand to her sequined mask, making sure it was firmly in place. "*Oui*, you frightened me, that's all." She hoped her best French accent from four years of studying the language was good enough to disguise her voice. "*J'ai perdu mon chemin*… I mean, I have lost my way and exited on the wrong floor. I've no sense of direction at all."

Her teeth caught her lower lip. *Would he recognize her and challenge her?*

"The party is down a couple of floors. Why don't I show you the way?"

He didn't recognize her. She exhaled a deep breath.

She had no choice, so she followed him down the darkened stairwell. "*Merci beaucoup* for your kind assistance."

Once they were in the hall, the doorman gave Trent a nod. Kate retrieved her ticket from her evening bag.

"Are you with someone?" Trent asked as he took her by the elbow and led her through the door into the ballroom.

At the feel of his fingers touching her bare skin, tingles ran up her arm, leaving her speechless. When he dropped his hand to his side, a wave of relief swept through her.

"I came with a friend, *monsieur*. She's here, somewhere?" She glanced around the elegant room, with its glass-topped, domed ceiling. Music, voices and laughter mingled in the air.

A woman in plumes walked by, followed by a man dressed in top hat and tails. Movie characters Dorothy and the Scarecrow danced together. On one side, there were three stages set up for different types of music. The rock band set down their instruments. At the middle stage, an orchestra began to play.

"Something for everyone," Trent said over the music.

Kate gazed up at him. As usual, he looked handsome and virile. *He was something for everyone.* She clenched her hands in the folds of her dress and frowned at her crazy thought.

She scanned the crowd. "I don't see my friend."

"Would you like something to drink?" he asked, nodding his head toward the bar.

"*Qui.*" Kate flicked her fan to cover her face. "Champagne would be nice."

"I'll be right back. Don't go anywhere." He gave her a smile that weakened her knees. He had never smiled like that at 'Dr. Meyers.'

Was she crazy? She couldn't let him get her a drink. If he knew she was Dr. Meyers—who he thoroughly disliked—and that she had intended to send him to prison, he wouldn't want to spend a moment with her.

Trent strode through the crowd of flamboyant costumes toward a bar lined with people. Knowing he'd only be away for a few minutes, Kate fled across the floor and found Darcy.

Kate gripped her friend's arm. "Trent caught me in the stairwell as I was going up to the offices."

"Yikes, Kate. What are you going to do?"

"He didn't recognize me, thank God. But I need to leave before he does. He went for drinks. He's by the bar at the main door." She swiveled toward the bar where she saw him speaking to the bartender. "Once he's away from the entrance, I'll slip out."

A waiter carrying a tray of hors d'oeuvres approached them. Darcy took a shrimp canapé. Kate waved him away. No way could she eat anything because of the knots in her stomach. "I guess I'd better go. It'll probably be worse if he sees us together."

A man dressed as Buffalo Bill sashayed up to them. He tweaked his mustache with his fingers. "Howdy. How 'bout if we rustle up a dance?"

His friend, a short cowboy in a tall ten-gallon hat, joined them. "Yeah, how 'bout it, pretty ladies?" he asked in a decent John Wayne accent. "Can we talk you into a round of foot stompin' on the dance floor?"

Kate shook her head. "No, sorry, I can't."

* * *

Holding a glass of champagne in one hand and a beer in the other, Trent scanned the ballroom for the Cinderella beauty. She wasn't where he'd left her. *Damn, where did she go?* He was definitely losing his touch. Dr. Meyers—the one woman he was interested in knowing better—disliked him immensely. She liked Greg, and his friend obviously returned her affection. Not only had Trent seen them in the hallway laughing about something two days ago, he had stepped into the Green Tree Restaurant and spotted them having lunch together. Both looked happy and were smiling. Trent had turned and walked out the door.

"Trent Farrington," a man bellowed from behind him.

The company's archrival bore down on him. In his fifties, rugged, and deeply tanned, Blake wore a gray pinstriped suit, right out of the 1930s. His salt-and-pepper hair was slicked back.

"How fitting, Blake," Trent drawled. "You'd make Dillinger proud." He sipped his beer and glanced toward the crowd.

"Not happy to see me?"

Trent shrugged. "Can't keep the riff-raff out. As you know, the party's open to anyone willing to pay three hundred dollars a plate." He leveled his gaze on Blake, not liking the idea of Blake being anywhere near Farrington's operations.

"How else would you see me once a year, if I didn't come?" Blake smiled and patted Trent on the back.

The man was as crooked as the teeth on a broken saw. At the deadly look Trent bestowed on him, the man wisely removed his hand.

"Ah, come on, Farrington. Let's forget the past. That was business. Now, how are you doing?"

"Hard to forget a vice president who quits and absconds with some of our best clients."

"Hell, they used their own better judgment and went with me."

Trent glared at him. "So what do you want from me?"

"I want to discuss business. Rumors are going around that your granddad's health is on the downhill slide. He's an old man. You should sell out."

"When he retires, I'll run the business."

Blake's laughter boomed. "Come on, Trent. You and your useless cousin? You'll both run the company into the ground. And you, you're still wet behind the ears. I'm willing to offer you boys a decent price. Sell and enjoy yourselves. I bet Roland would like that. You'd both be set up nicely for life."

"I don't care what your price is. The company's not for sale."

Blake snorted. "A man was killed, and now I've heard another burned his hands at your downtown site. OSHA's going to shut you boys down if you have any more accidents."

Trent barely restrained himself from grabbing the scum by the lapels. This wasn't the place to brawl, but he'd reached the limit of his control. "Are you threatening me?"

"*Threatening?* All I'm saying is if you have more accidents, you're going to bring the reputation of the company down."

"You seem to keep pretty close tabs on what's going on with *my* company?"

"Face it, Trent, you're not competent to fill James Farrington's shoes. Your granddad will listen to reason and sell to me."

"If that cold day in hell ever came around, he'd never sell to you."

"We'll see. Everyone knows Farrington Construction has had its day, especially when James Farrington steps away. Either way, Blake Construction is moving up. We'll steamroll over all our competition and be number one in the state."

"Try it."

"Just remember, I offered to buy you out. Listen to reason. Any more accidents and you'll want to salvage what you can, and then I'll pick up the company for a cheaper price." He gave Trent a curt nod and strode away.

Watching him go, Trent's mood blackened. Was that a threat? The crooked bastard would never get his hands on Farrington Construction.

"Guess who?" From behind him, Cecilia slipped her arms around Trent's waist and flattened her breasts into his back as if one date made them a couple. "Dance with me. It's my *royal* command."

He shrugged from her hold and turned to face her. She made a good Cleopatra with her shoulder-length dark hair, Egyptian headdress, and decorated dress, but he wasn't interested. "Not now. I'm looking for someone."

"Is that champagne for me?"

He shrugged and handed her the glass as *Cinderella* had all but disappeared.

"Your mother is over there. It would make her happy to see us dance together."

Cecilia pointed to where Eden sat at a table among a group of her friends. She nodded and had a faint smile on her lips.

Trent inwardly groaned. He glanced around for the woman in the silver-blue gown. *Had she left?*

"Trent, you're not listening to me. What does it take for a girl to get your attention?"

It depends on the woman.

Over Cecilia's shoulder, he spotted *Cinderella* across the ballroom. Something about her hit him like a tidal wave even now. "Excuse me. There is someone I need to speak to."

Cecilia clung to his arm. "Come home with me tonight."

"No." He shook off her hold and headed toward the girl in the silver-blue gown as if an invisible connection reeled him to her.

CHAPTER EIGHT

Under the ballroom's glittering chandeliers, Kate had watched Cecilia with Trent. They made a beautiful couple with their similar coloring. Rumors about their first date ran rampant through the office. Kate gritted her teeth. *He was a player.* How easily he passed himself around to every woman he met, making them each feel special for the moment. Well, Cecilia could have him.

Then his gaze had shot across the ballroom, meeting Kate's. The air escaped her lungs. By his expression, he didn't look too pleased that she'd not waited for him to return with the drinks.

Why had she stayed a moment longer, chancing she'd be discovered by Trent? Was she sabotaging herself?

Kate snapped out of her daze. "I've got to go."

Darcy's head jerked toward Trent. "Uh oh, he's headed this way."

Kate spun around and smashed into a portly batman. The man pulled her into a tight embrace, crushing her breasts against his plastic breastplate.

"What's this?" he slurred in a deep voice. "*Manna* from heaven?"

Kate struck him with her fist. "Let me go."

"Baby, why so fast?" He reeked of hard liquor.

"I said let go—now." She jabbed the heel of her slipper into his foot.

"Ouch." Batman released her. "Hey, the pretty kitten has claws. I only wanted a dance. This is a party, you know. That's what goes on here...*among other things,*" he said in a low growl near her ear.

"I don't dance with *drunks.*"

With hands on her hips, Darcy stepped beside Kate. "Is this guy giving you trouble?"

Kate straightened the shoulders of her gown. "Yes." She bestowed a nasty look on the out-of-shape man dressed in tights, then remembered her disguise and her French accent. "Who do you think you are, *Monsieur Batman?*"

A cocky smirk spread on his lips. "Oh, come on now, kitten— you know exactly who I am."

"I have no idea." She turned to Darcy. "I'm leaving…"

Trent bore down on her, through the crowd and gave her no chance to escape. What else could she do? Batman was the lesser of two evils.

She tilted her head up at him and mustered a smile. "I've changed my mind, *monsieur*. I'll take that dance."

He laughed. "So, you've finally realized who I am," he said drolly. "I knew you would."

Kate had never met the drunken man before, but if he kept her from facing Trent at this moment, she would do anything. She allowed Batman to lead her onto the dance floor. When a rock song broke out, she exhaled in relief, never more grateful for fast music in her life.

While they danced, Kate stole a nervous glance toward Trent. He was near Darcy, his arms crossed over his chest as if waiting for the song to end.

"What's your name, beauty?" Batman's slurred words broke into her thoughts.

"This is a masquerade, *monsieur*, so I'm not telling."

"The unmasking will be soon. I can *hardly wait* to find out who you really are."

"I'm new around here. You don't know me."

"All right, I'll play your game. I'm Batman for this evening, but I think you've figured out who I really am."

She blinked. *Was she supposed to know who he was?* "I still don't know who you are." She wanted to add that she didn't care, but the man had saved her from Trent. Now, all she had to do was get near the entrance doors and slip out.

He cocked his head. "Ah, not impressed? What to do? Does the name Farrington Construction ring a bell? *Hint—y*ou're at *Farrington Towers* and this is a Farrington function."

A soft gasp escaped Kate. "You're a *Farrington?*"

He chuckled. "Now you're shocked, but it's your lucky night. However, I'm not a Farrington in name. The name is Roland Sikes and I'm James Farrington's grandson."

Her heart raced. How had she not heard that there was another grandson? She choked out, "I assumed Trent Farrington was the last of the Farringtons."

"So he is, but what's in a name?" Despite the mask he wore, the mention of Trent brought a look of gleaming hatred to his pale blue eyes. His lips twisted cynically. "My mother was a Farrington. Hate to claim it, but Trent and I are cousins."

Kate's shoulders drooped. She had failed in her research. An article had stated Trent was the last of the Farringtons, but perhaps there were even more heirs with different last names. "Are there any other grandchildren?" she asked weakly.

He gave her a grim smile. "No, just the two of us. If you're trying to pick out which one you'd prefer, I can tell you my cousin isn't half the man I am." He was clearly jealous of Trent. "Ah, a slow dance."

Her luck had run out with the music. Reluctantly, she let him pull her into the dance. She stared into his breastplate. His heavy cologne and the smell of alcohol on his breath suffocated her, along with his overbearing personality.

While she moved with him, her mind reeled from the fact that there was now another grandson in the picture.

She did her best to maneuver Roland through the crowd, brushing by the other dancers to get as near to the exit as possible.

"I'm supposed to lead," he said dryly.

"Equal rights for women, *monsieur*."

"I like a woman who knows what she wants." He smiled and pulled her close. "Lead me wherever you'd like, baby." His hand slid down her back to her backside, where he squeezed.

Forgetting her accent, she shoved him away. "Stop it."

He gripped her arms. "I meant nothing by it, baby, but you do turn me on."

"This dance is over. Let me go." She struggled to free herself, but his hands were clenching her arms above her elbows, squeezing and hurting her.

"I'll let you go when I'm ready, kitten."

"You heard her," a familiar voice said behind her.

"Go to hell, cuz. This one is mine." Roland lunged at Trent who, in one swift movement, twisted his cousin's arm behind his back.

Trent growled in a low voice, "Do you want our grandfather to read in the papers tomorrow about how his two grandsons brawled here tonight?"

Roland shook his head, his breath coming in gasps. Trent released him. Roland took a step backward and caught his balance. He turned and raised a fist and looked like he might come back at Trent. Then reasoning must have taken over because he laughed as if it was a joke. "You'd like for me to make a fool of myself here. Won't happen. As I said, watch your back, *cuz*." He stalked toward the bar.

Kate gaped. Like a landslide, her brother's last words rushed to her, this time coloring her perspective differently: "Grandson... Trent...tell...found...Jeopardizes...integrity...building..."

She put her fingers to her lips. What if Matt had meant the other grandson and his message had been for her to *tell* Trent? If so, this was a huge error on her part. Trembling, she wrapped her arms around herself.

"Are you all right?" Trent asked.

Fighting the hysteria bubbling inside her, knowing she might have been after the wrong man all along, she nodded. "I'll be fine in a moment."

"Sorry about my cousin. He's drunk."

Steadying her nerves, she rubbed her arm where Roland had grabbed her. She'd have bruises tomorrow, but as much as he'd frightened her, none of that mattered. Her heart wanted to sing. Roland had to be the culprit—the man was obviously a creep. Everything else made sense now.

"*Monsieur*, I was having a nice time tonight until I met your cousin." She was surprised she spoke the truth.

His eyes gleamed. "Don't let him ruin your evening. Would you like something to drink?"

One drink with Trent couldn't hurt. "All right. Champagne, please."

"Another champagne coming up." He winked and linked his arm in hers. This time, it appeared he wasn't going to give her the chance to slip away.

His touch sent warm sensations sizzling through her.

After he procured two glasses of champagne from the nearest waiter, he gave her a sideways glance. "Would you like to sit somewhere?"

In spite of knowing that she shouldn't—it was a foolish risk—she found herself nodding. She hid a buoyant smile behind her fan at the thought that Trent could very well be innocent.

She followed him through the French doors onto the patio and into the balmy night. Potted trees, decorated with tiny orange and white lights, were scattered around the expansive terrace. Tables with white tablecloths held lamps with gently flickering flames. The city below was a sea of stars.

Once they were seated at a secluded corner table at the back of the patio, Trent said, "I thought I'd lost you in the crowd."

"*Lost*, Monsieur Zorro? I couldn't have been lost. I knew *exactly* where I was."

"But then were you trying to lose me?"

"*Non*," she said with a shake of her head, feeling daring. *Why not run with this?* With her disguise, and if only for this one evening, she had him all to herself. Now she was fairly certain he was innocent of the crimes she'd thought were his and she doubted her own rush to judgment that the accident was definitely his fault.

She smiled. "I was distracted by the crowd. Then I saw you talking with a pretty girl. You seemed quite occupied. She had her hands on you...in a most *familiar* way. Your girlfriend? I was most sure of it, *n'est-ce pas?*"

"I don't have a girlfriend," he said in a flat tone.

"Well, if not, this woman likes *you* very much," she teased.

He shrugged. "She's a family friend."

So his date with Cecilia had meant nothing? Truthfully? Even though his voice held a grim note, she couldn't resist teasing him further, knowing his family's desire for him to marry. "Oh, I see. Then you must have a wife? For surely, someone like you has one."

His lip curved in a grin that warmed her. "No." He chuckled and shook his head. "Not yet."

Thankful for the dim lighting, Kate sipped the bubbling champagne and contemplated the man who sat beside her. She found herself anxious to know if he was ruthless or a man of integrity.

"*Who are you really?*" she whispered. The words spilled from her lips before she could stop them.

"Why don't you go first," he drawled. He leaned back in his chair, his pose lazy. His dark eyes glinted through his black mask. "I'm much more interested in finding out who you are."

He was talking about names, of course, but she was thinking of who he was beneath the façade that everyone hid behind. There was no way she could reveal herself to him, but being alone with him made her feel a little reckless…and a bit giddy.

"I could not, *monsieur*," she said truthfully. "Besides, I thought the unmasking was at midnight."

"So it is," he murmured. "Why don't I guess who you are now?"

Panic flew through her for a moment, but she forced herself to remain calm. Her disguise was good. Her lips quirked. "But I am who I appear to be—just myself—as I thought you were, *Monsieur Zorro.*"

Trent chuckled again, and she liked the sound.

His brow furrowed. "I feel like I know you from somewhere. Have we met before?"

Her cheeks grew warm. "No, I'm sure we haven't…ever met."

Although she was glad for the sequined mask that covered her eyes and nose, she lifted the lace fan that dangled on her wrist and covered her mouth. She shouldn't let him get too many glimpses of her face.

He leaned across the table. "We'll see, after the unmasking. However, there is something familiar about you. But it's a *good* familiar I recall."

Had he liked her just a little as Dr. Meyers? Ridiculous hope sprang inside her that he had.

His seductive lips curved into a smile that sent a shiver through her. "Suddenly, I'm enjoying my anonymity," he said.

She snapped her fan on his arm. "If you have something to hide…*anonymity* could be beneficial. Do you, Monsieur Zorro? Do you have *something* to hide?" Was he as innocent as she wanted to believe, or was she only taken in by the way he made her melt into a heated puddle with one glance from those dreamy, dark eyes?

"Nothing to hide. But tonight, what you see is what you get."

"You sound as if you find it difficult sometimes to be yourself?"

His smiled. "At times."

Could it be hard to be Trent Farrington, *heir to a fortune*? He did have an enormous responsibility, too, with the company.

His face was half hidden by the mask, while his cologne, crossed the distance between them. Kate leaned toward him and dropped her gaze to his incredibly sensuous mouth, so kissable and close. Warm sensations bubbled inside her. Not only was she attracted to him, she liked all that she was finding out about him. She wanted to know more.

"I suppose you're Cinderella?" he asked, his voice smooth and seductive.

She laughed. "Actually, I'm supposed to be Marie Antoinette. And I should be losing my head very soon. In more ways than one."

"What a shame. It's such a pretty neck." He flicked her a smile and shook his head. "You're too beautiful to be Marie Antoinette. If I remember correctly, Cinderella, too, was in disguise."

At that remark, she jerked her head up. Too close to home... She was forgetting herself by staying here with him. She had to leave the ball before he recognized her.

Kate flicked up her fan again to shield her face. "I must find my friend."

"Darcy King?"

Blood rushed to her cheeks. So he had recognized Darcy? "*Oui.*" She cast him a sideways glance. Had he known her identity all along? Had he been toying with her?

"Can't she wait awhile longer? I have only a little time before I have things I have to do. Do you dance?"

"*Moi?*" Kate frowned. She couldn't. She had to leave.

His lips quirked. "Yes, *you.*"

"It's been awhile since I've danced with anyone, except for that *awful* Batman."

"Good, because I'm asking you. Shall we?" He extended his hand.

His eyes through the mask seem as soft as black velvet. Once again, she was drawn into their dark depths.

Was it such a risk? "All right, Monsieur Zorro. One dance."

Trent clasped her hand. They walked inside.

A man called out, "Hey, great party."

"Thank you." Trent kept on moving toward the dance floor. As he wove them through the crowd, her gown swished against the other dancers.

The previous song ended and Trent raised a palm to catch the maestro's eye. A classical melody filled the ballroom.

His grin was pure mischief. "How fortunate, a slow song."

He lifted her hand and placed it on his shoulder. His hand was on her waist, warm and strong.

While they danced, she found herself enjoying her time with him way too much.

She hoped she wouldn't have to pay for this tomorrow. "I see you wield such power, Monsieur Zorro. Is this *your* affair?" she asked coyly.

He winked. "It could be my costume. You know there is a sword that goes with it."

Kate laughed. "*Touché.*" Then she let herself be carried away in his arms around the dance floor. Happiness bubbled in her as time seemed to move in slow motion. Her head reeled, not only from being with him, but also from the thought of how perfectly they fit together.

Considering everything she had discovered about him, she was sure he was innocent. She smiled broadly.

"Why the bright smile?" he asked.

"Oh, nothing."

"Not laughing at my dancing, are you?"

"*Non.* I can tell you there is no fault with your dancing, Monsieur Zorro. I'm just surprised that you do so well in this day and age." There was no fault with him at all. Even in costume, she found him superbly gorgeous.

"Nice to know all those cotillion lessons my mother forced me to take as a kid at the country club paid off."

"Then you might want to laugh at me because I never attended such functions."

"None? Not in France?" he asked, a grin teasing his lips. She could tell he wasn't totally convinced she was French.

"*Non,*" she said, blushing guiltily. How many lies *had* she told him?

He stiffened and gazed down at her. "I just had a horrible thought. You're not a friend of my mother, are you?"

"You mean there is a *maman* of Zorro here tonight?" she asked, pretending to search around the room.

Trent chuckled. "Perhaps." He twirled her around. "You dance like an angel. A beautiful angel." He brought her back to him. "But then, why the smile earlier, if not at me?"

"I'm just surprised that I'm having such a nice evening."

"You expected to come here tonight and not enjoy yourself?"

Her cheeks heated. "I-I only meant that I'm having more fun than I expected."

"I'm having a wonderful night myself."

With a glimmer of shyness, she dropped her face to the level of his black shirt. If anyone had told her this morning that she would be dancing in Trent Farrington's arms this evening, and enjoying herself beyond belief, she would have told them they were crazy.

The music stopped abruptly. Eden Farrington strode across the stage and grasped the microphone. "Sorry for the interruption, but I wanted to let you know in fifteen minutes we'll have the unmasking." Her gaze flicked directly to Trent and Kate on the dance floor, while her lips flattened in a grim line.

Kate bit her lip. *Oh, my God, the unmasking.* She glanced up at Trent. "It can't be almost midnight."

He nodded. "But it is."

"In the meantime, ladies and gentlemen," Mrs. Farrington said into the microphone, "we have a few announcements to make. Trent, will you please come up?"

Kate had to get out of there.

When she turned to leave, Trent grasped her elbow. "I have some things I must do for the benefit. Don't leave—I don't even know your name."

She had to get out of here before he discovered her true identity. "But I must find my friend," she said, unable to meet his eyes.

"Darcy? All right, but *don't leave.*" Kate stiffened. It was so like him to give an order to her as Dr. Meyers, but this time he softened it with, "*Please.*"

She didn't know what to say. She wanted to stay, but how could she? He must have taken her silence for agreement because he strode toward the stage.

With him away, she rushed through the crowd to find Darcy. Trent's next announcement followed her trail. Despite her distress, she listened as he told the crowd, "My family's foundation will donate money for the construction of a new wing for the Children in Crisis Center. I'll personally oversee the building and design."

For the Children! Tears welled in Kate's eyes. She'd been so wrong. He couldn't be the ruthless crook she had suspected. If she wasn't careful, the only thing he'd be stealing would be her heart.

For one brief moment, she stared at Trent. "*Who is that man?*" she whispered under her breath.

"Trent Farrington," answered an older man beside her who had mistaken her meaning. "He's just like his grandfather, always ready to help those in need. And he'll be a good president for the company. I was worried Roland would be left in charge. That would be a disaster in the making if you want my opinion."

"Thank you," Kate murmured.

She hurried on through the crowd to Darcy. Her friend sipped champagne and laughed with a tall Arabian Sheik.

Kate walked up in time to hear the man say in a voice that sounded like Greg's, "You look amazing in that dress, Darcy."

Not wanting to be seen by him either, Kate ducked her head and pulled her friend aside. "I'm out of here before Trent discovers who I am at the unmasking. I'll catch a cab."

However, she hoped there might be time for her to do one more thing before she left the building.

* * *

Kate's gown rustled as she ran down the long, dark hall of the forty-fifth floor. The only other sounds were the gurgles from a water cooler, an elevator moving in a shaft, and her slippered footsteps on the carpeting. Except for several dim lights lighting the way, darkness shrouded the floor. Without people, there was something sinister about an empty manmade mountain of concrete and glass. A trickle of apprehension ran up her spine.

She removed the tiny flashlight concealed in a pocket of her skirt and searched every door until she found the correct nameplate. '*Roland Sikes.*' If by chance his office was unlocked, she would do a quick search. If not, she'd go home. After a glance over her shoulder to make sure the hall was clear, she turned the knob.

Kate quietly slipped inside the office, shut the door behind her, and strode to the desk.

"Who is it?" a man said. A lamp clicked on.

Sucking in her breath, Kate dropped her flashlight and whirled around to face Trent's obnoxious cousin. Roland reclined on a brown leather couch. His black Batman breastplate was discarded on the floor, along with his mask. Kate's heart hammered at the glitter in his eyes.

He tapped his finger to his cheek. "Ah, my first impression was correct," he said his words slurred. "Wise choice to ditch my cousin. However, I must say I am surprised to see you here."

Kate froze in place and searched her mind for an explanation. She could claim it was a mistake and make a beeline to the door, however, the company files piled on top of his desk beckoned.

She edged closer to read the names on the labels. "I needed to use the phone, but now that I'm here, I have to see for myself the office of the magnificent Roland Sikes. Is this where all those fabulous business decisions take place?"

He straightened up on the couch, sending her heart racing. "What type of decision do you have in mind at this time of night?" He smiled and eyed her breasts.

At his leering look and too-familiar tone of voice, she swallowed her fear. "I do so admire a sharp mind. You have a sharp mind, do you not, *monsieur*?" She searched for any awards to brag about and placate him. No such mementos adorned his walls.

"Sharp as any other. Sharper than my cousin if you'd like comparisons." He cast her a wary glance. "You're not by any chance an associate of Frank Blake? He's a competitor."

Who was this *Frank Blake* everyone mentioned? Kate shrugged. "I know of no such man." She made a mental note to check Blake out. "Actually, I was lost in the halls. Since I didn't bring my cell phone with me," she lied, "I needed to find a phone to call a cab. *Your* door was unlocked." She made out the name on the top file labeled 'Ace Advertising Company.' If she could just get a little closer, she might be able to decipher the names on the other files...

Roland rose to his feet, his big frame swaying. "Why leave so early, kitten? Although if I'd known you were coming, I would've had a bottle of wine sent up. I guess we'll have to make do with whiskey." On his way to his desk, he stumbled and caught himself. He tossed her a broad smile and continued toward his desk.

She went to the other side to keep the desk between them.

"I know just the place." He sat and reached inside a large bottom drawer and pulled out a bottle. Uncapping the lid, he extended his arm. "Care for some. I might be able to find a glass around here...someplace."

"*Non, merci*. I must go. I'll find a phone elsewhere."

"Ah, don't go." Smiling, he held out the telephone receiver to her. "Here, use my phone. Make your call."

Hesitating at that smile, she flicked her gaze to the phone near him. Her teeth sank into her lower lip as she stepped closer.

He was drunk and had proven himself to be lecherous in the ballroom. *Should she?* She wasn't sure she could outrun him to the door in a gown and heels. Not wanting him to see her panic, she punched in the numbers to a city cab.

He lunged and clamped his beefy hand on her wrist. She yanked her hand to get away, but his grip tightened.

Pushing the button on the phone, he disconnected the call. "What's the big hurry? It's barely past midnight." He moved around the desk and slid his other hand up her arm. "I'll give you a ride home." He licked his lips. "Later."

Recoiling in disgust, she tried to jerk away.

He grazed her lips with a knuckle that wielded a ring with a huge sapphire. "I like your mouth, baby. Why don't you take off the mask?"

"Let me go, or your grandfather will hear about this."

He eased his hold. "So, you do know James Farrington? Which means you've known all along that I'm his grandson. You also ran into me on purpose at the party. Now, you're in my office. Be honest about why you're here."

He lowered his face and tried to kiss her. She smacked the flat of her hand against the side of his head. "Let go, I said. I'm not here for anything. You're drunk."

He recoiled. "Stop playing hard to get. Let me see your face. Have I sampled your charms before?"

"No!"

He snatched her mask off, and with it, her wig. When the pins were yanked out it stung her scalp and her hair tumbled down her back. His fingers bit into her as he gripped her shoulders.

She punched his soft stomach. "Let go."

"Come on, kitten. Stop the innocent act. Sheesh, I'm not asking for much, just a *kisssh,"* he slurred again. He clamped his other hand on her waist.

"Stop," she cried. She tried to knee him in the groin, but he blocked it.

His fleshy lips descended on her. "All the girls want me. I get laid all the time."

She turned her head just in time so his disgustingly drunken mouth landed on her cheek.

He stuck his hand inside the shoulder of her dress.

At a ripping sound, Kate punched his chest. It was like a slab of pork. "Now you've torn my costume."

"I'll buy you all the dresses you want, spoil you, and pamper you. Take you down to Barbados for a nice long weekend."

"Your being rich might impress some women, but not me."

He backed her up against his desk. His hand on her shoulder, he pushed her backwards. Things started falling off the desk.

Kate raked her nails across his cheek.

He caught her hand. "I take back what I said. You're not a kitten. You're a little hellcat."

"Stop this instant. I'm warning you I *will* scream and bring security running."

Roland snorted. "So why haven't you?"

In desperation, she clenched her hands and shoved against his chest. "I mean it... I will scream. Now let me go."

"If you wanted to, you'd have done it. Stop playing games. You're starting to piss me off."

Kate struggled against the big man's restraining arms. As he pressed her further backwards over the desk, a surge of fright assailed her. She did not want to scream, and even if she did, would anyone hear her?

CHAPTER NINE

Where did *Cinderella* go this time? Trent tossed his hat, mask, and cape on a table, and surveyed the ballroom to no avail. On the dance floor, Cecilia twirled around in Frank Blake's arms. She raised her nose haughtily in the air, as if she thought to make him jealous. It didn't work.

He cornered Darcy, coming off the dance floor. "Where is she?"

She blinked. "Who?"

"The young woman I saw you talking to. *Cinderella*, or Marie Antoinette, or whoever she's supposed to be."

Darcy's face reddened. "Oh. I think I might recall who you mean…"

"Where is she?" Trent asked, nearly losing his patience.

"S-she… She said something about leaving."

"*Leaving*? She's taking this Cinderella thing too far. I asked her to wait." He leaned toward Darcy. Her eyes widened, and she stepped back. He hadn't meant to frighten her, but this was important. "Who is she? I have to find her."

"Ah, well…"

"*Darcy*," he snapped. "It's a simple question. She was with you. What's her name?"

"Grace," she blurted. "That's it. She's from France, and she's probably on her way back there now."

"Grace *who*?" he said, through tight lips.

"I can't think with you standing over me like that."

Blowing out a deep breath, he backed away. "All right, Darcy, but you either know her name or you don't. But then…" He narrowed his eyes and frowned. "She does look familiar. Does she work in the building? She reminds me a little of…*Dr. Meyers*. About the same height, her mouth…" Damn it. He couldn't, *shouldn't*, be seeing Kate Meyers—a woman who hated him *and* who liked his best friend—in every woman he met.

"Oh, no, Trent, that's because she's uh… They're *cousins*. Yes, that's it. And that's why the slight resemblance. Her last name is…*Guckenheimer*. I'm sure she's already on her way back to France. She hardly ever comes to the U.S. She won't be back for a while. Sorry."

He contemplated the information. "That explains it. Except for looks, she's nothing like Dr. Meyers. At least she doesn't look at me through thick glasses with contempt in her eyes." He muttered the last to himself, more than to Darcy. He wasn't surprised he'd been as attracted to Dr. Meyers' cousin because he'd been attracted to Dr. Meyers from the moment he'd met her, though *she* preferred Greg. Shaking his head to clear his thoughts, Trent added, "Never mind, Darcy. When did she leave?"

"About ten minutes ago."

He strode from the room and stopped by the doorman at the exit. "Al, did you notice a beautiful woman in an eighteenth-century ball gown walking out these doors?"

Al nodded. "Yeah, a real looker. Said she needed the exercise and took the stairs. I was about to go and check on her, because I saw through the glass window that she was heading up, not down, but I got a call. I should also mention that Mr. Sikes took the stairs, too. He looked a little worse for wear, like he might have trouble."

Trent stalked off toward the stairwell. On the top floor, he was greeted by the sound of something breaking. A female's screams sent Trent bolting down the hall. He burst into Roland's office.

Flicking on the bright overhead lights, he found his cousin had Grace lying over his desk, her fist beating against his broad back. The room was in disarray, a powered wig and mask lay on the floor. Her hair partially covered her face.

"Have you lost your mind?" Trent rushed toward them and gripped Roland by the shirt. Grace's dress, ripped at the shoulder, revealed a heart-shaped birthmark at her neckline, further angering Trent. He hauled Roland off Grace as she sprayed something in his cousin's face.

"Damn, kitten," Roland whined. A red palm print and scratches graced his cheek. "Why did you have to spray me with that shit?"

Shielding her face with her arm, Grace turned, sending a blast of the same spray directly toward Trent. She hit him in the eyes.

"What the hell?" Trent jerked back. His eyes burning and tearing, he could barely see.

"I'm so sorry, Monsieur Zorro," she said, her breathing coming in little rasps. "It's pepper spray." She moved off the desk and closer to Trent. "I did not mean to hit you with it, too. Just him. He frightened me."

"I was only trying to kiss her," Roland slurred.

"Yeah? Looked like a little more than that to me." Trent grabbed the heavier man by the collar and planted his fist into his bloated face. His cousin slumped, but Trent didn't release him; rather he held him up.

"She's yours, too?" Roland snarled. "She came to my office, looking for me to satisfy her."

Keeping a tight hold on cousin's collar, Trent turned his ire on Kate. "Is that the truth? You came to his office?"

"*Oui*, I did," she said in a low voice. "But I thought it was empty. I only wanted to use a phone to call a cab. His door was unlocked. When I came in, he attacked me."

"She led me on," Roland taunted. "Danced with me. Came in here with her little o*ui, oui, French accent.* Said she wanted to see my office," his cousin muttered, half out of his mind. "Stop trying to run my life, cuz. You're going to get your day soon, you bastard."

Trent cuffed Roland on the jaw. When his cousin's head lolled to the side, Trent eased Roland to the floor. "He has a drinking problem. He might not even remember this tomorrow."

His knuckles aching, Trent reached for Cinderella's hand. "Come."

* * *

Kate's stomach knotted with dread and she resigned herself to go with Trent. With his firm hold on her hand, she didn't think he'd let her slip away this time.

In spite of the darkness in the halls and his eyes nearly blinded by pepper spray, he knew his building well. He strode easily down the hall to his office and into his large, private executive bathroom.

She gnawed on her lower lip. Just how much of a glimpse did Trent get of her before she zapped him with the pepper spray? She felt horrible, but she'd had no choice.

Trent clicked on the bright lights. She gaped into the mirror. Oh, God, he would surely recognize her without the mask and wig.

"It's all my fault," she whispered. "*Everything.*"

She had a list of sins piling up, beginning with her lies to get the job, her credentials, her suspicions about him, and her sneaking around the company offices—and now shooting and hurting him with pepper spray.

Bending over the sink, he flushed his eyes with water. "Even if you did go into his office uninvited, there is no excuse for what he did."

At his misunderstanding of what she had meant, she sighed. "The sting should last about fifteen minutes." She barely remembered to use her French accent. How had this night come so far that she had ended up in Trent's bathroom?

While he splashed more water into his eyes, she checked herself in the mirror. With her wig in her hand, her real hair hung in a wild tangle of blond curls down her back. Her ripped gown revealed the top of her lacy bra. She pulled the pieces of the dress together.

Weary of the lies she had gotten herself into for her investigation, Kate choked back a sob. "I'm so sorry, *monsieur*."

Trent dried his face on a towel, then turned toward her. "None of this is your fault."

Ready to confess everything, she tensed and waited for him to denounce her.

He focused on her face. "My eyes are still blurry, but I can see a little better, Grace."

"*Grace?*"

"Darcy told me your name. I practically wrung it out of her. I owe her an apology."

He had not recognized her. Kate released a deep breath and collapsed against the edge of the counter. As much as she hated her stepfather, she guessed years of living with a conman must have taught her some acting skills.

Was there any way she could get out of here tonight without him discovering her true identity?

"Grace Guckenheimer," Trent said in a reflective tone. "Strange, a German last name… And Grace doesn't sound French either."

Her nerves jangled, she nearly choked out a nervous laugh and covered her mouth to stifle it. She coughed instead. "My father was German." She turned away to hide her burning cheeks. "And Grace is actually short for *Gracielle*." She hated herself for lying to him even more.

"And you're related to Dr. Meyers who works at Farrington Construction?"

That shocked the breath out of her and cut too close to home. "*Oui*" she said, wincing. Good Lord, she was digging herself in even deeper. How could she ever tell him the truth now? He'd hate her. "Please accept my apology for the pepper spray, *monsieur.*"

"You were only trying to protect yourself. My cousin was drunk and can be a bastard, but I've never known him to try to force himself on anyone before." Trent held out his hand. "Let's go into my office."

A guilty twinge hit Kate as they left the bathroom. "Does the spray sting badly?"

He shrugged. "I'll be all right. Now, sit here on the couch. Do you want to call the police? You have every right to have him arrested. I don't care if he is my cousin."

"I don't want to call the police. He was drunk and I'm fine," she said through chattering teeth.

Trent cursed, and dropped beside her on the sofa. "You don't sound like it. Are you sure?" He folded her into his arms.

It seemed the most natural thing in the world to allow him to comfort her. She pressed her face into his warm shoulder as a sob burst from her throat. How she wished she had never lied to him.

"My vision might be shot to hell," he said, "but I know when someone is upset. Now, breathe in and out slowly."

She nodded. He'd been her enemy up until this night. And, really, she had saved herself from Roland with the pepper spray, but leaning on Trent felt good.

As he held her in his arms, she reveled in his spicy scent. She wanted to stay there forever—never wanted to let him go.

He tipped her chin with his finger. "My vision is clearing somewhat. Are you better?"

She swallowed. "*Oui.*"

She needed to get out of there and fast. As much as she wanted to tell him the truth, self-preservation called out to her. It was likely he would be angry with her—very angry if he knew all of her lies—and she'd experienced his temper before.

However, as long as he couldn't see her clearly, she stood a chance of getting away with this evening.

His hand touched her shoulder. He swore under his breath. "That bastard. Your dress is ripped."

Trent released her and stepped to his desk. He returned with a stapler and sat beside her. His fingers grazed her bare skin above the bodice as he pieced the sections of the gown together and stapled them. A shiver ran through her. "We'll replace the dress, but this should hold until I can take you home."

"You are a most resourceful engineer, monsieur."

"How did you know?"

Her cheeks grew warm. "Uh, your cousin said something about that." To deflect from her misstep, she added in a lighter tone, "I should hope your buildings have more substance than these staples, Monsieur Zorro."

"Much more. I'll show you sometime."

When he leaned in, she moistened her lips with her tongue. She met him across the few inches separating them. His warm firm mouth pressed against her lips. She heard his breath catch in his throat. He took her mouth with his in a caress. Spiraling heat rushed through her entire being. He cupped her face with his hands, while his tongue explored her mouth.

His kiss became more urgent. Her heart raced as she put her palm to his nape. She wanted to run her fingers through his hair and wrap herself around him. She dropped her hand to Trent's chest and could feel his hot skin and the erratic beat of his heart beneath the fabric.

Her own moan snapped herself out of her daze. *Oh, my God, what am I doing?* She fought the mad desire rushing through her, tore her lips away, and jumped to her feet. "I must go, Monsieur Zorro. I'll call a cab."

"No, don't. And the name's Trent, Trent Farrington. Soon as my vision clears, I'll take you home."

She clamped her hands over her chest and took a step backward. "I can't stay, monsieur, and the ride is unnecessary."

"Then give me your phone number."

She frowned. "Why?"

"To call you. To go out," he teased. "You know, on a date." When she shook her head, he asked, "Why? You're not married, are you?"

"*Non.*"

"Engaged?"

"*Non.*"

"A significant other?"

Her shoulders sagging, she whispered, "*Non.*" What a tangled web she'd woven. "Pen and paper, *monsieur?*"

"On the desk."

Instead of a phone number, she scribbled, "Thank you for rescuing me." She folded the paper and handed it to him. He slipped the note inside his shirt pocket.

A dull ache settled in her stomach. This night with him could never be repeated. Her coming to the company with lies had gotten her what she deserved. She knew she had likely jumped to the wrong conclusion.

Tears sprang in her eyes. "I have to go." She turned away and headed to the door.

"No, wait. Just a few more minutes. My vision is clearing."

"*Au revoir, monsieur.* I'll find my way home. I'm sorry to have to leave you this way."

Fleeing down the hall, she heard him shout, "*Grace!*"

CHAPTER TEN

Monday morning, Kate sat at her desk at Farrington Towers with a hot mug of coffee between her hands. She had kept busy volunteering at the Children in Crises Center on Sunday and had tried her best not to think of Trent, but her thoughts continuously wandered to him.

He'd kissed her. And she had responded—wildly and with all of her heart. She touched her fingertips to her lips.

What had he thought when he'd read what she wrote on the piece of paper? How would she face him today and not give away her emotions or her regret for all her lies?

Should she go to him and confess everything? Her shoulders sagged. He liked her as Grace, but disliked her as Dr. Meyers. What would he think if he found Dr. Meyers and Grace were one and the same—and both were phony? Her spirits plummeted. Most likely he'd hate her even more. Still, she wouldn't trade that night for anything.

Someone banged around in the outer office.

"Darcy," Kate called out.

Her friend poked her head through the doorway. "Hi, Kate. Did Trent find you later that night at the benefit?"

"Yes, I did see him. He told me you said my name was Grace Guckenheimer, and that I was related to Dr. Meyers. Where did you ever come up with a name like that?"

Darcy stepped further into the room. "When Trent demanded I tell him who you were, all I could think of was God give me the '*grace*' to get through this." A sheepish grin spread on her face. "Then I thought of the strict German nun who taught me in religion class." She straightened her shoulders. "You're not mad at me for almost blowing your cover? That's why I didn't call you yesterday."

Kate chuckled. "No. Actually, it was brilliant. I know how demanding Trent can be when he wants something."

"Yeah, he wasn't too happy that you left the party."

"I can just imagine how hard he'd be to stand against if he wanted something." Kate's cheeks grew warm. If he ever wanted more from her, she didn't think she could refuse him. She frowned and didn't like the direction of her thoughts one bit.

"He said you looked vaguely like Dr. Meyers. I didn't know what else to say, except that you were cousins."

Kate grimaced. "That cuts too close to home. But thanks—you saved me."

"Did you find out anything important for your investigation that night?"

Leaning her elbows on her desk, Kate propped her face in her hands. "Yeah. Something big. I found out there's another grandson that I'll have to investigate—Roland Sikes. Perhaps he's the one Matt meant when he said 'grandson.' Sikes is obviously the black sheep of the family. And I'm no longer sure Trent had anything to do with the accident."

Was she letting her feelings and attraction for him weaken her resolve and cloud her thinking?

"Kate, I told you Trent wasn't a cheat. I knew it the moment I laid eyes on him."

"Yeah, but his cousin is a real monster. Do *not* let him get you alone."

"What happened?"

Kate explained Roland's actions and added, "I need more information on him. He's in the Sales Department. Seems like he takes a lot of time off, too, but his job would make it easy to order supplies and skim money. I'm going to have to make a visit to the Purchasing Department to see what I can dig up."

When the phone rang, Darcy reached for the receiver on Kate's desk. After a moment, Darcy put her hand over the receiver. "It's Eden Farrington. She says she wants to set up an appointment with you today, in her office—*asap*."

Kate's eyes widened. "What could she want? Tell her I'll be there in half an hour."

Darcy hung up the phone, her face concerned and curious. "Kate, have you seen Mrs. Farrington's assistant, Marc? Not bad looking. The body-builder type. Rumor has it they might be lovers. Melissa, the receptionist at the main desk, said he must like rich, older women by the way he paid so much attention to Mrs.

Farrington and not to Melissa. I think she's saying that because he's ignored her completely—even though Melissa's done her best to flirt with him."

"I haven't met the man. What's his full name? I'll pull his file."

"Marc Simpson."

The phone buzzed again. Darcy answered, then put the call on hold and blurted out, "It's Trent. He's asking if you're here."

Kate groaned and waved her hands. "Oh, my! I can't face him—not yet. Tell him I have an appointment. I'll just go a few minutes earlier to see Mrs. Farrington. I'll have to consider how to handle him."

Kate grabbed a few employee files to work on while she waited. As she rushed out the door to go to Mrs. Farrington's office, she overheard Darcy say, with a seductive edge in her voice, "Sorry, Trent. Dr. Meyers just stepped out. Anything I can do to help you?"

Kate winced. Now that Kate's suspicions that Trent was the culprit had nearly evaporated, nothing stood in Darcy's way if she wanted to go after him romantically. More reason, for her friend's sake, that Kate should step back. Darcy would be good for him. Not only was she nice, Darcy even had a normal family background.

* * *

Kate stepped into Eden Farrington's outer office. Unfortunately, her assistant, Marc, wasn't at his desk so she didn't have the chance to check him out.

"Don't worry, Cecilia." Mrs. Farrington's voice carried from her office. "You are understandably upset because he didn't pay attention to you at the benefit, but do as I tell you."

Kate moved closer to the doorway and suppressed her guilt for listening to the conversation inside. She justified it for the sake of her investigation, and she had to find out about everything that was going on in the company. Although she admitted to herself, this time the discussion sounded more personal and about Trent—and was likely none of her business.

"He spent most of the evening with *that* woman. *Who was she?*" Cecilia railed.

"Not to worry. I'll find out."

Kate bit her lip.

Cecilia muttered. "Trent doesn't act as if he likes me."

"Nonsense," Mrs. Farrington said. "You're a beautiful girl. He'll come around. Go to work, and then we'll go shopping and out to lunch. We'll think of something you can do to get his attention."

"All right," Cecilia said with a heavy sigh. "I'll see you later."

Realizing their conversation was at an end, Kate rushed over and dropped down on the sofa. She flipped open one of her files.

A second later, followed by Cecilia, Mrs. Farrington strode into the outer office, her gaze narrowing on Kate. "You're here early, Dr. Meyers.

"Yes." Kate rose from the sofa.

"I didn't expect you for another twenty minutes," Mrs. Farrington said, checking her watch.

With a sour expression, Cecilia raised her chin a notch. "We'll continue our talk at lunch, Eden." She flounced out of the room.

Trent's mother led Kate into the office. The feminine room was done in a traditional style with warm peach tones, cream-colored carpet and whitewashed furniture.

Mrs. Farrington sat at her desk and indicated a nearby chair for Kate. "I hope you like your job."

Uneasiness washed over Kate. She sat down. "Yes, I do," she answered warily.

"Good. I've called you here to get acquainted." Her shrewd eyes perused Kate. "And I want to discuss my...*my son.* If I ask you some personal things, will you think I'm a meddling mother?" Her blue eyes pierced Kate.

"What?" Kate didn't know what to say.

"I'm troubled about our family—Trent specifically. He met someone at the benefit ball. I don't approve of him picking up strange women, but he's never cared about what I thought."

"Oh?" Kate asked, in a non-committal voice. If Trent did have a problem, perhaps it had something to do with his overbearing mother.

"Most women are only after him for his money."

Kate nearly gaped. "Don't you think he has some other appealing characteristics?" she asked quietly, holding in her shock.

"Perhaps some." Mrs. Farrington pursed her lips. She picked up her letter opener on her desk and swished it in the air. "But I'm concerned for his future happiness. Trent's grandfather is adamant. He demands that Trent settle down soon, but James doesn't care *who* Trent marries. I do. I want him to marry someone of whom I approve—like Cecilia." Eden shrugged. "It was probably my mistake to tell him I thought he should date her. He has always done the opposite of what I wanted. Explain this to me, Dr. Meyers. Why do you think he is like that?"

Dazed by this woman's superiority complex, Kate stared at her. "I suppose it's human nature to resist authority."

A burly man with a weight lifter's build strode into Eden's office. "Excuse me. Should I bring the car around?"

"Yes, I won't be long." Mrs. Farrington turned to Kate. "Dr. Meyers, I'd like you to meet my assistant, Marc Simpson. Marc, this is Dr. Meyers. She is new on our staff."

So, this man was the infamous assistant and chauffeur Darcy had mentioned. He gave Kate a brief smile. "Pleased to make your acquaintance, ma'am."

After he closed the door, Trent's mother said, "Now where were we? Oh, yes, I'll get to the point. I'm concerned about my son getting married because Trent's grandfather is adamant this family doesn't die out. Trent's our future."

"I hear there is another grandson—Roland Sikes."

The older woman's face turned into a contemptuous smirk that sent a chill through Kate. "In every family there's always a relative one would prefer to keep locked up in the attic. *Roland* is *ours*." Was she speaking as a jealous woman who thought her son was the best in the family? Or was there even more to Roland, regarding his business dealings?

Mrs. Farrington must have read the shocked look on Kate's face. "I hope I didn't come across as being ungenerous to Roland. Perhaps I am being a little selfish. I would like nothing more than to see my bloodline continue and inherit. And Trent's duty is to get married and produce offspring. He's known this since he was a child—but it must be the right girl."

Kate was having a hard time liking Eden. Obviously no one was good enough for her precious son, except Cecilia.

Kate couldn't resist. "As you said, Mr. Trent Farrington met someone at the benefit ball. Isn't that a step in the right direction?" She couldn't believe she was discussing this with Trent's mother.

"We won't accept any *unknown* factors. What if this turns serious? Who knows what gutter she's from?"

Kate's cheeks warmed. Yeah, she was pure gutter trash, or at least that's what Eden would think if she discovered Kate's real background. Her nefarious stepfather would probably taint her life forever. Even if there weren't already too many strikes against her with Trent, his family would be disgusted to know she was related to notorious conman Bill Jackson. Another reason to avoid Trent.

In spite of those thoughts, Kate raised her chin. "What was wrong with the woman he met?"

"We know nothing about her. I'm asking for your help to find out what Trent thinks of her."

A flush heated Kate's cheeks. "*Me?* How can I help?"

"James had mentioned he wanted you to speak to Trent—as a psychologist. I want you to tell me everything Trent discloses. And I want you to express to him what a wonderful girl Cecilia is."

No way. Kate wouldn't recommend Cecilia to anyone. She seemed like a spoiled brat, but perhaps that was only Kate's jealousy rearing its head. "I'm not a matchmaker, Mrs. Farrington, and he's not speaking to me as a psychologist. Even if he did, anything he said to me would be confidential."

"No one has to know what you tell me—not even his grandfather."

"It isn't legal, Mrs. Farrington."

The disgruntled woman jutted her face toward Kate. "Well, it should be. What he does is of the utmost importance to me. You said you liked your job. If he chooses to confide in you, I'm sure you can bend the rules." She gave Kate a thin smile and stood. "For his benefit...and yours." Mrs. Farrington's gaze traveled down the length of Kate. "Now I hope we understand each other, Dr. Meyers."

Stunned, Kate couldn't believe the woman had just threatened her. "I assure you, he won't speak to me." Kate headed toward the door, her nerves simmering with disgust. Now she understood at least a part of why Trent was the way he was with women. What an awful mother. A twinge of sympathy for him washed over her.

But she couldn't get involved any more than she already was with him. She should leave the company as soon as she investigated the records more thoroughly...and Roland Sikes.

* * *

After his unsuccessful attempt to contact Dr. Meyers, Trent took a few business calls, then settled back in his chair, contemplating the crumpled note on his desk that thanked him, but was missing a phone number. *Grace did not want to see him again.*

Mrs. Nash buzzed the intercom. "None of the cities around here have any Guckenheimers listed. Should I keep looking in other counties?"

"No. That's not necessary." He knew where to find Grace's phone number. He'd speak to her cousin, Dr. Meyers, when she returned to her office.

After his vision had cleared on the night of the benefit ball, he'd been chagrined that Grace Guckenheimer had walked out and left him deliberately high and dry about how to contact her.

Normally, he didn't need to chase women and would have let it go. However, Grace was different. He was intrigued.

Before he'd been hit with pepper spray, he'd noticed the resemblance between the two women. Except, through the mask, Grace's dark green eyes had not looked at him with disgust like Dr. Meyers' always did.

Trent got up from his desk, stalked to the window, and gazed out. If Grace had kissed him, why wouldn't she give him her number? He thought dryly, did it run in her family that the women didn't like him for some reason?

At a tap on his door, he turned.

"Hey, morning. How's it going?" Greg stepped into the room. "Why the sour look?"

Trent pointed to the balled-up paper on his desk. "This is all I have left of the girl I met at the benefit ball. I asked for her phone number and she left a thank you note."

His friend chuckled and plopped his lanky frame on the sofa. "Sorry, but now you get to feel what it's like for the rest of us. I've had the old fake-number switcheroo a few times. You, bud, must be losing your edge."

"Maybe I should check my deodorant," Trent said dryly.

Greg grinned. "Dr. Kate has never seemed that impressed by you either. By the way, I didn't see her at the party."

"Perhaps she doesn't like people," Trent quipped sarcastically. "Or maybe it's just *me* that she doesn't like."

"She seems nice enough to me."

"She was always congenial to you. The woman I met at the party was her cousin. Dr. Meyers must have allowed Grace to use her ticket, or she came to the party with Darcy. I'll get her cell phone number from Dr. Meyers."

"Glad someone isn't falling at your feet."

Trent shrugged. "I've waited long enough for Dr. Meyers to return my phone call. I have the distinct impression she's avoiding me. But, that's not why I called you. Did you find out what Frank Blake has been up to lately?"

"Yeah, I did some research. He's up for the same award as you."

"Interesting."

* * *

"Is Dr. Meyers in, Darcy?"

Sitting at her desk, reading over an employee file, Kate tensed at the sound of Trent's voice outside her office door. Her time of avoiding him had run out.

"I'll buzz her," Darcy said.

"That won't be necessary." Trent strode into the room without knocking. Kate gasped at the intrusion.

He closed the door behind him, leaving them alone. "I left word for you to call me when you returned. Didn't you get my message?"

Just seeing him with his tall and handsome good looks knocked her senses off kilter, which wasn't a good thing. "I-I planned to call you in a few minutes. I've been preoccupied with something in the records." This was partly true. She'd been looking for Marc Simpson's employment file, to find out more about him. Curiously, his file was missing.

Trent crossed his arms over his chest. "So what was of so much interest?"

"Oh, nothing important, just a missing file on one of the employees. Now, what can I do for you, Mr. Farrington?"

"What can you do for me?" he repeated. "I met your cousin Grace at the benefit ball. Could you give me her phone number?" He seemed chagrined to have to ask her for anything, but obviously, he wanted Grace's number badly.

Inwardly she smiled that he had liked her. Then panic jolted her to her senses. He could never find out she was Grace—he'd have to forget about her.

"You don't have to frown. It's a simple enough request. You know your cousin's phone number. Would you please give it to me?"

Expelling a deep sigh, Kate sagged back in her chair. "Why didn't you ask *her* for it?"

"I did." He tossed the crumpled note on her desk.

Kate smoothed out the paper. At seeing her own handwriting, she stifled a smile. He must have been a bit irked when he opened it to find only a thank you note.

She lifted her gaze to his. "Have you considered she might not want you to have it?"

He scowled at her. "I should have known you would give me a hard time. What is it about me, doc? From the first you've been set against me."

She was remorseful about that, but she had thought Matt's last words implicated Trent.

Rising from the desk, Kate strode around to the other side to stand before him. "I could say the same thing about you, but no, I don't dislike you at all." *At least not anymore. Now, please don't give me another reason to feel that way again.* "I can tell you, Mr. Farrington, that I know Grace very well, and she is not right for you."

How true her statement was. His mother would be dead-set against her—even under normal circumstances—and perhaps his grandfather, too, if he found out she wasn't a psychologist. And she didn't even want to contemplate that her best friend, Darcy, was completely crazy about him—not to mention how Trent would feel if he knew how she'd come to the company on a mission to send him to prison. There were too many strikes against her.

He stepped closer and gazed down at her. "Dr. Meyers, I don't think I need you to analyze who is right for me—or who is not."

Irrational jealousy sizzled inside her. When he had discovered her snooping in his office, he had almost kissed her then, as herself. Now, all he could think about was Grace. That stung.

You're way too fickle, buddy. "Sorry, but I heard of your reputation and this in my cousin."

His eyes narrowed. "Why, I think you're jealous of your own cousin. You may not *like* me—but I can see it in your eyes that you're attracted to me."

He ran his finger slowly down her cheek. "Is that it?"

She shivered, and a tingle ran all the way to her toes, though she tried to hide her response to him—unsuccessfully.

She whirled from his knowing gaze. "I think *you* are used to getting your way with women. Maybe your grandfather is right."

There was one way to make him leave her office—and in a hurry.

She stepped to her desk and picked up her calendar and a pen. "I have an opening tomorrow at two p.m. Will that do for us to get together? I'll pencil you in right now. You can come here and we can discuss *all* your problems with women." She turned up a sweet face to him. "I'd love to help you overcome your *issues*—as would your grandfather."

"*And lie down on your couch?*" he said in a cool tone. He flicked his gaze over her breasts. "I knew you were interested." Then he raised his dark eyes. "Or do you mean for *analysis*? Cold day in hell on that one, doc."

It was obvious from his tone that he hated therapists...or women planted in his path by his family.

Kate didn't know what to say. She sighed. "Mr. Farrington... Grace, uh, she wouldn't like it if I gave you her number."

"All right, but trust me. I *will* find her. If she doesn't want to see me after that, I'll let it go."

The blood drained from Kate's face. His trying to find Grace might lead back to *her*. She blew out a deep breath and returned to her desk to plop down in her chair.

"This is outrageous," he said throwing out his hands. "You act like I'm going to *hurt* her."

Yes, he could hurt her—and deeply. She'd already fallen for him, but her past and her lies put him out of reach. There couldn't be a good outcome out of this for her. Her cheeks burned, too, as she realized *she* didn't want him to find out the humiliating truth about her family and past.

She had to shut him out of her life before this went any deeper—and she was used to shutting things out. She had suppressed her memories and shame for years. It was easier than facing that pain.

"I'm not concerned about her. It's *you*," she lied. "Grace is a heartbreaker. You should forget about her."

His brow furrowed. "Did I ask you to look after me?" he asked incredulously.

His cell phone rang. He answered it. "This afternoon? All right." After he disconnected the call, he turned to Kate. "Frank Blake must be at it again. It seems OSHA will be at the Karger site today. Someone reported a violation against us. Doc, I want you to be there at four p.m. sharp. It's time for you to find out what we do at this company. Since you are hiring construction workers, I'll give you a tour of the place."

The blood drained from her face. She hoped she would never see the towering building site again or have to visit the place where her beloved brother had fallen.

"What's wrong?" Trent asked.

She clenched her hands on the chair arms. "I told you before that I'm afraid of heights, Mr. Farrington. I don't really want to go up there just yet."

"We build high-rise buildings. You need to get used to it. *Be there*." He turned on his heel and strode out the door.

CHAPTER ELEVEN

As Trent strode out of her office, Kate expelled a ragged breath and sagged back in her chair. She'd like to burn holes into his back. Should she have given him her own home number and met him somewhere dressed as Grace? Then if Grace rejected him, would he leave her alone? And really, did she want him to? If she did nothing, how long would it take for him to trace Grace back to her?

Now, because she'd not given him the phone number, he had ordered her to meet him at the construction site. Was he trying to punish her and test her fear of heights?

Her shoulders sagged. Her time was definitely running out at the company. Today, she had to locate those damning orders for inferior supplies and try to get more information on who else could be involved.

When lunchtime arrived, Kate rushed out of her office and headed to Purchasing. Cecilia wasn't at her desk so Kate tried the door to the file room. When the knob turned, she exhaled a sigh of relief and entered. The place was silent and empty. Her nerves taut, she went up and down the several rows of Steelcase file cabinets until she located one cabinet labeled "Karger Building Project."

Kate flipped through the last six months of files and checked the invoices. Three of them caught her eye. Strangely, the last three orders of drywall had been shipped to a warehouse in a shady part of town, and not directly to the Karger site.

Kate wasn't sure what the purchase orders meant. She slipped the papers into her briefcase. She'd photocopy them and return the originals tomorrow, which shouldn't be a problem. If Cecilia left the door unlocked at lunchtime, security was probably lax in this office.

A tap on a metal cabinet in the next row reverberated around the room. Kate's heart raced and she froze in place. Several minutes ticked by.

Not knowing what, or who, had caused the sound, she edged silently toward the door and quietly slipped out of the room.

Her churning stomach was tied in knots by the time Kate reached her desk and collapsed in her chair. *Had someone been in the file room? Had she been seen?*

Kate checked her watch. She had missed lunch entirely. Her next appointments were back to back and would begin in a few minutes. She was to interview several potential employees and later meet Trent at the Karger job site as he had commanded.

Apprehension swept through her. She was concerned about stepping onto the building site where her brother had fallen. The memories were too recent and still too painful for her to fake a cool composure around Trent.

To top it off, now she wondered if whoever had been in the file room at the same time had seen her. Was she insinuating herself in too deep?

* * *

The afternoon sun lowered on the horizon as Trent strode through the construction site. As for the anonymous report of violations, OSHA had come and gone without finding any issues. Several men moved about completing various jobs before they wrapped up and left for the evening.

Two hundred feet away, Dr. Meyers paused outside the front gates. Her blond hair was knotted in a bun and gleamed in the late sun. Dressed in a drab white suit, she stood there staring up at the building, looking like a lost soul. Perhaps all this loud activity intimidated her, compounding her fear of heights.

Frowning at the uneasiness he might have caused her by making her come to the job site, he strode up to her. She whirled toward him, with an anxious expression. Taking in her pale face, he swore. "Hell, you look like you've seen a ghost. You actually do have a problem with coming here."

She raised her chin. "It's just that you startled me. That's all."

He shook his head in disbelief. "Yeah, right. I don't believe you're being truthful. I saw you from a distance and you looked like you were having an issue then."

"I'll be all right," she whispered, through pale lips.

"If you say so. By the way, doc, OSHA just left. Luckily, they didn't find any workplace violations."

"Th-that's good," she said, swaying slightly.

"Are you sick?"

She shrugged. "No. I'll be fine."

He studied her face. "Is it the height thing that's bothering you?"

She raised her chin. "I-I can manage."

"All right, but I'm not convinced. Why don't you tell me why you're afraid of heights—or whatever it is that's bothering you about being here?"

She raised gray eyes to him, distorted by the glasses, and something tightened in his chest.

She blew out a deep breath. "I suppose, like most people, you must think therapists don't have any problems. Let me just say I had a traumatic experience with heights when I was a kid."

"And...?" When she seemed reluctant to say more, he teased, "Should I guess? You fell out of your bunk bed?"

Her mouth curved upward, as he intended. "You read minds, too?"

"So you don't want to tell me the real reason?"

Her lips compressed and she shook her head.

"I understand entirely your not wanting to tell me," he said with dry sarcasm, "because then you'd have to explain why you went to work for a construction company that builds *high-rises*. You are an enigma, doc."

She gave him a sideways glance. "Perhaps I thought I'd only be working in the offices," she quipped.

"All right, since you're not going to tell me, come on. Let's go. I'll show you around. I'd like you to see what we do."

Glancing again at the building, she drew in a deep breath and squared her shoulders as if readying herself for the journey upward in the elevator. "I-It's one thing to ride in those enclosed elevators at work, but these are so open."

"If you're so terrified of heights we will avoid the elevators today. Our tour will only be on the ground—although the elevators are perfectly safe. And since you're here, you might as well see some of the site."

He picked up a hard hat for her from the stack by the entrance gate. Something caught his eyes. About thirty feet down the fence line, and partially hidden by equipment and pallets of construction supplies, a bloodied mass was attached to the chain link fence.

"What the hell...?" he asked.

Behind him, Dr. Meyers gasped.

They strode toward the object. Blood oozed from the eyes, mouth and the neck of a woman's severed head. Long, pale-blond hair spread out with a splattering of deep crimson red.

"Oh, my!" Dr. Meyers cried. "That wasn't here when I walked by only minutes ago."

"Don't panic. It's only a Halloween mask with some sort of fake gel to look like blood. Probably a kid's prank." Frowning, he stepped closer to the object. "I hope they're not taking up some stupid antics, trying to make this place appear haunted after the accident months ago."

He inspected the mask and found a cord with glasses dangling from the neck, just above the severed edge as if to appear a woman had been strangled first and then guillotined.

"Holy shit, doc—it looks a little like you." He glanced at her face, now whiter than the dress shirt he wore with his suit today.

"I, uh, Mr. Farrington... I don't feel well at all..."

When she sank toward the ground, he caught her by the waist and gently swung her up in his arms. Her glasses and hard hat fell off and landed on the ground.

"Hey, doc... Kate?" he asked.

Her head lolled on his arm and her shirt fell open at the neckline. His gaze dropped to a red heart-shaped birthmark at her collarbone, the same mark he'd seen the other night—*on Grace*.

When her eyes fluttered open, a jolt hit him. Now an exquisite gray color of steel mixed with blue sky, at one time he'd seen those eyes a different color. At the ball, they'd been a dark forest green. For a moment, her gaze locked on his.

She snapped her lids closed. "I-I'm okay. I didn't eat lunch."

"Are you sure that's the reason you fainted?" he asked in a controlled voice.

"Yes," she whispered.

If she'd been any other woman, he might have been tempted to dump her out of his arms for tricking him. However, now, instead of feeling stupid or angry, he couldn't stop a simmering satisfaction that he *had* found *Grace*. No wonder he'd been attracted to both women.

And this meant Dr. Meyers had not hated him on the night of the party—far from that.

She had obviously worn green contacts that night. Why had she kept her identity a secret? What was her game?

"I'm all right now," she muttered. "You can put me down."

Still stunned about her deception, he stood her on her feet. She turned away from him, but nearly stumbled.

He caught her around the shoulders. "No, you're not *okay*." Surprised by his own protectiveness, he scooped her up again and strode to a nearby bench. He sat her down.

"Can you please find my glasses?" She dropped her face into her hands, while he went to retrieve them.

Only when she had adjusted her glasses on her nose did she turn and face him again. "Thank you. I am so embarrassed."

"Are you better now?" he asked, after she'd rested a few minutes.

She nodded. "Yeah."

"Come on, you're shaking. If I've ever seen anyone in need of a drink, it's you. I'll have the thing removed while we go to the bar around the corner."

Leaning on him, she hobbled beside him over the gravel and to the work site exit. "Do I look like I drink a lot?

"No, but unless you've a reason not to drink, today you could use one."

When they neared the gates to exit the construction site, Greg strode through. "Hey, what happened?"

Greg's gaze swept over Trent's arm around Dr. Meyers' shoulders. Was that a flicker of jealousy in his friend's eyes?

"She fainted," Trent said.

Greg turned toward the thing hanging on the fence. "Yikes. Is that what upset you, Kate? It certainly is gruesome. Someone's got a depraved sense of humor."

"My thoughts exactly," Trent answered. "Must be a Halloween prank."

Kate nodded. "I-It was silly of me. I-I over-reacted."

"Would you get rid of it, Greg? I'm taking her to Hannigan's Pub."

On their way out of the construction site, Trent whispered to her, "And tell me the truth. It's wasn't only the mask, but you weren't feeling all too well before you got here."

She shrugged, but he had no doubt that her faint had been real. And with her withholding her identity from him on the night of the party, he felt he had every right not to tell her that he'd found her out.

She deserved a little bit of her own medicine, until he found out why she'd not revealed her true identity.

* * *

Away from the shadows of the Karger Construction site, Kate walked on trembling legs down the sidewalk toward nearby Hannigan's Pub. Trent's arm was draped securely around her shoulders. Despite her shock over the bloodied mask, she couldn't help but notice how warm he felt against her and how her pulses leapt at his nearness.

Kate reexamined the facts and tried to hold on to her fragile control as they walked on toward the pub. No doubt, the grisly mask had been meant for her. The resemblance was too close. Was it only a warning, or some kind of threat? Whoever did this must have discovered she had a connection to Matt and why she was at the company. If so, her days at Farrington were definitely numbered—she had to leave soon.

But who could have done it? Anyone could know she was going to be here because she'd posted her intent to visit the Karger Construction site early in the day. It wasn't Trent who placed it on the fence because the mask wasn't there when they'd passed that spot earlier and they'd been together since they arrived. Unfortunately, from the time she'd been in the file room to now, this person had plenty of time to hang it on the fence to frighten her.

With all she'd come to know about Trent, she was convinced his smarmy cousin Roland was the 'grandson' Matt had meant in his last words. Had Roland been the person hiding in the file room? Sending such a hideous warning, indicated someone with a dangerous mind. The idea that someone knew who she really was sent a shiver through her. However, she couldn't let fear stop her. She had to stay at the company and find out who was responsible for the equipment and the supply switches, which had caused Matt's death.

Trent squeezed her shoulders. "Hey, you're shaking. You can calm down now. It's only a Halloween prank. You all right?"

Fighting the urge to sink her face into his muscular chest, she nodded and swallowed a lump in her throat. "Yeah…probably just a Halloween prank," she said in a flat voice.

They soon arrived at the local Irish restaurant, only a few minutes from the construction site. Kate remembered hearing the place was a frequent happy-hour hangout for downtown business clientele and for nightlife.

Inside, the rustic pub had dark wood paneling, with candles flickering on the tables. When Trent removed his arm from around her, Kate sighed and took a seat across from him at the wooden booth.

After their drinks were served, Trent pushed the glass of blackberry brandy in front of her. "Drink some. It'll help."

As she sipped, the liquid burned her throat. She wrinkled her nose and glanced up to find him staring at her.

"You don't like it?" he asked.

She shook her head. "I'm not sure. It's strong."

"Seemed like you needed a stiff drink." He leaned back against the booth and studied her. "I'd say for a psychologist, you have a lot of phobias: afraid of heights, faints at the sight of fake blood. I could go on." He pinned her with his dark gaze. "What shook you up so much that you fainted?"

Kate dropped her gaze to the table. "At first glance, the mask seemed so real," she said in a low voice. That was the truth, but she had taken an extra jolt knowing it was meant for her. A chill prickled along the nape of her neck.

"But it wasn't *real*."

She toyed with the glass of brandy in her hand and tried to redirect the conversation, tried to gain her balance. "So I do have a lot of phobias. Have you ever heard the theory that those who go into the psychology field are likely people who are comfortable around psychologists—because they've been around a lot of psychologists?"

He chuckled. "No." He sipped his beer, but his gaze never left her face.

A blush heated her cheeks. "Well, it's true. I've had my share of problems."

Her statement made her sound like she'd been a patient, but actually her great-aunt had been the only psychologist Kate had ever known. Not that she couldn't have used some help after a childhood spent with Bill Jackson—but she'd never been professionally treated by anyone. Her aunt had tried to help, but unfortunately, she had died over three years ago.

Kate took another sip of the strong drink. One, to steady her nerves because she was affected by Trent and needed a break from gazing into his dark eyes. And two, she was almost certain, because of the likeness to her, that the mask had been meant for her. It seemed like a threat of some kind and she wasn't sure how serious. Was it placed there to scare her away? Or was it a more dangerous threat because she was getting too close to something?

With a shudder, she swallowed another gulp of brandy.

Trent leaned forward across the table and regarded her. "I see you're taking my advice to drink for medicinal purposes."

Kate gave him a faint smile and nodded weakly. "You sure you're not trying to get me drunk?"

"Would it help?" he inquired in a bland voice.

Heat rushed through her at the memory of him saying he'd be available for warming her bed. She flicked him a wary glance. "I've never fainted before," she said, ignoring his question. "But I think your suggestion to have a drink was wise. I'm better already."

"Maybe you should eat something, too, since you skipped lunch, or you actually might pass out again for drinking on an empty stomach. They have food here, or we can go to a restaurant on Las Olas."

That would be wonderful to spend more time with him. What was she thinking? Alarm swept through her. For the duration of her time at the company, she had to keep her relationship with him strictly dealing with business. "I can't do that, *Mr. Farrington.*"

"Sure you can. Just say, 'I'd love to go, *Trent.*'"

A pain tugged at her heart. She wished she could reveal herself as Grace and pick things up from there, with no lies, other than a name, to interfere between them. She'd thought their evening at the ball was special to him and she would treasure those memories for a lifetime. But she supposed his evening with Grace had not been special enough that he wouldn't hit on the first vulnerable woman, even one he'd shown little interest in before…

"But I work for you," she said weakly. Had he forgotten the romantic night he'd shared with Grace at the benefit ball? He was fickle and not to be trusted with her heart. "And did you forget about my cousin already?" she prodded.

His smile turned into a chuckle. "Sorry, doc, if I've given you the impression I was asking you for a date. Is that what you assumed? It's purely professional between us. I merely thought since you fainted I'd feed you and we could drop the sparring for the evening."

Her face burning, she nodded. Of course, he didn't like her the way she was, as herself. Perhaps he thought she was homely without makeup. Ever since her glasses had flown off her head, she'd been half worried he had recognized that she was Grace. She'd been waiting for his reaction and for him to denounce her. Obviously, there was no need. He still saw her as the plain-looking, unattractive doctor—which was exactly what she'd wanted him to think from the beginning.

She frowned and almost said something about men who were only interested in women because of the way they looked, when he held up a hand. "Now, Dr. Meyers, I'm not trying to make you angry. I only thought I would make amends for the way I demanded your cousin's phone number." He gestured to the space between them. "Nothing personal. You and I are hardly the same type, which we agreed upon before."

Her shoulders stiffened. She had the distinct impression she'd been insulted further. She should be relieved he'd not recognized her, but she wasn't. She regretted the entire charade.

"Deep thoughts?" Trent asked, raising his beer.

Her face warmed. "Yes."

"I have a few of my own. Since I potentially saved you from another nasty fall, I thought we might be friends."

"Friends? You want to be my friend?" She narrowed her eyes. "Or are you still trying to get Grace's phone number?" she asked in a sour voice.

Before she could say more, Greg strode into the pub. "I took care of the mask." He dropped beside her in the booth. "Are you okay, Kate?"

"Yes. I'm better."

Elbows on the table, Greg leaned toward Trent. "Wow. That was a terrible Halloween joke."

"Either that or someone hates Farrington Construction," Trent said.

Thinking the same, or that someone hated *her*, Kate's eyes widened… She gulped more brandy to calm her frazzled nerves.

Trent blew out a deep breath. "Maybe we should take the mask to the police for evidence."

"Not going to happen. It's already in the dumpster." Greg waved toward the waitress to catch her attention.

Trent lifted his beer. "Too many strange things happening. Jack from Western called about two hours ago and said he traced the elevator problems in Farrington Towers back to a computer glitch. I wonder if someone is hacking into our programming."

Adjusting his glasses, Greg straightened. "That's my area. I'll research it."

A frown creased Trent's handsome face. "And, damn it, with Frank Blake wanting the company so badly, I just don't trust that he isn't behind this. He'll do anything to bring us down."

Kate's stomach rolled. *Who was this Frank Blake?* She needed to find out more about him, and of course, there was Roland, the black sheep who was her main suspect. If only she could confide in Trent and relate her suspicions about his cousin.

Kate pushed away the rest of the drink. "I'm better now. Thank you. I have to go."

Trent and Greg stood while she grabbed her purse and slid out of the booth.

"Are you sure you're all right?" Trent stopped her with a hand on her elbow that sent a tingle shooting up her arm.

"Yeah," she whispered, alarmed that just the merest touch from him affected her like that.

"I'll walk you to your car, Kate," Greg said.

Trent's hand dropped to her lower back in a possessive move. "I brought her here, Greg. I'll take her to her car."

Greg raised an eyebrow. Trent dropped some money on the table and steered Kate by the elbow out the door.

Outside, darkness had fallen on the city. The street buzzed with passing cars. Some people strolled along the sidewalks, while others sat at tables on outside patios.

They neared her car in the parking garage at Farrington Towers. The seclusion of the parking spot brought back a vision of the horrible, bloodied mask. Kate shuddered, grateful for Trent's presence.

He opened the car door for her. "You can't be that cold as it's quite warm tonight. Are you sure you're all right to drive?"

Touched by his concern, she nodded. "I don't live far away. Thank you for your help tonight, Mr. Farrington." *Keep it professional, Kate.* She slid into the seat.

He leaned down, one hand on the car. "I meant what I said about taking you out to dinner."

"No. I couldn't. I'll see you at the office."

Earlier he'd made it clear their relationship was professional, yet now the sizzling warmth in his eyes sent heat flowing through her, unsettling her composure.

He cast her a brief ironic smile. "You understand what I meant before is that I couldn't ask you for a date. After meeting your cousin Grace…well, I liked her and I intend to find her. No rock will be left unturned. I can assure you of that."

Kate gulped and his intense gaze unsettled her even further. She turned the key in the ignition of her car and broke the momentary bond between them.

Trent stood on the sidewalk and watched Kate drive away. He'd nearly told her he knew she was Grace, but he'd been hoping she'd tell him the truth herself.

How far would she take this charade? Was it because she really wanted nothing to do with him? He didn't think so by just the way she looked at him at times, yet something always held her back.

Anyway, he was glad he'd found out that Grace and the little spitfire doctor, who had hated him with a passion since they'd met, were one and the same. He'd play along for a while.

Perhaps his judgment had deteriorated, because he wanted her like no other…wanted her in his arms, in his bed, and in his *life*. And the last… Well, he'd never felt that way before.

* * *

The next day at lunchtime, Kate snuck into the Purchasing Department. With her nerves stretched to the breaking point worrying that she'd be discovered again, she replaced the original invoices in the files.

Kate returned to her desk, sighing in relief, glad she hadn't been caught. With the palm of her hand propping up her chin, she stared at the copies she'd made of the last three shipments of drywall. What was this all about? Why hadn't the drywall been taken directly to the job site? Was she possibly onto something here?

Darcy strode into Kate's office. "What's up?"

Kate thrust the bills at her. "Look at this. Why would a shipment of drywall temporarily go to a warehouse before ending at the actual Karger Construction site? This can't be a usual practice—and this has happened on the last three orders."

"Huh?" Darcy shrugged. "Why do you think?"

"I think someone's doing something with the drywall before it's being brought to the site. If that is the case, this entire investigation is going in a different direction than I thought. Someone isn't just siphoning off money to pocket it—they're out to do damage to the building. I just read an article that some cheap foreign drywall has chemicals in it and can corrode metal, and make people sick. I'll have to go back to the Karger building site and get samples of the drywall."

"I'll go with you."

"I'd rather you didn't. I don't want to draw attention to us. Besides, if something should happen to me, I need someone to know the details..."

A stricken look crossed Darcy's face. "You're scaring me. You found that mask at the site. Everyone's already talking about it, saying it looked a lot like you. Damn, Kate, this is scaring me."

Kate pressed her hands together. "I hoped they'd all think it was only a coincidence?"

"No. It's out there. I don't know, but I wonder who—?"

"When I posted my plans for the day on the board, anyone walking by could have seen where I'd be at four p.m. There was plenty of time for anyone to orchestrate their little horror show."

"Is this going to get dangerous, Kate? I'm worried about you."

Kate rose from her desk. "I don't know. I hope not... Have you heard anything about Roland Sikes?"

"No, except that he's a womanizer and a partier—big time."

"Okay, but keep your eyes and ears open."

"Have you seen Trent today?" Darcy asked.

At the hopeful look on Darcy's face, Kate winced. "No." She headed toward the outer office, with Darcy following, just as Trent himself was striding through the door. Kate's pulse raced, while heat rose to her cheeks.

"Good afternoon, Darcy. Going somewhere, Dr. Meyers?" Trent asked.

He grinned at Kate as if he knew with just a glance that he could affect her. And the jerk found that amusing! And he liked her, but only as her cousin!

She squared her shoulders and stepped back, determined to stifle the sparks that sizzled between them.

Resolved to shut down her feelings, and to keep him at a distance, she gave him a cool look. "I'm not going anywhere in particular. I'm here if you need me." *Need?* Why did she say *that?* Oh, my, she didn't like the way he turned her into the high school wallflower, mesmerized by the quarterback.

His knowing gaze flicked over her, sending simmering heat through her.

Not amused by her physical reaction to a single look from him, she crossed her arms protectively over her chest.

Darcy's eyebrows arched. "Well, if no one needs me...I'll just go out to my office...and see what work I have to do."

Kate sat at her desk and while Trent closed the door, she discreetly slid the copies of the invoices into the top middle drawer so he wouldn't see them.

He turned from the door and smiled at her again. "Are you feeling better today?"

Nervousness gripped her at being alone with him and his strange friendliness today. She gave him a wary nod. "Thanks. I'm a little embarrassed about fainting yesterday, but I really appreciate your help."

He arched an eyebrow. "But you still won't give me your cousin's number?"

She blew out a deep breath. At least he hadn't seen through her cover. "Please. You've got to forget about Grace."

He nodded. "I'm taking your advice." An easy smile played on his lips.

"What? You mean you're going to give up on finding Grace?" She narrowed her gaze on him, wondering why he was giving up so easily.

"I believe you if you say that she's a heartbreaker, and that I should forget her. Will that make you happy?"

Frowning, Kate put her hand to her mouth and coughed. "So...what can *I* do for you today?"

"I'm here to talk to you as a psychologist."

"As a—?"

"Don't you remember the appointment you set up for me yesterday? It's on your calendar."

She gaped. "But I... You can't be serious?" She slumped back into her chair. "I don't think that's a good idea."

He came around to her side of the desk, leaned down, and placed one hand on her desk. "Why? Let see your appointment book." He reached for it. "There it is penciled in for two p.m.? You did make the appointment."

The challenging gleam in his eyes made her uneasy. She rolled her chair back, afraid he was going to put his hands on her shoulders. "I thought you were worried about 'playing into your family's hands'? You know, I might be part of a 'setup' by your grandfather. Remember all those things you told me."

Sardonic amusement twisted his lips. "So, tell me that you don't want to hear about my family? Or my mother?"

He couldn't know the bait he threw her. She definitely wanted to find out more about him, and anything else that could help her investigation, but that could be playing with fire. However, she needed to risk spending this time with him. She might find out more about the rest of the Farringtons in fifteen minutes than she had uncovered in her few weeks at the company.

"All right," she said with a nod. "Let's get this over with."

He cast her a hot glance. "Should I lie down on your sofa?" He smiled broadly.

She narrowed her eyes and nodded reluctantly. "I suppose..."

She didn't want him to notice how much he affected her so she turned away and gathered up a note pad. She didn't want him lying anywhere near her either and didn't believe for any moment that he was serious about this.

Ignoring her better judgment to be so close to him, she straightened her shoulders and resolved to get through this as quickly as possible.

"Do you mind if I make myself comfortable?" He peered at her intently as he removed his jacket, loosened his tie, and exaggerated the act of unbuttoning his shirt at the neck.

Kate couldn't stop the heat that rushed through her. He laid his jacket on the back of the couch, stretched out on her sofa, with his hands crossed behind his head and his nearly black hair against the pillow.

He was sexy and entirely too handsome. She cleared her throat and sat in the chair near him with her notepad, trying to assume the professional appearance of a psychologist. "All right. Go ahead. Tell me whatever you'd like."

Do anything, but don't strip naked. Oh, damn, she remembered him with his shirt off that day at the construction site. The tight jeans...

"All right. It all comes down to my childhood. Should I start at the beginning, after my father died?"

"Yes, go ahead." Keeping her back ramrod straight, she hoped she pulled off a professional appearance.

"My father died in a car accident when I was nine." She jotted down notes. "We were close. I was naturally devastated," he said.

"Most people would be."

"Is your father alive, Kate?"

She frowned at his use of her first name and met his gaze. "He died before I was born."

"So you had no father figure?"

At the usual sting of embarrassment burning her cheeks, she shrugged. She certainly was *not* going to talk about her stepfather Bill Jackson—the convicted conman.

"No, not really," she answered, somewhat truthfully because her stepfather had been nothing like a father should be. She'd been terrified of him and hated him all at the same time.

"You had your mother?"

"No," she said, shaking her head. "My mother died when I was two. Later, I went to live with my great-aunt." *That's it, Kate, skip over the fourteen years of unhappiness that was spent with your wicked stepfather, before she finally went to live with Aunt Kate at sixteen...*

"Sorry to hear that. Do you have brothers or sisters?"

She didn't like the direction his questions were heading. "A *brother*, but we're supposed to be discussing you, not me." Thanks to someone involved with this company, she didn't have a brother anymore either, but she had to steer this conversation away from herself. "*Mr. Farrington,* why don't you tell me about your cousin?"

He raised a dark eyebrow. "Call me *Trent.*"

Frowning, she poised her pen on the pad. He continued, "I used to look up to Roland, but things changed as we grew older."

"The reason?"

"Next subject."

"Can you tell me when you started having problems with Roland?"

He crossed his arms over his chest. "Next subject."

"But we're not getting anywhere," Kate said in exasperation.

He narrowed his eyes as if he also knew they weren't going to either.

"All right, then tell me about your relationship with your grandfather?"

"Our relationship is good, but he's persistent in wanting me to marry," he said softly. "But you already know all about that. I had never met the *right* woman…"

The look he gave her caused a current of sexual magnetism to leap between them.

She wanted to join him on the couch, touch her fingers to his neck and feel his smooth bare skin, taste his lips again.

Kate dropped her gaze to the note pad lying in her lap. She had to stop her thoughts about him. "Tell me about your relationship with your mother?"

"Strained."

"Why?"

"My father cheated on her. She blames me. I suppose because I remind her too much of him. Or it's because of her generally cold nature. I don't know. She's let me down more times than I can count."

"Why don't you start from the beginning?"

"What's to say? She was absent most of the time and was never around when I needed her. I grew up with a string of nannies. Then later I went to live with my grandfather. I learned to live with an uninterested, distant mother. I don't think about it anymore."

A pang of sadness for the lonely little boy he had been, tugged at her heart. "Is there something about your relationship with your mother that might make you distrust women?"

His brow furrowed. "Is that what you think—that my relationship with my mother makes me *distrust* women?" He shrugged and locked his gaze on hers. "Tell me, what do you think of her?"

Truthfully, Kate didn't know Mrs. Farrington well. The woman had not been pleasant on the few occasions she'd met her. However, Kate couldn't stop the strong desire to help him fix his relationship with his mother.

"Oh," Kate said, "I couldn't say as I've only recently met her, but you're lucky to have a mother, you know. I can't remember mine."

"Sorry to hear that."

"Can you please tell me more about your mother?"

"No."

"But I'd like to help you."

"Don't try. It's irreparable. She's lied to me too many times."

Kate flushed to her toes. What would he think of her if he discovered the truth about *her* and her lies?

"But she's your mother," Kate said weakly.

"I can tell you she doesn't care in the least about being on better terms with me. We're both fine with the status quo," he said, misinterpreting her blush. "Enough about her."

"All right, then let's go back to discussing *you*."

He gave her a brief, ironic smile, then shook his head. "Not my favorite subject," he said with dry sarcasm. "On that note, I need to get back to work."

He sat up and leaned so close to her that they were face to face, causing her pulse to race. "Your verdict, doc? Am I sane?" he asked in a teasing tone.

"That jury is still out," she said tartly. "I hope you feel better now that you've discussed a few *personal* issues in your life with me."

"Do you ever take off those glasses, Kate?" Her heartbeat quickened at the huskiness in his voice. His tone did incredible things to her insides.

"At night." She swallowed to relieve her dry throat. "I take my glasses off at night."

They stood.

He ran his hand up her arm, sending tingles through her. "Some night, I'd like to see your eyes, minus the glasses."

Alarm bells clanged inside Kate. She jerked up straight. "*Impossible.* Besides working together, we now have a doctor-client relationship, so anything between us other than a professional engagement is definitely out of bounds."

"Business be damned. What the hell are you afraid of?" He took her tablet from her hand, ripped off the top sheet, folded the paper and put it into his jacket pocket. "Whatever I said today was off the record, Kate."

He tossed the tablet on the sofa and turned to cup her cheek. His gaze dropped to her mouth. Excitement roared through her.

She licked her lips. "I only like *working* for you, as a part of your staff, Mr. Farrington," she said nervously.

"Call me Trent—and I don't believe you really mean that." He placed his hand on the back of her head and traced lazy circles with his thumb on her ear, then he lowered his lips to hers and kissed her senseless.

Too weak to resist him, she melted into his embrace and lifted her hand to his cheek. His hand rested on her hip. Kate moaned at the sensations from his kiss. He called her back to reality by raising his lips from hers. She gasped.

"That's how much you like me in a *business* sense, Kate."

"But we work together—you like my cousin," she whispered. She ran her tongue over her lips, while taking a step back from him.

"It's inevitable that we'll be together."

"I don't sleep around."

"You won't have to. You'll be with me."

"You're moving way too fast for me… This can't happen," she said weakly.

He buttoned his shirt and retied his tie. "Yes, it can, *Grace*."

She swallowed the lump in her throat. "Grace?"

He nodded and gave her a brief smile. "And I'm not sorry. You want me and I want you. Let's not make it more complicated than that. We've had some problems at the construction site down in Homestead. I'll be away for up to a week. I'll call you, when I return. We'll go out to dinner and talk. Please remember our kiss." He brought her hand to his mouth and kissed her fingertips.

This time there was no guile. She believed him.

After he strode out of the office, she released a shaky breath and raised her fingers to her throbbing lips. Her body trembled with unquenched desire—a desire that had been building since she had first met him, regardless of what she'd tried to tell herself.

CHAPTER TWELVE

Trent stayed in Homestead for one week, until he was assured everything was running smoothly. Then he returned to his main office at Farrington Towers in Fort Lauderdale.

He couldn't wait to see Kate and looked forward to surprising her at lunch and letting her know he'd returned. He talked to her only once on the phone where he'd asked her if she was thinking about *them*, and she had said a breathless, yes.

But for now, he had company work to finish. He scoured the documents on his desk, confident the building should win the State of Florida award.

Without knocking, Roland stalked through the office door. Jacketless, and his shirt soaked with sweat under the armpits, he flung papers onto Trent's desk. "Sign these, so I can get the check. I'll wait."

Trent stared into his cousin's red, swollen eyes. "Whoa. What the hell is wrong with you? And what's this new company—*Ace Advertising?*"

Roland blew out a breath. "We need more exposure."

"I disagree. The amount of advertising Farrington does is adequate."

"And I disagree with that. You don't know how it peeves me to have to ask for your signature now. So sign."

"Leave the papers. I'll look them over. I doubt I'll sign without more information."

"To hell with you." His cousin whirled and stalked toward the door as Trent's mother entered.

"You look in fine shape, Roland," Eden said as she stepped aside. Her haughty glance roamed over Roland. He returned a disgruntled snarl before striding out of the office.

Eden's cool gaze then focused on Trent. "Trent, darling…"

"*Mother*," he said, flinching. "What can I help you with? *Do you need money, too?*"

"So that's what the squanderer wanted?" She dropped into the chair in front of Trent's desk. "No, I'm not here for money, but to discuss several things with you. This company is like a small town, and rumors have a way of getting back to me. I have a few questions about our newest employee—Dr. Meyers."

Trent lifted an eyebrow. "Such as?"

"I heard last week she fainted at the Karger site. You took her to Hannigan's Pub and—"

"Your point?" He leveled his gaze on her.

"She always seems to be in some kind of trouble. Weeks ago, Cecilia told me Dr. Meyers fell in the lobby and you caught her. Now, I hear she's fainted and you apparently helped her again. I see a pattern here. *Have you gotten her pregnant?*" At his still expression, she shrugged and continued, "*Good*. Then I have to question if she planned these stunts because she has designs on you. Nothing unusual. Some women might find you fairly attractive. You're certainly rich enough."

"Thanks," he said through gritted teeth. Sighing, he unclenched his hand. "Now, why don't you tell me what you're really getting at and why you're here?"

She rose from the chair and moved to stare out the window. "Remember, Trent, when you were little and used to ask me, 'Mom, why are you never happy?' Well, I'll tell you why. I always wanted more children."

"You!" he sat back in his chair in disbelief. "You were never around for me. What would you have done with another child?"

His mother whirled and her icy gaze swept over him. "I might as well be forthright about this visit," she said, ignoring his question. "You're the heir to this company—our legacy. I want everything to stay with our side of the family."

He frowned. "I don't have a problem sharing with Roland."

"He'll destroy the business. I want grandchildren to secure the company's future—our future…through *you*."

"Since when are you jumping on the children bandwagon? You weren't particularly loving to me. You always gave me the impression kids were just a headache to be tolerated. How would you treat a grandchild?"

She blew out a deep breath. "I suppose I should explain why I have been the way that I am. I suffered so many miscarriages that holding a living child was hard." A bleak expression crossed her face as if this was a difficult confession. "And I was trying so hard to get your father back. I was losing him to yet another one of his *whores*." She nearly spat the last word. "Marry Cecilia, and give me those grandchildren."

"Give it up. That's not going to happen."

She returned to the chair across from his desk and leaned toward him. "Should I speculate there's someone else? If it's not Dr. Meyers...? Who?" She frowned. "The girl at the benefit ball? You seemed quite entranced with her."

He inwardly groaned that his mother had been watching him with Kate that evening. Time to turn the tables. "I don't tell you who to see, Mother, but rumors have it you've taken up with your assistant?"

"Marc?" she said with a dry laugh. "Ridiculous. However, I do enjoy having an attractive man show me around."

"And what does *he* get out of it?"

She clasped her hands on the chair arms. "None of your business."

"Then stay out of *mine*. You were never interested before, so stop interfering in my life now."

She smiled, but without humor. She picked up a paperweight from the desk and tossed it around in her hands. "You're the company's future—*our future*. If you settled down with the right woman, I *wouldn't* have to interfere. Besides, you might be surprised who I'm actually seeing."

"I don't care if he's *Jack the Ripper*."

She rose from the chair. Piercing him with her pale blue eyes, she gazed down her nose at him. "You can tell me if you're *gay*, Trent." Her lips curled in irony. "Then I would understand why you don't like a beautiful girl like Cecilia. However, it wouldn't change the way I feel about you at all."

Gaping at her, he slowly shook his head in amazement and lounged back in his chair, pressing his fingertips together. How cold-hearted his mother could be, but he was used to her calculated verbal blows—nothing new there. He knew she didn't believe that he was gay, but as usual, she thought she could strike a hit at him, thinking that would hurt him, just because she didn't get her way.

His mother strode to the door, then paused and turned. "I want to warn you about someone who I think *is* a problem at the company. Cecilia returned from lunch the other day and saw Dr. Meyers had just come out of Purchasing—and she was sure she'd been in the file room. What business would she have in there?"

"Maybe she went to speak to Cecilia."

Nearly snorting, Eden shook her head. "Call it women's intuition, but there's something about Dr. Meyers that I don't like."

She turned and swept out of his office, leaving Trent with this latest information about Kate to ponder. Why *had* she been in the Purchasing Department and in the file room? What had she been looking for?

He'd been looking forward to seeing her today. He wanted to trust her, but with this news about her potentially snooping around, his nagging doubts about her returned. Why *had* she kept her identity from him the night of the benefit ball? Was there more she was hiding from him, and because of his attraction and feelings for her, was he being duped?

Because she worked for the company, on the night of the benefit ball, she had known the building's floor plan. She knew exactly where the ballroom would be. However, she'd been going up to the offices when he first discovered her that night in the stairwell. Later, she'd been in Roland's office, saying she hadn't brought a cell phone and needed to use a phone, when she could have used the one in her own office.

His head beginning to throb, Trent pressed his fingers to his temples. Every fear he'd had of betrayal with women reared like an ugly beast inside him. Was she just another woman who lied and couldn't be trusted? Why had she been in Purchasing? Why had she not confessed she was Grace?

He swore under his breath, then said it aloud. "I can't trust her."

* * *

Her nerves on overload, Kate arrived at the construction site for her appointment to meet Bobby, Matt's friend. Near quitting time, the whirl of activity that usually took place had already wound down. She hoped to get a sample to prove her theory that a lower grade of Sheetrock was being used for the drywall.

Kate blew out a weary breath. She did not like coming here at all. While she waited inside the gates, she thought of Trent. She had heard he had returned from Homestead on Tuesday. Now, it was Thursday and she still hadn't seen him, and he hadn't stopped by her office either. Perhaps, he'd taken her advice and decided it would be wrong for them to see each other romantically. She tried to tell herself everything would be better this way, but if so, why did she feel this terrible and crushing sense of disappointment and loss?

Her eyes burning, she rubbed a weary hand over her forehead. She was being ridiculous. She'd been beyond stupid to allow her heart to become involved with him.

Besides, if her research turned out like she suspected and this sample checked out with the lab, maybe she could make a connection to the responsible party. Then she wouldn't be at the company much longer. This charade needed to end before she was caught, before whoever put that mask on the fence took another step.

The caged elevator lumbered down the vertical track running the height of the building. The doors opened.

Bobby stepped off and strode up to her. "Nice to see you, Kate."

"Thanks for meeting me."

"I'm sorry. I couldn't get those samples you wanted. Too many people around." He must have read the dejected look on her face. "Look, Kate, if I can get any, I'll drop them by your house and leave them on your porch. But from what I could see, nothing looks out of the ordinary."

"No? Well...thanks, Bobby. I thought for sure I was onto something. Have you noticed anything suspicious with the equipment or supplies? What if Matt had discovered something and someone didn't like it?"

Her brother's friend wrinkled his brow and he touched her arm. "I haven't seen anything, but I'll help you in any way I can." Concern flickered in his eyes. "Be careful snooping, Kate. Matt wouldn't have liked it if I let anything happen to you, too."

"That's so sweet of you to care." She gave him a faint smile to relieve his worry. "I promise I'll be careful."

"I don't like you're doing this on your own. You should go to the police again if you suspect anything."

"They didn't believe me then, and without evidence, they won't believe me now. Do you know of anyone who might want to hurt Farrington Construction?"

"No."

"Will you call me if you notice anything out of the ordinary?"

He nodded. "I've got to get to my doctor's appointment. They'll be closing up shop soon. Don't get locked inside."

She shuddered at the eerie thought of being locked in all night—alone. "I won't. Bobby," she said softly. "I'll just be here a moment longer to take pictures. Thanks for everything."

"Keep me posted."

At a sounding bell, a stream of workers clocked out and exited through the gates.

Kate strode to where the heavy machinery was kept and where the supplies were stacked on pallets. She pulled a small camera out of her purse. A few pictures and she'd be out before the guard locked the gates for the night.

About to round the corner of the stacked pallets, Kate spotted a man in a hard hat, sunglasses, and a brown overcoat. Her stomach knotted. She ducked behind a crane. *Who was he?* All the workers should be off the site.

She crouched down to look underneath the cab of the crane, but all she could see on the other side were the man's legs encased in jeans, work boots, and the edge of a long brown coat. When he neared the supplies, her heart increased in tempo.

Kate bit her lip, torn between walking around to see his face and fear that kept her remaining hidden. He could just be someone working late. Or, what if *he* were *the* perpetrator? Great—she cringed. She was alone with him.

Her heartbeat quickened. The only weapon she had was her pepper spray. She clutched the tiny bottle tucked inside her pocket— not totally reassuring, but better than nothing. If this man discovered her spying on him, and came after her, she had to hope the guard at the gate would hear her scream.

From under the crane, she watched the man's boots as he walked away. She released her pent-up breath and waited a few minutes, hoping he'd left the site. When he didn't return, hunching over, Kate backed up to find another way out. Her backside bumped into a hard, masculine body.

Strong muscular arms wrapped around her and clamped her arms to her sides.

She shrieked. "Let me go." Going a bit wild, she hit back with her elbows and stomped his foot.

"Kate, ouch. Kate, it's me," Trent said, with a groan in her ear.

Her breath rushed out of her lungs. She ceased struggling, although her wildly beating heart nearly burst in her chest.

He held her in a tight grip. "What the hell are you doing here...*again?*"

Panic swept through her at what he would think. "*Nothing*," she whispered.

He abruptly released her as if she was something too hot to handle. She thrust the camera into her pocket, then whirled to face him, forgetting she had the pepper spray in her other hand. Under any other circumstances, she would have welcomed the punch in her gut at seeing him dressed in the tight blue jeans and nicely fitting white t-shirt. However, she was enormously relieved he wasn't the man in the overcoat. At the same time, she wished for it to have been anyone other than Trent who caught her snooping around. And he already knew she was Grace, but still, he hadn't called her. Frowning, she raised her gaze to his. Perhaps he'd found out something more about her...?

"Put that thing away," he ordered, "unless you intend to spray me with it again."

"Uh, no." She slipped the spray into her pocket.

Trent narrowed his eyes. "Why are you here, Kate? And this had better be good."

"I thought you were at an important meeting with the city to recruit new contracts," she said, stalling.

"Never mind where *I* was. This time I want a *straight* answer. Why are you here and without a hard hat on? I've warned you. I know you're hard headed, but you still might need one."

Kate lifted her chin, searching for a logical explanation as to why she was in the supply area of the construction site. She couldn't think of anything.

He narrowed his eyes. "I thought after your last experience here, you wouldn't be so eager to return."

"I-I needed some info on an employee's records, which were incomplete."

"*Who?*"

She winced and said in a low voice, "Bobby Owens."

"Him again?" Trent folded his arms across his chest. "Now isn't that interesting? You're in the supply area, and I thought I saw him leaving for the day."

She swiped the back of her hand across her perspiring forehead. *What else could she say?*

He took a long hard look at her, and she didn't like the suspicion and distrust now reflected in his eyes *for her*. An ache of despair welled up in her throat. "My mother tells me Cecilia saw you walking out of the Purchasing Department, too. Why were you there, Kate? That's not your area or part of your job either."

So that was why she hadn't seen him since he returned from Homestead—he didn't trust her.

For once, she thought to be truthful. "Okay, I'll tell you," she said with a nod. "I've had some concerns about things going on in the company, and I thought I'd check things out for myself."

"Like what?"

"Perhaps someone is ordering inferior supplies—trying to save money so they can skim the profits."

"Why the hell didn't you come and tell me this?" he demanded.

She shrank back. "Because I didn't think you'd believe me. I wanted to check the records first and then check here." She took a deep breath. "You know, about the man who fell and died…maybe it wasn't just an accident."

"So you've read the newspapers?"

She stabbed the air with her chin. "Yes, I did." She hated herself for not telling him the entire truth. "And you also said the man who fell had not taken proper safety precautions. What if that weren't the case? I think there's a possibility he got too close to discovering something…*someone* who was stealing from the company by substituting inferior products." There she'd said it. Her shoulders sagged in relief. "What if his harness had been rigged so he would fall to his death, to silence him and cover up something?"

Trent hesitated and then blew out a deep sigh. "All right. I agree it's a possibility; he might not have been careless."

With a pained expression on his face, Trent glanced away, then looked back at her. "I'll clue you in on what I think is going on. Some would like nothing more than to see us fail. *Me*, more than the company. And namely—Frank Blake. He wants the company, and I think he'd do almost anything to get it."

"You think Blake would do almost anything…?"

"Yes, and then there's my cousin… Roland's been acting strangely, too. Kate, let's go somewhere private to discuss this. But there is something I have to do before I leave, and I really don't like leaving you here alone."

He strode to the gates. After signaling to the guard that he would lock up the site for the night and the man could leave, Trent returned and plunked a hard hat down on her head. "Sorry, about the hair," he said dryly.

"Funny."

"Since you're suspicious, too, I want you to see something."

Amazed that in a split second he'd decided to trust her, she nodded. However, when they reached the elevator, she paused. She wasn't so sure she could trust *him* at all. Perhaps he wanted to throw *her* from the building.

"I can't go up in that thing," she said in a quivering voice.

"I won't let anything happen to you. Trust me?" He held out this hand.

She hesitated and nodded. He'd believed her, when others probably wouldn't. She grabbed his hand and stepped with shaky legs onto the construction elevator. Being only a temporary device, the partially open cage was mounted to the outside of the building. The car traveled up a temporary track, attached with cables.

As they rode upward, she snapped her eyes shut and clenched her hands on the railing. Out of the shelter of the ground floor, the wind whipped stronger and blew against her face and jacket. She shivered, knowing how high up they must be in this ridiculous cage, and not feeling safe at all. She started shaking. Oh, how she hated heights.

"Oh, my God." Her head felt as if it were spinning, and she held her breath.

Trent put his hand on her back. "Kate, breathe," he said in a low, reassuring tone.

She nodded, keeping her sweaty palms clenched on the railing in front of her. "We're up how many floors?" she asked with a gulp.

"You don't want to know, but we're up nearly fifty. Don't look down. I found evidence of possible tampering in the penthouse area, and I want to check a few places before I call the police."

Relief swept through her, taking her breath away. She wanted to hug him. They were on the same page. Someone was doing this deliberately. Trent would help her find out who caused Matt's death.

When the elevator stopped, Trent stepped off. He held the gate open and reached out his hand, beckoning for her to follow him.

Before she could move, the car dropped an inch, then several more inches in small jerks.

The blood drained from her head. "Trent?" She caught his horrified gaze.

The elevator made a loud screeching sound. The car plummeted.

As the floor dropped beneath her feet, Kate clung to the railing and let out a blood-curdling scream.

CHAPTER THIRTEEN

After a few terrifying seconds, the elevator slammed to a halt a few floors down. Her breath solidified in her throat, Kate surveyed her surroundings. Aside from her legs and knees taking a pounding, she wasn't hurt, but exiting was impossible. The car was stuck between floors.

Dear, God. Was Trent trying to kill her?

"Don't move," he shouted from above her.

She blew out a deep breath of relief. "I'm not going anywhere," she muttered to herself and watched him climb down.

Without a safety harness, and like a superhero, Trent descended down the metal track.

Fear that he could fall caused her heart to trip. She'd never witnessed such an amazing feat. "Be careful," she yelled.

When he reached Kate, he crouched on the roof of the elevator cage and leaned over an opening in the top. "Take my hand. I'll pull you up."

She gripped the railing even tighter. "I can't move."

A few strands of the remaining cable pinged as pressure caused them to snap.

"Yes, you can, Kate. *Do it*," he said in a clear order. "Any minute, the last cable might break. And we'll both be done."

She thrust her hand upward. He grabbed her and lifted her through the opening in the roof.

He looped his arm around her shoulder. "Are you all right?"

"Yes," she said through chattering teeth. Her head whipped around as she took in the whirling blur of the city below. "I think so." She shuddered.

"Don't look down. We can get to the floor landing from here. If you sit down here, you just have to jump a few feet to the floor."

The elevator dropped an inch. Trent steadied her. A creaking sound came from the elevator. They exchanged looks of fear.

"No time." He grabbed her around the waist, and flung them through the opening to the landing. In a protective move, he took the fall with his back. His hard hat whacked the concrete and flew off his head as they slammed to the floor, with her landing on top of him.

Clinging to his chest, she lifted her head.

Inches away, the elevator let out a final screech just before plunging downward, leaving a severed cable whooshing overhead and whipping around in a dangerous loop.

Kate tried to sit up.

He groaned. "Don't move." He rolled over on top of her, shielding her with his body, his arms cradling her head.

An explosive sound echoed upwards through the shell of the building as the metal cage imploded at the bottom.

"Trent?" Her voice quivered. "Y-you can let me up now?" When he didn't respond, she rolled him off of her.

"Trent!" she cried, shaking his shoulder.

Blood dripped down his cheek. With his hard hat gone, the cable had caught his head. A cut streaked through his temple and into his hairline.

Reaching under her skirt, she removed her slip. With shaky hands, she folded and pressed the material to the wound on his head. "Speak to me, please," she cried.

His eyes fluttered open.

Relief assailed her. "Oh, My God. You're okay. I was so afraid. Why did that happen?"

"I'm not sure." With a groan, he pressed his hand to this temple and tried to sit up.

"No." She pressed her palm on his shoulder to keep him lying flat. Realizing she still had her purse on her shoulder, she retrieved her cell phone. "I'm calling an ambulance."

He grabbed her hand. "No, ambulance."

"Yes. You need medical attention."

Pain etched his brow as he struggled against her hold and sat up. "I was momentarily stunned, that's all."

"It's more than that. You're bleeding. Let me call 911."

Holding her slip to his wound, he rose to his feet. "No, Kate. No doctors. I don't like them—no offense—but not if I can help it."

"Well, you're hurt and this is ridiculous, but then we have another problem," she said in a shaky voice. "How are we getting down? Will we have to stay up here for the night?"

"There's another elevator on the other side of the building."

"Are you kidding me?" she blurted out. "I'm never going to get on one of those things again."

"We don't have a choice. The stairwell is not completed up to this floor."

"What if—?"

"I'll check the cables. I'll get us down." He pinned her with his dark eyes. "Trust me?"

She let out a deep breath and gave him a curt nod. She wanted to argue that he was supposed to have kept her safe coming up here, but then she supposed in the end he had.

"Thank you for saving my life," she said, giving him a brief smile. "I can't believe you climbed down to save me. You didn't even put on a safety harness."

"With the elevator cable frayed, Kate, there wasn't time."

"But you risked your life for *me*."

He shrugged. "I couldn't let you fall."

As they walked through the corridor, he leaned on her. She could feel him trembling. "Are you sure you're okay?" she asked.

"Yeah. You're a slight thing, Kate. Am I hurting you?"

She shook her head and bore his weight. "I like to think I'm stronger than I look."

* * *

Kate drove into a hospital parking space and shut off the engine, not caring that Trent wouldn't like it one bit. He was seeing a doctor—if she had to pepper spray him to get him into the emergency room. "Do you want me to go into the ER with you?" she asked sweetly.

He leaned back in the seat. "Why the hell are we here, Kate? It's just a minor cut, and I told you on the way over, you're wasting your time. I'm not going."

Kate exhaled a deep breath. "You banged your head, too. I'm not driving you anywhere until you go inside and have a doctor look at you."

"Stubborn woman."

"*Stubborn man.* I'll help you inside." In case he anticipated driving off with her car, she retrieved the keys from the ignition and walked around to the passenger side. When she opened the door, he grunted at her like a bear in pain—typical wounded man when injured.

"Come on," she said, grasping his arm. "Let's get this over with."

He pushed up and out of the car with a groan. "I admit I'm lightheaded. Maybe you're right."

Panic caused her to catch her breath in her throat. What if he was worse than she thought? "Should I get the paramedics?" she asked.

"No." He took a deep breath. "I can make it." She offered her support by putting her arms around his waist.

They checked in at the desk, then while they waited in the emergency room to be seen by the doctor, Trent called the police and reported the incident.

Afterwards, he punched in the number to the manager of the building site. "Sam, there's been an accident at the Karger site." Trent told him what had happened. "Tomorrow, you're to report this to OSHA and shut down the site. We'll stay closed until we can go over every piece of equipment to make sure it's safe."

* * *

Two hours later, and after a round of x-rays, Trent sported ten stitches in his hairline and a neat bandage. He was free to leave the hospital.

Kate winced when she saw Trent in his bloodstained t-shirt. They came so close to being killed. She wanted to put her arms around him, and press her face into his chest, but that wouldn't be appropriate. He was her boss, no matter how much he'd tried to sway her to become otherwise.

Brushing away the tears from her cheeks, she sent a prayer of thanks to God that Trent was alive. He could be gruff at times, and polished at others, but she thought inside he was a good person, if he'd let someone get close to him. She wanted to help him. Something about this man bore into her soul, even though she shouldn't let him. There were too many of her lies between them now, and he had his own trust issues.

"Don't worry, honey. He'll be all right." The nurse handed Kate a bottle of pills. She must have assumed they were something more than employer and employee. "Just make sure you check on him a few times during the night."

Those instructions left Kate with a dilemma that she pondered as she drove out of the hospital parking lot. "Where should I take you?" she asked, giving him a sideways glance. Concern washed over her that he looked a little worse for wear with his head leaning back against the passenger seat.

"To my condo."

"Will someone be there to help you?" she asked, trying to keep the jealousy out of her voice. Would he call a girlfriend?

"No, I'll be fine alone."

"You heard what the nurse said—you can't be alone. Should I call your mother?"

"No! Don't make a big deal out of this, Kate."

"Then I'm taking you to your grandfather's house."

"Absolutely not."

"Well, I find it strange that you won't even go to your family in a situation like this. You're lucky to have a family, you know?"

"I don't want anyone fussing over me."

"You mean like *your mother?*"

He snorted and gave her as much of a chuckle as a bear could in pain. "Kate, Eden's never been the type to hover over me when I'm sick."

"Any mother would be worried. You need to call her."

After setting the GPS system, he pressed the button on the door, lowering the passenger seat a little more to reclining. "You don't know my mother, plus it's just a scratch. Take me to my condo."

"As if ten stitches and a slight concussion are nothing serious? Frankly, I don't know what the problem is with you and your mother," Kate muttered under her breath. Then she blew out a frustrated breath. "You leave me with no alternative. You can't go home alone." She turned off the GPS.

"Damn it, Kate. I'd like to know what you propose to do with me since you've just passed my street. If you're taking me to my grandfather's, I assure you I will walk home. His health is deteriorating. I don't want him worried about me or about what happened at the site tonight."

"That's not where I'm taking you," she whispered.

A few minutes later, she pulled into her driveway and shut off the car. She had to be crazy to bring him to her house where he could find out so much about her. "You can stay with *me*."

He flicked her an ironic, but steamy gaze, so she quickly added, "In my *guest* room."

"And here I thought you were inviting me for more," he said dryly.

She gave him a retiring glance. "I don't think *you* are up for *anything more*."

"*Humph*. Don't count me out."

"I'm only taking pity on you and I'm helping you like you did for me the day I fainted. The only thing that would complete this is if you were wearing a hospital gown."

"Should I be hopeful you want to see my buff backside?"

She chuckled softly. "No comment."

He stepped out of the car. "What are you laughing about?"

"That image. That would take you down a notch."

"Ah, because of my arrogance, you think?" When he took a step, he winced, as if he felt more pain than he admitted.

Guilt swept through her. "Sorry. It wasn't nice for me to laugh when you're hurting."

After they entered the front door, she turned on the lamp. The warm glow filled the living area of her homey house. She'd have to hide Matt's pictures.

Trent appeared weak from the exertion.

Kate frowned. "Let's get you in bed... I mean to your room, so you can lie down in the *guest* bed." At the heat rising on her cheeks, she whirled to lead him down the hall. "Are you still in a lot of pain?"

He sat on the bed. In the light, his normally tanned face was pale. "Some."

She concluded he was hurting badly and had to curb her impulse to put her arms around him.

Oh, Dear God, help me. Getting involved with him would only bring her heartbreak.

Her eyes burned as she turned to the dresser. Opening a drawer, she extracted a large t-shirt that read: MUSCLEMEN ROCK.

He flicked his gaze to hers. "Ex-boyfriend's?" She noted a hint of jealousy in his eyes.

She shook her head and did her best to keep the sadness out of her voice. "No. I have a few things of my brother's here from when he used to stay overnight. There should be a pair of shorts in the top drawer. If you need anything else, just yell. The guest bathroom is across the hall. I'll put a new toothbrush on the sink and bring you a glass of water."

* * *

After sleeping for a couple of hours, Kate awoke and decided to check on her patient. She shuffled down the hallway to the guest bedroom and flipped on the light. Trent had dressed in sweat shorts and a t-shirt. He was sprawled on his back on the queen-sized bed. With his tousled, dark hair and, and one muscular leg that had worked its way out from under the sheet, he looked incredibly sexy.

He opened his eyes.

"I was only checking on you, Mr. Farrington."

"Are you back to calling me that? Call me *Trent*. After all, I am a *guest* in your house."

"All right, *Trent*. I'm sorry. I sort of kidnapped you, and you're in bad mood. Let me check your bandage."

He grimaced. "You're the doctor."

Guilt reverberated through her. How would he react if he found out she wasn't a psychologist at all? Biting her lip, she shoved the thought away for now. She lifted the bandage. "No bleeding. Go back to sleep. Okay?"

"But now I'm awake and thirsty. I feel too weak to even lift the glass of water."

Kate caught the slight curl of his lip. She narrowed her eyes. "Going to milk this for all it's worth?"

His lip slightly curved. "Why not, when I have my chance?"

Knowing she played with fire, she put her arm around his neck to lift his head. She brought the glass to his lips. As he sipped, she was conscious of how close his face was to her breasts, and by the gleam in his eyes, so was he. Slowly and seductively, he let his gaze slide over her. Her nipples tightened beneath the thin nightgown and robe, while desire sent her heart hammering.

Biting her lip, she lowered his head to the pillow. "I think you're feeling much better." She set the glass on the table and crossed to the door.

"I like your hair down, Kate. It's beautiful."

Blood rushing to her cheeks, she put her hand to her hair. She had forgotten to twist it up before she came to check on him. He already knew about her charade at the masquerade, but she'd hoped he wouldn't read more into why she had not told him up front about herself and ask questions.

Frowning, she headed to the door.

As if he read her mind, he murmured over his shoulder. "What I'm waiting for is for you to tell me why, Kate? Why did you hide your identity at the party?"

Her breath catching in her throat, she flipped off the light. *What could she say?*

After returning to her bedroom, she tossed and turned—unable to sleep. She'd barely dozed off and then she had a horrible nightmare that Trent had fallen from the Karger building.

Kate awoke with a jolt and rushed to his room. She turned on the lamp by the bed.

His eyes flickered open. He focused on her face. "Why did you let me think you were someone else the night of the party?

Heat flooded her cheeks. He wasn't going to let it go, so she gave him a half-truth. "You didn't seem to like Dr. Meyers, so I decided to play the part of my costume."

He grimaced. "I'll buy that, but only for the moment because my head hurts like I've been beaten with a sledge hammer."

Anxiety rushed through her and she forgot her own worries. "Is it worse? Should I call the doctor?"

Throwing his arm over his forehead, he closed his eyes. "I'll be all right…if I don't move."

She clenched her hands together. What if he was worse than they thought? "What if the doctor missed something? Should I call your family?"

"No. Absolutely not."

"Until I'm sure you're improving, I'm not leaving you alone. I'll be right back."

She pushed a small upholstered chair into the room, along with her alarm clock, a pillow and a throw. Wearily, she sank into the chair, resting her head on the pillow. She pulled the blanket over her legs.

"Go to your bed," he murmured. "I'm fine. You need your sleep."

"I've set the alarm for your next meds. I'm not leaving you alone."

"Then lie down here with me. There's plenty of room. I'm not exactly in any condition to assault you."

"But I can't lie down beside you," she said in a rush of words.

She wiggled around trying to get comfortable in the chair. He watched her, amused. The bed did look more comfortable…

"Oh, sure you can. But I can't argue anymore about it because my head is pounding like someone is jack hammering inside my skull." He patted the bed beside him and closed his eyes as if overcome with pain.

Kate jumped from the chair and hovered over him. "Is there anything I can do for you? I knew it; you should have stayed at the hospital."

"No, Kate. Turn off the light and lie down."

"I'll sleep in this chair, but if you're not better in a few hours, back to the hospital you go."

She flicked off the light and sat down again. Curling her legs beneath her, she covered herself with the blanket and fell asleep to the steady rhythm of his breathing.

Hours later, she opened her eyes. Light filtered through the blinds. Birds chirped outside—and a warm arm was draped around her and brushing the undersides of her breasts. Trent's arm! Alarm sailed through her. Oh, my God! How did she get on the bed?

Trent sighed and hauled her up snuggly against himself so her bottom rested against his thighs. Heat coursed through her. Wide-awake now, she looked over her shoulder. He opened his eyes.

Gasping, she threw off the comforter. She extricated herself from his arms and nearly jumped from the bed. "I don't know what happened. I must have walked in my sleep."

"No. I shut off your alarm. I picked you up, and put you here. You were so exhausted, you didn't even wake up." He gave her a lazy grin. "You must have been cold, too." He swiped a hand through his dark hair. She swallowed the lump in her throat. With the bandage at his temple and the dark morning shadow dusting his face, he looked sinfully handsome and more like a pirate than a construction executive.

Her gaze flew to the huge erection extending his shorts. She gulped.

"You've got to be starving since we didn't eat last night," she said in a breathy voice. "I'm going to shower, then I'll make breakfast."

As she fled the room, she heard him say, "Don't run from me, Kate."

CHAPTER FOURTEEN

Glad his headache had faded, Trent dragged himself out of bed. He entered the shower and let the warm water massage the aches from last night's horrific incident from his shoulders. Luckily, he and Kate weren't dead, but the company was in big trouble.

And then there was Kate. He was going to trust her. The memory of having her warm and next to him in bed flooded his mind, making him grow hard again. He groaned and quickly switched the faucet to cold.

After stepping out of the shower, he was in control of himself again. He dried off and searched for his clothing. She must have removed his things. After donning the large white robe hanging on the bathroom door, he entered Kate's cozy kitchen.

With her back to him, she was using a spatula to scramble eggs in a frying pan. Bacon sizzled in another. The smell of food wasn't what heightened his hunger. It was Kate. He craved a taste of her. If he was truthful, he would admit he'd wanted her from the first moment she'd landed in his arms in the lobby.

He obviously had a problem. Tugging the robe tighter, he was afraid he couldn't hide the evidence of his attraction to her.

She whirled from the stove and gave him a dazzling smile. "Hi."

He caught his breath. With her damp, blond hair hanging in ripples down her back, and those puffy high-heeled slippers, she looked like an angel or a fairy princess come to life. He never thought a woman holding a spatula and wearing a simple white robe could be so damned sexy. It was a good thing she wore longer skirts at work because he'd never get any work done. He wanted those slender but shapely legs wrapped around him.

He nearly groaned. Soon, if he didn't think about something else, he'd need another cold shower.

She poured two glasses of orange juice and sat them on the bar. "I thought you could use a hearty breakfast after last night."

With a sigh, Trent sat on the stool. "I'm hungry all right, but to be honest, at the moment, I'm not thinking of food." Not wanting to come on too strong, he knew he should temper his desire because he wanted to strip her of the robe and bare her before him—a primitive rather than a controlled response. He wanted to swoop her up in his arms and take her on the counter, or carry her into the bedroom, or lay her down on the first place he could find. He felt like a barbarian.

She must have seen the intensity in his expression because her smile faded. "If anyone would've told me a week ago that you'd be in my kitchen—after staying overnight—I would have called them crazy."

"I didn't expect this either."

"I'd better pay attention or I'll burn our breakfast." She returned her attention to the eggs. "Coffee?" she asked over her dainty shoulder.

"Sure." What he really wanted was to hold her and nuzzle his face in her fair hair and the crook of her neck. Instead, he poured himself a cup of black coffee and sipped.

Glancing at the clock, he frowned. "It's ten a.m.?"

She scooped the scrambled eggs onto two plates. "Yeah, since you turned off the alarm, we slept in. I'm going to be late for work today."

"If you call that sleeping in, I'd like to show you the real meaning of the words." As he intended when he said it, she blushed. He grinned, pleased that he could bring a rosy glow to her cheeks.

She crinkled her nose. "For some reason, I'm always saying the wrong thing to you."

"And I wonder why *I* enjoy that so much. Maybe you're saying the right things. You know, doc—like a *Freudian slip*."

She shook her head slowly. "No. Can't be."

"Kate, stop fighting what is happening between us. Come here." Despite the wariness on her face, she turned off the stove and did as he requested.

Encircling her in his arms, he drew her close.

Her long, blond hair brushed his chest. He didn't care if she knew how attracted he was to her.

She gazed at him with such unease in her gray eyes, it worried him.

He frowned and stroked his finger along her cheek. "What's wrong? I'm not going to hurt you."

"Are you sure about that?"

He tipped her chin. "Yes. I would never hurt you." He lowered his mouth and kissed the frown on her brow, then met her lips. She tasted of citrus. Heat spiraled through him. With his ramrod hard erection, it was sweet torment. He wanted to gather her in his arms and take her here, now, and later.

He inhaled deeply and gathered her close, resting his forehead on her head. "Do you know what you do to me?"

"Yeah," she said in a shaky voice, lifting her hand to cup his cheek. "Because you do the same to me."

She raised her lips. Unable to resist, he took the invitation and kissed her slowly and deeply. When he moved his hands slowly down her arm and finally cupped her firm breasts, she sighed. Through the thin fabric of her robe, he kneaded, then slipped his fingers inside the opening. Her bare nipple grew hard against his palm.

She arched her back. "Oh, my."

Heat flooded through him. He dropped his hands to her hips and pulled her against his erection.

"Kate, you're so sweet. To be honest, I've never wanted any woman in my life as I want you right now. I'm intrigued and I want you."

"We can't do this. You're my boss," she said, pushing her hands with gentle pressure against his chest.

"So, I'll fire you," he teased. At the shock on her face, he jerked his head back. "Kate, I'm joking. I don't care. There is something special between us. We can continue to work together, but do you really think I could walk out that door now?"

She shook her head and raised her lips to him. She kissed him first.

Then she pushed her hands against his chest, her cheeks turning red. "We shouldn't."

"We should. It's right."

"No."

"*Yes.*"

He silenced her with his lips and lost himself for a while in their kiss. Finally, he pulled away. "I don't know how much work we're ever going to get done at the company with this between us, but we can make it work. That is unless you want me to go and leave you alone? Am I being too pushy, Kate? I want us to be together."

"It's crazy—I must be crazy. But I don't want you to leave either." She lifted her arms around his neck and raised her lips to his.

His cell phone lay on the kitchen counter and buzzed. "Ignore it." He ground his mouth down on hers and lost himself in their kiss.

Trent bunched the thin robe upwards. He slid his thumbs under the sides of her panties, then cupped her bare buttocks. She shivered and moaned against his mouth.

He pulled his lips from hers and groaned. "Oh, Kate." He swooped her up in his arms with one destination in mind—the bedroom.

Before he could take a step, the house phone rang. They let it. The answering machine picked up the call. "Dr. Meyers," his mother rattled on in a shrill voice.

Breathing hard, Trent set Kate's feet on the ground and held her in his arms. Her face against his chest, he listened.

"Do you know where Trent is?" his mother asked. "I was told he was with you yesterday, and he was hurt. I don't want to notify the police, so call me immediately." *Click.*

His cell phone buzzed again. He reached for it on the counter. "Damn. I'd better take it." He picked up the cell phone. "Hello."

"The police are at the Karger site. They said you were in an accident last night. Why didn't you call us?" His mother was on a rant, her voice like the screeching of a bent saw blade whirling out of whack.

Trent brushed off his mother's concern for him. "I should have called the house... I'm all right." He grimaced and put the phone on speaker for Kate to hear, then he added, "Matthew Jackson's death might not have been an accident." When Kate flinched, he frowned at her with concern. "And now, Eden—with the elevator crashing yesterday—I suspect someone might be tampering with the building site. I'll be there to meet the police and OSHA."

"I've been to the Karger Building and your car is there. I'm sitting outside Dr. Meyers' house. Marc can drive us to the site."

He exchanged a glance with Kate. "I'll be out in a minute." He hung up the call. "Sorry, Kate. If anything, she's demanding. I have to go meet the police."

"Of course. And your mother has to be worried about your condition."

"No, Kate. If anything, she's worried about who would run the business if something happened to me."

"How did she know you were here?"

"Sam, who manages the Karger construction site, must have told her."

Trent followed Kate to the nearby utility room. She removed his clothing from the dryer.

"Later, we'll talk about *us*, all right?" he asked. Not waiting for her answer, he pulled her into his arms and kissed her fully on the lips. He cupped his palm on her breast. She sighed and buried her face in his throat. He groaned and stepped back and watched a blush creep over her face. "I'd better go. Today, while I'm gone, think about how much we want each other."

"I will."

The dreamy look in her eyes reassured him. "Damn it, if this weren't so important, I would stay and tell Eden she can wait in the driveway until hell freezes over."

He headed to the bathroom and dressed.

When he returned, Kate had slipped on a dress and sandals and held her purse. "I'll go with you."

"With Eden? I don't think so. I wouldn't put you through that."

"Okay, but wait one moment." Kate went into the kitchen and returned with a brown paper bag. "I packed your breakfast so you can take it with you."

"Nice of you." Smiling at her, he pulled her into his arms. He gave her another hot kiss on the mouth and desire ran rampant through him. Finally, groaning, he lifted his lips from hers and she gasped. Her lips looked fresh and dewy, and she appeared well kissed.

He groaned. "Don't look like that or I'll never leave here."

She flicked him a brief smile. "You'd better go then."

"Later, I'll tell you what I hear."

* * *

Two hours later, Kate arrived at the Karger site. She had to find out if this was sabotage, even though Trent might be angry with her for following him there. The information could shed light on who caused her brother's death. Two squad cars, several other vehicles, and Trent's Porsche were parked in front of the half-completed building. A limo zoomed away from the site. Kate assumed it was his mother's car.

After donning a hard hat, Kate strode to where Trent stood by the mangled construction elevator, along with the police, an OSHA representative, and several Farrington Construction employees. Another man, looking like a detective, jotted notes on a pad of paper.

Trent didn't appear pleased to see her and gave Kate an exasperated glance when she stepped up beside him. "Couldn't wait for me to tell you, huh?" Then he pivoted back to OSHA rep. "Was the cable partially cut?"

"No," the rep answered. "This appears to be an accident."

"Accident!" Trent roared. "I think someone is tampering with my building."

The rep shrugged. "All we've found is a tipped container. It leaked some type of acid, weakening the wires, until the cable snapped. We'll run more tests."

Trent's face twisted with anger. Kate caught his arm.

The man who'd been jotting down notes in a pad, stepped closer. "I'm Detective Stone, ma'am." He handed Trent a business card and a piece of paper. "Your report number and my contact information. Do you know of anyone who would tamper with your job site, Mr. Farrington?"

"I have one sure enemy—Frank Blake."

Kate bit her lip. She hadn't said anything about her suspicions about the drywall, or about the man in the overcoat on the jobsite because she might be wrong. How could she say something now? She had not one ounce of proof and Trent might wonder why she took such extraordinary steps to check out one of their products. For all she knew, the guy on the grounds could have been someone who was allowed to be there.

The detective closed his notepad. "I'll send a report to you and to your grandfather."

"No. Just to me," Trent said. "I'd like to keep that information away from grandfather as long as I can. He has a bad heart."

She hadn't realized the elderly man's health was so precarious. He had seemed perfectly healthy the last time she'd seen him.

After the OSHA Representative left, the detective said, "I advise you to improve your security and hire a night watchman. We'll be in touch."

While the police cars drove off, Trent glanced at Kate. She raised her chin, waiting for his reprimand.

He narrowed his eyes. "Why did you come here? We don't know what we're dealing with. We were almost killed here yesterday."

"Well, I had to be here. An employee of the company was injured."

He stepped close, until they were inches apart. "*Me?* You're referring to *me* as an employee?" he asked incredulously.

She smoothed the arm of her jacket. "*Yes*, so naturally I was concerned about what had happened on the site. It's my job."

"All right, Kate, but as your *employer*, I'm ordering you not to come here without me from now on." He clasped her shoulders and squeezed. "Please, Kate, listen to me, as someone who cares. *It's dangerous*. I don't want you to be hurt. It was too close last night. We barely escaped that elevator with our lives. Do understand?"

She nodded. "Yes, I understand what you're saying." While she was done with not being truthful to him, she skirted saying what he wanted to hear.

His face relaxed. He must have taken what she said for a yes, but she couldn't promise him that as she might have to come back here to gather more evidence. "Unfortunately, I'm going to be tied up all day with this. We both probably need some rest tonight, so don't worry about going to the office today. But tomorrow's Saturday, why don't I pick you up at noon? Dress casual, we'll go somewhere for lunch."

Although he released her arms, his gaze scorched her to her toes.

* * *

In a tree-shaded park overlooking the river, a man settled on a bench to watch the boats motor by. While the morning sun glinted on the water, a satisfaction simmered inside him. With the successful sabotage that caused the elevator to crash, he was one step closer to the end of his mission.

Two average-looking bimbos jogged by and gave him the once-over. After they ran on, he muttered under his breath, "Not tempting enough for me to give you what you deserve." Besides, he didn't like mixing business with pleasure. He had to control that impulse and stay focused on his work at hand.

For now, pleasure would have to wait. After the job was finished, he'd have the money and could get away with whatever he wanted. The rich always walked.

He smiled to himself, thinking that he was nearing his final reward. The police wouldn't be able to pin the incident on him, wouldn't even be able to prove the damage to the cable was intentional. Being the consummate professional in his line of work, he had placed containers of acid, normally used to etch the concrete, so they appeared to have tipped accidentally, as if they'd tumbled over in a rainstorm or as if a worker had been careless.

The acid had leaked onto the cable, making Trent Farrington look like he ran a sloppy operation, which was exactly what the boss wanted. Who knew that Trent Farrington himself would nearly be killed by it?

Boats cruised along the winding river. One day soon, his military training and stealth would finally pay off and make him rich. That was his little secret from the boss. Once the job was done, he could extort money from a turnip. Even if his boss had to steal to pay up, he'd get the biggest, fattest paycheck imaginable and maybe more.

He grimaced. Only one problem had arisen—little Kate Meyers. She wasn't even a real doctor. Lucky for him, he always liked to show up to pay his final respects to his victims. He'd seen her at Matt Jackson's funeral and had checked her out.

Nosey little bitch, but tempting, too. After she'd been snooping in the company records, he'd had just enough time to plan the little pleasant surprise that he'd left hanging on the fence for her at the construction site. He was surprised she hadn't run from the company with her tail tucked between her legs.

Brave or stupid—if she didn't take the hint soon and leave the company—he'd take her out. With pleasure. He might do it sooner rather than later because he didn't need her as a distraction and he didn't like to lose control while on the job. But one woman? Was it so risky? And she was a real beauty and would be a special treat. It would be slow and sweet—at least for him.

He chuckled. His prey never enjoyed those *tender* moments, but that only made his release all the more exciting. Since he had a job to do, he really should fight the urge or deal with it right away so he could relax.

CHAPTER FIFTEEN

Saturday had arrived. While she got ready for her lunch date with Trent, Kate gazed into the bathroom mirror and put in clear contacts. Then she applied makeup with a shaky hand, wanting to look nice for him. Her stomach fluttered as she slipped on dangling earrings and brushed her long hair, leaving it hanging down her back.

Decorated with beads, the lower neckline of her white blouse and the above-the-knee jean skirt, made her feel attractive. A pair of high-heeled sandals complemented her outfit and made her slender figure appear taller.

When the doorbell rang, excitement surged through Kate. She hurried and opened the front door.

At the warmth in Trent's dark eyes, a tingle ran through her. He was as handsome as usual in his casual shirt and slacks. He grinned and his gaze roved over her. "You look amazing."

"So do you. Your bandage is gone."

He flicked his fingers to his head. "But not the stitches."

Overwhelmed at the reminder of how close they'd come to death, she stepped into his open arms. "We could've been killed."

He hugged her tightly. "Coming close to death makes you realize how precious life is and how much one should value every moment of every day."

She nodded and buried her face in his muscled chest and breathed in his tantalizing cologne.

Were things moving at a faster pace with them because of their brush with death? Somewhere along the way, she'd grown to care for him, beyond a physical attraction, and didn't want to lose him now. Her eyes clouded and she choked back a sob.

He cupped her chin, forcing her to look at him. "Why the tears?"

Kate pulled her face away and blinked her eyes. "I can't believe what's happened these past two days and that someone might be sabotaging the company!" she blurted out nervously. "It's scaring me."

He gave her a quick kiss on the forehead. "Don't let it."

"I'll try not to."

"You want to go to lunch? If you stay in my arms any longer, I'm not sure I'll want to leave, and I'm starving. I didn't have dinner last night, or breakfast."

Outside, he opened the passenger door for her and she slid inside his black Porsche. They drove to a downtown bistro on the waterfront where he tossed the keys to the valet. "Here, Mike."

"I'll take good care of it, Mr. Farrington," the young man said.

Obviously, Trent frequented this restaurant. She wondered who he had dined with there in the past year.

Outside on the large patio, they were seated at a table overlooking the river and the marina. The day was pleasantly warm and a soft breeze stirred Kate's hair around her cheeks.

Though the restaurant was crowded, a waiter hurried over and took their orders.

Trent reached across the table and clasped her hand. As she sat staring at him, strong feelings of contentment washed over her. Even though she'd tried not to, she suspected she'd fallen in love with him. How had that happened?

His warm, dark eyes seemed to reflect her own feelings. He stroked his thumb on her palm, sending tingles up her arms. She shivered.

His face turned serious. "I want you to be aware that I think something is going on with Roland and somehow he's tied into all this. I'll have to watch him."

"I'll help."

"No. I'm only warning you about him so you'll be careful…to keep you safe. I don't trust him. He's not the person he used to be…not like when we were kids. But somehow he's involved."

"What makes you think so?"

"He was asking for money for advertising. I felt like the entire company he was trying to hire was a sham." Trent caught her gaze. "And I'm asking you, Kate—for my sake, if not for yours—please, no amateur sleuthing." He rubbed her hand between his warm palms. "Damn it. I wish I knew what we're up against. We almost died when the elevator fell."

At the memory, a shudder shook her shoulders. "We were up so high…"

Trent caught her with his gaze. "Tell me. Did something bad happen to you to trigger this fear of heights?"

Now was her chance to tell him the entire, sordid truth about her background. She searched for words, but she'd spent a lifetime burying her memories. To now dredge up the past for Trent to hear and to judge…for her to *relive*? Nausea overwhelmed her. She wanted to tell him but the words died in her throat.

His face darkened with concern. He squeezed her hand over the table. "Damn it, Kate, what happened to you?"

"Nothing—it's nothing." She feigned a laugh, even though her hands were clammy. Used to hiding her feelings, she quickly composed her face. "You know, a lot of people are afraid of heights. I just am."

He pinned her with a pointed stare. "But not like you. One day, even if it's no big deal, you'll tell me?"

She blew out a breath. "Okay."

The waiter delivered their food. While he savored his meal, she nibbled on her food—chicken—just like herself. *At least tell him about your brother, and why you lied to get into the company. If he thinks less of you and hates you, it's better to know now before you become more involved.*

"You're quiet. What are your thoughts?" he asked after they'd eaten the food.

She swallowed the lump in her throat. "I have something to tell you. Something that might make you not want to see me again."

He placed his hand over hers and then trailed his fingers along her arm, making her feel warm all over. "Tell me what I should know about *you* that could possibly change *my* mind."

"It's hard enough, but I can't think when you're touching me."

He lifted her hand to his lips. "Good." He kissed the inside of her wrist, then her fingers. "Because nothing would stop me from wanting to see you. *Nothing.* Whatever has happened, we all have a past. I don't care…"

Not like mine. "Trent, I—"

"Damn it to hell," he said as his gaze shot past her shoulder. "Eden and Cecilia are inside by the windows. My mother's probably been watching us the entire time."

Kate stole a quick glance. The two women stared back with pursed lips. The look his mother gave Kate chilled her to her toes.

Turning to Trent, Kate murmured sadly, "I don't think your mother likes me."

"I don't care what she thinks, but I'm sorry if she's bothering you." He squeezed Kate's fingers. "Don't let her spoil our day? Let's get out of here." He gestured to the waiter. "Check, please."

After paying, Trent led Kate out of the restaurant. While they stood on the stone walkway waiting for the car, the sound of high heels clicked on the pavement behind them.

"*Trenton Farrington*," Eden said to their backs in an irritated voice. "I know you saw us. Why didn't you come over and say something to Cecilia and me?"

When they turned, Cecilia mumbled as if in shock, "The girl from the benefit ball…"

"Or were you *too distracted*?" his mother asked dryly.

"Why, yes, Mother, *we* were distracted. Since it's a holiday weekend, I'll see you at the office on Tuesday."

Eden deposited her hands on her hips. "Aren't you going to at least introduce us to your friend?"

"But you've both already met *Dr. Meyers*," he answered flatly as the valet drove his Porsche up to the curb. "Good afternoon, *Mother*. Cecilia."

Cecilia's mouth gaped like a fish out of water, and Kate stifled a grin. She wouldn't have traded that look for anything. She guessed she had a little feminine competitor in herself after all. A smile edged her lips as she slid into the car.

Mrs. Farrington gave her a frosty glare through the window and Kate's heart skipped a beat. She wanted his mother to like her. Would Mrs. Farrington eventually forgive her for getting in the way of her plans?

Trent drove the car out of the parking lot. "It's just a short drive to Key West. Since it's a long weekend, you want to get out of town with me?"

Smiling, Kate shoved away her worries about his mother. "Yeah, sure. I'd love to go."

A trip with him was a big step, but for once she felt ready to grasp something good in her life.

* * *

After stopping at their respective homes to pack for the trip, Kate settled into the seat of Trent's car again to enjoy the four-hour trip to Key West. Sometime during this weekend, she'd tell him everything about herself.

When they stopped at a light, he placed his large palm over her slender hand. "Do you believe in fate, Kate?" He chuckled. "Hey, that rhymes."

She smiled at him. "You were saying?"

"Fate? Kate, do you believe in it?"

"Yeah. I suppose I do." But it wasn't always kind. If she'd been fated to meet Trent because her brother died, she would rather have met him some other way.

It was a glorious day for a drive. A string of bridges crossed aqua-blue water and linked tropical islands to the final large island of Key West.

They discussed many subjects, except what she *should* tell him. There didn't seem to be an opportunity. She was a little annoyed at herself, but she just couldn't bring herself to ruin the moment.

He told her about his life, where he'd gone to college— Princeton. He liked motorcycles and mountain climbing. "It's in my blood. Heights don't bother me."

"No wonder you can build those incredibly tall buildings."

After they arrived on the island, and drove through the small town, Trent parked the car at the entrance to an old Victorian-style hotel.

A white sedan with tented windows pulled in behind them as Kate and Trent got out of his car. The climbed the steps to check into the hotel.

He gave her a pointed look. "One room, Kate?"

"Yes," she whispered in an excited breath. She was going to take a leap of faith that everything would turn out all right with them. However, once their luggage was wheeled away, nervousness flitted through her.

At the hotel desk, the clerk informed them that the room wouldn't be ready for another hour.

Trent glanced at her with chagrin. "Could there be any worse timing?" he asked wryly.

She grinned. "Not really. So we have some time to kill? I've lived in South Florida all my life, but I've never been to Key West. And here we are."

"Never?"

"No. And it's beautiful here." Her self-centered stepfather never spent money to take his family on vacations, but instead he went with his friends to his usual haunts, like Las Vegas. Even though it was illegal and dangerous to leave elementary-aged children alone, he'd stock up the refrigerator and leave Kate and Matt to fend for themselves at home for up to two weeks at a time. She had been glad for the reprieve from her stepfather—and she and Matt became self-sufficient.

Trent grasped her fingers in his warm hand and her thoughts of her selfish stepfather faded away. "Why don't we walk down Duval Street and get something to eat? I'll show you around."

In the warm, breezy air, Kate and Trent ambled down the streets of Old Town already filled with other contented pedestrians. They passed by old houses and shops.

Several squawking roosters ran in front of her and mingled with the crowd. Kate turned to Trent and laughed. "Chickens? In town?"

He smiled. "You can see anything and everything down here."

Tourists cruised by on mini-bikes and bicycles, occasionally beeping their horns. Kate liked the relaxed atmosphere and loved being on this mini-vacation with him.

Cars whizzed by. The white sedan with the tinted windows drove past. Kate frowned. That was odd. It was the same car that had parked behind them at the hotel and had been there when they'd walked out after checking in, too. Had they been followed? Chalking it up to nerves, she decided to keep a lookout in case she saw the car again.

"Ernest Hemmingway had a home nearby," Trent said as they made their way down the street.

They stopped at a restaurant and saloon. The band's music, and the delicious smell of food, wafted through the air.

After they were settled at a table on the patio, Trent held her hand and her gaze. The heat was rising between them. "Taste this, Kate." He fed her a shrimp, popping it into her mouth.

They savored grouper sandwiches, conch salad, and frozen margaritas, and then strolled out of the restaurant.

Arm in arm, they walked down the sidewalk. "It's beginning to look like rain. Our room should be ready. Should we go back to the hotel?" Trent asked with a warm gleam in his eyes.

"Sure." The margaritas had made her lightheaded and more relaxed. Kate forgot about the car. She smiled, blissfully happy, although she was nervous about what would happen once they entered *their* suite. However, she wanted to make love with him, wanted to take this irreversible step.

Rain burst through clouds in a downpour that battered the rooftops and cooled her skin. Kate laughed as Trent pulled her along to the nearest overhang of a small shop. They were soaked.

Trent rubbed his hands on the thin white gauzy material that covered her arms. "Damn, we didn't make the hotel, and all I want to do is get you there."

Two men stepped under the overhang with them to get out of the pouring rain. One man ogled Kate's chest. She lowered her gaze and realized the wet, gauzy white shirt was nearly transparent. She clamped her arms to cover herself.

Trent pulled her against him. "You do have a problem with the shirt, sweetheart," he whispered against the top of her head.

"Problem?" she said lightly. "Not if I'm in your arms."

He leaned against a wall, taking her with him. "Glad to take care of it."

Kate wrapped her arms around his back and lingered in his arms. She heard the footsteps of the men as they walked on.

Once they were alone under the overhang, she glanced around his shoulder. "The street is nearly deserted."

"Ah, so it is." Trent lifted her chin, dipped his head and kissed her. He tasted like the margaritas they had with dinner.

Heat simmered within her. She molded herself to his muscular body and his hand slipped between them to fondle her breasts. Her nipples tightened, and she thought she would die from his touch through her wet shirt. He made her dizzy with his kisses. She moaned against his lips, while the rain kept a steady beat on the tin roof and the paved street.

In the storm, a couple of teenagers streaked by on skateboards. One shouted, "Get a Room!"

Trent dragged his mouth across Kate's cheek to her ear and chuckled. "We have one," he murmured, squeezing her waist. "Maybe we should go there, Kate."

She giggled.

He smiled, then plundered her lips once more with a long, heart-stopping kiss. Her toes curled.

The rain slackened to a sprinkle.

"Let's go, Kate. Might as well, we're already wet."

The streets were nearly abandoned when they stopped once more in a dark, secluded doorway that jutted in to a closed shop.

He pulled her close and ground his mouth down on hers. Cupping his hands to the sides of her face, he kissed her, their tongues entwining, his taste filling her senses. Warmth rushed to her core. She moaned her desire. She needed him against her, within her. The kiss turned fiery as urgency exploded between them.

Giving his own savage moan, he lowered his warm mouth to her breast and took her nipple through the thin wet fabric of her blouse and bra. Her knees nearly buckled. He returned his lips to hers and pushed up her skirt, putting his knee between her legs. His hand dipped beneath the fabric of her underwear.

His fingers touched her intimately. "Trent," she said through a gasp.

"Kate," he said, blowing out a breath, "you're in my blood." He smoothed her skirt down, then caught her again up in his arms and kissed her. "Let's get back to our hotel or we'll never make it."

As they neared the hotel, the rain stopped completely and stars popped out in the sky.

They shared a smile and charged up the stairs. Once they were in the suite, he kissed her while his hand slipped under her shirt and cupped her breast. All thoughts of taking time to tell him about herself, and to clarify the truth, left her mind with his touch. She sighed.

Rising on her toes, she pressed into him, needing his hard body against her, wanting to feel the strength of his arms encircling her. He bent and kissed her with such fierceness that it swept her away. They clung together, passion blazing as his tongue thrust into her mouth, while he undid the buttons of her wet blouse.

Her hands unbuttoned and freed his wet shirt from his slacks. He shrugged out of it, revealing his perfect chest, broad shoulders, and six-pack abs. The sight sent her pulses to pounding and she touched his skin as she'd longed to do for weeks.

He unhooked her lace bra and slipped the straps and wet shirt off her shoulders, then unfastened her skirt and slid it along with her underwear down to the floor.

Trent swung her up in his arms and carried her to the bed. He yanked back the comforter, and settled her on the cool sheets.

Gazing into his heated eyes, she lay back on the pillows consumed with desire and beyond protesting or slowing things down to tell her story.

Trent returned his hands to touch her, sending shivers running through her. "You're ready for me." He undid his belt and pants, kicked out of them, and joined her on the bed.

She touched his bare shoulder and pulled him to her. "I want you," she murmured. He moved over her, and she ran her hands through his dark hair.

With a groan, he caught her hips and moved his erection between her legs, with his naked body, and his hot flesh, against her. He slowly pushed inside her, filling her up. "Kate...so tight."

She didn't think she could stretch any more. Desire shot through her being. "Oh, my," she murmured in gasps.

He kissed her throat, the curve of her jaw. "You are more than any man deserves."

She was unprepared for the unbridled passion and fire that engulfed them. She met him thrust for thrust, over and over again, wave after wave building inside her until she exploded, crying out, "Trent!"

He shuddered and gripped her hips, while she clutched his broad shoulders. He surged into her, meeting his own need, his liquid heat pooling inside her.

How violent and incredible their lovemaking had been. They both lay back on the pillows in an exhausted heap. He was everything she'd ever wanted. He rocked her world.

After a few minutes, her eyes popped open. They hadn't used birth control. And she'd not told him anything about herself, but she still thought they could get through this. He'd just have to believe her that she'd come to the company for a good cause, to find out what really happened to her brother. Trent had said as much recently, that Matt's death might not have been an accident... He'd be receptive. She was sure of it.

Trent gathered her close and kissed the top of her head. "I've wanted you for a long time, Kate, from the first moment I held you in my arms in the lobby, your first day."

"Do you mean that?"

"Yeah," he said with a chuckle. "You've driven me mad ever since."

"Mad, I do believe," she said, giving him an impish grin.

"Mad and crazy, lustful… I could go on."

They rose from the bed. She stood bared before him. Heat rising on her cheeks, she crossed her arms to cover herself.

"No, don't be embarrassed. You're lovely," he murmured. "I want to look at you, touch you…and more."

She closed her eyes as he trailed kisses down her neck to her shoulder. His fingers grazed her stomach where she had a raised, two-inch long, scar. "How did you get this?"

"Childhood accident," she muttered weakly, and somewhat the truth, although how it happened wouldn't be anything like he could ever expect. "I hope you don't find it too ugly."

"No, Kate. Nothing about you is ugly."

She switched the subject. "I want to look at you, too. I remember that day on the construction site, you were bare-chested and wearing those tight jeans."

"You liked what you saw?"

She giggled. "How could I not, Mr. Farrington?" She placed her hand on his smooth, warm abs, as she'd longed to do for weeks.

He pulled her into the shower. There they explored each other with their hands, tongues, and hearts.

"Your skin is like satin." He lowered his head and nibbled on her shoulder.

She stroked him and he grew hard in her hands. "And you're so big and strong," she teased.

"Nice to hear it," he said, with a chuckle. "Ah, Kate. What you do to me is incredible."

He pulled her back to him, kneading her breasts, and lightly squeezing her sensitive nipples as the warm water streamed over them. She arched her back.

Damn, Kate." He had her bend over and brace the wall, and standing behind her, he clasped her buttocks and then stroked her intimately until her womanhood throbbed and was aching to be filled. He slowly entered her wetness. With his hand, he fondled her breasts, while she moaned her pleasure. He withdrew and thrust forward, again and again. She took every inch over and over again, until she was writhing in ecstasy and tightening around his hardness. His fingers found her most sensitive spot. Her body quickened. She climaxed hard and clenched him tightly.

He shot his seed into her. "Oh, Kate," he muttered near her ear.

Her legs were shaky and she would have collapsed if he hadn't clutched her to him and held her up

After drying off with plush hotel towels, they returned to bed and lay together in total exhaustion.

He grinned. "Sweetheart, that was the best sex I've ever had. *Twice.*"

"You were wonderful, too."

He nestled her in the crook of his strong arm. "That's what I like to hear." They dozed for a while.

Kate awakened a couple hours later to moonlight shining through the drapes. "Trent?"

"Yeah?" he asked in a husky voice. His eyes hooded, he reached out and stroked her cheek.

A glimmer of insecurity washed over her. She hadn't told him the truth about herself, but she just couldn't tell him now, in bed, and ruin their weekend.

"Just hold me," she muttered.

He gathered her in his arms and brought his lips to hers. More heat spiraled through her. She lifted her arms to wrap them around his neck. He groaned and deepened the kiss.

Suddenly, he broke away. "I'm not sure what you're doing to me, but I like it."

"I do, too."

"I didn't protect you—both times. We can't keep doing this. Next time I have to use a condom."

"Trent, I'm not on birth control pills. I never expected anything like this to happen between us."

He flicked her nose. "You seemed to detest me when we first met."

"I was so wrong about you. You're not the arrogant, careless playboy I assumed when I first met you. You're *amazing*…in so many ways." Her lips curved with delight.

"I never envisioned myself in this situation either, at least not until recently… I'm not playing games here, Kate." He kissed her mouth again and trailed his warm lips and tongue along her neck. "By the way, what did you want to tell me earlier that was so important?"

She thought he cared enough for her that when she told him the truth he would know she'd been driven to her charade to get justice for Matt. "Oh, I can tell you later."

Because he'd probably be a little upset with her, and she might have to soothe him, she didn't want to tell him tonight—not their first night together. She'd tell him at the office when his lips weren't nuzzling her ear and neck, or when his fingers weren't caressing her bare stomach. She'd just have to convince him that she had come to the company for a good cause, and that she was worthy of his love. Together, they'd find the perpetrator at Farrington Construction.

Trailing kisses over her cheek, he molded his palm over her breast while he flicked his thumb across her nipple. "I want you again," he said in her ear.

She pushed back a lock of dark hair that had fallen on his forehead. "I'm glad. I never want this night to end."

He kissed her nose. "I promise you this night isn't over. Expect to sleep in tomorrow and get back to town very late on Monday."

"Thankfully, it's Veterans Day weekend."

Trent caressed her hot flesh. When he kissed her, she almost believed everything would work out between them. Not wanting to think about anything else, she sighed, deliriously happy. He trailed hot kisses on her breasts, her stomach and everywhere, and brought her to the edge of insanity with his mouth. This time when he moved over her again, he wore a condom. The fire in his hungry lips met hers in a deep kiss as, once again, he branded her as his own.

CHAPTER SIXTEEN

On Tuesday morning, Kate awoke alone in her own bed and back in Fort Lauderdale. She and Trent had returned late Monday evening, after the best weekend of her life.

Smiling to herself, she leisurely stretched. Her muscles ached, not surprising after their vigorous lovemaking. Except for a few walks near the water, and watching the sunset on the ocean, they had spent most of their time in Key West—in bed—and with room service.

She already missed him.

Earlier that morning, he had disentangled himself from her arms, brushed a kiss across her lips. Then he covered her with the comforter. "Kate, you're too exhausted to get up. Stay in bed. I'll cover for you at the office."

Silently agreeing she was too tired to get out of bed, she snuggled back into its warmth and watched him head out her door. Impulsively, she rose up on her elbows, but caught herself before she murmured the words, 'I love you, Trent.'

It was too early to tell him her feelings for him—feelings she hoped he shared.

Falling back into an exhausted sleep, she later awoke with a jolt. She glanced at the clock. Nine a.m. In spite of what Trent said, she had a job to do. In addition, the last thing she wanted was to draw attention to the fact that they were seeing each other.

If she hurried, she wouldn't be significantly late for work. Not wanting to change her normal routine at the office, but wanting to look nice for him, she dressed for work in a more form-fitting gray suit with a crisp white shirt. She arranged her hair in a softer bun, with a few tendrils at the sides. Then she popped in contacts and applied makeup—she didn't have to hide anymore. She wanted Trent to like the way she looked and she planned to go shopping this week.

On the drive to work, her thoughts began to nag her again. She hadn't told him anything about her deception to get into the company. What would be the best way to confess? "Trent, there are some things you need to know about me. For one, I'm not a *real* psychologist." She clenched the steering wheel. "Yeah, right—he'll like that one."

Oh, God, how was she going to tell him the truth about herself? How would he take it?

"Trent," she said, practicing again what she'd say, "I had to get into the company to nab the person responsible for my brother's death...*namely you.*" Sounded better, but she should definitely leave off the last part. She didn't want to hurt him by letting him know he had been her prime suspect.

Kate blew out an exasperated breath, not ever wanting to lie to him again. She'd just have to explain that she meant no harm to anyone who was innocent.

When the time came, she was sure the right words would come. Trent would believe her because she was sure he cared enough about her to forgive her.

He would hear her out.

* * *

At ten a.m., Kate stepped off the elevator. When she walked by Purchasing, she noticed Cecilia wasn't at her desk. The file room door was slightly ajar and the hall empty so Kate took advantage of the opportunity and retrieved a few more suspicious purchasing invoices from the file drawers.

A few minutes later, she entered her own office. The sight of a single, red rose in a vase brought a smile to her lips. She inhaled the sweet fragrance, then sat at her desk to study the purchase orders.

With a quick tap on the open door, Darcy bounded into the room. She shoved her hands on her hips. "I wondered when you'd show up. So glad you're okay after that accident, but *okay* is an understatement. Boy, do you have a healthy glow. Your hair is not so severe. And you ditched the glasses. Good for you."

The news she was seeing Trent might hurt Darcy. Kate's cheeks heated with guilt.

"And by the look on your face, Kate—and not to mention that incriminating rose—I'd say you had one heck of a great weekend. Someone here at work? Who's it from?"

Kate winced. "Oh, you'll be surprised."

When Darcy frowned, Kate was reminded just how much Darcy had wanted Trent. "I need to tell you something. This is so hard for me. Trent and I…" Tears stung Kate's eyes as she rose from her chair. "Darcy, I know you sort of liked him, but after the accident, we ended up together this weekend. It just happened. I didn't plan it. Please don't hate me."

Darcy didn't bat an eyelash, but rushed to fling her arms around Kate. "It's all right. I want you to be happy. I suspected he was attracted to you anyway. Trent wasn't right for me, but he is for you."

"The last thing I'd want to do is hurt you. I didn't expect this to happen."

"It's okay. Sure, he's delicious, but I saw sparks flying between you two at the masquerade ball. Matter of fact, lightning nearly struck every time he was in this office. And even though he seemed angry at you at times, I saw the way he looked at you."

"You did?"

"Yeah. Actually, I want to tell you something, too. I went out with Greg this weekend to a football game. You were right about him. He's sweet and fun. Maybe I'll go for a nice, easy-going guy for a change."

Kate hugged Darcy again. "You and Greg. That's great."

"Well, it's only one date—we'll see what happens. But you, you'll have your hands full with Trent. He seems strong willed and compelling. Greg is like a cupcake in comparison."

Kate smiled. "And you were so right about Trent. He's fantastic and he makes me so happy. And I know he isn't responsible for Matt's death."

"I never thought Trent was a criminal."

"You had more faith in him than I did."

Darcy shrugged. "And you've experienced more rotten people than I have—if you don't count my ex-boyfriends."

Kate chuckled. "I want to help Trent, too. I think he has some deep issues."

Darcy laughed. "You always wanted a project."

"Yeah, and he's it." Then Kate sobered quickly as panic rushed through her. "I need to tell him everything. I'm afraid he's going to be upset with me when he hears it all."

"He should believe you." In spite of her words, Darcy looked a little worried.

"Is that wishful thinking?" Kate asked, frowning. "He also suspects someone is sabotaging the Karger site, just like I do."

"You mean someone is intentionally harming the company?"

Kate nodded. "We're not sure who. I have two suspects. Trent says Frank Blake wants Farrington Construction, and Roland seems jealous of Trent. All the problems on site could be to make Trent or the company look bad. Or someone is trying to get even for something... Anyone could be responsible. When Cecilia was on break this morning, I went into Purchasing to get to the bottom of this and I found these."

After spreading the purchase orders out on the desk, Kate's eyes fell on an incriminating signature—*Trent's*. "That's puzzling," she said, taking a closer look. "Trent authorized this change order?" She whirled to her computer and pulled up the equipment files. "This model—I'm not sure, but I don't think it's intended for heavy commercial use. Why would he do that?"

"Substandard equipment?" Darcy frowned. "*Trent?*"

"Maybe it's just a mistake, or I'm not reading this right. I'm going to him with this to get his opinion. Perhaps it's nothing."

* * *

When Trent glanced up from his desk to find Kate standing in the doorway, a warm glow spread through him. Was this what love felt like? He'd never thought it possible.

He smiled at her. "Rested enough?"

She grinned back at him. "Pretty much, considering the weekend we had. Thanks for letting me *sleep in*," she teased.

He stood. "Any time."

She waved the papers in her hand. "I have something important to show you."

"Sure, but come here first." She walked straight into his arms. "You smell so good," he whispered against her hair. "I'd like to see you tonight." That was an understatement. He wanted to see her all day, all afternoon, and all night...

"I'd love that, too."

"How about if I pick you up at six. For dinner and more?"

"Yeah, I'd love it."

He lowered his head and brushed his lips across hers. "I could stay over, or..." He kissed her ear and then her earlobe. "Or you could come to my place?"

Clasping her arms around his neck, she smiled up at him. "Either one works for me."

He squeezed her waist, then he dropped his hands to her buttocks. "Ah, Kate," he said, with a low growl, hauling her tightly against him. "What are we going to do about...about *this*?"

"I don't know," she murmured.

"I do...later...tonight," he said each word seductively. Gazing down at her, he was satisfied by her dreamy gray eyes that she had been just as affected.

He ran his thumb over her bottom lip. "I can barely keep my hands off you now." He smiled and cupped her silky cheek. "I'll be taking cold showers at work, regularly. Damn—wish we could leave now, but I have too much work to do, and I need to go to the Karger site in a few minutes."

Using all the will he possessed, he dropped his hands and stepped back from her.

"I understand. We both have work. And I have an important issue to discuss with you. I want you to look at some purchase orders and tell me if anything seems wrong—"

The intercom buzzed. "Greg is here," Mrs. Nash announced in her raspy voice.

"All right. Send him in. Sorry, Kate. I have a meeting with him now."

Greg ambled into the room. His gaze flicked to Kate. He seemed startled to find her here and the door closed. Trent sighed. Later, he'd tell his friend about his weekend with her.

"Should I leave?" she asked.

"No. I really want you to stay. There's something important I want you both to hear."

Trent returned to his desk, while Kate sat in one of the chairs across from his desk.

Trent explained the details of Friday's accident to Greg. "I'm fairly sure the cable was deliberately sabotaged and to make us seem like a sloppy operation in front of OSHA."

Blowing out a deep breath, Greg dropped into a chair. "Who'd want to hurt Farrington Construction?"

Trent crossed his arms over his chest. "I don't know, but we're going to find out."

Mrs. Nash buzzed the line again. "Sam's on the phone. OSHA has already arrived at the Karger building site. Are they going to shut down the project for longer than this weekend?"

"No. *We're* going to." Trent clicked off the intercom.

"But that will put the work behind schedule," Greg sputtered. "Won't be good."

"Greg, we have to find out what damage has been done. The elevator was rigged to fall. Safety on the site is my first concern."

His friend nodded. "But shutting the site down? Stopping construction? Seems whoever is doing this is getting exactly what they want—the job stalled."

"That's right." Trent rose from his desk. "Let's go see what OSHA has found." His gaze moved to Kate who'd been silent through their conversation. "Kate, since the entire site might be booby-trapped, I want you to stay here. We'll discuss what you wanted to talk about when I return."

* * *

Several hours later, Trent returned to his desk, determined to call Kate. He was punching in her extension when there was an insistent knock on his door.

Without further ceremony, his mother thrust the door open. "Trent, dear, am I interrupting something?"

His stomach knotted as it always did whenever she used an endearment. Perhaps he *did* need therapy.

She strode into the room. "I heard OSHA was at the Karger site again. Did they find out anything? I also want you to tell me about your weekend."

"If it's about Farrington Construction, I'll tell you. As to telling you anything about my personal life—you're out of luck."

Sighing, she seated herself in a chair across from him. "All right, if you're not going to confide in me, tell me what's going on with OSHA."

"We're waiting for the report. In the meantime, we're tightening security at the site."

"But wasn't the elevator breakdown an accident?"

He considered whether to tell Eden his suspicions. For her safety, he decided she needed to know. "We need to make sure no one has sabotaged the Karger project. Can you keep this information from getting back to my grandfather? I don't want him worried."

"Oh, my, I should have known... I should have told you my suspicions earlier." She put her hands to her cheeks. "I shouldn't have held off."

"What are you talking about?"

"I don't know how to tell you this. I discovered some information about one of our employees—and I think this may clarify some things for you."

He frowned. "Which employee?"

"There is no way I can spare you."

Anger ratcheted inside him. "Just say it," he ground out.

"It's about...*Dr. Meyers*. You've never been able to pick out the right women—you've always had a blind eye."

By the slight smirk curling at the edge of his mother's mouth, he had the impression she was elated to dish out some dirt on Kate.

He clenched his jaw. His heart pounding, he picked up the top letter in his stack of mail. "I'm busy," he snapped. "Get to the point." What could be so terrible his mother had rushed in here like this?

"I didn't trust her from the beginning, and rightly so—and to think she had you at her house."

Trent stared at his mother as he became increasingly uneasy...

"So, darling, I took the liberty of hiring a private investigator. He easily found this information for me." She thrust a folder in his direction. "My intuition was correct. She is not what she said, or what she seems—as if she is a nice girl. Perhaps *she* has something to do with what's going on. You'll see she has reasons for coming to our company..."

"Kate couldn't be involved in what was going on in the company."

Eden placed a picture of Kate before him. "This is her *mug* shot."

A punch in his gut couldn't have been more effective. He shoved his hand through his hair. He couldn't, wouldn't, believe anything this bad about her.

Still, nausea rolled in his stomach like a rogue wave. He shrugged, then stabbed his mother with his gaze. "She might have been arrested for anything...stopping a tree from being bulldozed in a parking lot. A war protest...jaywalking. This means nothing."

Glancing at him coolly, his mother raised and eyebrow, then set various articles and more pictures on his desk. "Keep reading."

He scanned the report. As he went through the photos and newspaper clippings of Kate being arrested for fraud, hurt and pain riddled him like bullets. He clenched his fists, his blood pressure rising. What a fool he'd been—an idiot. He'd let down his guard. He, a man who never trusted any woman, had trusted *her*. The truth about her pierced his heart as painfully as any sword.

His breathing labored, he remembered Kate at the benefit ball, in costume, toying with him and hiding her identity. He'd even caught her ensconced in his office after hours.

And to think he'd thought she'd been worried about him hurting her, when it was he who was about to take the tumble...

The blood roared to his head. He'd been blind, as his mother accused. In his mind's eye, he went over his weekend with Kate. Had he been fooled by her smiling, beautiful face? By how happy he'd been—how happy he thought *they'd* both been to have found each other?

Why the lying, conniving *witch* was a scammer. It had all been acting on her part. She'd set him up. Could she have something to do with what was going on in the company?

His insides aching, he barely heard the rest of what his mother said, but Eden's voice recalled him to the present. "Her stepfather was conman Bill Jackson, if you can believe it. The man was notorious."

"I've heard of him."

"And she was prosecuted for being involved in at least one of his crimes. For goodness sake, she's not even a real psychologist. She used her late aunt's credentials to worm her way into our company."

"And her *real name* is?" Trent snapped.

"Nearly the same as her Aunt Kathryn. Accept her name is Kaitlyn. So being *Kate* Meyers made it easy for her to lie to us." Eden thrust a photo at Trent. "Here's her Aunt Kate's picture."

His shoulders hunched as he scrutinized the middle-aged, gray-haired woman, who slightly resembled Kate. "This woman died?"

"Yes. A few years ago. Now, here's the bio on the fraudster, the young *faux* Dr. Kate Meyers, and the reason for her youthful appearance. She's not thirty-four, but a mere twenty-six. She has a bachelor's degree in psychology, but she is far from being a doctor."

Anger and pain raged through him. How had he been so stupid, so blinded by her? The reality was Kate's sweet innocent face was a sinister mask.

"By trying to set you up with all these women, your grandfather overlooked what should have been obvious. She was here to con us." Eden handed him another report of unending dirt on Kate. "She was engaged to Jeffrey Cooper, III, heir of the Cooper fortune. Shortly after the engagement announcement, the wedding was called off—*by him*. He must have found out about her checkered past."

Kate's betrayal slammed him as if he'd been hit with a cement truck. His mind reeling, Trent recalled how expertly she had hidden her identity from him at the benefit ball. He clenched his teeth. *What a little actress.*

And what about him?

He was a damned idiot. Although all the warning signs had been there waving like red flags, he'd only seen what he'd wanted to see. *Fool!* Her betrayal, and his own embarrassment to admit his mother might be right, crushed his insides like a wrecking ball.

"I'll get more information to you as soon as I can. Trent, I'm so sorry I had to be the one to bring you this terrible news."

He didn't believe his mother's sympathetic demeanor one bit. He wanted to tell her to go to hell, but he didn't want to give her the satisfaction of knowing just how painful a blow she had dealt him. He knew hiring the detective had not been for him, but for her own gain. Her real motive had been to bring Kate down so he might want to marry her precious Cecilia. And maybe she was right... His judgment with women stunk.

Trent sagged back in his chair and thought back through events. It was obvious Kate had gone to a lot of effort to get into the company. She had hidden her beauty and played hard to get. *But why?* Was she involved in the sabotage? If she had come here to hurt the company or to steal, what had she wanted so badly from him that she'd slept with him? After she'd landed a job with the company, had she decided it was more lucrative for her to marry the heir than for whatever she'd wanted to steal...or do to the company?

Damn it. He had played into her hands. Over the weekend, he'd even told her he wasn't playing around in their relationship, hinting their connection was something serious. Thank God, he hadn't told her how much he cared for her.

Anger simmered inside him like a pot of boiling oil. He needed time to cool off because he was tempted to wrap his hands around Kate's slender, beautiful neck. And he wouldn't give his mother that satisfaction.

Crossing her arms over her chest, Eden pinned him with her blue eyes. "You can thank me, Trent. I couldn't let this woman make a fool out of you any longer—as she did."

"You've given me the information about her," he said flatly. "You can go now."

His mother rose from her chair. "Have you decided what you are going to do about this…this *fraudulent* person?"

All the warning bells had sounded and he'd ignored them. His mother was right—fool…fool…fool.

Shaking with anger inside, he controlled it and steepled his hands before him on the desk. "Don't worry. I'll take care of *Dr. Meyers.*"

CHAPTER SEVENTEEN

A chill edged Kate's spine as she paced across her office floor for the umpteenth time. Why had Trent not called her directly yesterday? Instead he had Mrs. Nash make the call and tell her, 'Trent said to tell you that something came up and he has to cancel your plans.'

Here it was, one full day later, and he still hadn't heard from him. That hurt. Had their weekend together meant nothing to him, not even enough to come and explain what was going on? In addition, she needed to go over the purchase orders with him. They lay on her desk, waiting.

Darcy strolled into Kate's office, sipping a cup of coffee. "What's up?"

Kate took a seat behind her desk. "Several things. Bobby left drywall samples on my porch yesterday. I sent them to a lab. And I also found more change orders signed by Trent." Kate tapped the papers with her pen. "See here, he placed the original order for the correct supplies, then went back a few days later and changed the product to something I'm pretty sure is below code—just as Matt suggested. But I don't believe Trent would do anything like this knowingly. I'd trust him with my life."

"Maybe there's an explanation."

"I'm going to find out why he changed these. I can't wait any longer."

With nerves stretched to breaking, Kate headed for Trent's office.

His secretary wasn't at her desk. Kate tapped directly on his office door. "Trent, it's me. It's Kate."

"Come in."

Trent sat at his desk with shoulders hunched, pen on paper, writing. When he didn't look up, worry squeezed her like a vice.

She approached his desk. "I know you cancelled our date yesterday," she said nonchalantly, "but I wanted to invite you to dinner tonight…at my house, if you're free." Her voice wobbled. "I make a really great spaghetti sauce. And I have a few things I need to discuss with you about the company. It's important."

Finally, he looked up from his desk and pinned her with hard eyes that cut her to the core. He rose from his desk, strode to the door and locked it. He returned and stood so close to her she had to tilt her head up to see his face. Why was he reverting back to the suspicious man she'd met when she'd first arrived at the company?

Her throat ached. Had something else happened? "What's wrong?" she whispered, afraid to hear what it was.

"No, *Kate*," he said cryptically, in a voice cold as ice. "You first."

Something *had* happened. Her knees knocked together.

Although the frosty look in his eyes frightened her to her toes, she lifted her chin and stood her ground. "I've been looking at some purchase orders. We need to go over them? I think someone has access to Purchasing and is switching products that you ordered."

He crossed his arms over his chest. "Really now?" he scoffed. "Someone in my company is a *crook*? I find that hard to believe."

Taken back by his sarcasm, obviously meant to hurt her, she reared back and frowned. "Y-yes. Cecilia works in the department, and she's careless. She doesn't lock the doors when she's away. Anyone could walk in and change things. Your mother is often in Purchasing too… I just don't understand why they haven't noticed this switch-down issue before now."

He let out a harsh chuckle. "So you want to beat them to the *blame* game. How did you hear?"

"Hear what?" she whispered, not liking the sound in his voice at all.

"Yesterday, my mother brought me some interesting news about you."

"*Me?*" Kate retreated a step, but he only moved toward her, backing her against his desk.

The look on his face was one of displeasure. "Yeah, *you*," he said in a flat voice.

Closing in on her, he traced his finger down her cheek. Then his hand slid into where her shirt opened at the buttons, and curled around her neck. "How can you be so innocent looking and yet so treacherous?"

Alarm shot through her. "I'm not...*treacherous*, Trent. Why don't you tell me what you're talking about? I'm sure I can explain everything."

"Oh, you're a *good talker*, I'm sure. You've known how much I wanted you from the start, didn't you?"

"What?"

"Oh, sure you did." He cradled her head in his hands and with his thumbs, traced lazy circles behind her ear. She couldn't think clearly with him touching her. "Thought you could bring me to my knees if I got my hands on you. You are beautiful though. I'll give you that."

Was he angry, or what? He lowered his mouth to her ear. His warm breath sent a shiver through her.

"Trent, don't. Let's talk first."

"You blindsided me. I admit to that."

"No. Please, tell me what you're talking about? What did your mother say about me?"

Not answering, he seemed distracted by her hair. He dragged the pins from her bun, sending her hair cascading down her back. He ran his hands through the strands. "And it's just that I wanted you so damned much." His hand dipped along the edge of her throat.

"I planned to tell you everything...I tried to."

"What took you so long?" When he dropped his lips to hers, she melted into his embrace. Pulling away, he gazed at her with a bitter look. "Damn my soul, but I want you even now."

Frowning, she pushed at his shoulder. "What's going on? Explain to me why you canceled our date?"

His hands tightened on her waist. As if she weighed nothing, he lifted her and sat her down on top of his desk. He didn't answer her question but asked his own. "Was it your goal...to make me trust you?"

He knew. "Uh, well...I *have* been trying to tell you a few things."

"Why did you wait so long?"

"The time never seemed right."

He cupped his palm on the back of her head and pressed his lips to hers. While he gave her a soul-searing kiss, he unbuttoned several buttons on her shirt and slipped his hand inside her bra and kneaded her breasts. She whimpered, while her nipples hardened beneath his thumb and heat flooded to her lower region.

"Oh, Trent." She couldn't think and was lost to his touch.

"Hell, I still want you." He bent to pull off her high heels. Then he ran his hands under her skirt and tugged her tights down her legs.

"Trent, you'll put a run in my stockings, and I don't think we should do this here. Plus, you're angry with me—I can tell. I'd like you to tell me what it is that is bothering you first. Okay?"

He didn't answer. He ran his fingers beneath the silk of her panties. She shivered. She gave no more resistance when he slipped them off her legs, or as he returned his hand to caress her, stroking her intimately as he stood between her spread thighs, sending heat through her.

Then fire combusted between them. He opened her mouth to his and kissed her with a burning passion. He trailed his lips down her cheek to her neck.

Her thoughts gone, she gasped at the sensations he stirred inside her. With a moan, she pressed her palm to his hard erection through his slacks.

He groaned and then reared back. He pushed her hand away. Breathing hard, he gazed down at her, shock written all over his face at what had nearly happened.

His eyes, like black granite, glowered at her as she half lay on his desk with her clothes half-stripped off her. "Damn it, Kate. You can certainly be hot if it suits your cause, but I suggest you find a change in your taste in partners, *sweetheart*."

Kate blinked. Stunned, she focused on his harsh face. "What do you mean?" She sat up on his desk.

"Because I know all about you. My mother brought me a little report about you—from a private investigator."

The blood drained from Kate's face.

"So *you do* understand my meaning? Yeah, you forgot to tell me about your wonderful stepfather and all the dirt I would find on you."

"I wanted to tell you and was afraid you wouldn't understand. I tried, but we ended up…you know…busy," she said, wincing.

Anger etched his brow. "Hell, I thought you were going to tell me you'd been married before or something. Not that you and your father are damned *swindlers*… Bill Jackson of all disgusting creeps."

She cringed. It hurt to have him think such a terrible thought about her.

Trent looked like he could strangle her. "Damn it to hell, Kate—and that isn't even your real name—just how long did you think you'd get away with proclaiming to be a psychologist while sleeping in my bed?"

She ran her tongue over her dry lips. "I promise…I planned to tell you everything."

"Too late now," he roared. "I won't believe your excuses." He gripped her shoulders.

"What are you going to do?" she cried.

He gave a laugh, without humor. "*What should I do about it?* You do give it your all, though, I have to say that for you. How many of your victims have you slept with?"

"None! And I don't have any *victims*. My stepfather wasn't the nicest of men, but he died a few years ago."

"Great—he *was* a conman, and if he hadn't died you'd probably still be working with him. You even lied to me about your age. You're *twenty-six*, which explains a few things." He grabbed her chin roughly. "Did you come here to steal or do something to my company?"

"No—"

He tightened his grip on her chin. "Once you found out how hot my family was for me to marry, did you think that route would be more lucrative?"

"No. I swear it." She pulled her face away from his touch. "Nothing like that occurred to me at all."

"So you admit trying to con us?'

"No!"

"And do you have sex with men without birth control? Or was that just another lie… were you trying to trap me into marrying you? Have I caught something?"

"No, Trent! Listen to me. I'm not anything like what you're thinking." She slid off the desk and pushed down her skirt. "I know this looks bad, but please, I can explain everything, if you'll just let me."

"However good your charade, I won't be lied to again. You played me for a fool? Do you think I'd believe you now?"

"Well, you could *listen* to what I have to say."

His expression was implacable and unnerved Kate. "Do you know what happens to frauds like you? *Prison*, sweetheart."

Frowning, Kate bit her lip, drawing blood. "But he was my *stepfather*," she said weakly, dabbing her thumb at the moisture on her lip. "I tried to explain to you before, but I was afraid you wouldn't think much of me if you knew about him."

"You were right." He grabbed her arm and shook her. "You worked with him. Damn it! You were arrested and prosecuted in one of his schemes. What could you possibly say to clear yourself?"

"I did work for him a few times," she said through rubbery lips. "He told me I had to earn my 'keep.'" Tears burned her eyes. Except for her Aunt Kate, she had never told anyone how badly her stepfather had treated her. Even she didn't want to think about all he'd done to her. She swiped her eyes with her fingers. "I didn't work for him in the Wallingford Case. I was exonerated."

"But *did* you do it?"

"No! He used my name. I was only *eighteen* and completely innocent of any involvement...that time."

"That time?"

Her cheeks heated, while hot tears rolled down them. How could she raise her horrible past up to the light, when all she'd ever tried to do was bury it as deeply as possible? She wanted to get out of Trent's presence, go somewhere, and curl up into a ball. "Bill Jackson was a terrible man. H-he made me do certain things...or...or..."

Dark memories rushed back to her—memories that she didn't want to think about. She wanted to tell Trent everything, but at the disgusted look on his face, the words died on her lips. Her vision blurred and all her insecurities as an abused child returned.

He'd never believe her now. Probably never would have, no matter when or how she'd told him. She clutched the back of the chair for support.

"Your stepfather's been dead for three years. You did this con job at my company on your own."

A shock of defeat swept through her. He had her on that issue. "I did this for my *bro*—"

"I won't listen to your lies, blaming anyone else for your coming here. Doesn't matter anyway. Since I won't publicly humiliate myself, I'm not about to have you prosecuted. *You're fired.* I want you to get the hell out of my company. If you're anywhere near here or our operations—if you have anything to do with what is going on with my company—I'll be sure to make you regret it."

"But... I—"

"Shut up, Kate, or I might change my mind and call the police *now*. Just be glad you're getting off so lightly."

Anger darkened his expression. Knowing he would never trust her again, Kate nodded as tears sprouted in her eyes.

Trent shoved his shirt into his slacks. "You can stop the phony tears, princess. You're the worst of women. Lying, cheating, sleeping with your victims—it makes no difference to you. You'd do anything for money."

She shook her head. "Trent, I—"

"Spare me—I hate liars. Everything you've told me from day one has been a lie, *Doctor Meyers*. Can you deny that?"

Kate winced. "Not everything. I was with you because you really meant something to me." She searched under the desk for her underwear, but only found her tights. She thrust them in her pocket and stepped into her high heels.

"Stop acting like there was something special between us, when you're nothing but a lowlife con artist," he ground out.

The *lowlife* remark sliced her to the core and brought a fresh welling of tears to burn in her eyes. Deep inside, because of her stepfather, she'd always felt that maybe this was true about her, even though she'd tried to make a life of her own away from the taint he'd marked her with. It must be true. The crushing pain in her chest took her breath away.

Even though she couldn't find her underwear, she couldn't stay a moment longer in Trent's angry presence. "I tried to tell you everything, about my brother and why I was here," she said, using her last defense. "But I was afraid you would think the worst of me, and you wouldn't give me a chance to explain. Turns out, I was right. Which just proves that I would never have been good enough for you—even if we'd met under the best of circumstances." She'd never tell him now. She was done.

"You are correct." He pointed toward the door. "Now out. I know all about Jeffrey Cooper as well. Seems like your fiancé found out what a treasure you were and dumped you. Do you think I'd want to be involved with a criminal or a gold-digger like you?"

Her cheeks felt on fire. He couldn't have hurt her more if he had struck her. "I wasn't after his money. He never said... I had no idea Jeff...was...was—"

"One of the richest heirs in the country?"

"No, I didn't know. And his mother didn't like me for the same reason you're blaming me—because of *my stepfather*. I can't help it if my mother chose to marry Bill Jackson. She died within a year of marrying him. I had to live my entire life with *her* mistake."

Whirling away from the disbelief simmering in his eyes, she swiped away the humiliating moisture sliding down her cheeks.

"Your tears won't work with me, princess. I know you for what you are. Your excuses can't explain your lies to get into my company—or the fraud you perpetuated on me."

She cringed. *Oh God, he was right.*

He reached for his wallet and tossed several hundred-dollar bills on the desk. "I've never paid before, but in this instance, I want to make sure you get something for all your trouble. I enjoyed the sex, but in spite of what you thought, your little scheme would never have worked."

Now shaking, she ignored the money. "You have a right to be angry, but you've got me all wrong."

Only moments from breaking down, Kate elevated her chin. She hung on to her crumbling composure as she marched toward the door.

Pausing, she faced him once again. "Be careful," she said, her voice low with strain. "I think whoever is sabotaging your company has access to Purchasing. You need to check the equipment records."

Disgust for her was written all over his handsome face. "The number one person in this company I can't trust is *you*." He thrust his finger toward the door. "Now take your things and get out.—or I'll have the pleasure of *throwing* you out. Understand?"

Numbly, she nodded.

On shaky legs, she walked as composed as she could out of the office. Mrs. Nash's mouth gaped open. The woman said nothing about Kate's hair hanging in a long tangle down her back, or anything about her face that must surely be a mess with her new use of eye makeup.

Kate stepped into the hallway and exhaled a deep breath. Thank God, it was empty. Hugging herself, she hurried toward her office. Did she deserve this gut wrenching pain? Had she perhaps been wrong to come here, especially by lying to get the job?

She'd not exactly had a normal upbringing. Had she been so accustomed to her stepfather's con games that she'd gone a little too far by coming to the company to investigate on her own? Had there been another way? What was the old saying? 'Oh what a tangled web we weave, when first we practice to deceive.'

She had come to the company on false pretenses—but what else could she have done to find justice for Matt? No one at the police station believed her because of her stepfather's criminal past. And actually, she'd found that everything going on at the company was different than she'd expected.

Now, she had to leave when she was so close to finding the person responsible for Matt's death. And she had lost her heart in the process and badly hurt the man she loved.

CHAPTER EIGHTEEN

Trent followed Kate out of his office and watched her retreating back as she rushed down the hall. He hoped that was the last he'd see of scheming Kate Meyers. In spite of all the warning signs about her, he'd let her into his heart. What a fool he'd been. He'd trusted her.

He blew out a deep breath. For once, he was glad his mother had interfered. She'd saved him from making the biggest mistake of his life.

On his return to his reception area, he ignored Mrs. Nash's furrowed brow and proceeded into his office. Trent shut the door and sat at his desk, aching like hell from the blow Kate had dealt him.

Unbelievable, the spell the witch had cast over him. A moment ago, he'd nearly lost his senses and made love to her again. He'd been about to drive into her like a raging bull—like an idiot…an unprotected idiot. And she'd been just as receptive.

He sighed, glad he had taken care of birth control over most of the weekend, except for the first two times.

Now, if he could, he had to shut her out of his mind and his life. What he'd done today had been the most difficult thing in his life: throwing her out of his company. At one point he'd nearly weakened, and had wanted to believe there had been some reason— any reason—but that had made him even angrier at himself so he had struck out hard. He had resorted to being nearly cruel to her about the money he'd tossed at her—to remind himself what she was—when all he'd wanted to do was to clutch her to his chest and for her to once again be the woman he'd come to care for.

He grappled with the pain, the twisting in his gut, the emptiness in his heart. She had been nothing but an illusion. He had to remember what she was…whenever he weakened. She'd put him through hell.

Feeling something under his shoe, he rolled the chair back and discovered her panties.

He bent down and dropped the bit of black lace in the trashcan. She deserved to feel uncomfortable with a naked butt for conning him and his family.

He should call security to escort her out. Better yet, he should go over to her office soon and make sure she'd vacated the premises and do that job himself if she was still there.

"Trent," Mrs. Nash said over the intercom. "I didn't want to interrupt you when you were with Dr. Meyers, but your grandfather called awhile ago."

He frowned. "Is he all right?"

"Yes. He said he was feeling a little weak today and planned to stay in bed, but for you not to worry. He wants you to call him when it's convenient. Trent, but before you do, I must ask you, is Dr. Meyers all right?"

"She's fine." He punched in his grandfather's phone number.

He didn't want to talk about Kate, or think about her. He blew out a deep breath. He felt as if he'd been beaten to a pulp and it was still early in the day.

"I hope you're taking it easy," Trent said when his grandfather answered the phone.

"One never rests when one is neglecting his duties."

"Stay in bed. You don't need to worry about anything."

"Shouldn't I? I heard about the elevator accident." Leave it to his sharp grandfather to sniff out any detail.

Of course, Trent thought dryly, and elevator crashing was a huge deal. "Don't worry. I have everything under control," he lied into the receiver.

"I have some important issues to discuss about the future direction of the company. I want you to meet me on the yacht, Saturday, at three p.m."

"Do you care to enlighten me now on what this meeting is about?"

"No. I'd rather review my plans to everyone all at once." He ran through a few names and Kate's name was on the list.

"Dr. Meyers?" Trent muttered. "She can't make it."

"This is a mandatory meeting. She must be there. The dear girl didn't quit? I don't think my heart can take much more worry."

Trent hung up the phone. *Dear girl...?*

More like *conniving viper*.

* * *

Still trembling from head to toe, Kate stepped inside her outer office and closed the door.

Darcy glanced up from her computer. "What's wrong, Kate?"

Tears burning her eyes, Kate shook her head numbly, unable to speak.

Darcy jumped up and rushed to her. "What's happened to you? You look like you went through a blender. Did someone hurt you? That damned Roland Sikes? Oh, my God. What did he do to you?"

Wagging her head from side to side, Kate let the tears spill down her cheeks.

"Well, then what? Did you find out who caused Matt's death?"

Kate shook her head. "Trent," she managed in a hoarse whisper. "H-he knows..." Her mouth curved downward. "And he's put the worst spin on everything. He wouldn't even let me explain."

Darcy's face fell. "Oh, goodness..." Then she let out a deep breath. "Okay. Okay, let's think about this." She frowned. "What does this mean for *us*?"

"It means *we're fired*. We're lucky he's letting us go without charging me with a crime. He thinks I was here to steal. So pack up—quickly."

"But, what happened? You really like him."

"No," Kate rasped, "I never want to see him again." Her despair sunk into her like a stone in a lake, and she hurried into her office to pack.

Darcy followed behind her.

At the sight of the red rose from Trent on her desk, a strangled sob burst from her throat. Kate pressed her knuckles to her lips. "No...no—I won't cry anymore. It's done—finished." She straightened her shoulders and marched to the closet to retrieve the empty box she had standing ready for this inevitable day when she must leave. "Better to know now that I would never have been good enough for him—because of my stepfather."

She wouldn't try to get him to believe her again. No point. After all, she was a conniving lowlife. Her throat ached in despair.

"Oh, Kate... Can't you just explain to him?"

Kate dropped down at her desk and began to pack. "I tried, but he didn't want to listen. My stepfather will forever taint my life," she said, her chin trembling. "I didn't even want *you* to know just how bad my life had been with my stepfather. 'Earning my keep' was better than the alternative Bill Jackson gave me. I *had* to help him several times in his cons—but I was just a kid." She choked back a sob. "No, I won't cry anymore."

Raising her hands to her burning face, she told Darcy the things she'd tried to bury so long ago—memories of her stepfather holding her on his lap.

"I know your stepfather used to hit you, Kate, but did he rape you?"

At the thought, Kate cringed even now. "No...but he touched me! I would have done anything—walked over hot coals—to prevent him from putting his hands on me." She shuddered. "I realized later that he knew just how to manipulate me to get me to do whatever he wanted."

"Kate, and your fear of heights?"

Kate swallowed a lump in her throat. "He made me go out on a seventh-floor ledge and into another office to unlock a door so he could enter." She swiped away those tears she couldn't stop now if her life depended on it. "I was eight and Matt was too big. I was the only one small enough. I failed anyway. I froze and was stuck on the ledge, for the longest time. My stepfather finally coaxed me back, and then he slapped and hit me. I couldn't go to school for a week. He told them I had the flu..."

Darcy rushed to Kate and hugged her. "I always suspected something bad had happened, and wondered if that was why you were so involved with Children in Crisis, but I was afraid to ask."

"You're a good friend and I thank you for that. I only wanted to forget those dark parts in my life."

"Listen, you didn't have a choice about your stepfather. If Trent Farrington doesn't understand that, well, he's not worth it."

"Darcy, even if Trent could get past Bill Jackson being my stepfather—which he won't because of his high society background, especially with his mother—he's not going to forgive me for lying about my credentials to get into the company. I shouldn't have done that."

"You, too, Darcy?" They whirled to find Trent filling the doorway.

Heat searing her cheeks, Kate stood up, wondering how much he'd heard. She swiped away her tears. "No, she's innocent. I alone am to blame."

Apparently, he thought so little of her because he nodded in agreement. "Yes," he said. Then he turned to Darcy. "Now, let's just say your boss has gotten herself into some hot water."

Kate thrust her chin up. "I'm packing up and leaving like you ordered."

He crossed his arms over his chest. "I've changed my mind. You're not leaving right away," he said in a cold voice.

After the way he'd spoken to her in his office she'd never stay, besides his face was one of anger and not of someone who'd come to apologize.

Kate threw the pens into the box. "Pack your *personal items*, Darcy."

"*Stop,* Darcy," he growled.

Kate grabbed her purse. "I was fired, remember? We're leaving."

He stepped into her path. "Leave us, Darcy. You're not fired," he ordered.

Darcy sent Kate a sympathetic look but did as she was told. "Kate, I wouldn't step out, if I didn't think you two needed to talk." After Darcy left the office, Trent closed the door, leaving Kate ensconced with him, alone.

Kate stepped back and pinned him with her gaze. "There is nothing for us to talk about—and no worries, I'm not staying here."

"You'll stay, or shall I'll call the police and report the whole sordid story?"

Her entire breath left her on the exhale. When she glanced at him, she couldn't stand the hatred in his eyes. He meant what he said. Kate shook her head. She whirled away, unable to look at him.

"I didn't think so. My grandfather wants us all on the boat on Saturday. He specifically asked for you. His health is bad, so you're to be there. I want to let him down easy because he thought a lot of you. And if you cause problems…"

She turned back to him and glared. "I'm sorry about his health, and I wouldn't want to hurt him, but *I* can leave right now."

"*Can you*? You're in a lot of trouble. I can make sure this time you don't get away with your little schemes, doing the public some good. You were practicing without a license, which is *fraud.* Do you understand? *You could go to jail,*" he said hotly. "I could have you prosecuted."

"But I never actually practiced with anyone…" *With him, she had.* She swallowed that truth. "It wouldn't look good for me, having been arrested before…"

"You're right, and you wouldn't last long in prison. Physically, you're too fragile. They'd eat you alive."

She gulped and didn't think she would either. She'd been jailed before—after she'd been arrested for the Wallingford scheme that her stepfather had perpetuated by using her identity for his cover. Thoughts of one of the scariest nights of her life whirled through her head. Most of the women had been nice to her, but a couple of them had threatened to beat her up. And a male guard said he had other plans for her…

Light-headedness struck Kate, and her knees buckled.

"Sit," Trent ordered. He put his hand on her shoulder and propelled her into a chair. "Put your head down."

She dropped her head into her lap, letting the dizziness recede.

"Let's just say, Kate, I hold all of the cards to your future now. My grandfather doesn't know anything about this. He's called some of us together and you're on the list to meet on Saturday. And you're going to go on Saturday because you're going to appease a sick man." He folded his arms over his chest. "Practicing medicine without a license is a serious offense."

Blood rushed to her head. She didn't think he could prevent her from getting her degree in the future, but he might be able to stop her from getting her license or a job. The Farrington's were powerful in the area.

"Do you understand what I'm saying?" he asked.

"Yes," she whispered.

"So we've come to an agreement? You're not to go anywhere until we know what my grandfather wants and until I see what you've been up to in my company…until I say so. Agreed?"

She raised her head and nodded. "Okay."

"Did you steal money from the company? Not that your word is worth much."

Kate clutched the arms of the chair. "No. I never took anything…"

Her face burned with shame. She had stolen cash out of someone's desk once for her stepfather when she was a little girl. She had been too terrified to refuse him. She didn't even want to think about her stepfather's threat right now or she'd throw up all over the Farringtons' beautiful office—or Trent for that matter.

She took in a deep breath and glared up at him. "Let's get one thing clear. I won't stay at the company to be humiliated or insulted by you. I was acquitted of being involved in my stepfather's scheme in the Wallingford case because I had nothing to do with it. I was innocent in the crime. My stepfather used my name to cover his tracks in the incident. I'm nothing like him. I wish you would believe me."

He crossed his arms over his chest and didn't have to say a word. The look on his face confirmed he would never again believe a word she said.

"I'll stay," she said in a low voice, "but don't ever touch me again."

"I wouldn't dream of it, princess," he said, scowling. "I'll admit you had me fooled for a while, but I'll be lucky if I haven't caught a disease."

Her cheeks stinging, she gaped at him.

He pivoted on his heel and strode from her office.

"I thought you were responsible for my brother's death," she said to his retreating back. She had to tell him at least that part of this mess, but she wasn't sure he heard her. At this point, she didn't think it would make a difference. He'd probably think that was just an excuse to come to his company and steal.

CHAPTER NINETEEN

Anxiety gripped her stomach as Kate drove her car to James Farrington's mansion for the yachting trip on Saturday. Her hair was secured in a French-braid. She wore white Capri pants and a pink shirt with matching tennis shoes for the day on the water. Having to face Trent today, she felt like a woman set to go before a firing squad. She just had to get through today.

Since their fallout on Wednesday, she'd only seen him once. He'd been dining with Cecilia at the Green Tree Restaurant. Sitting close, the two had seemed rather cozy together. Cecilia smiled up into his face and looked enraptured by whatever he had said. Then his gaze had snapped to Kate's across the room. The cold look in his eyes shattered Kate's heart, along with her composure. She'd turned and walked out of the restaurant.

Their nights of making love seemed like a dream now. Her heart ached though she kept up appearances at work. He'd stripped her of her duties and had told her he'd watch her every move.

After appeasing his ailing grandfather today, she assumed Trent would let her go for good. Obviously, he couldn't wait to get rid of her. And she just wanted to be as far away from the Farringtons as possible.

Tears pricked her eyes. She'd be glad to leave. When she'd come to the company, she didn't expect to land herself in such a heap of trouble or endure so much pain. While she'd known the risks, she hadn't planned to stay long enough to get caught.

Stepping out of the car, she was glad her new transition-lenses changed with the light. The sunglasses shielded her reddened eyes after a fresh bout of crying on the way over here.

A male crewmember in a white uniform met Kate on the lawn and led her around the side of the two and-a-half-story, red brick mansion overlooking a magnificent vista of the river. The house had a large patio and a balcony that ran the entire length of the second floor. Tied to a dock, a massive, luxurious yacht floated on the water along with several other boats of varying types and sizes.

Kate boarded and steadied herself to the gentle rocking of the ship. The crewmember led her to the back of the boat where Trent's grandfather, his mother, and Cecilia sat around a table. In casual wear, Trent leaned against the bar. He was so incredibly handsome he hurt her eyes.

By his hardened expression, she knew she could never make amends. Never again would he look upon her with a warm light in those dark eyes.

She supposed she should be grateful he hadn't had her thrown in jail—at least not yet. Regardless of what he planned now, she'd found out he could change his mind in an instant.

While he didn't smile at her, he did dip his head to acknowledge her presence. "*Dr. Meyers.* What an *honor* it is for you to join us," he said sarcastically in a low voice.

Kate cringed. If this was how he was going to act, the day would be depressingly long. "Thank you, Mr. Farrington," she said through tight lips. "I was *delighted* to be *invited.*"

Trent's mother eyebrows drew together in a frown. "Dr. Meyers, I'm surprised you're here today." She threw a puzzled glance toward Trent.

"Your son insisted I come," Kate answered truthfully, knowing Mrs. Farrington had arranged for the investigation on her.

"Ah, he did?" Trent's mother then turned a cold shoulder toward Kate and proceeded to act as if she didn't exist.

Cecilia sent a snarky grin toward Eden as if they had won the game and Trent was the ultimate prize.

"Please forgive me for not rising. These pesky health issues," Trent's grandfather said, placing a hand over his heart. "Welcome, Dr. Meyers. So good to see you. May I call you, Kate?"

She nodded. "Yes, please do."

Trent rolled his eyes. "Why don't we *all* call her *Kate,*" he snapped. "Dr. Meyers seems a little formal, doesn't it?"

Kate clenched her teeth.

James Farrington beamed a smile. Obviously, he mistook the informality as meaning she and Trent were on good terms. He couldn't be more wrong. "Sit here, dear. Trent, why don't you pour Kate a drink?"

Trent stepped to the bar. "Sure. Pick your *poison*."

Kate winced. For most people this would be a cliché, but for him, no doubt, he meant every word. "A Mimosa, please. Hold the *hemlock*."

He made a pretense of looking through the items on the bar, then he shot back, "Fortunately for you, we're out of hemlock today. Would *arsenic* do?"

Daunted, she shook her head, and warily sat down, feeling like the virtual 'captive audience.'

Had he told his grandfather that she was a criminal? Seeing nothing but humor—or was it satisfaction reflected in the older man's eyes—Kate relaxed her shoulders and settled back into the chair.

"Thank you," she murmured when Trent handed her the drink. She didn't bother to meet his eyes. It hurt to see how much he hated her. While he had good reason, because she'd lied to him from the first, at least he could have heard her out and let her explain herself and what she'd done and why.

Shoving aside that painful thought, she sipped the tangy orange juice and bubbling champagne drink.

"I'm glad you're feeling well enough to make the trip," she said, bestowing a weak smile to Mr. James Farrington.

"Thank you, dear. The doctor said my health would improve as long as I live stress free. That's one of the reasons I brought you all here. We'll get on with the business portion as soon as everyone arrives."

Trent drained his glass quickly and poured himself another, straight from a bottle of whiskey. Was he concerned about this meeting and needing to bolster his confidence with alcohol, or was he drinking because of her?

"Ah, there is Roland coming down the dock," Eden said dryly. "He looks a little unkempt, as if he's been hitting the booze hard again."

Although Trent's older cousin was Kate's prime suspect, Eden appeared cruel where Roland was concerned. Uneasiness settled in Kate's chest. Didn't the woman know her actions pitted cousin against cousin?

"Sorry, I'm late, Grandfather," Roland said as he entered the deck. With sweat beading on his brow, and his shirt wrinkled, he swiped at the fair hair hanging limply across his forehead. It was obvious that at one time Roland had been attractive, but he could never have compared to his gorgeous cousin.

Thankfully, Roland had stayed clear of her since the benefit ball and seemed embarrassed by his actions of that night. Or was there another reason he avoided her? Could he have been the one to leave the mask for her? She was certain it had been whoever had been in Purchasing on that day she'd heard a noise.

"Take a seat," James Farrington said, waving toward the table. "Ah, and there's Frank Blake coming down the dock."

"Frank Blake!" Trent blasted. "Why the hell is he here?"

"I invited him, so be civil," James ordered, just before Blake strode onto the back deck where they had all gathered. "Glad you could make it, Frank. Trent, notify the captain that we're all on board."

After Blake settled into a chair with his drink, James leaned toward his guest. "Frank, have you met Dr. Kate Meyers?"

With salt and pepper hair, a mustache, and overly tanned skin, Frank Blake had a set of gleaming brown eyes that could send a chill up a polar bear's spine.

Kate shivered. This was the first time she'd met him in person. There was something a little familiar about him perhaps because she'd met his type before. He was the creepy kind her stepfather occasionally brought to their house.

He appeared to be nearly Eden's age. Through his glasses, Blake perused Kate. "No, we haven't met. I'm sure I'd remember someone as pretty as she is." His eyes narrowed, then he turned and winked at Eden. "Why, James, she's as lovely as your daughter-in-law here."

Mrs. Farrington lifted an eyebrow. "I remember you were always a sweet talker, Frank," she said dryly. "You still are." Even to Kate, Blake seemed to be groveling as he spouted off his praise for Eden—as if he were schmoozing her. How could Mrs. Farrington not be aware of this?

Blake chuckled. "It was nice to renew our acquaintance at the benefit ball this year."

Trent's mother raised her glass in salute. "I was surprised, too. I thought you'd forgotten all about me these past ten years."

"Eden, I've been a fool," Blake said coyly. "Do you mind if we speak together privately?" They drifted to a small table at the back of the yacht.

The engines rumbled to life. The crew cast off the lines and the vessel moved away from the dock. Picking up speed, the boat pounded over the waves in the Intracoastal Waterway. The breeze cooled Kate's face.

"Trent, why don't you sit here between these two lovely ladies?" James Farrington swept his hand toward the chair between Kate and Cecilia. Kate narrowed her eyes. Did he know she and Trent had spent a weekend together? If the grandfather did, he didn't let on. "Two fine-looking, young women. I'm not sure how you can resist?"

Trent sat down between them, slightly turning away from Kate. His body language spoke volumes and showed that he'd rather be anywhere but near her. And that hurt. But what about Cecilia? Had he gone out on a date with her—been with her, too? The idea brought pain to Kate's heart, but she put on a mask of cool composure. She had to play along so Trent would set her free and she could move on and try to pick up the shambles of her life.

When James stepped away from the table to speak to a crewmember, Cecilia scooted her chair closer to Trent's. "I enjoyed the party last night. Rob and Karen said we should all go out one night next weekend."

Trent didn't comment. So they *had* gone out... A sense of loss hit Kate. Perhaps he was uncomfortable with her being here and didn't want to discuss his private life with Cecilia. He'd moved on so fast. If only she could forget him as quickly as he had her. Tears teased the back of her eyes. The sooner this day was over the better.

A crewmember brought out appetizers. Kate tasted a bite of a sushi roll, but found she could barely eat anything. To distract herself from Cecilia's endless chatter to Trent about the damned party they'd attended, Kate strode to the back of the boat. She clasped the railing, breathing in the salt air, and taking in the passing view. She soon regretted her move.

"I'd love for Cecilia and Trent to get together," Mrs. Farrington said from a few feet away at a smaller table where she sat with Blake. "And I think it's possible now. Frank, you won't believe it, but I saved him from making a disastrous mistake with a woman who is virtually a criminal."

Kate pursed her lips.

Blake lifted his drink. "Really now? Lucky break for you."

"Yes. I'd never tolerate someone like *her* in Trent's life. Thankfully, this woman won't be around much longer." Eden shot a chilling glance toward Kate.

Kate frowned unhappily, wishing Trent's mother would just leave her alone. After pacifying his grandfather tonight, Trent would dismiss her for good, so why didn't she ease off? Soon Mrs. Farrington would get her wish and Kate would be gone for good. She was already halfway out the door and definitely out of Trent's life. Eden must be ecstatic.

Raising her chin, Kate did an about-face and headed back to the table.

The yacht cruised past houses and condominiums. The tendrils of loose hair around Kate's face blew in the light breeze. While the ride was nice, she just wanted to go home.

A crewmember directed everyone to the dining room for dinner. Lobster, fish, and steak were on the main menu. Kate didn't think she'd be able to eat much of anything.

One member of the staff set a special diet plate before James. James picked up a carrot and wrinkled his nose at the rest of the healthy food. "Ah, this is what happens when you live to the ripe old age of seventy-eight. They conspire and feed you tasteless food." He crunched on a carrot. "I should have been a rabbit."

"Now, James," Eden said with a smirk, "I told the cook, no more steak. We want you around for a long time."

The elderly man sighed. "I may die of culinary boredom."

The rest of the conversation was mostly between James Farrington, Trent's mother, Cecilia, and Frank Blake.

To Kate, the dinner seemed to last forever as she picked at her food. When it was over, everyone returned to the tables outside on the deck. Decaffeinated coffee was served and the glasses of wine refilled.

James Farrington said over his coffee cup, "I suppose you all are curious to know the real reason I brought you all here. We should get on with the meeting. Don't you think so, Frank?"

Blake sipped his wine before setting down the glass. "All right, James. Have you considered my offer to buy the company?"

"Yes. It's a little low. However, my health is not as good as it used to be. I'm willing to put the past behind us, Frank, and consider your offer."

Kate gasped, along with Mrs. Farrington. Cecilia's and Roland's mouths dropped open.

"Are you serious?" Trent jumped to his feet, his eyes revealing his shock. "You can't do that without consulting the rest of us."

"I own the company," his grandfather pointed out.

Trent pounded his fist on the table. "You're willing to forget that generations of Farringtons built the company, not to mention when Blake quit he absconded with a fourth of our clients? And, now, who the hell knows what else he's been up to. We've had problems lately on our sites."

Blake clenched his hands on the arms of his chair. "See here, Trent. I had nothing to do with your problems. Don't blame me."

Trent jutted his face toward the man who he considered their enemy. "I've never been *certain* of anything where *you are* concerned, Blake."

Stunned, Kate couldn't believe James would do this to Trent. Trent loved the company. She noticed Roland's face reddened, but he didn't offer any protest to the sale. Why wasn't he just as upset as his cousin to be losing the company he thought he'd inherit?

James narrowed his eyes. "Trent, I'm as *serious* as a man can be. You, of all people know where I stand on the issues with this family." He folded his hands like a steeple on the table. "Frank, here are my concerns. If this deal were to go through, would you keep all of the employees? I want my grandsons assured of jobs as well."

Cold fury rose on Trent's face. He seemed to have trouble containing his anger. "Work for, Blake?"

Smiling, Blake raised his wine glass in a salute. "Why, yes, of course, Trent. You have particular talents, being an architect as well as an engineer with some good ideas."

"That means so much to me coming from you, Blake," Trent ground out sarcastically.

Eden cleared her throat. "Trent, I think we should be grateful Frank wants to take over the helm of the company. You don't need the stress."

Roland stood, shoving his chair away. "I think Frank coming on board would be the best thing to happen to Farrington Construction. I won't stand in the way of that decision." Roland took his drink and strode out of the area.

Kate flinched with shock that Roland didn't care for, and love, the company as much as Trent did.

Blake chuckled and winked at Trent. "Even Roland thinks I'll be good for the company."

The look Trent returned was deadly. And Kate knew what that was like.

Blake picked up Mrs. Farrington's hand. "I'm so glad you like the idea, Eden. You think I'll be good for the business?"

She smiled at him. "Yes—in spite of being a shrewd cutthroat at times."

Blake gave her a sharp glance. "Eden, don't think of me that way."

Eden's lips curved. "I'm wise enough to know that Trent's not ready for the responsibility. And, heavens, Roland couldn't run a shoe store."

His face ablaze with anger, Trent rose from the table and pinned his grandfather with his ire. "I can't believe you'd sell to Blake. You want some immoral cutthroat to take over Farrington Construction?"

Trent strode to the bar and poured another glass straight from a bottle of liquor. He tossed the amber liquid down his throat. Then he poured himself another drink. He turned to the group again. "Mother, you would trust a man who used you years ago to get to our clients and then dropped you like you were nothing?"

Blake's face reddened. "I-I—"

"It's all right, Frank." Eden leaned across the table and patted Blake's hand. "You've explained to me that all those years ago you thought I hated you after you left me."

The man nodded. "I couldn't face you."

"You believe him?" Trent asked in a low, angry voice. "He used you to get to us—then dumped you. Damn it. He doesn't deserve Farrington Construction now. Sell, but I won't work for Blake."

James Farrington held out his hands, palms up. "Don't make this any harder. Trent, I've told you I won't hand over the company to you or Roland, as you've not proven yourselves responsible. You know what I require from you, but year after year, you ignore me."

Trent tossed down his drink and deposited the empty glass on the table. "All right." His gaze landed on Kate and his eyes hardened as he contemplated her. Then he turned and thrust his hand toward Cecilia. "Care to take a walk with me around the yacht?"

Suddenly Kate couldn't breathe.

"I'd love to." The pretty brunette glanced at Kate, giving her a haughty tilt of her nose. Trent didn't glance Kate's way again.

He stopped by the bar, thrust a bottle of whiskey under one arm, and allowed Cecilia to cling to the other.

Kate's stomach knotted, while a flash of grief consumed her as she watched Trent leave with Cecilia.

* * *

Anger seeped from every pore Trent possessed as he guided Cecilia to the staterooms. He knew exactly what his grandfather had just blackmailed him to do—sell his soul to secure their dynasty, as if they were medieval aristocrats and he had to beget their heir.

Farrington Construction had been the one sure thing in Trent's life, but to marry someone he had no feelings for just to keep the company—could he do it?

Even his great-great-grandfather, Joshua Farrington, had married an English, mail-order bride, not for love, but to secure his future and to have sons. Eventually, she had become the love of his life.

Trent felt a headache coming on. His mother was right. When it came to women, his judgment was faulty, so what difference did it make who he married? He'd run out of chances to choose his own wife. And he had been brutally burned by the only woman he thought he cared for and could trust.

This afternoon, when Kate had boarded the boat, he'd been freshly hit by her beauty—and her betrayal. And when his treacherous body had noticed her sexually, he was angered at himself even more. He still wanted her in his bed, his traitorous, beautiful Kate, even though her duplicity had cut him like the sharpest of blades.

He shoved his hand through his hair. Hell, she had never really been his—in bed, yes, but not in heart. It had all been a horrible game on her part. What she did to him tore him up inside. Even his dreams wouldn't let him forget her—but he couldn't think about her now.

On the walk through the yacht with Cecilia, he'd considered the idea of letting the company go, and the thought sent defeat rippling through him.

"Is something bothering you, Trent?" Cecilia broke into his thoughts.

"No." Getting quite good at lying, he steered her by her elbow. "I wanted to find a quiet place for us to talk. Will my cabin be all right with you?"

Her eyes lit up. "You never asked me to your cabin before." She swayed. He suspected more from drinking than the rocking of the yacht. Both were under the influence of alcohol. Planning to ask her to make the most important decision of their lives, might not be the wisest thing to do at the moment.

Perhaps they could come to an agreement and make a marriage work for both of them. He'd explain the marriage would be a business deal. They would sleep together to have children. He'd be upfront with her that he didn't love her, and she couldn't expect that he ever would.

All the happiness he thought he might have had with Kate lay like trampled dirt on a construction site. He had to forget her. She had used him, tricked him, lied to him.

"*Actress,*" he swore under his breath.

"What did you say?" Cecilia asked.

Trent shook his head. "Nothing." He refused to think of Kate now. She had to be wiped from his life, his heart.

He and Cecilia would have the children his grandfather and mother wanted so desperately. Then perhaps they could live separate lives. Would she go along with that arrangement? He didn't think so as she seemed the clingy type. That would leave his entire family and her happy—everyone except him. If he downed more whiskey, would this sound more palatable?

Trent stopped at the galley and said to Beasley, "Send champagne and two glasses to my cabin, plus another bottle of whiskey."

Beasley raised a gray eyebrow.

Trent ignored the little man and led Cecilia to his large stateroom where a crewmember set up the champagne before departing.

Trent offered Cecilia a chair at the table. After handing her a glass of champagne, he sat down on the bed. "Do you have any idea why I brought you here? I've been thinking it's time I got married."

Cecilia giggled and acted a little too giddy for his tastes. "And you want me? Your mother said from the beginning that eventually you'd come around and would marry me."

Anger sizzled inside him at how much his family interfered in his life. He looked at Cecilia. She was attractive, but he realized he had not an ounce of desire for her.

However, he needed to take control of his company. *They'd all* pushed him toward this. He felt like a bastard. Cecilia deserved better than this.

His thoughts rushed back to Kate up on the deck, a woman who definitely deserved less. Damn. He hadn't even decided what to do about Kate. Let her go after tonight without punishment? And if she had to be punished to learn a lesson, did he want to be the one to administer that punishment, strike back at her to make her feel a little of the pain that he felt? But if that involved getting too close could he keep his hands off her?

Cecilia moved to the bed, threw her arms around his neck and pressed her lips to his cheek. Not only did this not feel right, he hadn't yet told Cecilia what type of marriage this would be. He pulled away.

She laid her hand on his thigh. "We can stay together tonight. No need to wait. *I love you.*"

He sobered. "Hold on. We're still discussing this. Did you say *love*? If we do marry, you understand it's for convenience—for both of us. I'd pay your family's debts and you…" He looked down into Cecilia's hopeful face and felt nothing for her, except compassion. She deserved a better marriage than the one he offered.

"If we were to go through with this," he said flatly. "You have to know up front—I don't love you." He felt a dull ache of foreboding. He wanted to tell her he was sorry—that this wasn't going to work.

She smiled rather brilliantly. "For now, I'm not worried about you loving me. I'll be *Mrs. Trenton* Farrington. I want a huge diamond ring, and for the wedding dress, I know just the designer in Paris…"

As she rattled off more demands, Trent felt the noose tightening around his neck. *Holy hell, what was he getting himself into…?*

* * *

The yacht glided down the Intracoastal Waterway on the way home. Kate's hands clenched on the railing, she watched the sunset on the horizon and the rippling dark waves. The breeze was chilly now, so she had slipped on her light jacket. This had to be 'up there' as one of the worst days in her life. She loved Trent, but to maintain control of the company, he was going to appease his grandfather.

Feeling wretched, Kate listened to James Farrington's voice travel in the air as he told stories about the company, the Farrington family, and especially Trent. Trent had been loved and that was so far from her own experiences as a child, without her mother to protect her. Trent would never have understood what she had to deal with growing up with her stepfather, and that she hadn't had a choice of parents.

Kate bit her lip. She was tempted to find Trent and to beg him not to marry Cecilia, but she knew he wouldn't care about her opinion now. Reluctantly, she turned from the railing. Trent's grandfather, Mrs. Farrington, and Frank Blake relaxed close by in the outdoor lounge area.

"James, I don't like that particular part of your story," Eden grumbled. "You make it sound like I deserted Trent."

"You *are* his mother."

"I knew Trent was in good hands with you, James. He needed a father figure."

Kate kept glancing toward the doorway to see if Trent and Cecilia were returning.

Frank reached over and patted Eden's hand as she sat beside him. "I'm sure Eden was a good mother to that boy, which is what I think of him, James. He doesn't have the experience to control this company."

James raised a wrinkled brow. "Of course, he seems young from your age or mine, Frank, but Trent's thirty-two, with enormous business sense. We're proud of him. I was younger than him when I took over. Of course, I was married and settled down. I don't go for all this carousing and living together that young people do these days. A man and a woman need to bond for life." James glanced at Kate. "Why don't you join us, dear? You seem restless."

Kate neared the table. "Mr. Farrington! Why would you sell? You know how much Trent loves the company," she said, surprising herself as she blurted out the words.

Just at that moment, Trent and Cecilia neared the entrance to the back deck. Kate's face heated. If he had overheard her sticking up for him, he didn't acknowledge it.

Was he going to marry Cecilia? She didn't get a chance to analyze the couple walking toward her when Mr. Farrington gasped. He flattened his hand on his chest and fell back in his chair.

Kate rushed to him. "Mr. Farrington…?"

"Pressure…here," he gasped. He placed his hand over his heart.

"Oh, dear," Eden cried.

Trent strode up to Kate's side. "What's going on?"

Kate shook her head and leaned over the elderly man. "I don't know. Perhaps a heart attack?" She loosened James's collar. "Mr. Farrington, are you all right?"

Clutching his heart, his grandfather managed to sit up. "Whew. I was a little lightheaded for a moment, but I… I'm better now."

"Lightheaded?" Trent growled. He turned and strode to the intercom. "Captain," he barked, "return home—now." He glanced at his grandfather. "Or should we dock somewhere else and get an ambulance?"

"Stop. I'm fine, Trent. Don't worry about your old, decrepit grandfather." Under his breath, he muttered, "*or the future of this family*." In a louder voice, he said, "It's probably just indigestion."

"Indigestion, my ass," Trent muttered.

Frowning, Kate gave Mr. Farrington a sideways glance. Moments before, the elderly man had seemed perfectly fine. Only when Trent and Cecilia were heading their way—and James must have seen them—had he had his episode.

"Trent," Mr. Farrington said, "just get me home."

"If you think you're all right…" Trent's brow furrowed as he gave his grandfather a long, hard look. "But tomorrow you're seeing your doctor."

"I'll do that." James nodded. "Just for you, Trent. Now, don't worry about me."

Kate noted that the elderly man's lips curved slightly. *Was he using his illness to manipulate his grandson?* Perplexed, she stopped hovering over him and sat down at the table.

"If everything is fine with James, Trent, why don't you and Cecilia join us?" Eden asked. She looked radiant, probably because her son had spent time with her chosen daughter-in-law-to-be.

Jealousy spiraled inside Kate. Would this evening ever end? She wanted to go home. She wanted to forget Trent and how much his pairing with Cecilia tore at her insides.

"Well, grandson, do you have news to cheer up an old sick man?" James asked.

"I do," Trent said, while Cecilia clung to his elbow. He wasn't slurring his words, but Kate thought he might have had too much to drink tonight. She hoped he wouldn't make a stupid decision to pacify his grandfather.

Trent extricated his arm from Cecilia's tight grip. She obviously didn't want to let him go. "And it might surprise you all."

Flicking a glance toward Kate, Trent strode to stand behind her chair. He placed his hands on her shoulders, sending a wary chill through her. Her eyes widened. *What was he up to?*

"We spoke about this before, didn't we Kate?" he said in a cool voice. "But we wanted to surprise you all. I can tell by all your faces that we have succeeded. Don't you think so, *sweetheart?*" Trent gave her shoulder a little pinch and smiled at everyone. "Kate and I are planning to be married."

Speechless, Kate gaped over her shoulder at him.

"What are you saying?" Cecilia sputtered. "I thought…you and me."

Kate rose from her chair. What was he talking about? He couldn't stand the sight of her. After having spent a weekend of making love with him, she knew he was not looking at her with tenderness or even kindness. There wasn't any forgiveness in his face either.

"Excuse us," she said through tight lips.

No way was he going to use her just to keep his company. She would get off this boat, even if she had to jump off and swim.

He must have seen she was half thinking about running for it.

He took her elbow. She hated herself for the way heat spiraled through her at his touch. She didn't want to feel anything for him, knowing the way he thought of her.

"Yes, excuse us for a moment," he said, glaring down into her eyes. "We have a few things to discuss, don't we, *sweetheart?*" He gave her a grim smile, without any humor.

Kate clenched her teeth. As much as she liked the idea of running, she thought dryly, the water was too cold and she wasn't the best swimmer. With a resigned sigh, she allowed him to lead her away—still virtually, his captive.

Once they were out of sight, he dropped her arm as if she were something too hot to handle.

She whirled on him. "What's this about? You abhor me. *Have you lost your mind?*"

"That's the point. I'm not crazy. This is about revenge."

Tears burned the backs of her eyes. She'd had enough. "Now you want to *marry me* to get *even* with me?"

"Not a chance," he said, crossing his arms over his chest. "Do you think I want to tie myself to someone like you, but this will be your payment to me, princess. You owe me for not hauling you off to jail. Although I do appreciate your sincere comment to my grandfather about me loving the company." He rolled his eyes.

She raised her chin. So he had overheard. "I meant that. But I won't marry you under these circumstances."

"Ah, but you were willing to before?"

"I wasn't trying to trap you into marriage! But you won't listen—"

Backing her against a railing, he put both hands on either side of her, trapping her with his body. "You were hotter in the sack than any woman I've ever met. You were after something."

He must have thought better of being so close to her because then he swore under his breath and stepped back. "Listen, I only intend for us to have a short engagement, just long enough to prove to my grandfather that I don't need to be married to have a stable enough life to run the company."

"*You'd lie to your grandfather?* And with what you think of me, why should *I* agree to do this? And you think I'm a liar. What makes you also think I'll keep my word if I agree to this?"

He raised a dark eyebrow. "Because I hold the upper hand in this case. 'Pretend engagement' or jail… It shouldn't be a hard choice." Then he nodded toward the lounge area at the back of the boat. "Now let's go and give the best performance of our lives and pretend we're a happy couple."

"You're unbelievable, and you think I'm a scammer," she muttered.

Gritting her teeth, she followed him back to the table. Cecilia was not there, and neither was Eden or Blake.

"Eden's consoling Cecilia down below." Trent's grandfather waved them over to sit with him. "The girl thought you were going to marry her, but I'm happy with your choice."

They sat. Trent put his arm around Kate and squeezed her shoulders. She frowned up at him. Damn that wasn't gentle—he'd obviously intended for the squeeze to be too hard. When he forced a smile toward her face, her heart shredded. She returned a weak smile of her own, still very aware of how much he despised her.

Trent secured Kate's hand in his. "We're engaged. She just has to pick out a ring to make it official."

Frank strode onto the deck. "Cecilia is taking this badly."

"Sorry to hear that," James said, raising his glass of ice water in salute. "But I have happy news. Trent and Kate will be married." He smiled. "So Frank, it looks like I won't be selling to you after all."

"What?" Blake sputtered. "B-but—"

"As soon as the nuptials take place, I'm turning the company over to Trent. Now if Trent reneges on the wedding, I'll sell to you Blake. You have my word that we'll sit down and negotiate a deal."

Blake's tanned face reddened as if his head would explode.

Kate glanced at Trent. On the exterior, he appeared calm, but his hand tightened on hers. His grandfather's face seemed to say 'Don't bamboozle a bamboozler.'

James calmly turned to Kate. "I couldn't be happier that you'll be my granddaughter-in law. You may call me *grandpa* now, dear. I'll arrange for a minister to perform the ceremony in two weeks."

"We don't want to rush things," Trent said. He looked to Kate for support.

"Yes, Mr. Farrington...*grandpa*. I'd love a big wedding...but one like that takes time. Uh, I'll need a good six months, or perhaps a year to plan."

"I never believed in long engagements. You made the decision. Now, go through with the marriage. Trent, make an honest woman out of this lovely young woman before someone else does."

Kate's face heated. Obviously, there weren't many secrets around Mr. Farrington. Did he know about their weekend in Key West?

Under her lashes, she glanced at Trent. Had he thought with his grandfather being so sick that they might not have to take this step if the engagement was a long one? He'd said he planned to take back the proposal once he proved to his grandfather that he could run the company without a wife...

Trent's plan for a long engagement had backfired. He returned a shuttered gaze and squeezed Kate's hand. "My lovely bride-to-be and I have a few more issues to discuss. Come with me, *sweetheart*."

With her hand clasped tightly in his, they once again returned to the railing on the other side of the yacht. He released his grasp immediately, indicating that holding her hand had only been for show.

"I know what we can do," she said in an excited whisper as the thought occurred to her. "We'll stage a fight just before the wedding. I'll break it off. Then he can't blame you."

Trent shook his head and scowled. "No. As wonderful as your *acting* skills are, and as good as you are at *conning* people, he'll still blame me."

She narrowed her eyes. "You don't have to get nasty. I was trying to help."

"We may have to go through with this wedding. It might be the only way."

"No," she said, shaking her head in disbelief. "You *hate* me. Marry Cecilia."

"Unfortunately, you're the only one I can divorce. I don't want to *hurt* Cecilia."

"But me?"

He gave her a look that crushed her. "You can't be hurt. You have no feelings."

Her throat seemed to close and tears sprang up in her eyes. "No, Trent, I *do* have feelings. I'm not what you think, and you can't force me to marry you just to use me. I won't do it."

"Oh, no?" He backed her against the railing. "I'll have you prosecuted, starting tomorrow. It's a serious crime practicing as a doctor when you aren't one."

The blood drained from her face. "But I want to be a psychologist. I plan to finish. This would destroy any chance for a career…"

He glanced away. "You're right. You'll never get your real license. And you've been in trouble before. It won't look good for you with the police."

"*You'd do that to me?* You'd ruin my life?" she rasped.

"Kate, you had no qualms about using me in the worst way a woman can use a man—and I need to use you now. Fair's fair. To keep me from being fleeced, you'll sign a prenuptial agreement. Look, I'll throw in $200,000 for each year of marriage. You couldn't make that anywhere else—*honestly.*" She stiffened at his dig. "You'll be well-paid for your services." He flung it like an insult.

Her cheeks stung in return, and her legs nearly gave out. "With the way that you feel about me, I won't sleep with you."

He grabbed her arm to hold her up. "Ah, you mistook my meaning, princess. Look, as delectable as I might have found you before I knew what you were, I've no intention of sleeping with you again either. You're safe from me."

"How long would this marriage last?" she croaked.

"As short as possible—and two years at the most—just to make it look legitimate. Then we'll divorce. That's all I'm asking."

Her shoulders slumped in defeat. Two years with a man who hated her? A man she loved... He really planned to go through with this. How would she stand being near him? She had cared for him and each day he'd be tearing her apart more and more.

"When we finally get a divorce, how will you break the news to your grandfather?" she finally choked out.

"He's so ill... I hope he makes it, but when the time comes, I'll tell him we're not getting along. I'll also confide in him that you'd previously had a hysterectomy without telling me until after we were married. Believe me, he'll be glad we're divorcing if he thinks you can't have children."

She rolled her eyes. "Nice. He'll hate me, too. And I never thought you could be so ruthless and heartless."

He shrugged. "Sometimes it's necessary. In exchange, I'll let you go with all your good qualities intact." He released her arm and let his gaze rove over her body as if she were something reprehensible. "You're used to con schemes. This should be easy money for you."

"I hate you." She didn't mean what she said. She loved him, but anger caused her words to slip out.

"The feeling is mutual," he said as he turned to go back to the lounge area.

The blood drained from her face because she knew *he meant it.*

CHAPTER TWENTY

A week later, Trent called Kate to his office. "For appearances sake, we'll take a weeklong trip out of town," he suggested.

She frowned, surprised he'd want to be anywhere near her.

At her raised eyebrows, he added, "*Not together.*"

Her shoulders drooped. "Of course."

"And after lunch, I've scheduled an appointment for us with my attorney."

They met at his lawyer's office for the meeting regarding their prenuptial agreement for this marriage that he'd blackmailed her into.

Even though Trent had suggested she should have her own representation, she shook her head. "I don't have an attorney. I'll sign away my right to one."

"I can get one of my partners down the hall to represent you," his lawyer said. Another lawyer was quickly brought into the room.

Glancing at the contract, Kate frowned when her gaze fell on a certain line in the agreement.

"Yeah, that's right," Trent said. "If anything should happen to me, my assets will be split between charities and my family—not you."

Tired of his constant attempts to hurt her and his accusations against her character, she shrugged numbly. She didn't care about making money. However, if Trent died and Roland was in line to inherit money, there was more reason for Roland to make that happen—at Trent's expense.

"Here's what you get." Trent pointed to a line in the contract. "You'll receive $200,000 for each year—upon the breakup of the marriage."

Kate jerked her head toward Trent's attorney. "Mr. Smith, please strike that sentence. I don't want *any money* allocated for me in the prenup."

Trent raised a skeptical eyebrow. "She'll take it. Of course she wants the clause."

She clamped her arms over her chest. "No," she insisted, "I don't."

"Could we have a moment alone?" Trent asked the attorneys.

After the lawyers left the room, so they could settle their dispute, Trent grumbled, "I'm not insisting on this for your sake, Kate. My attorney said if you don't take something in the agreement, it might invalidate the prenuptial."

"Oh," she said her shoulders sagging. "But really, I don't want anything from you." He cast her a suspicious glance. Damn him. He wanted to think the worst of her, so let him. "Then when this farce is over, Trent, I'm going to give the money to the Children in Crisis Center."

"Right," he said, rolling his eyes.

She blew out an exasperated breath. "If you don't believe me, suit yourself." She skimmed through the prenuptial. "Thank you for the *future* donation to the Center," she said firmly as she signed on the signature line. "They can always use the money for the children."

And Trent had his ironclad agreement so she couldn't fleece him—that was what he thought of her character.

* * *

A week later, the weekend after Thanksgiving, the wedding ceremony was to be held in a small chapel.

Kate hadn't slept any the night before, so her skin looked pasty white when she'd looked into the mirror that morning and applied makeup. The blush didn't help. Instead, it seemed garish against the pretty ivory cocktail-length dress and her pale face, so she wiped off most of the makeup.

Before the ceremony, Trent's grandfather seemed concerned when he took in her appearance. He patted her hand. "Come on, honey, smile. I promise you that you and my grandson will be good together. You'll have lots of babies, too."

She mustered up a smile for his sake, but guilt ground into her stomach at the deceit they played on him by going ahead with this sham of a marriage.

Kate couldn't stop trembling as she stood beside her soon-to-be husband. Darcy and Greg stood in as their best man and maid of honor. Since Kate didn't have family, a private affair was fine with her. However, this wasn't the wedding of her dreams where love flowed between a man and a woman.

In Trent's family, only James and his Aunt Vera sat in the pews.

Although Mrs. Farrington wanted Cecilia for Trent's bride, Kate couldn't believe she wouldn't attend her only child's wedding. However, Eden came in at the last minute and sat in the back row of the church.

Kate met Trent at the front of the church. He wore a dark suit and looked incredibly handsome. Instead of devotion, her groom gave her a cool glance as if he despised her, and she nearly began to cry again.

Her fingers were stiff and cold when he took her hand in his warm palm. He smelled so good, and all male. From his shuttered gaze, she couldn't tell if he was nervous too. After the vows, he kissed her—she knew for appearances' sake. He pressed his warm lips to her cold ones just long enough to satisfy his grandfather. But this wasn't real and she thought she might cry. If Trent had ever had any feelings for her, they had crystallized to disgust.

Swallowing the despair that threatened to overwhelm her, she lifted her chin and walked out of the chapel ahead of Trent who assisted his grandfather.

* * *

After the tiny wedding reception at James Farrington's mansion, she drove alone to Key West and spent the next agonizing week alone in a hotel that Trent had booked for her. She spent most of her time wondering where her new husband was and if he thought of her at all.

Thankfully, he'd chosen a hotel on the newer part of the island for her. To stay where they had once made reckless love would have been excruciatingly painful. Perhaps, on his part, he didn't want her to dwell on their weekend at the older Victorian hotel either.

She had no idea where he went for the week. Trent was, after all, her employer—which was how he treated her now—not as any loving husband would.

During her stay in Key West, she made two decisions. The first was no matter what happened, she wouldn't lie to him ever again. The second, she'd make the most of her time left with the company, and track down the saboteur. If not Roland, her other instincts pointed to Frank Blake.

Had Blake given up trying to buy the company now that she and Trent were married and it looked like he would take control? Now, with the hope of heirs, it was unlikely James Farrington would sell, no matter how many times Blake tried to wreck the company's reputation. So maybe his scare tactics would cease. Perhaps Trent thought the same.

Since the wedding, the only contact she had with him was an email to ask her if she'd arrived at the hotel and that he wanted her to email him everyday to let him know her status. For a moment, she'd thought he might care just a bit, but then reality set in. He was probably protecting her as his investment.

On her return drive from the Florida Keys to Fort Lauderdale, Kate wondered if Trent would allow her to remain in her own house. If only she could go to her own home, she thought she could begin to heal from the devastating pain that she'd brought on herself.

Or would he think it necessary for her to live somewhere near him to maintain their front? Hopefully not. Her emotions were too raw, and it was better for her if she saw him as little as possible. She was sure he'd want it that way, too.

With the week up, she hadn't tried to call to let him know she was on her return to Fort Lauderdale. And since he hadn't made other suggestions on her living arrangements, she pulled into her driveway, assuming she'd be staying in her own home.

The only thing good about the situation was he had said before she'd left for the trip that she could keep working in the offices. Of course, even if he stayed out of her face, she was sure he'd watch her every move. He didn't trust her enough to leave her alone.

* * *

On her first day back at the office, wearing her frumpiest brown suit, thick glasses and tight bun, Kate sat at her desk and opened her briefcase.

Darcy strode through the doorway. "I'm glad to see you. I'd say something about your appearance—but I don't think you need to hear it from me."

Kate nodded. "Thanks."

"I thought you might have skipped town—permanently."

Kate shrugged. "I wanted to leave. Thought about it, too," she said with a wane smile.

"Did you tell Trent everything?"

"I haven't seen him since the wedding. He refused to listen to me."

Kate hated to admit even to Darcy that she had tried at the small reception, when they'd had a moment alone on their wedding day. Trent was in a bad mood the entire day. He put his finger on her lips. "I don't want to hear one word." He had turned and walked away.

Kate's cheeks burned at the memory that he thought she was nothing but a liar. She began checking her emails. "I'm sure I must have a lot of work to do after being away." Trent had given her back her duties, but any decisions she made had to be under his complete supervision.

"He came back to the office on Friday. Are you going to be all right?" Darcy asked.

"Yeah, sure," Kate replied in a low voice.

Trent strode through the door. "Of course she's going to be all right, Darcy. And I need to talk to her…*alone.*"

Putting her hands on her hips, Darcy whirled on Trent, surprising Kate. "She's not anything like what you think she is."

"It's okay, Darcy," Kate said. "I don't need anyone to stand up for me."

Darcy marched out of the room.

Trent looked as handsome as ever in a dark suit and just as unforgiving as the last time she saw him. "I thought you would at least keep the reason for our marriage between us."

Taking a deep breath, Kate dropped her gaze to his gray tie. There was no point in seeing the hatred she was sure she'd find there if she looked.

She picked up the file on her desk and opened it. "Darcy guessed something was wrong. I couldn't keep this from her."

Kate didn't elaborate further. She had broken down in tears after the reception. How could she *not* tell Darcy? Darcy had been the one to help her pull herself back together. During her week in Key West, Kate had finally accepted the marriage for what it was—a marriage done because he needed a pawn for a wife.

"You're not to tell anyone else, Kate. Is that clear?"

Still not looking at his face, she gave him a curt nod. "If that is your wish." She had no one else she wanted to tell, and it was too humiliating anyway.

"That's what I *expect.*" Trent handed her an envelope. "I'm dropping off your copy of the prenuptial agreement."

Signing the papers had seemed a million years ago. "Thank you."

She waited for him to leave, but when he didn't, she raised her eyes. "Yes? Now what else can I do for you?"

"How was your honeymoon?" he asked.

"Fabulous," she quipped. "And yours?"

"Just great. Couldn't have been better."

"Where did you go?" she asked. She could have bitten her tongue. "Never mind." She turned to her computer screen. "I shouldn't have asked. It's none of my business."

"It's not like you ever really cared, Kate." She opened her mouth to say she had, but the look on his face stopped her. He added, "I'd never believe you now."

"If you think I'm such a liar," she said with exasperation, "then why aren't you leaving my office? I've done my part."

"There might be a little more you have to do for me. And I'm paying you well."

Heat flooded her cheeks. He intended to insult her—again. "I told you I don't want your money. None of it." Then she gasped. "That is unless you don't plan to pay me a salary for working here..." Perhaps he'd reap his revenge in another way, by causing her to lose her house. *He couldn't.* Her spirits plummeted. *He just might.*

She would look for a job elsewhere if he did not plan to pay her. There was nothing in their agreement saying she had to stay here and work...but it could take weeks to find something else, and she'd gone through most of her savings. It was a sure thing that he wouldn't give her a good reference.

Tears pricked her eyes. "I do need to make enough money to cover my car payment and my mortgage. I don't want to lose my home. I've worked hard to make the payments," she said in a rush of words. "You don't hate me enough that you'd do that to me, do you?"

"I have every reason to want revenge, Kate, but hold on. You'll get your salary, and I'm not criticizing you over the prenuptial money either. I have something I want you to do. Your first acting job as my wife has come up. Wednesday, I'm up for an award by the state. Seven p.m." He wrote on a piece of paper and handed it to her. "Here's the address of the hotel. I think it's best if you meet me there."

Kate realized that he didn't even want to pick her up and arrive with her. Perhaps he thought she wasn't even worthy of that courtesy. She held back her tears and built a wall around her emotional self. After all, she'd had years of practice. She had to cut her feelings for him from her heart. Their relationship was strictly a business one as he'd reminded her time after time.

With the sting of this latest insult, she raised her chin and tried to put some lightness in her voice. "As you order. I'm your employee—I'll be there."

"Good, but only after you go shopping. You're done with your *disguised act* and wearing those frumpy, old-maid clothes."

She made a frustrated sound. "These are my clothes. They're no act."

"Right," he scoffed. "Now go shopping and buy yourself some clothes for someone worthy of being a Farrington—even if you're not."

Gasping, she rose to her feet. "You're insulting me again."

"You work for me personally now, Kate. You're *acting* as my wife. I'm not asking much, and I want to see you in a new wardrobe. Is that clear?"

She clenched her hands. "Yes, you are *very clear*, and I'm not happy to be told what to do at every instance."

"I'm not happy about this arrangement either."

She stamped her foot. "But you're the one who made it. You could have married Cecilia and been as happy as two clams in a clamshell."

Ignoring her statement, he handed her a credit card. "I'll make arrangements for you to have your own account—with limitations, but I'll be generous."

Of course, he didn't trust her with limitless funds. "Thanks, but no thanks. I told you I don't want your money. I'll buy anything I need from my salary."

"Oh, come on, Kate, cut the crap. You signed the prenuptial agreement with just a token protest, for affect. You might fool others, however, I know you for the con artist you are."

"Do you, Trent? I came to the company to find out who caused my brother's death. That's all."

"Now, you've lied to me again. Matt Jackson was your *stepbrother*. I read it last week in one of the reports that you were related."

Her face burned that Trent was still having her investigated. "Matt was my *brother*."

"And you write a column in the local newspaper, which you didn't tell me about. And one article was about rich men getting away with murder and the injustice." Her throat went dry and he went on, "So you came to the company to set a trap for me, Kate? Great job."

"I didn't set a trap, Trent. I did think…at the time…that you *were* guilty, and I wanted evidence, but I soon realized you weren't the one—"

"Spare me," he said, putting up a stopping hand. "You even slept with your suspect. While I am sorry that Matt Jackson died at this company, I don't buy that you cared about your stepbrother that much. I think you thought the company was a good place to work one of your con jobs, and once you got here and realized how hot my family was to marry me off—"

"That's not true at all."

"Listen, I've had more experience with gold-diggers than any man should have. Now, take the card. You can't afford the kind of clothing you'll need as my wife."

"There's no way I can prove to you…" She whirled away from him. "Oh, you'll never believe me… I'm not taking your card."

He blew out a deep breath. "Don't make a big deal out of this. Most women would love to go shopping with a man's credit card. Of course, you're not like most women are you? Most women don't have an arrest record or have to falsify documents to get hired by a company."

She wanted to smack him, but he was right. Her shoulders sagged in defeat. "I'll take the card."

"Also, my mother suggested Marc drive you to certain shops on Las Olas, so you'll know where to go."

Kate gaped at him in disbelief. "I can't believe your mother thought of me?"

"She'll want you to be dressed to her standards."

"Of course," Kate muttered. "You're right. With the way your mother wanted you to marry Cecilia, she'd more likely want the man to drive me out of town. If you give me the addresses of the stores, I can drive myself. I wouldn't want to embarrass your mother wearing something that wouldn't be up to her *standards*."

"It's for your safety, too. While nothing else has happened— and maybe OSHA is right that the cables were weakened from an accident with chemicals—we're not positive someone isn't sabotaging the company or trying to harm one of us. Now that you're a Farrington, it might be a good idea for you to go with my mother's driver as you'll be in and out of the stores."

A small part of her buoyed that he might care for her safety, which meant there might be a chance for them. She raised a hopeful face and met his rigid expression and any thoughts of reconciliation sank like a stone.

He stared down at her. "Don't ever make the mistake of thinking I care and that I'll fall for your schemes again, Kate. I'm only doing this show for my grandfather, because I *care* for him and I want him to retire."

Kate plucked the card from his hand. "Then why try to protect me? If I die, you'd get your wish. You'd be single again. Your grandfather wouldn't be able to complain." Then realizing what she'd said, she flushed and frowned unhappily. "Maybe I shouldn't give you any ideas."

"I don't want you hurt."

"Are you sure? You could've surprised me."

"Kate, are you pregnant?" he asked her with a pointed look. "I didn't use protection a couple of times." When a hot gleam flashed in his eyes, her entire body burned with desire as she remembered the intimacy and passion of their weekend together.

Her shoulders tensing, she met his gaze. "No," she whispered. "You don't have to worry about being permanently trapped with me. You're safe from my grasping claws."

"In spite of everything," he said softly. "I would have taken care of you and the baby. Thank you for telling me."

He walked out of her office.

At the possibility of what could have been between them, and what was now ruined, her cheeks flamed and more tears pricked at her eyes.

CHAPTER TWENTY-ONE

The hotel was one of the oldest and finest in Fort Lauderdale. Expansive glass windows overlooked a crimson sunset and the New River. Yachts paraded by, whooshing waves against the seawalls. People strolled down the brick path along the waterway, where numerous boats of all sizes were docked.

Dressed in a tuxedo, Trent proceeded up the steps and into the ballroom for the Award's Ceremony. Soft music filled the air.

His mother had already entered and looked well in a blue evening gown. Trent's stomach tightened in a knot. Would she be proud of him tonight if he won? He didn't want to care, but never having pleased her, he found that he wanted some sort of gesture that she was happy with his success.

His grandfather leaned on his cane and hobbled across the floor toward Trent. Worry swept through him. He strode to the older man's side, afraid his grandfather would overdo it tonight.

"Hello, Trent. I might seem weak and feeble," his grandfather muttered, seeming to read Trent's mind, "but I'll make it."

Trent took his arm. "Let me help you."

"If you must," his grandfather said with a sigh. "Actually, I should thank you. You're a good grandson in my time of need."

Eden trailed behind them. "If you're this bad, James, we could have brought you in a wheelchair, but for your pride you'd risk a fall. We'd all be devastated if something happened to you."

His grandfather grunted. "Would you, Eden? Trent, help me to the table and don't make any big deal about me needing help. Just pretend I twisted my ankle," he added sarcastically.

The last thing his proud grandfather would want was to appear weak. "Sounds dainty of you," Trent said with a chuckle, "but I understand." He shouldered the elderly man past the tables displaying the building models up for the award, to a reserved, white linen-covered table near the podium. Aunt Vera sat waiting.

Trent settled the man into a chair. "Hello, Aunt Vera."

His grandfather turned to his daughter. "Where's, Roland?"

Trent's timid aunt blushed and her blue eyes paused on Trent. "Sorry, father...Trent. Roland said he might not be able to make it here tonight."

"Ah hah, Roland, can't make it for his cousin's big night." His grandfather threw Trent a glance. "There was a time when being in this family meant something."

"I'm not bothered if he's not here, Aunt Vera," Trent replied, kissing her cheek. Matter of fact, he preferred that his cousin wasn't here. Roland had always been a pain in the ass and jealous—even more so now that Trent was officially president of the company.

His grandfather pointed to the two chairs next to his. "Trent, you sit there, and then save this seat between us for your lovely wife. By the way, where is Kate? In the powder room?"

"No. She wanted to drive separately. She should be here soon." He hated to lie to his grandfather, but he had to follow through with this farce.

When he'd last seen Kate in her office, after their separate honeymoons, he found himself far too attracted to her, in spite of the ridiculously baggy and unattractive suit she'd worn—because he knew exactly what she hid under the outfit. He'd thought it best to avoid being alone with her as much as possible.

He'd been angered, too, for she'd had a rosy glow on her face as if she'd spent time outdoors, while at his honeymoon destination he had worked hard on business—and on forgetting her. Her radiance was obvious proof he alone had suffered for her deceit.

His grandfather gave Trent a shrewd glance. "In my day, we escorted our wives to such events."

Trent glanced at his watch. "Kate had some errands and was running late," he lied. "She insisted I drive on ahead of her." He wouldn't be surprised if she didn't show up after his dictatorial demand about how she should dress.

Disobeying his first order? Hell, he probably deserved it after his treatment of her that day. He'd never treat a *real* wife as he had her, but he had wanted...to do what? Hurt her? For the way she tore him up on the inside?

Mayor Smith ambled into the ballroom with a few guests.

Behind him, Kate stepped through the doors. Trent sucked in his breath. She gave the true meaning to the term "drop-dead gorgeous." As she stepped down the stairs, she dazzled the eye in a shimmering red gown. Her blond hair was partially swept up. Nothing about her beauty simulated the hardened criminal she truly was.

Her gaze met his from across the room. Even though he knew she was good at disguises, and this was but another one that hid the negative, something like electricity still sizzled between them.

He strode to meet her and took her hand. She looked entirely too beautiful and sexy with a fair amount of her breasts plumped up for his view.

Though he hadn't wanted to flatter her, he couldn't stop himself. "You look lovely."

She smiled hesitantly. "Sorry, I'm late. The transformation took some time."

With everyone looking on, Trent leaned in and kissed her cheek. He instantly regretted the move because when he inhaled her floral scent, desire rushed to his groin.

He took a step back. "I assure you the result was well worth the time."

She gave him a weak smile. "Thank you. You look handsome tonight, yourself."

"I tried to call you this afternoon, but you didn't pick up."

"Oh? I must have been busy getting ready and missed your call. Sorry."

As he escorted her across the floor to their table, every man in the room stared at her. Jealousy rippled through him—the power of it shocking him. He had to get a grip. She was his temporary wife, by his own fault. He slid his gaze over the large diamond earrings dangling from her earlobes. "I see you didn't have any problems spending my money," he said dryly.

Her eyes widened. "But you told me to."

He sighed. "You're right. I did."

She blew out a deep breath that sounded like relief. "By the way, the jewelry is imitation. You always think the worst of me."

"I have good reason."

"I'm not a gold-digger. I told you why I came to the company. I wanted to find out who was responsible for Matt's fall and have justice served."

"I'm not convinced, Kate. He was your stepbrother."

"Matt was my *brother*, and I loved him. I wanted whoever caused his death to be caught. I still want that."

"Kate, how many times was your stepfather sent to prison for fraud?"

A frown etched her forehead. "He has nothing to do with this...or me."

He shrugged. "Why should I believe you? Like father like daughter. You were prosecuted. Let's just hope you can play the devoted wife as well as you can take an order to spend money."

Her face paled.

Trent blew out a deep breath. "I apologize. You don't deserve that either. You've done everything that I've asked." He held out his hand and guided her toward their table.

Eden flicked her discriminating gaze over Kate. "At least you had the sense to dress for the occasion."

Kate's hand tightened in Trent's.

His mother thought he'd foolishly fallen for Kate, in spite of what the two of them knew about her. He didn't have any guilt for not telling Eden the truth now. She shouldn't have interfered in his life. He'd have words with her later and tell her that she was to treat Kate with respect.

He realized then, and was astounded that in spite of what she'd done to him, he wasn't going to let anyone, including his mother be unkind to Kate. It seemed only *he* could be the one to cut her down...

His grandfather snorted and held out his arms to his new granddaughter-in-law. "She looks more than nice, Eden. I thought you were a movie star come to grace our table, Kate. So elegant tonight. Sorry, I can't get up. Give me a kiss."

She bent over and kissed his cheek. "Thank you, Mr. Farrington."

His grandfather chuckled. "*Grandpa*, remember? You remind me of someone...someone I used to know. Admit it, Eden. Kate is by far the loveliest woman in this room and in the city for that matter. Much prettier than Cecilia."

Eden's face turned into a sour grimace.

His grandfather patted the chair beside him. "Kate, take this seat. Trent, you on her other side, by your mother." Once they were all seated, James turned to Kate. "Now, how are you, my dear? I hope my grandson is treating you as you deserve." He shot a glance toward Trent.

Kate frowned. "Y-yes, of course. Our marriage is wonderful."

Trent narrowed his eyes. She wasn't too convincing. He assumed she was a better liar. Perhaps she was only a great actress when the occasion suited her. Or perhaps she was subtly undermining him to get even. That thought ground in Trent's stomach.

James chuckled. "I am pleased. There is no doubt I'll have fine great-grandchildren."

Trent sighed at his grandfather's words. The man was like a bull when he wanted something. Hopefully, his grandfather wouldn't start pushing in that area, or two years would seem an eternity.

"Leave them alone," Eden said, pursing her lips. "They're barely married, James." Trent was surprised she'd stuck up for them, but then she paused. "Frank Blake is here. I'll wave him over."

"Mother," Trent said in a low voice, "can't you see he's using you to get to the company?"

"Should we talk about *who* is being used by *whom*?" Eden snapped back near his ear.

Glad that Kate was in discussion with his grandfather, Trent leaned toward Eden and said quietly, "Blake wants the company. He'd like to ruin me. If he is hanging out with you, he has an angle. He used you years ago, and he's using you now. *Wake up.*"

"Thanks for your vote of confidence in me," Eden said through her teeth.

"I don't mean that as a put down. I don't want you hurt needlessly, and we can't trust him."

Eden gave Trent a wry look. "I think Blake has changed. Why not? People can change, can't they?"

"There's an old saying that a snake might shed a few layers of skin, but it's still a snake."

"You need to learn that lesson for yourself regarding your new bride. But no, you're making a fool of yourself. You should have married Cecilia."

Trent ground his teeth together. From Eden's point of view, she must think he was an idiot to have married Kate.

A horrible thought occurred to him. "Just don't make Blake my stepfather," he grumbled. Could his life get any worse?

His mother's mouth curved into a wry smile as if to goad him.

"Speak of the devil," Trent muttered as Frank Blake strode up to their table.

"Hello, Farringtons. One thing about being in the running for the same award is that my table is next to yours." He leaned over and kissed Eden's cheek. "Lovely as always, Eden." He turned to Trent with a smile. "You did a fine job with your design and building, Trent. I think your mother has reason to be proud of you."

Eden smirked. "A mother *should* always be happy with her child's achievements. And, Frank, you did well for yourself. If I were the judge, it would be hard for me to decide who to honor with the award."

Blake shot her a glance. "Why thank you, Eden. That's a nice compliment, coming from you."

Trent sighed, not surprised. She had never been the devoted mother. Why should tonight be any different?

His grandfather leaned back in his chair. "I'm surprised, Frank, you feel that way about Trent's design, since if he wins—you lose."

Blake shrugged. "I might not win the State's award, but I have other irons in the fire, so to speak." He turned to Kate. "Don't tell me this vision of loveliness is the new Mrs. Farrington? A quick marriage—with such haste. Will we be hearing happy news soon?"

The insinuation was obvious—that Kate was pregnant—and by the pink coloring her cheeks, Trent's stomach clenched with uncertainty. While Kate had told him that she wasn't pregnant, what if she were lying? He had learned he couldn't trust a word she said.

Kate smiled brightly and took the man's insult in stride and returned the barb. "We're hopeful that will happen soon. Trent tells me everyday how much he's looking forward to children, and a whole bunch of Farringtons to take over the company."

"That's nice, ma'am." Leaning closer to her, Blake peered into Kate's face. "Mrs. Farrington, have we met before? I wasn't sure the other day on the yacht because you wore glasses, but now I'm sure we have. Somewhere, several years ago, was it?"

The smile faded from Kate's lips and a pained expression settled on her features.

"I don't think so, sir," Kate replied in a demure voice that made Trent uneasy.

Blake tipped his head and drawled. "Oh, I think it's possible, ma'am."

At the way the man's gaze slithered over Kate in an almost obscene way, Trent wanted to grab Blake by the throat.

Was she hiding something else from him? Did she know Blake? Anger sizzled inside Trent. He would have to speak to his *faux* wife about the connection—tomorrow—as he didn't trust himself alone with her tonight.

Blake turned his attention to Eden and tapped her on the shoulder. "I hope to get the chance to dance with you this evening."

Eden beamed a smile. "That would be marvelous."

By the look on her face, Eden was enamored with Blake. Because of her unhappy relationship with Trent's father, she needed to find some happiness in her life. Tonight, Trent noticed her face was less harsh, making her more attractive.

Blake smiled at Eden. "Would you mind if I speak to Trent alone for just a moment?"

Trent raised an eyebrow. Then gritting his teeth, he rose from the table and followed Bake to an alcove on the other side of the room. "What's this about, Blake—my company or my mother?" *Or my wife*, he wanted to ask, but he was afraid to hear what Blake might have to say.

"No need to take that attitude with me. Your mother is a charming woman, but this is about the company."

Trent sighed and couldn't help being relieved. *This wasn't about Kate.* "What my mother does is her business, but I warn you, don't use her to get to Farrington Construction."

Blake placed his hand over his heart. "You think so little of me?"

"Why shouldn't I? You stole our clients and records when you left our company. And I must say I'm surprised you're here. I didn't think you'd want to witness this event that I'm going to win."

"Why not? My architects did a fine job or we wouldn't be up for the award? I realize you probably think with all the praise for your building designs that I don't stand a chance to win, but I can run a company better than you can. And what better way to become number one than to buy you out—for the right price, of course, Farrington."

Trent restrained himself from shoving Blake against the wall. "You resort to unsavory tactics in running your business. I'd never let you bring that to Farrington Construction."

"A man's got to make a profit. Even if I don't win tonight, you'll be working for me one day—I promise you. I won't mind taking over your designs."

Trent snorted. Blake gobbled up companies to make his empire grow and his tactics were ruthless. That was the reason his company now ranked number three in the state. He looked down his nose at Blake. "You forget we've dealt with your dirty tricks before. You won't get Farrington Construction. The company's not for sale."

"OSHA's on your tail. I doubt you're as clean as you profess, or why would there be so much trouble at your sites? You'll need someone like me to head the company…or your building just might not come to completion."

Trent glared at him. "Is that a threat?" He wanted to wring Blake's neck, but the mayor walked over, shook their hands and congratulated them on their projects.

* * *

While Kate watched Trent and Blake across the ballroom, she couldn't shake the sickening feeling that had settled in her stomach after Frank Blake's words to her. *Did she know Blake from somewhere?* Her stepfather had always dealt with the most unsavory characters, and this man definitely fit that bill.

And Blake did seem to want Farrington Construction badly, which would make him a prime suspect in anything going on at the company. If Trent failed because his job sites had too many accidents, Blake could benefit as the new buyer—Kate had heard of companies using unsavory business tactics. Also, Blake's hungry gaze had roved over her, revealing he was not as enamored with Eden as he acted.

Aunt Vera stood up from the table. "Excuse me. I see friends."

"Vera," James said, "while you're away, dear, why don't you give Roland another call? Tell him I said it's an order for him to get over here and support his cousin and the company."

"Roland wouldn't come anywhere near us if he didn't have to, to get his allowance," Eden retorted.

Vera blushed. "Eden, please…"

"Call him, dear," James Farrington said. "I want my family united tonight. Tell him I said that this is important."

Kate felt sorry for Trent's aunt who was mild mannered and seemed embarrassed by her son's behavior.

After Vera walked away, James turned toward Eden and lowered his voice. "After what Frank Blake did to us years ago, quitting and taking our best clients, using our company plans and undercutting us—tell me, just why *are* you seeing him?"

Eden's mouth curved into a wry smile. "You invited him on the yacht. I was sure you'd forgiven Blake when you considered selling the company to him."

"Eden, I knew Blake was hungry to buy the company, and I had to somehow convince Trent that he needed to settle down—*or else*. I want you to break it off with Blake. I don't trust him."

"Don't interfere in my life. You've done it before." Eden lifted her glass of wine. "Besides, I find Frank charming. Why shouldn't I enjoy myself?"

"Can I trust you to keep the company's business private from him?"

"Of course. Haven't I always done what you wanted?"

"*Eden*... Can I trust you in this matter?" he repeated, raising a gray brow.

Trent's mother folded her arms across her chest. "I wouldn't do anything to hurt your precious company or *our dear* Trent. He is my son and Farrington Construction is his legacy, after all."

Mrs. Farrington's gaze held ire, puzzling Kate, but at least the woman must have some love for her son, as most mothers do.

Mr. Farrington let out a deep sigh. "All right, Eden, I believe you." He smiled at Kate. "I'm sorry, dear, we're having this discussion as if you're not here. It's important Frank Blake doesn't know our company's private business."

Kate nodded in agreement. She had distrusted Blake from the first moment she'd met him on the yacht. However, since Blake's question earlier, it was impossible to get rid of this gnawing feeling in her stomach that perhaps she *had* met Blake somewhere before that event. And that couldn't be a good thing.

James patted Kate's hand. "You're going to think we're a dysfunctional family."

She gave him a weak smile. "I suppose all families have issues."

Her perception of the Farrington family *had* changed. In the beginning, she'd thought Trent had everything—family and fortune, but she now knew his family had as many issues as any other. Well, no family could ever be more dysfunctional than hers had been, but now she saw that the Farringtons were far from perfect.

"Everyone has a few skeletons in the closet," Mrs. Farrington said with dry sarcasm, her gaze landing on Kate. "Don't they, Kate? And some more than others?"

Kate's face heated. She nodded and sipped her wine to cover her blush. She supposed she should be grateful Eden hadn't told James that Kate had falsified her employment records or that her stepfather was a career criminal. She didn't want to see disgust for her in his eyes, too.

When Trent rejoined the table, Kate sighed with relief, hoping that this conversation would come to an end. However, when he sat down, his expression was stony.

"What did Blake say?" James asked Trent.

Trent blew out a deep breath. "He mentioned wanting to buy the company again. Nothing I want you to worry about. He knows we won't sell."

Kate was relieved that Trent's face softened slightly when he looked at her for an unguarded second. Whatever Blake had said had not been about her.

Eden rose from the table. "Excuse me. I'm going to mingle."

Trent's mother strolled to a woman at a nearby table. She spoke a few words, and then she walked directly to Frank Blake on the other side of the room. Placing a hand on Blake's arm, Eden threw back her head and laughed at something he said.

"Now that I have you two alone, tell me how my honeymooners are?" James asked. "Am I going to hear the pitter patter of little Farrington footsteps soon?" He wiggled his eyebrows.

"Please, don't rush us," Trent muttered.

Kate's cheeks heated. "I'd love to have children one day," she said honestly, even though she would never have babies with Trent. And she had to remember that Trent's future plan was to lie to his grandfather and say that she'd had a secret hysterectomy before they married—Trent's perfect excuse to get rid of her.

However, Trent didn't seem perturbed by her answer. He took her hand in his. Of course, the gesture was for his grandfather, but his touch sent warmth curling low within her. Kate glanced at him from beneath her lashes. He was so handsome and virile...his sensual mouth so kissable. She loved his lips. She couldn't forget what had been between them, Trent's tenderness when they'd made love. Did he ever think of those nights?

When the waiters served the salads, Trent released her hand. She sighed.

With a florid face, Roland staggered up to the table and dipped his head toward his grandfather. "Sorry." He turned to Trent. "I hope I'm not too late for this *happy* celebration." Roland's words dripped with sarcasm.

Kate inhaled a whiff of strong drink from the man.

"Roland, nice of you to support your family and the company for such an important event," James said dryly.

"You did *insist*," Roland said as he pulled out a chair at the table and sat. "I'm here to witness Trent in all his glory. That's if he can pull off a win."

Trent didn't say a word. Aunt Vera, and Mrs. Farrington with Blake in tow, returned to the table. Eden bestowed a smile of adoration on Blake before he returned to his table.

Kate lifted her fork to eat her salad and watched Eden out of the corner of her eye. She hoped for Trent's sake his mother wasn't being used. If it became serious, Blake would have easy access to the company to do his dirty deeds.

Perhaps he already did.

* * *

Even though they weren't on good terms, Trent exhaled a relieved breath when Roland and the others settled at the table, interrupting his grandfather's chance to probe about the conception of his first great-grandchild. The question had put too many thoughts in Trent's head about sex with Kate.

Dinner was a meal of stuffed Cornish hens and prime rib. Trent noticed Kate didn't eat much, but only picked at her food with her fork.

She looked stunning tonight, and he was aware of that, too much for his own good. He couldn't forget the intimacy they shared, even if she had been using him. He wanted to hear her whimper with pleasure and to hear her cry out his name. That part had been real, unless she was the best actress in the world. He was very aware of her sitting so close to him. He watched her mouth as she took a bite of chocolate cake and had to force his gaze to his own plate.

He was relieved when the dessert plates were cleared away. Soon, couples packed the dance floor.

Roland stood and said dryly, "Excuse me, dear family. I'm going outside for a smoke."

"Does he do anything good for himself, Vera?" his grandfather grumbled after Roland had walked away. "Didn't you raise him to have any sense at all?"

Aunt Vera's face reddened. "Father, he makes his own choices. Please excuse me while I go powder my nose."

Trent made a mental note to speak to his grandfather about his treatment of his aunt whenever the conversation turned to Roland. Aunt Vera wasn't to blame for the way Roland had turned out.

Blake sauntered up to Eden. "Care for a dance?"

She rose and took his hand.

And he realized then that his mother needed someone to make her happy. He just hoped it was not Blake. Trent shook his head in disgust when she walked away with him toward the dance floor. However, he had to give Blake credit for one thing—he'd managed to make the woman crack a rare smile.

Trent glanced at Kate. If she had been his wife in reality, he would have asked her to dance, too, and hell yes, he would have been planning to take her to bed tonight.

If he hadn't found out about her treachery, he would still be making a fool of himself, drowning in her beautiful misty-gray eyes. He'd probably be professing his love by now and blabbering like a damned idiot. He clenched his hand on his wine glass.

His grandfather glanced toward him. "Have you two had a disagreement?"

"No," Trent said.

"Not at all," Kate added.

Trent peered over his wine glass at his grandfather. "Why do you ask?" he asked as innocently as he could.

"You're not dancing with your wife. Need I remind you that I wasn't born yesterday? I can tell when something is wrong. Have you two been arguing?"

"We aren't arguing," Trent said gruffly.

"No? Then to appease an old, sick, dying dog, kiss each other, or you'll have me worrying unduly." His grandfather placed his hand to his heart. "I don't think my old ticker can take it."

Trent rolled his eyes at Kate. He gave her a faint smile. "You know, he's milking this sickness to the hilt. Do you mind?" He leaned toward her and gave her a peck on her silky cheek. He inhaled her fragrance and scent.

Grandfather snorted. "You call that a kiss? I'll never have great-grandchildren at that rate."

"We're in a public place," Trent replied.

The elderly man wiggled his gray eyebrows. "Everyone is preoccupied. Show me I have nothing to worry about."

Trent turned to Kate, feeling awkward. She had never really liked him. It had all been an act on her part. Could they continue this performance? "Kate?"

She nodded her consent. He placed his hand on her warm arm and pressed his lips to hers. With just the touch of his mouth on her lush lips, desire hammered through his body as if he were on fire and it rushed to his groin. She raised her hand to cup his cheek.

Frowning at his own reaction and the touch of her palm on his face, Trent pulled away.

By the dreamy expression in her eyes, and her slightly parted lips, he thought that while she might have been only using him for her own gain, she felt the same electricity he had during the brief touch of their lips. Her breasts in the low cut gown seemed to swell up to entice him to delve inside her gown.

"Thank you," James said, with a heavy sigh, startling Trent out of staring at Kate like a witless fool. "That makes me feel better. I'm sure you two can work past any argument, and I just might live long enough to see my great-grandchildren."

Trent narrowed his eyes. "Slow down and you'll live to be a hundred."

"Trent, I'm a sick man and don't like anyone fussing over me, but I feel a little tired. I'd be grateful if you two would stay at the house tonight—just to know you're really close in case I should need you."

Time to act before his grandfather tried to throw him into Kate's vicinity. With the way they had both been affected by that kiss, this was dangerous territory.

He glanced at Kate. "That's impossible. We need our time alone tonight, don't we, sweetheart?"

"Yes, sorry. We can't stay," she said, a little too emphatically for Trent.

He gave Kate a sharp glance. He'd not been able to get in touch with her today. Just what *did* she *do* in her spare time? It never occurred to him she might be planning to meet another man—perhaps even tonight. Jealousy roared to life inside him, and he realized when it came to this woman his feelings or emotions seemed to run out of control. She might even have a *significant other* that he wasn't aware of. After all, he'd been nothing to her but a con job.

"Why can't we stay, *sweetheart?*" he asked, in a barely perceptible cutting tone. "Do *we* have *other plans* for this evening?"

She blushed, satisfying him that she understood exactly what he meant.

"I only have plans for *us* tonight," she said in a low voice, as if she got the message.

Trent clenched his teeth. *Disappointed, Kate,* he said with his eyes? *Who the hell are you sleeping with?* He was sure the last thing she wanted to do was to spend time with him, especially now that she would be financially rewarded for just *playing* his wife. Did she think she could collect his money and sleep with as many men, on the side, as she desired?

So, why shouldn't she do exactly whatever she wanted? He had a sickening feeling inside that he had no right to make these demands...

He was relieved from his spiraling downward thoughts when the announcer picked up the microphone. "Welcome to our annual State awards." He proceeded to hand out the acknowledgements. "And now for our most prestigious award of the evening. The winner is Trent Farrington, of Farrington Construction."

Applause broke out in the room.

Trent exhaled a deep breath. His hard work had paid off. This would put his mark on the family company for the next generation. In that moment, he understood what his grandfather meant about the sense of pride in accomplishment. What Trent did with his company was the legacy for the Farringtons who would follow after him.

Trent strode up to the podium, took the award and plaque and spoke into the microphone. "Thank you. I'm honored. The company is honored. We look forward to building the best buildings possible."

He said a few more words about his vision for the future direction of the company. Then he made eye contact with Kate. He was surprised to see pride shining in her eyes.

* * *

There were a few speeches, then congratulations accepted, and Trent stood there with Kate playing the beautiful and devoted wife at his side. He found he enjoyed the support, and that having her there eased him through a time he would otherwise want to avoid. When dancing resumed in the ballroom, Trent considered asking Kate to dance—for appearance's sake.

Before he could ask Kate, Eden sauntered up to him. "Trent, would you mind dancing with me?"

Trent glanced toward Kate. "Excuse me for a moment." She nodded her approval and went back to the table to wait. Like a dutiful wife.

He led his mother onto the dance floor.

Before the music started, she laid her hands on the lapels of his jacket. "I just wanted to say how proud I am of you tonight. Your father would be, too, if he were here to share this evening with us."

Her words startled him. "Thank you..." Trent kept his tone level. He wasn't going to question her sincerity this evening.

Then a twinge of guilt about their relationship hit him. She had been acting odd lately. Perhaps she was sincerely trying to reach out to him, to become more involved, and wanting—in her own cold way—for them to be a real family. If she changed, could he forgive her after all those years...?

She seemed genuinely happy tonight. Perhaps things could get better between them. Now, if only he could get her to see Blake for what he was before it was too late.

While he slow danced with his mother, Trent said, "You're intelligent, interesting and still attractive. There must be someone besides Blake who could make you happy."

"Why, Trent, that's the nicest thing you've said to me in a long time."

He didn't know what to say. He and his mother getting along—wonder of wonders.

The next time he glanced toward the table, Blake was hovering behind Kate's chair. Jealousy slammed Trent. Was she interested in Blake, too? Maybe she worked over many men.

"In spite of everything we know about her," his mother said, intruding into his thoughts. "You didn't just use her to make your grandfather hold onto the company—you're in love with her, aren't you?"

Her words stunned him, whirled around inside his mind, and nearly brought him to his knees at the truth of something that could never be. This had to be squashed—more reason to keep Kate at a distance. He gave his mother an uneasy glance.

Eden sighed. "I won't say anything more. I don't want to ruin your night. Perhaps we'll both be happy one day. Wouldn't that be nice?"

***

While James Farrington had been talking to some of his friends who gathered around him, Kate watched Trent dance with his mother.

A hand groped her bare shoulder, sending her nearly flying out of her chair. She twisted her head to find Frank Blake standing over her.

"Mrs. Farrington," he drawled. "Why don't you and I share a dance?"

It wasn't a question, but a demand.

Anxiety pummeled Kate. She bit her lip, wanting to say no. Then she reluctantly decided to find out what he wanted and followed him to the dance floor.

The band played another slow song. At the touch of Blake squeezing her hand, she tried to pull away, but he gripped her waist and held onto her hand.

"What is it you want, Mr. Blake?" she asked through tight lips.

"I didn't recognize you on the yacht, but tonight, without the glasses, I remembered. Someone as pretty as you shouldn't be forgotten, but has it been ten years ago already? You landed quite well for yourself as Mrs. Farrington, *sugarplum*."

Her eyes widened. "But I don't know you—"

"You don't remember me? I'm crushed. Darker hair, no gray." He held up a finger to cover his mustache. "Ah, yeah, you were little more than a child—sweet sixteen if I remember correctly—but the resemblance is still there…the golden hair. I'm surprised you'd forget our evening together. How is my good friend Bill Jackson?"

Her heart hammered in her chest as the memories of the past tumbled through her mind—memories she'd tried to block. That night the hotel room had been dark when she had entered, a cowering girl. She'd been unable to look at his face, except for a glimpse. She had not wanted to see the man who would do this to her for money. She'd been terrified to do what her stepfather forced her to do, and scared to death not to. "If you were his friend, you would have heard he was shot and killed by someone that he tried to con," she said, doing her best to hang onto her crumbling composure.

Blake chuckled. "So that's why I haven't seen him around. Ah, but he taught you well, *sugarplum*. Good job landing on your feet, especially after your brief touch with the law. Trent Farrington is worth a fortune."

"I was innocent!" She wanted to flee, but he clasped her hand tightly.

"Now, now, *Mrs. Farrington*. Not so fast. Does Trent know all about Daddy Jackson?"

A moan of distress escaped Kate. "Yes," she rasped out. "*He knows everything.*" However, seeing this 'friend' of her stepfather's, reminded her she hadn't shared the complete truth.

"*Everything?*" Blake chuckled. "You're lying to me, Mrs. Farrington. Why I'd say those perky breasts are as enticing...as the last time I touched them." He whispered a vulgarity in her ear.

Shock nearly knocked her off her feet. She didn't want to be reminded of that night.

Blake hauled her closer to him. "Damn, I could have had some fun with this. Oh, I wonder what you would do to keep your secret. Maybe even slip into the sheets with me." He squeezed her fingers.

Rearing her head back, she wanted to slap him. "Let me go."

He smiled and let go of her hand. "Your husband is approaching. I imagine he hasn't heard everything about you or Bill Jackson or you wouldn't look like you're about to faint. I think I should tell him."

Her heart was racing and she choked on her words. "No...please, don't." Trent already knew too much about her... And she didn't realize how much she hoped with time that he'd come to see she was truly a decent person—that she'd only been a little impetuous to find evidence on who was responsible for Matt's death—but with what Blake had to say, Trent would never think so.

Blake chuckled. "Don't look so worried, Mrs. Farrington. I won't say anything. I don't want any more bad blood between Eden and me, or Trent for that matter—as long as I get what I want. I'd love to get my hands into your pants, but I'll be discreet. We'll take this up later and finish what we started."

"You're a bastard. If you said anything, I think Trent would punch you in the face for what you tried to do to me."

"Does Trent know his bride was for sale, for her virginity no less?"

Kate shook her head vehemently. "That's because you offered my stepfather so much money! You knew he couldn't resist. And I wasn't going to let him turn me into a prostitute."

"You ran away before I got what I'd paid for, but Bill didn't believe me. You owe me a $10,000 roll in the hay."

"Go to hell," she said through clenched teeth. She wanted to run off the dance floor, but she wouldn't make a scene here in front of everyone. This was Trent's night and he deserved for it to go smoothly.

Blake shot Kate a wicked grin. "Oh, I'll go to hell all right, *Mrs. Farrington*, but I wanted to make my position clear. Just make sure you put up no resistance if the Farringtons decide to sell the company to me. Or else I'll be telling Trent a few details, I'm sure you won't want him to know. We'll be talking. That's a fact."

Dread washed over Kate.

Trent strode up to them. At the deadly look in his eyes, Kate's throat went dry. She had to quickly compose herself. She couldn't bear for him to hear this horrible story about her past.

"May I cut in?" Trent asked. She had the impression he might pound Blake into the floor if he refused.

"By all means," Blake said with a smile. "I don't like to keep a bride from her husband's *enjoyment*."

Clenching her jaw, Kate struggled to regain her composure as Blake walked away and Trent picked up her hand.

"Did you like dancing with him?" he asked coolly, his dark eyes studying her.

She shrugged and lowered her gaze to his crisp white shirt with the black bowtie. She had promised herself she wouldn't lie to him anymore, but if he asked her about Blake? Perspiration beaded on her top lip.

If Trent found out she'd met Frank Blake before, that her stepfather had sold her to him for a night, he might consider that additional evidence that what he thought about her was correct. She couldn't bear that. How many women of his acquaintance would have gone through such an experience? None she was sure. Tears burned the backs of her eyes. Yes. Her virginity had been sold by her own stepfather.

Trent clasped Kate's hand in his. "Your hands are clammy and you're trembling. What did *he* say to you?" he demanded.

Holding her tears inside, Kate pulled herself together and shook her head. "I just don't like him."

"That makes two of us."

The song was slow. For a moment, she allowed herself to relax in the security of Trent's arms. She wanted to weep and tell him everything about herself. But even though she knew none of this had been her fault, she thought that Trent would somehow think she'd been responsible.

When the song ended, he held her a little away and gazed down at her. "Why did you dance with him, Kate?"

"Why? I—"

He put his finger on her lips to silence her. "How can I trust you to tell me the truth?" He glanced over her shoulder and swore. "My grandfather's watching. Act as if you're enjoying yourself. You know he wants us to stay at his house tonight."

Kate glanced around Trent's shoulder and toward the table. Blake gave Kate a heated glance, which thankfully Trent did not see.

Her temples pounded into a roaring headache. "Sorry, I can't tonight. I don't feel well. Please give your regrets to your grandfather. I'm going home."

She had to get out of there. Right away.

* * *

Like a pressure cooker with its lid blown off, thoughts exploded in Kate's mind—her life with Bill Jackson, her wicked stepfather, and more vividly, that awful night with Frank Blake. Oh, my God. She couldn't stop the dreadful memories. That pervert had touched her!

Her stepfather's actions that night had been the final straw. He'd dressed her up like a hooker in a cheap sequined black gown and forced her into Blake's house. She had escaped that wretched night, but she'd nearly died. She'd cut her stomach badly on the glass when she wiggled out the bathroom window she had to break to escape.

Once outside, she'd called her stepbrother. With Matt supporting her around the waist, they had traveled on foot to her aunt's house, dripping blood along the way.

Aunt Kate had been furious and threatened her stepfather with child abuse. She had taken her niece to the emergency room, and then into her custody. Afterwards, Matt had also moved in with them, and they had a few blissful years.

On shaky legs, Kate stepped out the hotel's front door and handed the valet a tip and her ticket. "I can't wait for my car. I'll get it myself."

He handed her the key. "All right, ma'am. At the back of the parking lot."

With tears blurring her eyes, and her stomach rolling, she lifted the skirt of her expensive gown and hurried in that direction. Suddenly a wave of nausea washed over her. She found her car and crouched by the hood, glad the bushes blocked her from anyone's view.

Cigarette smoke wafted over the bushes. Her stomach heaved at the smell and she threw up. Taking a deep breath, she swiped her hand across her perspiring forehead, then struggled to her feet.

She had to get into her car. If anyone saw her like this, she would be mortified. As a member of the Farrington family, she was under scrutiny from the press. Reporters loitered near the front door like hyenas waiting for their victims. She didn't want a picture of her like this, to land in the papers. She had been lucky so far that after the announcement of their marriage, the media had not mentioned she was related to Bill Jackson.

She couldn't face Trent with this last humiliation hammered home by Blake, not now... It all made her feel so dirty. Swiping at her tears, she took a deep breath. Since Blake wanted to ingratiate himself back into the family, she was probably safe—for now. She just wanted to go home, take a warm shower and curl up in bed...and forget.

A man's voice, low and muffled, drifted over the bushes. "Have patience. There wasn't an opportunity. Believe me, Farrington will suffer...before he dies. Won't be with the new bride for long."

Her heart beating rapidly, Kate's hand flew to her mouth. Trent! *He was the object of the sabotage, not the building. They were trying to kill him!*

Someone truly hated him. She had to get a glimpse of the man who spoke, but the bushes were too thick to see through. She followed the nearly inaudible voice down the line of shrubs, but the cigarette smell faded along with the voice. By the time she rounded the other side to get a glimpse, there was no one there.

Would this man be waiting for Trent out here in the dark tonight? She had to warn him. Regardless of what he thought of her, she would do everything in her power to protect him.

She strode back to the valet and handed him her keys. "I've decided to stay for a while."

Kate headed to the restroom. Thankfully, it was empty. She splashed cold water on her face and rinsed her mouth. She popped in a breath mint and reapplied her lipstick.

She intended to tell Trent what she'd heard, but would he believe her?

As she turned to leave the restroom, Eden stepped through the doors. Her expression darkened. "Are you all right? Are you ill?"

"N-no. Thank you. I'm fine." Kate didn't think she should tell Eden what she'd overheard. While she didn't think the man who had spoken was Blake, Blake might have been the person making the phone call.

Eden's gaze swept around the bathroom before locking on Kate. "Let me apologize for my rudeness tonight. While you do know I wanted Trent to marry Cecilia, I do want to make the best of the situation. I want Trent to be happy. Call me *Eden*."

Her eyes misting, Kate stared, tongue-tied. It was not quite acceptance, but it was in the right direction. "Thank you."

Maybe Eden wasn't so dead-set against her, after all. And the Trent she'd fallen in love with—before he became the harsh man seeking vengeance—could he step forward again?

Could he grow to love her? With his mother's support, was there a chance for him to realize she wasn't the awful person she appeared to be? Then her shoulders drooped—not if Blake told Trent his story that her stepfather had been her pimp.

They returned to the dinner table.

Trent, who was helping his grandfather to his feet, gave her a sharp look. "I thought you were going home...*ahead of me*."

She forced a smile. "I think we should take up your grandfather's offer. I would love for us to stay at his house tonight."

Trent's eyebrows drew together in a suspicious frown. As soon as they were alone, she'd tell him what she'd overheard.

"Now, that's more like it." James beamed, which added a robustness to the ill man, making him look healthier than he seemed. "What do you think, Eden? They're staying the night at the house with us."

Eden nodded, and her lips curved into a slight smile. "A wonderful night for you, Trent, and I'm proud of you. I want nothing more than you to find the blissful happiness you deserve."

* * *

Kate followed Trent's Porsche and the limo to the mansion, then parked in the circular driveway. Marc let out Eden, Vera, and James. Then Marc helped Trent get James Farrington up the steps to the front door.

Once everyone had stepped into the house and the door was closed, Trent dropped the smile, and pulled Kate aside on the front porch, beneath the light. "What is this about? Why the change of mind to come here, Kate?"

She sighed in relief and clutched his arm. "I need to talk to you alone. I didn't want us to be overheard."

Trent pulled back from her touch. "You went outside and Blake followed you. I saw you both. What is between you and him? Do you work for him?"

"No!"

"Don't lie to me," he rasped.

She gaped. "I didn't see him. If he was outside, it had nothing to do with me."

Trent clasped her forearms and propelled her against the brick wall, pressing his body against her. "Damn it, Kate, *what the hell are you?*"

"I don't work for him."

He released her abruptly and stepped back.

Kate's knees buckled. She leaned against the wall.

"I know damned well he has someone on the inside. It must be you. And now you're my wife—"

"If he does have someone on the inside, it's not me. If you'd been listening to me, you would realize I've only done one thing you should be angry about. I did lie to get the job, but only to find out who was responsible for the death of my *brother*. He died while working for you. OSHA and the police seemed to act as if his life was worthless—or that's how it seemed to me, since nobody was brought to justice. Your company got away with his murder."

He folded his arms over his chest. "So you think I'm a murderer?"

"No! At the time, I thought you were cheating on the products, and not dealing with the safety issues, and you were getting away with it because your family has money."

"And now?"

"I know you're not like that. I know you have integrity. Please, believe me. I came here tonight to warn you. I overheard someone on a cell phone saying he would kill you. *You*, Trent. I didn't recognize the voice, but you say Blake was outside?"

Trent pierced her with a deadly stare. "What kind of con game are you trying to pull on me now? Don't try to turn this around. I think you're in on it. You, with your angel's face, and the heart of a liar... You expect me to stand here and believe you?"

"Yes! Listen, to me, Trent. I thought it was the company, but *you* are the target. Someone is changing the orders. What about Roland? You've got to believe me. I heard—"

"Ahem," said a voice from the doorway of the house.

Kate and Trent whirled.

"Trouble in paradise again?" James asked.

"No!" Trent retorted. "And why aren't *you* in bed?"

"Why aren't *you two* in bed?" James asked blandly.

"Grandpa, stay out of our business," Trent said.

His Grandfather put a hand over his heart. "But I couldn't sleep, worried about my newlyweds."

"We're not *your* newlyweds, and we're going to bed," Trent ground out.

James scrutinized both their faces. "Why aren't you two happy?"

Trent firmly put his arm around Kate and pulled her close. "We *are* happy. Kate is a treasure. Life is paradise with her. We couldn't be happier. Right, sweetheart?"

Kate nodded and turned to bury her face in Trent's chest. She couldn't stop the tears in her eyes. She was grateful that he shielded her face.

"We were just getting ready to come inside," Trent said more calmly over her head.

"All right, I'll leave you two alone, but I'm worried about you."

"Don't worry," Trent said.

James blew out a deep breath and nodded, but still a frown creased his brow. "Why don't I show you to your room? You can help me up the stairs, Trent."

After James had turned away, Trent gave Kate a cutting glance as if he didn't believe her or trust her.

Kate shoulders drooped. He thought she'd invented the latest threat against his life.

CHAPTER TWENTY-TWO

Kate had never been in Trent's bedroom at his grandfather's house. She tried not to look at the king-sized, four-poster bed. In the sitting area was a loveseat and chair. French doors overlooked a balcony, giving a direct view to the pool and the wide waterway. A luxurious carpet, mahogany furniture, and blue and tan furnishings completed the room.

Turning away from the window, she felt awkward. Perhaps, she should have told him what she'd overheard while they were at the hotel instead of here.

She cleared her throat. "I have nothing to sleep in."

Icy contempt flared in his eyes. He stalked to the drawer and tossed her a t-shirt and boxer shorts. "You can use the bathroom first. A new toothbrush should be in the middle drawer near the sink."

She flinched at his coolness and headed into the bathroom. All marble and granite, the large room had double sinks, a whirlpool bathtub, and a huge shower with all kinds of sprays.

After showering in luxury, she dressed.

Trent took his turn in the bathroom, while she blew her hair dry in his bedroom.

She glanced around the room and found not many personal items. Trent must have been living in his condominium for some time.

He walked out bare-chested and dressed in sweat shorts. "I usually sleep naked, but I thought I'd spare you."

Heat rose on her cheeks. He was going to make this night difficult. "Thanks," she murmured.

Trent stepped closer to her. "But then," he said in a husky voice, "I thought you might not mind at all, as you came here to seduce me...to continue whatever is your plan. I'd hate for you to have wasted your time. I suppose you're still not on birth control, so I'll make sure to protect myself." He dropped his gaze to her lips and slid his hand up her arm, curving his fingers around her nape. "You're too beautiful, Kate, and you know it."

She stared at him, going blank as she watched his lips descend. His mouth took hers in a caress that sent heat flooding through her. He forced her head back as he kissed her, his tongue twisting in her mouth. His hand landed lower and kneaded her breast through the thin t-shirt.

Instead of fighting against what he probably considered punishment, she raised her arms around his neck, giving herself to him. She pressed into him, then felt him grow hard, then rigid against her. He splayed his hands across her bottom and pulled her even closer. He groaned and gathered her up into his arms and deepened the kiss.

Finally, he raised his mouth from hers and stepped back, leaving Kate with a rush of regret.

"Now you can see," he said, breathing hard, "that no matter how desirable I might find you, I have no problem resisting you. So you can stop your games...including whatever reason you have to ensconce yourself alone with me tonight."

Stunned, Kate lurched back at his calculated, verbal blow. "I am not playing, nor have I ever played games with you. Really, you have to believe me. I heard someone saying he was going to kill you."

He raised a cynical eyebrow. "Tell me exactly what you overheard."

"This man said—to whoever he was talking to on the other end of the phone—something about having patience, and that there wasn't an opportunity. He said *Farrington* would suffer before he dies, and that you wouldn't be with your new bride for long. That can only be you—and not Roland."

Trent blew out a deep breath and dropped down on the loveseat. "This is a bit coincidental, Kate. You go outside. You hear someone threaten my life. Why should I buy it? If anything, you're in on it. If this is another tactic to get me to sell to Blake, it's not going to work."

"No, and I'm not in on anything with Blake. I'm telling you the truth."

Her stomach clenched at the thought that even if she wanted to tell Trent that Frank Blake was an associate of her stepfather, it would only look bad for her now. Besides, she'd had nothing to do with that disgusting man, but one night of pure hell—a detail she'd rather keep buried in her mind. She had to.

She bit her lip.

Trent narrowed his eyes. "What's the matter?"

"Nothing."

He snorted. "I'll take the warning, Kate, but I don't trust you. I'll sleep on the floor."

Exhaling an exasperated breath, she asked, "How can I get you to believe me? Everything was real between us."

"Real?" he scoffed.

"No matter what I say you'll never believe me, will you? You'll always put the worst spin on it." She *had* to tell him about Blake—no matter the consequences—but his next words stopped her.

"I am onto you, Kate. If I die, you would benefit."

Her breath caught in her throat.

Trent yanked the cushions from the love seat and tossed them on the floor. He went into the walk-in closet, returned with sheets and blankets, and spread them on the cushions.

Kate pulled back the comforter and the sheet and lay down on the bed. "Our being married was your doing," she said in a shaky voice. "You can't blame that on me." She sank her head into the pillows. "Besides, I thought you had your ironclad prenuptial and a will. So what would I gain?"

He switched off the light and settled down on the cushions on the floor. "I'm sure you would appeal to my grandfather's kindness and get your hands on my money somehow. I've decided to tell Greg all and leave a letter to that effect with my lawyer. If something should happen to me—if I were to die—the police are to consider you and Blake as prime suspects."

"Trent, you're wrong about me. And I only care about keeping you safe."

She squeezed her eyes shut. Oh, God, she'd be blamed? She couldn't think of that because she didn't want to think about Trent being hurt or worse. She would stay by his side until he was safe.

She wanted him to believe her…wanted him to love her. She'd just have to hope that Blake, or whoever was sabotaging the company, was arrested soon.

They lay in silence in the room.

"Trent, I know you won't believe this," she whispered, "but I love you. I would never hurt you."

She didn't think he heard her and that was all well and good because there was no future in their relationship.

* * *

Kate woke to an empty bedroom and spent breakfast with Trent's family. Trent had gone to the office early, while she had to endure the shrewd, speculative eyes of his grandfather on whether his grandson had done the deed, and whether there was a grandchild growing within her.

Her entire Thursday workday went by without seeing Trent. *Was he avoiding her?* In a way, she was glad because she didn't want them to have to pretend to be the happy couple in front of others.

Trent had nothing to worry about with her trying to *ensconce* herself with him again—she still had more pride than that, even if it had been shredded. Still, she worried about his safety when she couldn't see him. Maybe she needed to hire a bodyguard for her husband?

Without any other commitment for the evening, she decided to go to the Children in Crisis Center for her usual Thursday evening hour of reading to a few kids. Maybe she'd stay longer.

Kate was thinking about that as she stepped inside the parking garage elevator. Cecilia was inside with tears streaming down her face. She turned her back on Kate.

Frowning, Kate didn't say anything. When the elevator doors opened, she headed for her car. As she was pulling out, she noticed Cecilia striding in her high heels down the ramp.

Concern washed over Kate. She stopped her car. "Cecilia, are you all right?"

"Yeah," Cecilia mumbled and continued to walk. "I was looking for someone leaving who might give me a ride home, but everyone I know has already left for the day."

"I'll give you a ride."

"You'd do that for me?" Cecilia asked, staring at Kate warily.

"If you need it," Kate said.

Cecilia opened the passenger door and slid inside.

Kate pulled out onto the street. "Where am I taking you?"

"You're going to the Children's Center, right? My townhouse is nearby."

The hair on the back of Kate's neck prickled. "How did you know where I was going?"

"Eden mentioned you went to the Center on Thursdays."

On their way, Cecilia burst out in a round of tears, then finally caught her breath. "I-I can't drive because I went to court today. My driver's license has been suspended because of a DUI—my second. If my parents find out...or if Eden…" Cecilia wiped her eyes. "One thing, they'll all find out eventually, too, is—*I'm pregnant!*"

Shock rushed through Kate. She pulled the car over and stared at Cecilia. "*Trent?* Does he know?" she choked out, barely able to speak the words.

"Trent? Are you kidding? If only he'd slept with me, we wouldn't be having this conversation. I was supposed to seduce him, but he wouldn't sleep with me. One night I went out with some girlfriends, I picked up some man in a bar—and just one night— bam, I'm pregnant. I don't even know his name. Hell, I don't even know if I could recognize him in *a police lineup*. I was so drunk."

"You were going to pass off the baby as Trent's?" Kate asked, still stunned.

"Yes! If I had to. I was that scared at what I'd done. Now, I'm too far along. My life is falling apart. I'm not the Miss Perfect that Eden thought, and it's you who seems to have it all. You have everything I *wanted*." She ground out the last word.

Kate's mouth flattened into a thin line. "Cecilia, I'm pulling over and getting you a cab."

"No, no, please. I'm not blaming you. *You've won.* I'm giving up. I'm leaving. I'll have to go up north and live with my parents as soon as I start to show. I'm done with South Florida." Cecilia's chin quivered. "I just wanted him, but he wanted you from the first moment he saw you. It was so obvious."

Kate winced. "Well, uh, maybe," she said weakly. She couldn't tell Cecilia her marriage was a sham, and Trent really hated his temporary wife.

"I'm going to tell you something else because you were nice enough to give me a ride. Things are going on in Purchasing. I think someone has been slipping in while I've been out and changing some of the orders. I told Eden, but she said not to worry. She thinks she knows who's behind this, and she'd tell Trent."

Kate tensed. Eden probably thought that *person* was Kate. Oh my, the last thing she needed was for Trent to think *she'd* made the changes to the purchase orders. What if Eden built a case against her? She'd go to jail. No one would believe her. Her word was worthless to Trent and to the police. She'd certainly be prosecuted and maybe convicted.

"What makes you think someone's been in the department?" Kate asked in a shaky voice.

"At first, I thought I imagined a few things out of place on my desk, but then it happened several more times. Orders were changed—and I did not remember running them through the system."

Kate frowned, remembering how easy it had been for her to get into Purchasing. Anyone could have gotten in and changed the purchasing orders if Cecilia left access on her computer. "Thanks for the information, Cecilia. Until you leave the company, will you please make sure the doors to your office and the file room are locked whenever you're away from your desk?"

Glancing in the rearview mirror, Kate found a truck bearing down on her bumper. The high beams burned her eyes. "Some idiot is following too close." The driver of the truck honked impatiently as if he wanted her to move over—or be run over. Kate was already driving in the slow lane.

Cecilia clutched the passenger strap. "If he's such a damned speed demon, why doesn't he go around?"

"Maybe he'll get off at the next exit."

The truck didn't, and the closer tailgating had apprehension racing through Kate. "I'm going the speed limit, but still he's on my bumper."

Kate gripped the wheel of the car as they traveled up one of the highest and most dangerous curves on the highway.

Cecilia stared out the back window. "He's scaring me."

"Yeah, me too." Kate slowed the car, hoping to force the jerk to go around her. Finally, the man drove his truck into the left lane as if to pass them.

Kate exhaled a deep breath and kept her hands tightly on the wheel. "Crazy South Florida drivers," she muttered.

Then the truck pulled beside them and slowed, cruising at their same speed. As they crested that dangerous curve, Kate glanced at the person in the truck. He looked big, and burly, but she couldn't see his face with his sunglasses and his hat pulled low over his brow.

A second later, he edged his truck into Kate's lane. A squeal of metal to metal emitted when the truck and her car contacted. The man effectively forced her to move her car partly into the emergency lane.

As they rounded a high corner, he brushed them again. Panic rushed through Kate.

Cecilia leaned over and gave the man the finger. "Asshole. Where's a cop when you need one?"

The trucked swerved out of their lane and zoomed away.

Kate clutched the wheel, but that last bump caused her to lose control. The car screeched down along the guardrail with a loud crashing sound of twisting metal …

Cecilia screamed.

CHAPTER TWENTY-THREE

Hannigan's Pub was lively with music and the after-work crowd. Dropping money on the bar, Trent ordered a beer and a shot of whiskey. He'd been working for a couple hours at the construction site. Tired, he needed a break from work and the potential enemies that surrounded him—his wife included. Her latest revelation last night floored him. He had no idea if it was the truth. And in spite of what he'd told her, he'd been barely able to tear himself away from her arms or her lips—which made any proximity to her dangerous territory.

He threw back the shot of whiskey and then nursed his beer. Sleeping on the floor last night, with Kate so close, had driven him crazy. As had the question foremost on his mind: Was she sincere when she denied she'd had no involvement with Blake?

He wanted to believe her, but another part warred with himself that he couldn't trust her.

Greg strode through the pub room door. "Hi, buddy."

He settled on the adjacent barstool. Trent signaled the bartender who set two more cold beers and two shots in front of Greg and Trent.

"Thanks for coming," Trent said, raising his shot glass in salute.

"You're getting trashed, huh?"

"Yeah, I am. Drowning my troubles, Greg. You?"

"I can't drink the hard stuff tonight. Darcy is meeting me after her exercise class."

"Sounds serious with you two."

"Might be."

Trent's smile dimmed. "I hope you can trust *her*."

"I do. She explained everything to me. She and Kate came to the company because of Kate's brother. Can you believe Kate thought we ran a crooked operation?"

Trent hunched his shoulders. "That's the story Kate tells me."

"I believe her, man. Now, how about a game of pool?"

While Trent got change for the pool table from the bartender, Greg went to rack up. Trent barely had time to contemplate Greg's statement about Kate when he felt a soft hand caress his shoulder.

Kate? He turned.

Erin Duggan, a slim redhead he'd only casually dated, smiled back at him. Disappointment surged through him. He had to get a grip on his feelings for his temporary wife.

"You haven't been around here in ages," Erin cooed. Dressed in skintight leggings and a filmy low-cut blouse, she looked ready for an evening on the prowl.

"I'm married now," he said dryly.

"Word gets around, but I didn't buy it. Not you—*married*. That *hell* you used to talk about must have frozen over for you to have tied the knot."

Although his marriage was as phony as the overdone purplish-red color of Erin's hair, he needed to keep up appearances.

Trent narrowed his eyes. "It's the truth."

"That's too bad," Erin purred in his ear.

Trent shrugged and gulped down his beer. Where in the hell was his *wife* tonight? He couldn't stop his thoughts from circling back to Kate.

Erin placed a hand on his chest and squeezed his pectoral muscle. "You know me, hon. Your being married doesn't matter one bit. I don't see any wife around here. I can overlook her, if you can." She glanced toward her table across the room. "I'm with some girlfriends, if you want to remember some old times, stop by and see me."

"I'm in a lousy mood. I'd be bad company." He motioned to the bartender. "Send a round to that table, and get a drink for the lady here. And another shot for me."

Erin took the martini the bartender quickly mixed. She sipped her drink and gazed at Trent over the rim of the glass. "So by the looks of you, I'd say you've already found out marriage sucks. Been there a few times myself. I tell you, hon, I don't care." She brushed her breasts against his arm.

Greg handed Trent a pool stick. "Hey, remember you're married now."

Trent returned a bland look to convey he didn't care what Greg thought because Greg wasn't the one married to the *liar of the century*.

Greg started shooting pool, and one by one, the balls thumped into the pockets. He seemed to forget that they were supposed to play a game.

"Hey, Erin. Listen, I *am* married now." Trent hadn't been with Kate since they had signed their faux marriage on the dotted line, although he'd sure wanted to be last night. And why the hell was he still thinking of Kate? He drained the shot of whiskey. The liquid burned his throat.

Erin leaned in and kissed his cheek and put her hand on his ass. The thought of him being seen with a woman in public who was practically molesting him—snapped him back to his senses. In spite of his sham of a marriage, he had to admit he'd feel guilty cheating.

He took Erin's elbows and set her aside. "Listen, Erin, you'll have to find someone else. I'm married."

Erin pouted. "But you're the one who's always said 'marriage is for fools.'"

"Most join the club, eventually."

"Call me when you realize marriage is for *suckers*." She brushed her palm across his crotch. "You need that itch to be scratched. You aren't fooling me. You're as horny as hell. Where *is* your wife?" She whirled around then flounced toward her table.

He frowned. She'd come closer to the truth than he'd like to admit. *Where was Kate?* The possibility she was out carousing like Erin, or with another man, blackened his mood even further. The sweet girl he'd thought Kate had been, especially on their weekend in Key West, had turned out to be all smoke and mirrors. He had no idea what she was really like.

"Dam it to hell," he muttered under his breath. He turned to the bartender. "I'll have a beer, and send another round to the girls at that table. On second thought make mine a shot of whiskey." He'd get a cab home tonight and leave his car in the garage at work.

Unless he worked hard to focus on something else, his thoughts turned to Kate. Even though he tried to set them aside, he couldn't get her out of his mind, no matter how much he drank.

Damn it, he hated the idea she might be sleeping with other men. Maybe he should have thought through the details when he'd planned this farce. It's not that he suspected she did, but it was that he had no idea. Next time he saw her, he'd make one thing clear, she was to be faithful to him for as long as they were married and that had to be part of the deal.

He didn't care if she'd had a string of different bed partners every night in the past—as long as she was married to him, she was to remain as pure as the proverbial driven snow.

Greg strode up to the bar just as Trent was pointing at the bartender and giving him sound advice every man needed to know. "*Women*," Trent said, "are nothing but trouble."

The bartender raised an empty glass in mock salute. "I'll drink to that."

"Sheesh, I would, too," Trent said slurring his words, "but I think I've had enough for one night."

Greg clapped Trent on the back. "I'm glad you did the right thing—and you're not driving anywhere."

"Didn't plan to. I'm drunk," Trent said, slurring his words. "I can't even cheat on my sham marriage. And it's worse than I thought with Kate, Greg. I think she might be working with Blake to bring the company down...to ruin us."

Greg shook his head. "I don't believe it."

"She makes my mother look like Bo Peep, whoever that was."

"Kate is nothing like your mother."

Trent laughed, but with bitter humor. "Oh, you don't know. She's just as treacherous, just as deadly to my soul."

"Man, you just don't trust women."

Trent took the last swig of the whiskey the bartender placed in front of him. "I only have examples from the best to form my opinions."

"Is that why you're drinking tonight?" Greg asked.

Trent nodded. "My beautiful, beautiful Kate," he muttered, "is an angel on the outside, but a boa constrictor on the inside, waiting to strangle me when I'm not looking." He grabbed Greg's shirt. "I think she might want to kill me... Seriously."

"Man, you've fallen hard. You'd better get a grip on yourself and straighten things out with your wife. I thought I'd never see the day."

"You're wrong... No way have I fallen for her." Could he love her? In spite of knowing everything about her? No way. But he sensed there was a stupid truth to Greg's words. It explained why he'd been so bitter and angry at Kate's betrayal.

Trent's cell phone rang.

He fumbled for his phone and then listened to his mother's screechy pitched voice. What she said scared the hell out of him. He disconnected the call.

He turned to his friend, dead sober from the shock. "Greg... I've got to go to the h-hospital. Kate..." he said tripping up on the words. "There's been an accident. I'm not sure what happened..."

* * *

In the hospital, the waiting room held a chill. Kate wiped the tears from her cheeks with a tissue and took a chair by the window. She trembled all over. Someone had tried to scare them—and badly. Luckily, she'd not been hurt, only bruised. Cecilia was being checked, but she seemed okay, too.

The front door flew open. Trent and Greg rushed in.

Trent strode across the floor. After taking one look at her tear-stained cheeks, he pulled Kate into his arms. "Oh, My God. I didn't know... Are you all right?"

"Barely," she whispered. She clung to him, more tears blurring her vision. She wanted him...needed him to hold her.

If she closed her eyes, she could still hear the screech of metal, Cecilia's screams. Feel the car careening, nearly flying...

Her arms clung to his waist and she nestled her face into Trent's chest.

"You sure you're all right?" He nuzzled his cheek against the top of her head.

She nodded, sending pain shooting through her neck. "Yeah, I'm okay, nothing serious."

"What happened?"

"A man tried to run us off the road. He must have been trying to scare us—"

"*Us?* Who the hell were you with?" Trent demanded.

She stiffened at his accusations, felt the loss of his embrace as he stepped back—when she needed him the most. The movement sent more pain shooting through her shoulder and back. "Of all the times for you to be angry with me! I was almost killed." He just stood over her asking stupid questions, when all she wanted was to go home and lie down. "I was giving Cecilia a ride home, if you must know. I'm so tired—"

"Cecilia?"

"Yes!" She stabbed him with her gaze. "She needed a ride! And you? Where were you? You've been drinking. You want to know everything I do, but I don't see you reporting to me on everything you do."

Eden stepped into the waiting room with her arm around Cecilia and an ER intern at her side. Cecilia was sobbing and shaking.

Kate walked over to them. "How is she, Mrs. Farrington?"

"She'll be all right, but for heaven's sake, Trent," Eden snapped, "they could've been killed."

Kate swiped at wetness from beneath her eyes. "He had us rammed against the wall. I don't know why he stopped. One more pounding and I know my car would have flipped over the overpass."

"Why were you two together?" Eden asked.

"I was giving her a ride home," Kate said, bristling. She was tired of the inquisition. "I'm leaving. I was only waiting to make sure Cecilia was okay. The officer said I could go home, but my car..." She rubbed her eyes. "My car is destroyed. I'll have to call a cab."

Kate turned and strode to the exit.

Trent followed her and caught her arm. He took her aside. "First, are you sure you're not hurt?" he asked softly. "I'd rather have a doctor check you out."

Kate gave him a sideways glance when she heard the concern in his voice, and then reality seeped back in. He was only asking because they had an audience in Eden, and he needed to appear as if he cared. She straightened her shoulders and shook her head. "You don't have to worry about me. I'll be fine. I'm only a little bruised. I just want to go home and go to bed."

"All right, but with all that's going on, I'm taking you *home* to my grandfather's house. It's safer there with the alarm system. I'll post a security guard there tonight."

Too tired to argue, Kate nodded, but she wasn't too pleased to go back there after last night...when he accused her of ruthlessly plotting to be with him in his bedroom.

* * *

Once he and Kate had arrived at his grandfather's house, Trent said to Beasley, "Send up a light meal to our room."

Kate did not miss the 'our room' and only wished this wasn't one more charade he played.

When they were inside his bedroom, Trent closed the door and leaned against it. "Who's after you, Kate? Someone else angry about another con job you've pulled?"

"No! So that's why you wanted me to come here, so you could question me more on my morals?" Irritated by his constant accusation against her character, Kate whirled toward the window and clamped her arms over her chest. "As usual you think the worst of me."

"I think I have good reason, Kate," he said more calmly. "But I wanted you to come here for your safety...until we figure out who's behind this."

She took a deep breath and turned back to him. "Okay. Who could it be? Remember the Halloween mask on the fence? It looked like me. Someone knew at that time I was at the company, trying to find out what happened to my brother, and they tried to scare me away. But I don't know what any of it means, especially since I heard the conversation about someone being after you."

"This accident was more than to scare you, Kate. You were nearly run off the road, at a dangerous point. Did you see who was driving?"

"He seemed big. I didn't get a good look at his face. Cecilia was just telling me someone has been slipping into Purchasing, and I wondered if it was Blake. Perhaps when he visits Eden at the company? Without your mother, Blake wouldn't normally have access to the products."

"So you're really not working with Blake?"

"No, I'm telling you the truth."

Trent blew out a deep breath. "All right. So you think he's using Eden to get inside?"

Kate shrugged. "Trent the last thing I'm going to do is implicate your mother in something like this."

His dark gaze leveled on Kate's. "I never thought she'd be so stupid, but Blake could be manipulating her. It's also possible, someone wanted to kill you tonight because you are *my wife*."

Her cheeks warmed at the reminder. "Too bad they don't know I'm just *your employee*," she quipped.

It was going to be a long night... She wanted him to pull her into his arms and comfort her, for him to tell her that he was glad she didn't die, but that wasn't going to happen because he still thought she was the most evil woman on the planet...

Wincing, she sat down in the winged-back chair, dropping her face into her hands.

"What hurts?" Trent asked.

Besides her heart? She didn't want to look at him or tell him her entire shoulder and side ached. On some level, she wanted to keep him at a distance because he had the power to hurt her far more than a few bruised ribs.

Besides, if he showed any sympathy for her, she'd fall apart. "I'm fine," she whispered. "No, I promised myself I'd be truthful to you, and the truth is I am really hurting, but I'll live."

She heard him sigh. "All right," he said with concern in his voice. "Should I run the bathtub for you? A warm soak might do you good."

She nodded. Soon, she heard water rushing into the bathtub. When he returned, he said, "There are several robes in the bathroom closet. We'll go over to your house in the morning to pick up your clothing. I think it's safer for you to stay here until we find out and apprehend whoever is responsible for this."

She rose from the chair. "But I can't stay here more than one night," she blurted uneasily. He might be able to handle it, but she couldn't live so close to him with the way things were between them.

They went into the bathroom. Kate struggled with the buttons on her shirt. Trying to lift her arm sent excruciating pain ratcheting through her neck and shoulders. How was she going to undress?

She glanced sideways at Trent. "I need your help."

"Screw it," he said, surprising her. "We are married, even if it's only a temporary business deal." When she widened her eyes, he caught her gaze. "I promise no more digs tonight. I owe you that, at least. You were almost killed because of me."

He slipped the blouse off her shoulders. His fingers touched her skin and sent tingles through her. He lowered her skirt and slip. She was left in only her underwear.

His gaze swept to the bruise on her side. "My God, Kate. Let me see your hip."

Her face grew warm from embarrassment and something else, but she turned sideways.

"Damn it to hell. No wonder you're in pain. You're going to be sore for a week."

She turned her back to him. "Can you help me with one more thing?'

His warm fingers grazed her back as he unhooked her bra. "Do you think you can manage the rest?" he asked, strain evident in his voice.

She held her loosened bra to her breasts and glanced over her shoulder. "Yeah, I think it's better if I finish the rest myself," she said, her voice quivering. "Thank you."

"I'll be in the bedroom. Yell if you need anything."

She managed to strip off her underwear and stepped into the bath. She sighed as the warm water floated around her and soothed her aching muscles. She tried to raise her arms to wash her hair, but the pain and stiffness was too much so she decided not to.

After washing as best she could, she stood up in the tub and tried to reach for the towel, but pain shot through her shoulder.

After a knock on the bedroom door, she heard Trent speak to Beasley.

Kate frowned, contemplating how she'd reach the towel. She was too stiff to sit back down in the tub.

"Food's here. Do you need…?" Trent asked from the bathroom doorway.

A soft gasp escaped her as she realized the door was open. She stood naked before him, frozen and unable to drop back into the water.

He sucked in his breath and his eyes swept downward over her.

A warm flush spread over her body. She used one hand to cover her breasts, and extending the other, pointing toward the towel. "I can't reach my towel."

Trent lifted his gaze to hers. His dark eyes smoldered with desire. It was no longer about the bruises, but the heat that flared between them.

He broke eye contact first, leaving her feeling bereft.

He handed her the towel so she could cover herself and helped her dry off. "Let's get this robe on you," he murmured, "before I forget you're only my temporary wife."

"Trent…?" She wanted to say she didn't want to be just his temporary wife, but stopped herself, knowing that to him she'd be forever the con artist. "Never mind."

She tried to hold the towel with one hand, while he helped her slip her other arm into the navy-blue robe, but the towel dropped to the floor.

"Ahhh," she cried out.

"Kate, I've seen you naked before."

"But not this way. Not since things changed between us."

Slowly, because of her injuries, he helped her into the robe. She couldn't help the blush that heated her cheeks. Once she was in the garment, he straightened the robe around her and tied the belt.

He raised his dark eyes to her face. "It's the smallest I own and you look swallowed up in it." He gave her a long perusing look, then sighed. "Beasley brought us food. Let's eat before everything gets cold."

They returned to the bedroom. On the coffee table was a tray of covered plates and drinks in front of the love seat.

Kate was surprised at how hungry she was.

Trent poured her a glass of red wine. "Perhaps you'll need this to relax you. I've had enough."

She sipped, hoping it would dull the pain in her shoulder.

He poured water into a glass for himself and he contemplated her as she ate a sandwich and the accompanying food. He poured her a second glass of wine, which numbed some of her soreness. "So, who do you think did this to you? Blake? Roland? Someone else?"

She stopped eating. Her stomach sickened at the thought that not only could Blake be causing all this trouble, he was her stepfather's old acquaintance. She couldn't think about that right now. "I don't know. Do you mind if I lie down? I really need to."

He strode to the bed and pulled back the comforter. After freshening up in the bathroom, Kate kept the thick robe on and wiggled her aching body between the cool sheets.

"I'll be back after I shower, Kate."

* * *

Trent stood in the doorway of the bedroom, while Kate lay on his bed with her eyes closed, looking small and too delicate to have a killer after her. A surge of protectiveness nearly undid him. Although he had considered sleeping in another bedroom, and didn't think his grandfather would be patrolling the house tonight, she looked too vulnerable to leave.

She was his wife, at least for now. He'd stay with her to be certain she wasn't hurt worse than she let on. He'd protect her as long as they were together... And this time, he wasn't sleeping on the floor.

However, after he lay down on the edge of the bed, sleep eluded him. After a while, he heard a stifled sob.

He rose on his elbow. "Kate, are you in pain?"

"Did I wake you? I'm fine. Go to sleep."

He sat up on the bed and clicked on the light. "Damn it. I should have made you see a doctor at the hospital. What is it, baby?" He leaned over her.

She sniffled. "It's not the pain. It's just that everything has gone so horribly wrong." She started sobbing.

He slid closer, gathering her in his arms. "Tell me if I'm hurting you."

* * *

He wasn't hurting her, Kate thought, as she snuggled up to him in the soft king-sized bed. "I'll be fine." She choked out a sob again. She wanted to be optimistic but there was no chance things would work out between them, no matter how nice he was being now. "I didn't come to the company to trick you or con you. I just wanted to avenge my brother's death. I only wish I could somehow prove to you that I'm not as bad as you think—"

"Don't try, Kate," he said in a soft voice.

She nodded. "I know." She sank her face into the crook of his neck. "In spite of everything…you smell so good."

"So do you."

"Do you think you will be able to sleep like this?"

"Sleep? Are you kidding? I don't think I'll catch a wink with you in my arms?" His lips met her cheek.

She raised her lips to his. "I don't want you to sleep. I want you to make love to me. The wine is making me feel better…warmer…"

"Kate, this won't change anything between us."

"I know. *Please*?"

Trent was bare-chested and only wore boxer shorts. He leaned over her, untied the belt, and opened her robe. His eyes gazed upon her as he gently lay his hands on her breasts and smoothed his palms over her sensitive skin. He flicked his thumbs over her nipples.

She closed her eyes in pleasure. A moan escaped her lips.

He ran his hand down to her flat stomach, stroking her belly. He circled his fingers in her belly button, and then lower to the curls at the juncture of her thighs. She sucked in her breath as the throbbing ache between her legs heightened. Forgetting the pain in her shoulder, she rose up to meet his hand. He touched her, stroked her, and caressed her.

"No matter how out of control you make me, I promise I'll be gentle."

He brought his lips to her. The kiss made her dizzy with desire and a passion she'd never imagined she could feel. She clung to him wanting to give him everything of herself.

He kissed her breasts again, one at a time, twirling his tongue around her nipples…teasing, sucking. She tensed as he worked his way downward, over her stomach, and his tongue delved into her bellybutton. He moved lower on the bed, until his shoulders were between her bent knees, and then he reached under her, cupped her buttocks, and brought his mouth and warm tongue to her to drive her crazy. Quivering beneath him, she clutched his hair with her hand.

"Oh, Trent. I want you now."

"Easy, baby, you've been hurt. We don't have to."

"But I want to."

"All right, I'm with you, but we'll take it slow."

Then he reached over to the nightstand and took out a foil package. He sheathed himself, and slowly sank inside her. He entered her over and over again in a slow, steady rhythm.

Reaching such great pleasure, she soared in his arms as a fiery storm continued to build inside her. Her nails dug into his back, and then she climaxed. As she did, he surged into her and met her release with his own.

As she drifted back to reality, she wondered, if, with time, she could convince him that she was worthy of his love. That they were meant to be together. They were married after all.

When it was over, he lay back on the pillows and flung his arm over his head. "Damn, that was great, Kate. As long as we're married, I want you to drop whoever else you're sleeping with."

Her breath solidified in her throat. Her cheeks burned and a mixture of anger and hurt whirled inside her. *He thought she was sleeping around.* She was glad the lights were out so he couldn't see her shock or her pain at his words. "I understand," she whispered.

Yeah, she understood all too well what he thought of her. The frequent words of Bill Jackson rang in her mind, *"Piece of shit. Useless…stupid… Worthless trash. Should have dropped you in the gutter where you belong."*

And tonight, though she thought she had left that behind, she was battered and bruised and a whore—the destructive picture she'd tried so hard to run from, now complete. Trent thought she was easy. There would be no second chance with him. No second chance marriage. She'd never be good enough for him.

Her dream—the dream she hadn't realized she'd ridiculously held onto—died and blew away like ashes in the wind. The sooner she woke up to reality and got that message through her 'thick, stupid skull'—as her stepfather used to say to her—and shut down her feelings for Trent, the better off she would be.

She would not try for happiness again with him. She'd not let all the hard-fought self-esteem she had worked to build since she'd left her stepfather's house crumble any further. Tomorrow, she'd tell Trent that tonight was a big mistake, and that she wanted to return to being just his employee. There couldn't be a repeat of this night.

After a few minutes, with an aching heart, she rolled over on her side away from him and let the tears silently slide down her cheeks.

CHAPTER TWENTY-FOUR

The next morning, in his office, Trent poured over one of the reports he had Mrs. Nash compile. Everyone hired this past year checked out. There wasn't anything unusual on record and all the employees held clean background checks. Except for having falsified her educational records, having a notorious stepfather, and having been arrested once, Kate's records were even clear.

Were her claims that she had nothing to do with Frank Blake true? Had she truly only come to the company to find out what had happened to her brother? Was she innocent of everything else?

Leaning back in his chair, Trent pressed his fingertips together and contemplated the phenomenal chemistry between him and Kate. He had been riveted by their lovemaking. The sex had been hot, too hot, and any other relationship he'd ever had paled in comparison. She'd dozed off immediately. He had wanted to wake her up in the middle of the night for more, but he let her sleep, knowing she needed to rest after her ordeal. He'd been tempted to hold her in his arms while she slept, but he didn't want to hurt her.

But then, he had never doubted the chemistry between them. It was her character that had and still concerned him.

He blew out a deep breath and returned his attention to the reports. The next report listed all the change orders that had been done in the past year. A few alarmed him. He linked those to the purchase orders and found that someone had changed the orders for products and equipment he'd not approved.

Many had been before Kate worked at the company so she couldn't have been the person who tampered with those. He blew out a deep breath. *Had she been telling the truth?* He wanted to believe her.

He strode to the outer office. "Mrs. Nash, put out a memorandum to Purchasing. Nothing gets approved or changed without me signing off—*in person*. Someone has forged my signature."

Trent returned to his desk and called Sam, the manager of the Karger building site. "If you see anything suspicious, let me know. I want a moratorium on building. We will check the quality of every item to verify that we have the correct products. All the machinery has to be checked for safety, down to each miniscule part to make sure it hasn't been tampered with."

"This sounds serious," Sam said.

"It is. The entire crew needs to be on alert for possible sabotage." Trent hung up the phone. He would go through all the records and find out who was responsible, then go straight to the police.

While he'd like to relay this disaster to his grandfather, he couldn't. The stress might send the elderly man into heart failure. And if Roland had something to do with this, Trent would kill his cousin with his bare hands.

And the next time he saw Kate, he'd ask for her version of everything. This time, he would hear her out.

* * *

Kate strode through the parking garage, planning to go out for lunch and run errands instead of hanging around the office. At the sound of footsteps behind her, and still jittery after the accident yesterday, she whirled around.

Trent was behind her.

"Oh, it's you," she cried out with relief. Still, her defenses rose to protect her. This man could do more damage to her heart and soul than anyone else.

"Would you like to go to lunch?" he asked, closing in on her.

Tensing, she shook her head, wondering what he had to berate her for now. "I have errands to run." She turned to walk away.

"I'll give you a ride to the house later. All right?" he said to her back.

She stopped in her steps and gritted her teeth. He had a lot of nerve. She had lain awake for hours last night, hurting. He'd practically called her a whore. He said he thought she was sleeping with other men while she had been married to him. He probably thought she had been all the time she'd known him!

She stiffened. "No…thanks. I have a rental," she said flatly, over her shoulder.

"Kate, look at me." When she turned, he persisted, "I'll buy you a car. Just tell me what you want."

Why was he being so nice? Frowning, she walked on. He strode with her to the tiny leased car, the cheapest she could find. "That doesn't even look safe, Kate. How old is it?"

Kate shrugged. "It's fine. It'll do." She had to conserve her funds so she could buy another car.

Why was he still here?

When she raised her face to him, he smiled. "I have a great idea, Kate. Why don't we go shopping for a new car for you this weekend?"

She was startled by his suggestion. Desire sizzled in his dark eyes and she couldn't look away. He touched her arm, sending warmth flooding through her. His gaze dropped to her mouth. She moistened her lips with her tongue and her mind went blank.

"Are you thinking of last night?" he asked, rubbing her arm.

Her knees grew weak. "Yeah," she whispered.

Then Kate snapped to her senses. She remembered what he'd implied last night about her morals. She clenched her hands and regained her composure. So, that's why he was being so nice. He thought she'd whore for him again.

Kate raised her chin and resolved never to be alone with him again. "Last night was a fluke. I'm not about to add temporary sex to our temporary marriage, and I can't accept a car from you either. Thanks for the offer, but no thanks." She opened the rental car door. "I'm having an alarm installed at my house. I'm going there tonight. Remember our relationship is a business arrangement, so I'll just head on my way to do my errands—"

"Don't be ridiculous about tonight." He grabbed her arm. "It's not safe for you to stay at your house alone. You're coming with me. You were almost killed yesterday."

She clenched her hands at his highhanded, overbearing attitude. "Are you planning to kidnap me? Because that's the only way you can force me to stay with you."

"Of course not, but I'm pleading with you…for your safety, Kate."

"You're not thinking of having any fringe benefits, are you? Well, I'm taking your advice and cutting out all the men I sleep with—and the *all* is only *you*."

"I couldn't be sure what you were doing, and I couldn't handle the idea of you with anyone else. Our relationship hasn't been exactly normal, and I wanted it clear where I stood on the matter. I didn't mean to hurt you."

She jammed her finger into his chest. "Well, you did hurt me. You made me feel cheap. Came just short of calling me a whore. So thanks for everything, but I'll take my chances on my own. I'll do whatever you want in front of your grandfather, but really, the sooner this pretend marriage is over, the better it will be for me."

"I want to believe you, Kate… I want to believe there were no more lies between us than your credentials and getting into the company, and the issues that went along with that."

Kate stared at him in shock. "Are you beginning to believe me? I know I was probably wrong to take the matter into my own hands coming to the company, but I felt I had nothing else I could do to find out who was responsible for Matt's death—"

A silver corvette roared into the garage and pounded up the ramp, precariously close to where they stood by Kate's car. Trent pulled Kate away from the danger and into the safety of his arms. The car barreled off and screeched to a halt in Roland's parking space.

"Roland!" Trent released her. "Damn. He must be drunk again. He'll need to be drunk to take what I'm going to do to him."

Trent strode to Roland's car and jerked open the door. He grabbed his cousin by the collar and hauled him to his feet. "You could have killed us, or anyone else."

Kate gasped at the bruises, torn shirt, busted lip, and blood dripping from Roland's nose. Trent's fist stopped inches from Roland's face, then he dropped his hold.

Roland inhaled a deep breath and swayed back against his car.

"What the hell happened to you?" Trent demanded.

"He's going to kill me, if I don't come up with the money."

"Who—damn it? Let's go inside and you can explain." Trent glanced at Kate. "Will you come, too?"

Still sizzling about Trent's treatment of her last night, Kate folded her arms over her chest. "But only to find out what happened."

While they rode up in the elevator, Trent seemed barely able to hold his anger in check. "You've been cooking the books and stealing from the company," he accused.

"Yes." Roland seemed relieved to tell the truth.

Trent furrowed his brow. "You're in a lot of trouble."

Roland nodded. "I know."

The elevator door opened on the top floor. Once they were inside his office, Trent turned to his cousin. "What the hell is going on?"

"If I tell you, I'll be killed."

"If you don't tell me, *I'll kill you*," Trent said, fisting his hands. "You've been sabotaging the Karger building, bilking us for money. A man has died. You're going to jail."

Roland's face reddened. "No." He slumped down on the couch and dropped his face into his hands.

"What did you think would happen to the building, when you swapped quality products for inferior ones?" Trent asked.

Roland loosened his tie and shirt buttons and ran his hand around his sweaty neck. "I wasn't swapping anything. I did take the advertising money from the account, but I didn't sabotage your project."

"Someone is," Trent said.

"Blake, I'm sure," Roland mumbled. "I needed money to repay a gambling debt. He was so willing to lend it to me in the beginning, but then he turned on me."

"He was willing because he was setting us up," Trent said.

Roland swiped his hand across his bleeding face. "He told me not to interfere with the sale or he'd beat me to a pulp. Since he's not getting the company now that our grandfather won't sell, he's demanding his money back. *Right now.*"

Trent went into his bathroom and returned with tissues and a damp towel. He tossed the towel at Roland.

Roland blotted his bloodied nose. "Shit. I thought his goons were going to kill me. I'm dead anyway. I can't pay. I tried to triple the money that I took to the casino, but lost everything." His face creased. "I can't believe he let them beat the crap out of me. He told me if I didn't convince you to sell the company, I might not walk away the next time."

"How much do you owe him?"

"$325,000," Roland answered. "Now, growing $5,000 a day."

"I'll get the money for you, and you'll repay me out of your salary. Damn you, if you bring this hell down on our heads again. If I find you've been involved in substituting the products or sabotaging the building—and helping Blake, you'll go to jail. A man died."

"I'm not involved." Roland blew out a deep breath. "Man, thanks. I owe you. But I have to warn you that Blake plans to use your wife to get to you. He said he has something on her that would make her squirm if you knew what it was."

Frowning, Trent glanced at Kate. "You know about this?"

The blood drained from her face. "Can we talk privately?"

"In the bathroom." Trent followed her through the door and closed it.

His brow furrowing, he stood over her.

Her knees trembled.

"Just when I think I can trust you..." He threw out his hands. "You told me you didn't know Blake."

"No. I didn't say that. I said that I didn't work for him."

He swiped his hand through his hair. "Damn it. Splitting hairs, Kate? Why can't you ever tell me anything straight? And what the hell does he hold over you to blackmail you? Obviously something that's going to piss me the hell off."

Kate raised her chin. "I didn't remember Blake at first," she said in a rush of words. "I never knew his name—but at the awards ceremony he said he knew my stepfather—and then I remembered *him!*" She grabbed Trent's arm. "When I realized I'd met him before I was afraid to tell you, exactly for this reason! I knew you'd think the worst. There was never anything between Blake and me. Nothing that pertains to you or that you should be upset about." She did not want him to know the sordid details that Blake wanted to spill about her. "It's personal and nothing that mattered—"

He shook off her hand. "You and Blake... It's more than business, isn't it? You don't work for him—you work with him...and more. And you showed up at Farrington Construction around the same time that he tried to get back into our lives. Damn it to hell." He turned and strode out of the bathroom.

"It's not what you think," she called out to his retreating back. She followed him out to the hallway, where he stepped onto the elevator and the doors closed. She headed to her own office to calm herself. "Darcy…" she said as she walked through the doorway.

Her friend turned from her computer screen. "What's wrong, Kate?"

Kate stared at Darcy, in shock. "Trent and I… It's even worse. He thinks I'm in cahoots with Blake…and sleeping with that disgusting man, too."

Darcy handed her a letter. "This looks important."

Kate gasped. "It's the drywall report from the lab." She opened the envelope. "The drywall contains a radioactive phosphorus substance, which contains radium…and several more hazardous toxic substances. I have to give this to Trent."

* * *

Ten minutes later, while driving toward his grandfather's mansion, Trent swore under his breath. Were there no women he could trust, or was it only the ones closest to him that had no scruples? Kate had more skeletons in her closet than Jack the Ripper.

She and Blake…

Jealousy he'd never experienced raged inside him like an ugly beast. The thought of them together rolled his stomach into a nauseous wave.

The marriage had to end. He couldn't remain married to her, not a minute longer. He stalked into his grandfather's house. He'd gladly give her double the money from the prenuptial agreement just to get her out of his life. He hoped that his grandfather's health could hold up to all the truths he had to tell.

One thing nagged him and didn't make sense. If she and Blake were together…why would the man have tried to kill her?

He'd seen photos of the wreckage and the perilous angle at which the car had nearly gone over the steep ramp. This could not have been a stunt to make her look innocent, to fool them—because if the car had plummeted the hundred feet, she would surely have been killed. And the mask that day on the construction site…she had been upset, enough to faint.

Trent stepped into his grandfather's house.

Beasley entered the foyer. "Mr. Trent? You caught me by surprise."

"Where's my grandfather?"

"He's in the library. Allow me to notify him."

"Thanks, Beas, but I don't have time to wait—"

"But Mr. Trent…"

Trent strode down the long marble hallway and into his grandfather's study. The patio doors were opened to the side yard where his grandfather was practicing a golf putt on his personal green, looking as fit as a man of seventy-eight years old could look.

"I'm surrounded by liars," Trent muttered as he took in his grandfather's appearance. The man seemed to be the picture of health.

A guilty look rose on his grandfather's face. Then the man had the nerve to place his hand over his heart. "Trent. You surprised me."

"I'm sure I did," Trent said dryly. "You're quite active today for a man on his death bed."

"I was only stretching. I think I'll rest now, as I do feel weak. I didn't expect you."

Trent crossed his arms over his chest. "Obviously."

The elderly man sheepishly put his golf club down and shuffled into his study. "Now tell me what this is about?"

Trent blew out a restless breath. "First, you can knock off the sick act. Let's be honest with each other. Your poor health is a ruse, isn't it?"

His grandfather shrugged and sat on the leather sofa. "I had a scare, but I'm healthier than I led you to believe."

"Did you have to *scare* your family as well," Trent blasted.

"I wanted to retire, but I couldn't with my grandsons *Players of the Month*. I needed them to become responsible *men*."

"Okay your truth is out, now mine, and I think by your golf action you're strong enough to handle what I have to say. All is not going well at the Company."

Trent filled his grandfather in on the sabotage. He left out the part about Roland. He would give Roland the chance to return the money he'd taken from the company, but Trent did reiterate his suspicions of Blake.

"Trent, I do believe Blake could be responsible. He's an unethical scoundrel."

"I can get extra security to protect our assets, but there's something else you need to know." He told his grandfather the rest. "I only married Kate because I could divorce her when I wanted to. I had something to hold over her head to force her to marry me, in a temporary agreement."

Yes. Saying it out loud made it sound nasty. Damn it, *he* had forced her to marry him, then treated her badly for doing what he wanted her to do. But he had also wanted her like no other woman…

"Do you mean your marriage to that dear girl is a sham?"

"I guess shams run in the family."

His grandfather ignored the comment. "Her aunt was a fine, lovely woman. We might have become more if she hadn't died. To be honest, Trent, I knew on the day Kate applied for the job that she wasn't yet a psychologist. But I thought you might like her. I'm sorry I lied to you."

"I'm sorry I lied to you, too, but you forced this marriage."

"And you only said you would marry her to humor me?"

"Yeah, and I'll take my own blame for lying to you." He had to admit to himself that this wasn't the complete truth. In a possessive way, he had wanted to bind Kate to him. He realized that now... He hadn't wanted to let her go.

"I don't want you to be miserable in your marriage, but tell me, what has she done? She seems like a sweet girl."

"Sweet? I'm not sure that's the right word for Kate."

"What?"

"Never mind, but I just need out." He had wanted to give them a second chance, but the woman he wanted her to be was an unobtainable dream—and involved with Blake. The thought of a divorce brought an ache to his heart that she would never be his.

"I'll have our attorneys make the arrangements for an annulment, if that can be obtained. Or you can divorce her."

"No, don't do that. Tomorrow, I'll make the arrangements and draw up a settlement. I want her out of my life immediately and completely." It was the only way he could deal with how she tore him up inside.

"Trent, I'm sorry for this outcome."

Trent blew out a deep breath. "So am I. I'm going to the Karger site."

* * *

With the drywall report clutched in her hand, Kate stood near the half-opened door of James Farrington's study and listened to Trent and his grandfather discussing her. Her heart constricted in her chest. Trent could have his annulment or divorce, or whatever it took to be rid of her. She'd come here to give him the report and to tell him the entire story about her encounter with Frank Blake.

However, the gritty details would be nothing like Trent expected. When she was younger she'd blamed herself, but no matter how she might have attracted Blake, she knew that it wasn't her fault—it was her stepfather's. She should have told Trent, even if it was humiliating, but now, she wouldn't have to tell him about one of the most horrific and painful days of her life.

He'd be sure to misinterpret her involvement anyway. That was his way when it came to her. She was better to get out while she could. And get as far away as possible. But if it was better this way, why did she feel such a terrible sense of loss?

She swiped at the tears on her cheeks. Perhaps she'd just mail the report to Trent. Let him find the culprit, and then Matt's death would be avenged. If Blake was behind the sabotage, the paper in her hand proved he had to be crazy—making him dangerous.

A horrible thought rushed through her. What if Trent thought she'd falsified the document? Who knows why, but he might! Her shoulders sagged at that possibility.

As a hand pressed against her back, Kate whirled around.

"I heard everything, too," Mrs. Farrington whispered. "Why don't we talk?"

Kate numbly nodded. She followed Trent's mother down the hall. Even though she hadn't meant to overhear the conversation, she didn't want Trent to catch her here because there was no doubt he'd add eavesdropping to her list of sins against him.

Once they were out of the line of sight, Eden stopped. "Why is he divorcing you?"

Steeling her pride, Kate straightened her shoulders. "The marriage was wrong. That's all."

"Good. Now Cecilia will have her chance. I'm leaving my money to her. She's a distant relative on my side. I wouldn't have left anything to Trent if he stayed with you. Can't you see how continuing this marriage would harm him?"

"If money is all that matters to you, and not your son's happiness, I think you'll get your wish. You don't even care that your precious Blake is out to hurt Trent." Kate raised the paper in her hand. "Here's the proof."

Eden dropped her gaze to the report. "What proof? Something Blake did?"

"Blake's been sabotaging the materials and the building. I just need to link him to a warehouse to prove it."

Eden grasped for the paper. "Not Frank. Give me the report. I'll give it to Trent."

Kate shook her head. "No, thank you. I'll make sure he gets it. I'll probably mail it."

She didn't trust his mother to give him the evidence. Eden could be so blinded by her love for Blake, she might not think the report was important—or if it implicated Blake, she might even destroy the paper.

Eden Farrington stared down her nose at Kate. "I'm sorry for you in this divorce. Truly, I am. Trent might have thought he was in love with you, too, but he'll soon realize Cecilia is the right wife for him."

More tears burned Kate's eyes. His mother was so wrong. Trent had never loved her. "One day, will you please tell him the truth that I never worked for Blake, or had anything to do with him?"

"Perhaps... But only when he's safely married to Cecilia."

Blowing out a deep breath, Kate nodded weakly. "If that's the best you can do..."

Kate turned on her high heels. Her footsteps clicked on the marble as she strode out of the mansion, probably for the last time.

***

With her hands clenched on the steering wheel, Kate drove through the mansion's wrought iron gates. Just ahead of her on the main boulevard, Trent's car headed toward downtown and the Karger site.

She lifted her chin. She wasn't going to run or cower as she had with her stepfather. In addition, she was over the initial shock of hearing Trent tell his grandfather how much he wanted her out of his life. Face to face, like mature adults, she'd give him the lab report and tell him what she had overheard.

She took a deep breath. Now that she'd shielded her heart, she could handle facing his news and if he wanted a divorce, they should just do it.

Then she would say good-bye and get on with her life—away from him.

Kate slid out of her car and met him at the gates of the Karger construction site. "Hi," she said in a breathy voice with a reserved edge. If this was over, she'd face it head on.

"Why are you here?" Trent asked.

"We need to talk about a few things. Why are *you* here?"

He nodded to the security guard who opened the gates. "Kate, if you want to talk, you'll have to come with me." He put on a hard hat and handed her one.

She followed him to the elevator. "Uh... You know how hard this is for me. I can't go up there, especially after what happened the last time."

"Then stay here." He stepped into the open-cage elevator. "I'm not really in a good mood to talk about anything at the moment."

Kate sighed and reluctantly stepped on. He shut the door.

"Trent, you know I don't like this. Why does everything have to be so hard with us?"

His dark eyes shuttered, he shook his head. "It's brave of you to trust the elevator."

"Brave or stupid? I'm not sure which."

The elevator lumbered up to the top floors. Trying to breathe evenly, she shivered and pulled her thin jacket closer around her. Why hadn't she just given him the papers and told him she'd heard him talking about the divorce down on the ground? She must be a glutton for punishment... She kept her eyes closed until they stopped.

When Trent stepped out, she followed him. Her stomach rolled at being so high.

The late afternoon sun was already making pink streaks in the western sky, while the unfinished building seemed to gape to the open air. The wind caught her and she stumbled from the force of the breeze.

He grabbed her arm and steadied her. "Don't get near the edge. A gust could pull you over."

Her shorter skirt whipped around her legs. She clung to his arms. "Not a chance—I have no intention of getting too close."

He pulled her hands off his arms and moved away. "I wasn't trying to scare you."

Trent stepped to the ledge that had a two-foot-high wall running around the outside. He sat, stretched out his legs and leaned against a pillar, probably because he knew she couldn't go anywhere near him with her fear of heights.

Kate stood ten feet away. "I wish you wouldn't do that. If you were to fall..."

"I'm not going to jump, if that's what you're thinking. And if I fell, scaffolding is a few feet below the edge."

"Oh, that's a relief," she said dryly.

"I'm not afraid of heights. However, I do have a healthy respect."

"Trent, I'm sorry about all the issues you're having with your building."

"I'm sorry, too."

"So why did you come up here?" She shifted uneasily and waited for an answer.

"I'm here to reflect on my projects. My life. My failures. But really at the moment, I'm waiting to see why you would follow me up here, knowing how you feel about heights."

She squeezed her hands together. "The reason I came up here...is to face my fears and be brave enough to tell you everything about my past. Besides coming to the company to find who caused Matt to die, I should have told you about my stepfather. For beginners, I'm afraid of heights because of him. He was an evil, terrible man. I didn't have a choice that he raised me... H-he involved me in one of his schemes...on a ledge..." Her voice trembled.

"Blaming him for everything?"

"No. But I should have told you about me—about him—but I was afraid you wouldn't accept me for it..."

She paused. Here she was about to bare her soul and he didn't say anything, but just waited for her to say more. "What's the use? You'll never believe I was an innocent victim of my stepfather." She shoved her hand into her jacket pocket and pulled out the report. "I have something important to give you."

"What is it?" He got up, strode to her and took the paper.

"Farrington Construction had several orders for drywall that were rerouted to another warehouse before being brought to the Karger site. The drywall is intermingled with drywall that is laced with toxic chemicals. This is the report from the lab. These last batches were slated for the top floors of the building."

"What the hell—"

"Whoever is sabotaging the company, is only doing a little here and a little there to harm you. Mostly, it seems, they were sabotaging the equipment to wreak havoc. But I don't understand what the toxic chemicals on the top floors were for. None of it makes sense."

Trent studied the papers, then glanced at her. "The replacement with low-grade equipment was probably done to make us look like we ran a sloppy operation and to wreak havoc. However, I agree that the drywall substitution doesn't make sense. If Blake wanted the company, and this project, I'm not sure why he'd sabotage the actual building. And if he planned to take over our company and this building, his offices would be where the drywall was installed—where I had planned to have a penthouse apartment."

"I wanted to make sure you had the information before I left the company. I'm moving away… and I probably won't see you again—"

"*You're leaving?* I haven't told you I've released you from our deal yet."

"I overheard you telling your grandfather about the divorce, getting him on your side, when I came to give you this report. I didn't mean to eavesdrop—"

"You were outside the door listening?" he asked quietly.

"Yes, I heard it all! Count that against me! He's agreed and so did your mother. She can't wait to get rid of me. You'll be free to marry whomever you want—perhaps Cecelia—your mother's favorite. You won't have to deal with me anymore. I'm leaving now. Oh, God, I'll even face the elevator alone."

She turned to go and Trent followed and caught her arm. "I thought you had other things to tell me? Tell me the rest…about you."

"What's the point?"

Before she could hit the call button, the elevator moved in the shaft.

Trent gave her a sideways glance. "Someone else is here. I'm not expecting anyone. Are you?"

Her stomach knotted. "No."

The doors of the elevator opened and Frank Blake stepped off.

Kate's heart pounded at a bursting speed. "*Blake,*" she cried.

Trent threw her a dark look. For one moment, hurt flashed in his eyes, but it was quickly replaced with distrust. "So this was your plan, Kate? Both you and him here to trap me?"

"No," she said, shaking her head vehemently. "You've got to believe me. I don't work for Blake. I have nothing to do with him."

"Don't trust your wife, eh?" Blake chuckled. He walked around in the open air and spread out his arms. "See this view? I'll put my office up here. I'll be *King of the Hill.* You've built residences, recreation, shopping centers, and businesses all in one…a small town feel in a huge building."

Hands on his hips, Trent strode to Blake. "How did you get past my security guard?"

"Your guard has seen me here with your mother several times. I told him you were expecting me. Farrington, I'm a rich man, and I want to be a part of what is going on at Farrington Construction. We could make a fortune with this design. This is the wave of the future."

Trent glared at him. "Are you crazy? You've been trying to wreck my building. It will take months to find out what damage you've caused."

Blake jutted his face toward Trent. "Don't blame me for your failures. That's why I'm offering to buy the company. You'll work for me. Under my supervision, we'll prosper."

"Get it through your thick skull, Blake. Farrington Construction is not for sale."

"Why are you playing this game with me?" Blake snapped. "Your mother said you agreed to sell. She called me—"

"I don't care what she said—I don't even know why she said it—but you've been using her. Now get the hell off my property," Trent demanded.

Blake's face reddened. "Why you… Eden said you would accept my offer. She told me to come down here."

Trent stepped closer to Blake. "I said nothing of the kind. Now leave."

Blake shoved his hand against Trent's shoulder. "If you don't sell, I'll bring OSHA down on you."

Trent pushed back at Blake. "You've been interfering with the completion of this building and harassing Roland. Leave my family alone."

Blake snorted. "Then why the hell did you call me down here?"

"I didn't call you. There's no sale." He threw Kate a hostile look. "You and Kate can look elsewhere for a company."

"*Your wife?*" Blake chuckled. "What does she have to do with this? Oh, jealous of me and the beautiful wife. She told you? I'm surprised. She does owe me, don't you, Mrs. Farrington? I paid a pretty penny to get between her legs."

"Is this true?" Trent turned his ire on her.

"I don't owe him anything," Kate lamented.

Trent grabbed Blake's lapels. "As long as she's my wife, you stay the hell away from her."

Frank Blake jerked his jacket out of Trent's hold.

Kate stepped closer. "Trent, he's trying to make it sound like there was something between us. There wasn't. It was easy for our paths to cross, because my stepfather knew every shady, slimy character in town—"

"Tell me what it was, Kate?" Trent bit out, his eyes narrowing as he glanced at her.

She put her hand on his arm. "Let's go. I'll tell you everything in private...but not here. I can explain it so you'll understand that what happened wasn't my fault."

Blake pulled out his cell phone. "Come on up, boys." He turned back to Trent. "Farrington, I guess I'll just have to prove I mean business. I don't like it when someone refuses my offer. I don't like it when you have me come down here and then lie to me. What do you need, more convincing? You'll come to your senses after my boys are through with you."

"You can't use your strong-arm tactics to get my company. And don't ever play loan shark with Roland again. Do you understand me?"

"I don't give a damn about your useless cousin, but I want Farrington Construction. Financially, I need these projects."

"So that's why you want to buy so badly. Not my problem."

"I had to stomach your nauseating mother to get close to you and your family, but the wife?" He chuckled. "Now, I'll gladly do that job. I'm sure she's learned from the best with her stepfather, and you fell for it. Nice breasts, and that teeny tiny heart-shaped birthmark on her collarbone, just so." He stroked just where the birthmark would be on Kate's body. "How many other men have *paid* for her services?"

Trent jerked his head toward Kate. "Is this what I'm thinking this is about? You're a *hooker?*"

"It's not like that. My stepfather...my stepfather made the deal with him!" Kate said. "It wasn't my fault."

Blake scoffed, "It is like that, Farrington. I paid $10,000 for one week with her. No other way to slice it, my dear. Farrington, you turned out to be a hell of a sucker."

Trent shoved Blake and he stumbled and landed on a pallet of supplies. The outraged man struggled to his feet and dusted off his clothes.

With the wind whipping her hair around her face, Kate grabbed Trent's arm. "Trent, don't listen to him. He's making it sound worse than it is. Let's go so I can explain."

"How can you explain something like that?" The cold look Trent cast on her made her shrivel on the inside.

Blake struggled to his feet and Trent stepped closer to him.

They were too close to the edge. "Please, stop," Kate pleaded. "This is dangerous."

"You're not so hot, Blake, without your thugs around," Trent said.

Blake whipped a pistol from beneath his jacket. "Oh, yeah? If you don't sell the company to me, you'll have nothing but trouble. OSHA will be there every day until Farrington Construction comes to a screeching halt."

Kate's heart pounded as she moved out of sight behind a vertical beam and punched out 911 on her cell phone. "Please, hurry to the Karger building site." After giving the police the directions, she hung up.

Trent hit Blake's wrist and the gun went flying. Blake swung at Trent and landed a punch to his chest. Trent shoved Blake backwards.

"Stop!" Kate cried. "I've called the police and they're on their way."

She was looking for something to use for a weapon when the elevator door opened and three burly men got off. One of them tried to break up the fight, another rushed toward Trent and shoved him from behind. Trent's hands were clenched on the lapels of Blake's jacket... They both tumbled over the edge.

Kate screamed, "No!" With her heart pounding, she rushed to the side. Blake landed on the flat surface of the scaffolding, while Trent dangled precariously from the ropes.

"What in the hell, Farrington? Are you trying to kill us both?" Blake demanded as he stood upon the platform.

"Please," Kate begged. "You've got to help him, Blake."

"Not my problem. If he falls, that's one way for me to get the business."

"That's murder."

Blake had his feet close to the edge of the scaffolding where Trent managed to wrap his fingers around a metal bar and began to climb up on the platform. Kate held her breath. All Blake would have to do is stomp Trent's fingers or shake the scaffolding and Trent could fall to his death.

With squealing sirens, police cars surrounded the building.

One of the henchmen asked, "What do you want us to do, boss?"

"Help me get off this scaffold, stupid." Blake snarled down at Trent, "I hope you can hang on long enough for the police to reach you, Farrington. Come on, boys."

In the wind, the scaffolding pitched sideways a few inches. At the sound of ropes snapping and the pins in the scaffolding pinging, Blake scowled as if he became aware that the platform was dropping beneath him. He reached out with an outstretched hand to grab on to anything. A fleeting glance of terror passed over his face as he grasped empty air. His scream echoed off the downtown buildings.

Trent! Her heart racing, Kate rushed to the side.

One of Blake's henchmen yelled, "Let's get the hell out of here."

Kate leaned over the edge. Trent dangled from the last remaining rope of the scaffold. "Trent! Oh my God. What can I do to help?"

"Just step back," he rasped hoarsely.

He pulled himself up with the rope, then scrambled over the ledge to safety and then collapsed in a heap.

Sagging in relief, Kate dropped down beside him and put her arms around him. Tears streamed down her face. "I was so scared."

They sat for a few minutes, while the terror of his near falling to his death subsided.

"Kate, Kate," he rasped. "Why are you doing this to me?" Then as if he remembered, he shook off her hold. "You...and Blake! Others?"

She gaped at him. "*No!* I can explain everything. I'm not what you think and I certainly wasn't involved with Frank Blake in hurting the company—"

The police stepped off the elevator and approached them. Police officers set to work with tape, gathering evidence and recording the crime scene. For the second time within a year, someone had fallen from the job site.

"We'll have to take you to the station for questioning," a police officer said, gesturing toward the elevator.

CHAPTER TWENTY-FIVE

With two officers flanking them, Trent and Kate rode down in the open-caged elevator in stony silence. With one glance toward Trent, Kate could tell he had cut himself off from her completely.

On the ground, the police were already outlining Blake's lifeless body. She shielded her eyes as they walked past. His henchmen were loaded into a couple of cop cars.

After a short ride in the back of another police car, Kate and Trent were ushered into the station and into a room with mirrored windows and several long tables.

Kate accepted a cup of bitter-tasting coffee from a clerk. As she sipped the brew, she still trembled from the fear that took hold of her when Trent nearly fell to his death. Trent thought the worst about her, even worse than before.

Would he tell the police she worked with Blake in sabotaging the building? Could she prove that she didn't? She might be facing years in prison if they wanted to prosecute her as Blake's accomplice.

She was even less sure they would believe her when the detective on her brother's case strode into the room. *Detective Martin!* Months ago, he had thought she'd fabricated the story when she claimed some shady things were going on at the construction site. There had been no evidence other than the words of her dying brother. No one else had been close enough to hear so there was no one to corroborate her story.

Another detective jotted notes on a tablet. "Mr. Farrington, now tell us again what happened from the moment Frank Blake arrived at the building?"

"I've already told you everything," Trent said to the detective. "Blake cornered me at my building, demanding that I sell my business to him. We fought. We landed on the scaffolding, which broke. The weak scaffolding was probably due to Blake's sabotage orders at my company, just one of the many disasters Blake orchestrated to make me look bad so he could come in and buy us cheaply. If you research his business you'll find he was in financial difficulty—at least that's what he claimed minutes before the accident."

Eden strode into the room. "Frank's dead?" she rasped, anger etching her face. She pointed her finger at Trent. "*You...killed him.*"

"I did not," Trent said with a groan. "He came to me at the job site, demanding that I sell. He said you told him to come meet me and that you told him I was ready to. He was furious when I said I didn't want to see him, let alone to sell the company to him. He threatened that his men would beat me up if I didn't agree—"

"You've always hated him—ever since he stole our clients." Eden folded her arms over her chest.

"This has nothing to do with years ago."

"How could you?" Eden cried. "You know I cared for him. Why?"

"I didn't push him. And he said some nasty things about you. He had no intention of being with you after this take over. He was using you."

Eden pursed her lips. "Anyone could have arranged these schemes. You had nothing to lose if the building failed. We were insured... Perhaps *over* insured on the project. Trent, you just did not want me to ever be happy." His mother dabbed a tissue to her eyes.

Detective Martin shook his head in disbelief, as he listened to their conversation, his forehead furrowed in thought. "Mr. Farrington, one of Mr. Blake's employees said you pulled Blake onto the scaffolding—"

"That's because one of his other thugs shoved me, and I had my hands clenched on Blake's jacket," Trent said through gritted teeth.

"I was there," Kate said, speaking up. "Trent didn't push Blake. It's as he says. They did fight, but one of Blake's men shoved Trent, Trent and Blake both went over the side. After the platform collapsed, Trent managed to climb up the rope. That's the entire story."

"Which man shoved him, Ma'am?"

"The tall, beefy man with red hair."

"Thank you...?" The detective took another glance at Kate, squinted at her, and then looked back at the report. "*Mrs. Farrington?*" He cocked his head toward her. "Don't I remember you as *Kate*

Meyers? Earlier in the year, didn't you claim Trent Farrington was cheating on products? You claimed he caused your brother to die when a subpar harness broke and he fell to his death…all because of Farrington Construction's 'shady business practices,' you said. At the time, you *demanded* Trent Farrington be *arrested*? Said he was a coldblooded murderer."

"Yes, I did," Kate answered in a matter-of-fact tone.

"And you said you couldn't wait for him to rot in prison for the murder of your brother," the detective added.

"You said this, Kate?" Trent asked.

Her heart hammering, she bit her lip and locked her gaze on the detective, and then stood. "Yes, I said all this, but all before…before I got to know Trent. When I took a job there, I found out the truth. He wasn't skimming from the accounts to save money. Someone else has been cheating *and* sabotaging the building…but not him."

"*Or*…has the story changed because your *circumstances* have changed?" Detective Martin looked over the rim of his glasses. "You stand to make a lot more from this as *Mrs. Farrington*. I'm sure you'll protect your interests."

"Oh, it's the same as before, Detective Martin. You don't believe me, do you?" Kate cried.

The detective shrugged. "How can I? Does the name *Bill Jackson, convicted criminal*, ring a bell? You were arrested in one of his schemes."

"I was innocent! My stepfather used my name as a cover to save himself if he was ever caught."

"The acorn doesn't fall far from the tree."

"That's what I overheard you saying the last time," Kate snapped. "Don't you have anything new to say?"

"Birds of a feather, flock together." He gave her a cheesy grin.

She clenched her hands. "Listen, I'm nothing like my stepfather. I was just an innocent child forced to live with him. I was his foremost victim."

"Okay, ma'am. I've heard every excuse, but I just want *the facts*." Detective Martin turned away to jot a few more notes. "After you've given your full statement, Mrs. Farrington, you may go. We're holding your husband for more questioning."

Kate glanced at Trent. She wanted to stay with him until he was released. He leaned back in the chair, his arms folded over his chest, his gaze shuttered to her. "Go on home, Kate," he said gruffly. "When I get out, we'll make our arrangements…"

Her shoulders sagged because she knew what Trent meant—the divorce. She nodded and should be grateful that he didn't say she worked for Blake or she would have been held for questioning, too. There was nothing she could ever do to prove to Trent that she loved him—that she really was a good person. Her one sin—she'd lied to get into the company.

The Detective turned to Eden. "Would you stay, ma'am? We'd like to ask you a few questions about anything you remember that pertains to this case."

"Of course." Eden swiped her eyes with a tissue. "My daughter-in-law here wouldn't want Trent in trouble—she only wants him for his money and he'd have done so much better if he'd married the girl I'd wanted him to. But *I* can't lie about it—even if I am his mother. Trent hated Frank with a passion."

Frowning, Kate bit her lip. Trent's mother wasn't helping him at all.

"You're under arrest, Mr. Farrington," the detective stated.

"Call my attorney," Trent said as his hands were handcuffed behind his back.

"But I have proof that Blake was sabotaging the company," Kate said.

"All right. Let's see it."

She rummaged through her jacket pockets and then her purse. Not finding the report, she winced and looked at Trent. "Do you have it?"

His eyes narrowed to slits, Trent slowly shook his head. "Regrettably not."

"The report must have blown away during the scuffle," Kate said. "I'm sure I can call the lab on Monday morning and get a copy."

"Monday morning is three days away," Trent said in an ill-humored voice.

She didn't actually have proof Blake was responsible, but she had invoices that provided a trail to the warehouse. If she could link Blake to that warehouse…

Kate turned to the detective. "May I speak to my husband privately?"

"You have three minutes."

Detective Martin stepped out with Mrs. Farrington and into another room. Kate saw them talking through a large glass window.

She sat in the chair beside Trent.

He gave her a sideways glance. "You got what you wanted, Kate. I'm going to jail for Blake's death. And you can probably convince them that I killed your brother, too."

"You know I don't believe that now."

"Why didn't you just tell him you have the evidence against me? All the purchase orders that were changed have my signature on them. Or there's a builder's risk insurance policy on the building. Matter of fact, my mother says we're over-insured. There you go. Great reason for me to want the project to fail—to get that extra money."

She held up a hand. "Stop! We both know someone is trying to frame you. We can pull the original invoices and prove your signature was forged on the change orders."

"So you believe in my innocence now, when my own mother doesn't? Why should you, Kate? You have what you wanted. I'll go to prison for Blake's murder even if they don't prosecute me for your brother's death."

Kate took a deep breath. She wanted to tell him that she loved him, but there was no point. With what he thought of her, she had to leave South Florida as soon as she could make arrangements.

"I know you hate me, Trent, but I'll do everything in my power to clear you."

He narrowed his eyes. "I don't hate you. That's the last thing I feel."

"I never worked for Blake. The only real lie I told was to get into the company. That was no worse than when you lied to your family that we were a happily married couple."

"That's different."

"Is it?"

He didn't answer.

She blew out a deep breath. "I don't expect you to believe anything I say, and I'll sign the divorce papers…whatever you want. But before I leave, I'm going to help clear you."

She started to get up, but then dropped back into the chair. "I have to tell you…and this is so difficult." She brought her hands to her burning cheeks. "Okay, I don't really want to talk about this—it makes me sick to think about it. My involvement with Frank Blake is nothing like you're thinking. If you still blame me after I tell you, I just hope one day you'll find it in your heart to forgive me for something I had no control over. And he's dead so now I have no proof for my story."

She fanned her face with her hand. "Oh, I don't even want to tell you the details—because *I will* break down." Despite the fact that she was already close to 'losing it' and tears stung her eyes, she continued in a low voice, "Most of my life, I lived in fear. My stepfather was abusive, so maybe you can understand why I'm involved at the Children's Abuse Center, because that's where I should have been placed…to protect me."

Tears trickled down Kate's cheek as she went on, "I was sixteen. Blake saw me and offered my stepfather a large sum for my…for my… I can't even say it—*my virginity*! It's not something a nice father would do, is it? But my stepfather was a greedy, nasty man. He couldn't refuse such easy cash—$10,000. It was clear on my stepfather's face, that with that offer, he'd found a way to make money from *me*. And he sold me for one week to be that man's plaything. It didn't matter to my stepfather what happened to me. And that's when I realized that he'd never, ever, change."

She raised her eyes to find Trent's brow furrowed. "Oh, I'm going on too much. Do you want to hear the rest of my horrible, horrible childhood?"

"Yeah, tell me the rest," he said.

Kate dropped her gaze to her clenched hands in her lap. "So everything you think about me is true. I was a hooker…but for only one night. My stepfather drove me to Blake's house. And I was going to go through with it. I was so scared. If I refused what my stepfather had arranged for that kind of money, he said he'd hurt me badly." Tears trickled down her cheeks. "Although my self-esteem was at a low point, I decided then and there that I'd rather die than let him turn me into a prostitute.

When I refused to go through with it, Blake ripped my dress from neckline to hem. I threw up all over myself and him—a slight bit of revenge. He let me go into the bathroom to freshen up. I locked the door and ran the bathtub to cover the noise, while I escaped through a window—that I had to break. That's how I got the scar."

She pointed to her midsection. "I took a big risk because I nearly died… Matt was my hero. He helped me get to my aunt's house that night. I was in the hospital for a little while. My stepfather came looking for me, but my aunt threatened legal action. After that, I went to live with her. She stepped in to take over custody of me and she took in Matt too. I didn't tell you because I really want to forget that part of my life and I was worried what you'd think about me. It's always been humiliating—shameful."

Shock was evident on his face when Trent leaned back in his chair, his handcuffed wrists behind him.

"See why I didn't want to tell you. It's not pretty, but disgusting," she said in a low voice.

His brow furrowed. "It's an overwhelming tale, Kate."

She didn't think he bought her story, or at least not the part where she wasn't to blame. "Oh, I don't expect you to believe me. And it's hard for me to remember and talk about it, but when my stepfather was around my life was worse than bad... I know it won't make a difference with us, but you deserve to know the truth about me and my involvement with Blake. It wasn't something I wanted— it was something forced on me. In a way it feels like a relief to tell you." She swiped the tears from her cheeks, then stood and headed toward the door.

"Where are you going?" he asked. "To your house or my grandfather's?"

She called over her shoulder, "Neither. I'm going to the warehouse. It's partly my fault you're being blamed."

"Kate, no! His thugs are still out there."

She couldn't look at him and once again see the disgust for her in his eyes. "No, they were arrested. I'm going to see if there is any evidence to tie them to the place. Then I'm going to Farrington Towers and get the duplicate copies of those purchase orders. I should return in a couple of hours."

"Don't go, Kate."

She started toward the door again, then paused. "The detective isn't going to believe me without cold, hard proof. I'm a lowlife con artist to him, too."

"Wait until I get bond. I'll go with you."

"I have to go alone," she said flatly. "If possible, let's handle the divorce by mail. I'll sign away my rights to the pre-nuptial money—I don't want it. I wish you well."

"Don't go, Kate. Come back. We need to talk."

She shook her head. "There's nothing left to say. You'll never believe that I am the girl that you met and that our weekend was real, or that I'm worthy of your love. But I'll never forget you."

"Kate!" When he started to follow her, one of the police officers stopped him.

She kept walking. She didn't want him to see the tears flowing down her face, or the shame burning her cheeks. She didn't want to see the revulsion in his eyes, to see what he thought of her past. He knew the worst. Her life was nothing like the women that he would have known, or the woman he should marry. He knew all about her dark, dirty secrets. So regardless of what she felt, their relationship was now over.

Dredging up all the old memories made her feel as worthless as she had when she was young. Aunt Kate had taken her and loved her and made Kate believe she was a wonderful human being. She wanted to feel that way again.

She'd clear Trent somehow. And then she'd leave Florida and try to put him and the past behind her, but she was sure it would take a long time to get him out of her heart.

* * *

Kate parked her car around the corner from the warehouse. Her adrenaline was pumping as she strode down the sidewalk with her mace in her pocket and a flashlight in her hand. She found a smaller door that led to the office. She tried the knob, but the door was locked. She wasn't willing to risk breaking the window—not with *her* background. Besides, it was wired with an alarm system.

Peering in the window, she saw stacks of drywall. She was about to return to her car, when she noticed one of the huge doors to the warehouse was slightly ajar.

Kate pushed open the door, just enough to slip inside the cavernous room. An office nightlight shone dimly through dingy glass windows, but otherwise the warehouse was completely dark and dank, and smelled of dust.

She used her flashlight to illuminate the drywall. There were foreign language symbols that she could not read. Had the drywall been shipped here to disguise the markings before being sent to the Karger site?

Something scurried against the toe of her high heel. She slapped her hand over her mouth to stifle a scream. She flashed the light around the area and saw pallets of drywall everywhere.

A car roared into the parking lot. The tires screeched to a halt. Kate's heart hammered. She moved further back into the eerie warehouse to hide herself. Minutes later, the lights in the office brightened, sending light through the interior windows and into the warehouse. Mumbled voices carried from inside.

To hide, Kate ducked behind a mound of empty crates, shoving the flashlight into her pocket. Drawers opened and closed in the office. Did Blake have more henchmen than the three who were arrested?

The door from the office to the warehouse swung open. Footsteps trampled down the steps in her direction.

Her heart beat rapidly as she crouched down behind the crates.

"One part of the job is done," a man said, flicking on the overhead lights. "The little bitch really got in our way, but I didn't expect her to tie in a connection to the drywall. I'll take care of her tomorrow. In the morning, we have to arrange for this to be loaded on a truck and dumped far away from here."

Had she heard the man's voice before? There was another voice, lower and undistinguishable—feminine.

Kate wanted to peak over the crates, to get a glimpse, but she couldn't risk it. She strained her ears to hear more.

Her cell phone rang and shattered the quiet. Panicking, she slipped her hand in her pocket and clicked off the phone. Her heart pounded as she held her breath, hoping against hope that they had not heard the sound.

"Someone's here," the man barked.

He rounded the corner. Kate gasped and tried to run, but she was backed into a corner. She tried to scramble over a crate to get a way.

"It seems the wife is snooping and wants to throw another glitch in our plans," the man said.

He jerked Kate up by the back of her jacket collar as if she weighed nothing. Before she could make out his features in the dim light, he swung his fist at her. Pain exploded in her head, while total darkness descended upon her.

* * *

Trent told the police his side of the story and reminded them that he'd reported issues before about the building site. In one incident—the crash of the elevator—he had been nearly killed.

In the early hours after midnight, after his bond was paid, Trent was given back his cell phone. He called Kate. When she didn't answer, he drove to her house. She wasn't there. Finally, he stopped by Greg's condo to get Darcy's home number.

"Have you seen Kate?" Trent said, practically busting into Greg's condo when Greg opened the door. Darcy walked out of the bedroom, wearing a robe. If Trent had found the two together at any other time, he would have smiled for his friend, but now the situation was dire.

Darcy thrust her face toward him as if she wanted to claw his eyes out. "No, I haven't heard from her since this afternoon. She went to give *you* a report about tainted drywall. In spite of the terrible things you think about Kate, *she* wanted to make sure *you* got the report. She feared *for your safety*. If you've done something to hurt her—"

"*Done something to hurt her*—I'm trying to find her!"

Darcy put her hands on her hips. "Listen, Trent, Kate's a great girl, and if she hasn't told you, I will. The only thing wrong with Kate was her stepdad, and if you think she's anything like him—you're not worth the trouble. Thank God, that horrible Bill Jackson is dead. She used to come to school with bruises. Now, don't *you* hurt her anymore. She's endured more pain than anyone should—"

His eyes burning, Trent blew out a deep breath. "Darcy, she told me some of her story tonight. But why didn't she tell me all this weeks ago?"

Darcy shrugged. "She has her pride, I guess. I'm sure she wants to forget that part of her life, certainly not have it shape her future. And she didn't think you'd believe her."

"I have to admit she was probably right."

"You don't know the horrible things that man has done to her—and she was one of the people most victimized by her stepfather's crimes. She didn't even want to tell *me*—her best friend. And I only found out recently that once he'd made her go out on a ledge to try to get into another apartment so she could unlock the door for him. Seven floors up. She told me she was petrified and frozen on the ledge. That's why she's afraid of heights. She was eight years old, Trent."

"She started to tell me tonight..."

"She said the bastard had to coax her back to him. He beat the living daylights out of her after she got off the ledge because *she'd* ruined *his* plans."

"Darcy, if he wasn't already dead, I'd like to beat Bill Jackson to a pulp." Trent ran his hand through his hair in frustration. "I'll make things right with Kate, but I can't find her. She went to a warehouse to find evidence to clear me. I don't have an address... I don't know where to look... I'm worried..."

"I know where the warehouse is." Darcy grabbed her purse. "Why don't we go with you?"

Kate had been afraid to tell him about her past. "She thought I was too much of a snob to accept her with her background, and I proved her right. I'll make it up to her. I swear, Darcy." Guilt seared Trent as he climbed back into his car.

When they arrived at the warehouse, Trent jumped out and paused beside Greg's car.

Greg rolled down the window. "Would she have come here alone?"

Trent leaned his hand on the car door. "Yeah, I'm afraid she's brave enough. She wanted to find evidence that would clear me."

Darcy nodded. "Yeah, Kate's a little brave and might try it. She's fiercely protective of the people she loves..." Trent's gaze locked on Darcy's at those words. She shrugged and added, "Which has gotten her into trouble before, if you know what I mean."

Trent and Greg entered the warehouse and found that a scuffle had gone on there. And a high-heeled shoe that looked like the ones Kate wore that day, lay on the floor.

Dread soared through Trent as he rushed the shoe outside to Darcy. "Something's happened to Kate."

Darcy put her hands to her cheeks. "Yeah, there's no way she'd leave one of those shoes behind," she said cryptically. "Expensive."

* * *

While Greg and Darcy went to check for Kate at the offices, Trent strode into his family's mansion. Trent found his grandfather in the living room.

"Has Kate been here?" Trent asked.

"No. Why?" His grandfather's forehead wrinkled with concern. "Is something wrong?"

"Yeah, everything's wrong. And I can't find her."

"Trent… You're finally coming to your senses about that dear girl."

"Something's happened to her, and I don't know where to look. And Blake is dead. It's hard to believe he'd even come into our building if he thought it was booby-trapped. Maybe that wasn't him who was rigging things at the building. And if he's not responsible for the sabotage, who else would have it out for the company, me, and now Kate? Could it be Roland?"

"Roland?"

"It's someone in the company—it has to be him. And my mother is acting crazy, she sent Blake to the construction site, saying I'd agree to a sale. He was furious at me, accusing me of playing some kind of game with him, as if to anger him. I feel she's pitting us against each other, and I don't know why. Then she accuses me of pushing Blake to his death. On her testimony alone, I might get convicted."

"Oh, boy." James dropped down in a chair and rubbed his cheeks. "It's not Roland… I can't believe it."

With a stunned look on his face, his grandfather rose from his chair and strode to his study. Trent followed.

On the way, they passed Vera. "Have you seen Kate or Roland?" Trent asked.

"Or Eden?" James added.

Vera shook her head and strode with them down the hall. "I haven't seen Roland, but your mother and her assistant took out the yacht. It was strange, normally they would have turned on the dock lights, but tonight they didn't."

Trent blew out a frustrated breath. "Perhaps Kate's with them. She'll be all right. I'll radio the boat."

His grandfather scratched his head. "Maybe not. I was becoming suspicious… You have the right to information that I've withheld from you."

Trent frowned. "What information?"

"I'm sorry Trent. I did it for you! I'll explain. I brought this on you. I didn't know how dangerous my meddling could be."

His grandfather bent to open his safe and brought out an envelope. With a trembling hand, he took out papers and handed them to Trent. "Forgive me. I should have told you a long time ago…"

CHAPTER TWENTY-SIX

Trent glanced at the papers. "This explains everything. You're saying she's my adoptive mother. Why do I have the feeling you had a heavy hand in this?"

"I never intended to hurt you, Trent. I only wanted to help. You needed a mother, and she was married to your father."

"Did you force Eden, coerce her...manipulate her into raising me as if she'd given birth to me?"

"*Yes, I did,*" his grandfather rasped. "I didn't want a scandal. And if she's built up anger and resentment against you and me, it's all my fault."

"This still doesn't explain why she hates me."

"She wanted children and had a series of miscarriages. As it didn't look like she'd ever carry a pregnancy to term, I insisted she raise her husband's love child—*you.*"

"What happened to my mother?"

"She died having you. I thought I did the right thing."

Trent blew out a deep breath. "I can't believe this."

"I'm sorry I meddled in your life. Eden lost a baby the same day you were born. I thought you would fill the void."

"Do you realize that she's never liked me? I must have been a bitter reminder of all she lost. In addition, a reminder that my father cheated on her... And then to have me brought into the mix. Damn it, if Eden's been out for revenge, and Kate's with her, Kate's in grave danger."

After they left the study, Roland walked through the front door.

Trent was relieved his cousin wasn't with his mother. "Eden's played us against each other, throughout our lives, now more than ever."

After explaining Eden's story and her motives for wrongdoing, Trent added, "She had Blake and me—and even you—at each other's throats, and why after bitterly hating Blake for years, did she start dating him again? She was setting us all up. If she's working with anyone, it has to be her assistant, Marc Simpson. And if they have Kate, they mean her harm. I'm going after them. Will you drive the speedboat?"

Roland straightened his shoulders and nodded. "I owe you, Trent. I'll go with you and help in whatever way I can."

Trent strode into his grandfather's study and unlocked the gun case. "Marc Simpson has military training."

After taking a knife and a pistol, he handed a gun to Roland. "You might need this."

* * *

Kate's eyes flickered open. Above her clouds rolled across an ebony sky where stars splattered like diamonds on black velvet. The December breeze was about sixty degrees and she shivered in her light jacket. Her short skirt rode up high on her thighs, while the thin stockings offered no protection from the cool night air.

Her arms tingled from the position behind her back and her head ached. She tried to move, but her hands and feet were bound. She still had on one high heel. Alarm shot through her. *What had happened?*

Her mouth was parched and she lifted her head and tried to speak—but a gag prevented her. She dropped her head back onto the hard surface.

Where was she? The smell of salt water mingled with diesel fuel. Engines rumbled beneath her. A boat! Her memories surged back to her of what had happened in the warehouse. That reminder sent alarm rushing through her.

Kate turned her head. About ten feet away, in the pilot's house of the Farrington yacht, Eden Farrington stood with her assistant, Marc Simpson. The doors were opened wide to the outside patio deck where Kate lay.

Why would Eden leave her daughter-in-law trussed up on the deck? Kate's heart beat at a rapid tempo. Had she and Eden been kidnapped? First Blake had tried to kill Trent, and now Eden was with Marc? It didn't add up. From Kate's position on the deck, she could see the lights of condominiums and the tall mast of a sailboat sweeping by. They must be on the New River.

"I'd better check on her," Eden said.

Kate squeezed her eyes shut. She lay unmoving as realization sank in. Trent's mother—*Eden*—was in on her kidnapping. Kate was at their mercy. The woman hated to have her for a daughter-in-law, but this was taking things to the extreme.

Eden nudged Kate with the toe of her shoe, then returned to the console. "She's still out cold."

"Good," Marc said. "My job will be easier."

Kate's cell phone rang.

Who was calling? No one would miss her in the middle of the night.

"Damn it." Trent's mother returned to Kate, thrust her hand in her jacket pocket and withdrew the cell phone.

After the voice mail beeped, Eden played the message. "It's Trent. He's out of jail and looking for her."

"Thought of a *Plan B*?" Marc muttered.

"No. This wasn't supposed to happen, but we have passports and access to more than enough money. I've made your payments, so you can't complain. I don't think Trent or anyone else will suspect me of sabotage, but we'll have to wait it out in the islands until we see if our leaving raises any red flags with the authorities."

Kate couldn't believe Eden was responsible for the drywall and equipment changes. How could Eden think to sabotage the family company and hurt her son? It didn't make sense.

Marc put his arms around Eden's shoulders. "It could still work."

"It's not working if he's out of jail, and if he's not blamed for Blake's murder." Eden shrugged off Marc's hug. "Then everything I've done has failed."

Kate winced. Eden had wanted to pit Trent against Blake— It was more than obvious she hated her own son!

"Let's drop her in the water soon, Marc. I don't like this. Weigh her down with something heavy. I want to make sure she's never found."

Oh my God! They were going to kill her—now! Kate's heart tripped painfully in her chest.

"Throw her here? And have the authorities track the last cell phone call?" Marc asked sarcastically. "They'll put two and two together later, and remember we are out here in the yacht? They'll dredge the water and find her. No. When we get out to the ocean, we'll drop her by one of those concrete buoys where the fish like to feed. There the sharks will make quick work of her."

Fear sent chills through Kate. She nearly lost her control, but for the sake of staying alive she lay still and let them think she was out cold. She only took glances through the slits of her eyes.

Eden choked out a laugh. "You are ruthless, Marc, but she deserves it. I owe you."

"I plan to collect, Eden," Marc said in a low voice. "You know what I want."

"Marriage? Are you joking? I don't want another person controlling my life."

"It's your money I want to control, Eden. That's the deal—I want marriage or else."

Eden poked her finger into his chest. "Are you threatening me? You work for me."

"Either that or I want double what you owe me—ten million dollars," he told her.

"I don't have access to the kind of money you're demanding and won't if we don't get away with this. I'll be stuck out of the country forever. All because that bitch ruined my plans. He was supposed to marry Cecilia and bring my bloodline into the family, and then I wanted him *dead*."

"As you say, Eden, but when everything is back on track with our plans, I mean to collect. We have a deal." Marc's voice was flat when he added, "We need to get far away before daybreak."

Kate's head ached badly. Was she dreaming? Why would Trent's mother hate him? They turned away and Kate could barely hear them.

After a while, she assumed from the different type of movement that they were out in the ocean. She no longer saw buildings from her position on the floor. All she could see were stars, while the yacht rolled over larger waves.

"She's awake," Eden hissed.

Kate winced that she'd been caught.

The ship-to-shore radio beeped.

"Answer it," Marc snapped. "Be careful what you say."

Eden clicked on the radio.

"Oh, that's marvelous, Trent... I'm sorry about what I said to the police about you hating Blake... No, I haven't seen, Kate. Oh, dear, I hope you find her." Eden rolled her eyes at Kate.

Throwing an accusing glare at the woman, Kate struggled with her bonds and tried to scream through the gag, "*Trent, help me,*" but it was useless as her words were muffled. Tears trickled down the sides of her face and despair overcame her.

He wouldn't know she was on his own family's yacht—or that she really loved him in spite of everything. They'd kill her and she'd never see him again.

"Kate told me that she heard you discuss with your grandfather about ending your marriage," his mother said into the radio. "She said something about leaving town. Perhaps she already did. Anyway, darling, don't worry. Even though I never thought Kate was right for you, call me when you locate her. I wouldn't want anything to happen to that dear girl."

After Eden hung up, Marc murmured, "Good job."

"I'm sure the bastard believed me. He said she'd told him the same thing and perhaps she did want the divorce. That maybe she *did* leave him."

Kate's hopes that Trent would come after her, sank like her chance to live if they threw her into the water with a weight.

Eden strode to Kate, bent over her, and roughly dragged the gag from her mouth. "Now, you may scream all you want. No one will hear you."

"Why?" Kate asked in a hoarse whisper. "You're his mother. How can you hate him so much?"

"Oh, you think a *mother's* love is special? Think about that when you've sunk to the floor of the Atlantic Ocean—food for sharks. As you sink, think about just how much I love my dear Trent."

Sheer fright spiraled through Kate. She had to convince this maniac to keep her alive. "What if I'm carrying your grandchild? I might be pregnant."

"So, Marc," Eden said sweetly as she crouched beside Kate. "Let's hide her away somewhere safe …until my grandchild is born. Does that work for you, Kate?" Eden's words belied the angry look on her face.

Kate nodded emphatically. "Yes. Please don't kill me."

Eden grabbed Kate's hair and yanked back her head. "Just to let you know, this is what I think of Trent having a baby with you." She stomped her foot on Kate's stomach. At the excruciating pain shooting through her, Kate doubled over onto her side. Hot tears burned the back of her eyes. If there had been a remote chance she was pregnant, this might have ended it.

"I…don't…understand," Kate said through her sobs, swallowing hard as the waves of pain ebbed.

"Shut up, bitch. Trent isn't my son. He's the whoreson of the woman who stole my husband. His grandfather forced me to adopt and raise Trent as my own. It's high time I repaid them both."

"Does Trent know?"

"He hasn't a clue—the stupid bastard."

"But you raised him. You must love him."

"I was around him as little as possible. I detest him." Eden pursed her lips. "I had no idea at first you were Jackson's stepsister, but it was lucky for me that Marc recognized you poking around at the site. He'd seen you at the funeral for your brother. So I had you investigated. Marc left the Halloween mask on the fence to frighten you to leave the company, but you weren't buying that we were serious. You should have. Now, you die."

"But you can't kill me."

"I will because it *will* hurt Trent." She chuckled. "I hate the bastard, but you won't get the chance to tell him how much I do, Kate. He'll get over you, and if he doesn't go to jail, he'll marry Cecilia. If she hadn't been in the car with you, Marc would have rammed you off the road at the overpass."

"So that's why he stopped… He saw Cecilia in the car."

Eden smirked. "If Trent goes to jail for Blake's murder and yours, all the better. I want the bastard to suffer before he dies. Hopefully, Trent will get the death sentence."

Kate clamped her mouth shut. She hoped Trent would put the facts together and realize Eden hated him—before it was too late.

Eden turned to Marc. "It's time to get this done. We're out in the ocean. Get rid of her. Tie her to an anchor and throw her in like you did Carr."

"Stephen Carr…he was my brother's supervisor. *You killed my brother!*" Kate cried.

Marc left the helm. "He questioned the equipment orders so he had to go. I swapped his harness with a damaged one a week earlier and then pushed him. His damned supervisor found me on the site and figured out what I'd done. As for Carr, he was okay with looking the other way, as long as he was paid. He was already stealing from the company, but he was gullible. I told him I'd pay him to keep his mouth shut and he could quit working. Worked for a while, until he got greedy. I convinced him to take a ride with me in the yacht. Got him drunk. I gave him a one way ticket to hell at the bottom of the ocean. Like you're gonna get."

Marc crouched beside Kate and leaned over her. She stared into eyes so flat it seemed he had no soul. He touched her hair. "What a beautiful babe. It's a shame to kill you outright. You deserve more." He ran his hands through strands of her hair that had long since come loose.

Kate jerked her head away.

"Your hair's like fine silk and so long." He lifted a strand to his nose, then his mouth turned downward. "Your scent... I know your type. You taunt a man with your looks. Twist his head in a vice." Marc hauled Kate to her feet and swung her over his shoulder.

Kate's heart pounded. "What? No, no! Please...*please*, don't throw me in!"

He kept on walking. She fought like crazy, jabbing him with her shoulders and trying to bite him, even head butting him...until she realized he was taking her toward the staterooms.

"Where are you taking me?" Kate cried out.

"Yes, damn it," Eden snapped, following behind them. "Where are you taking her? Tie the anchor to her and throw that bitch overboard."

Marc shouted, "Eden, drive. I have to prepare her first. Follow the arrows on the GPS. We're headed to the islands." He kept on walking.

Fright shot through Kate as he took her into a large elegant stateroom with mahogany walls. He threw her onto the king-sized bed. He turned on the bright lights and hovered over her.

"What are you doing?" she asked.

"Too many questions. I'll have to shut you up."

He slammed his fist into her jaw. Blackness overtook her.

* * *

When she regained consciousness, Kate found herself still in the stateroom. Her arms were raised and she was tied by her wrists to a chandelier. The raw material of the rope cut into her skin. Her feet dangled off the ground. Her jacket and shirt were gone. She still had on her bra. For a brief moment, she'd wondered if the worst had happened, but she still wore her skirt and tights and didn't feel like she'd been molested.

Someone help me. She wanted to scream, but there was no one to help. No one was going to rescue her—particularly not Trent. She had to find her way out of this herself. She hadn't even had a chance to ponder a way to escape when the cabin door swung open.

Marc entered, eating a hunk of cheese. He waved a bottle of wine in her face. "Like some?"

Kate's heart beating at a rapid tempo, she shook her head.

"Oh, come on. Cat got your tongue? Sure, you'll have a drink. All sluts like booze."

The way he had tied her, she hung by her wrists. With his tall height, she was two inches below his eye level and her feet dangled off the ground.

He yanked her head back by her hair, and poured wine into her mouth. "It's Farrington's finest. It's your fault you're here, you know. You have to pay for your sins for looking the way you do—twisting a man all up inside."

Marc ran his hand down her sides and leaned in. He touched his nose to her skin. "Ah, delicious. The boss insists I dump your ass in the ocean, but I got turned on just touching your hair. I wanted you the first time I saw you. It would have been quicker for you if I drowned you right away. I'd planned to resist you—but you provoked me. It's not nice to taunt a man so he can't think straight. I knew I had to have a piece of you first. The way I like it, bloody and begging me for every inch."

He clamped his hand on her waist.

"No." Kate tried to hit him with the spike of her high-heeled shoe, but only scraped his pants leg.

He yanked off her shoe. "You force me to do this, but you won't be able to tempt any more men. Don't worry about drowning later, you'll be dead before you hit the water."

"No," she cried.

He placed the knife at her throat and scratched the blade across her skin. He didn't cut her, but she took the warning and ceased struggling.

Marc ran his hand up her side. "Nice bruises. From your husband?"

When she didn't respond, he held the knife to her breast, "Answer when I ask a question," he snapped.

"No!"

He chuckled. "Ha! Fooled you. I know they're from when I tried to run you off the road. You wouldn't be alive if Mrs. Farrington's pet Cecilia hadn't been in the car. Now your lesson begins. It's what you deserve, taunting me with that face and with that ass."

"I don't taunt anyone."

"If I say you do—you damn well better agree." He slipped a rope loosely around Kate's neck and tied the ends to the chandelier. "Here are the rules, when I ask a question, you respond and you say 'yes, sir.' Do you understand?"

Trembling, she nodded.

"You forgot 'yes, sir.' Failure to follow orders…" He made a tiny cut on her chest. Kate cried out. "Like this and then *cut*." He reached up and sawed just a little through the rope that bound her hands. "My game of 'chicken' for sluts. You don't want your hands to become untied now, or it's, '*tada,*' you'll hang by your neck. Your choice is to accept me as your commanding officer and obey orders."

He trailed his lips over the two-inch scar on her abdomen just above the edge of her skirt. "Nice scar."

Kate shivered with revulsion.

He drew the knife around her skin, seeming to take delight at playing with the blade where her breasts mounded over her bra. She raised her knee to kick him, but couldn't get any leverage.

"Rules are rules. You lose on that one. You know, eventually this rope will give." He sawed a little more through the rope that bound her hands. "So you have two choices, and after you're marked, and you beg me to cut you down, you'll do anything I ask."

Kate trembled as he lowered the knife to her neck. "I'm studying to be a psychologist. I can get you the help you need. I'll do whatever you want. Just let me down and we'll talk—"

"*Doctors?*" he roared. He raised the knife to her lips. "Talk like that again and those will be the last words you ever speak out loud. *Do you hear me?*" he shouted those last words in her face.

She nodded weakly. "Yes, sir."

Marc lowered the knife again, trailing down her skin to her skirt. "You should already be at the bottom of the ocean," he said, more calmly, "but you provoked me, didn't you?"

"Yes, sir," she whispered, shaking with fear. Her arms ached, from her weight and from lack of circulation.

"Do everything I say and I'll cut you down, alive—at least for a while. Makes no difference to me."

He was going to torture her, rape her, and kill her, and she didn't even know in which order. And there was nothing she could do to escape. Her pepper spray was in her jacket, and even if her hands were free, the rope hung around her neck like a noose...

Marc ran his palms up her stomach and touched the fabric between her bra cups. With the knife, he sawed at the thin material.

His eyes lit with excitement. "Don't move or I might accidentally cut you." He chuckled. "We wouldn't want that to happen. I'll get you out of the rest of your clothes and then you can pay for your sins for seducing me, slut. I'll tell you just how bad of a girl you've been... And then when I'm ready..." Marc chuckled as if making a joke. "I'll give you a special gift for Christmas."

CHAPTER TWENTY-SEVEN

Trent steered the speedboat away from port. He hoped Eden and Marc would believe that he searched elsewhere so they could overtake the yacht. He didn't want them to know he suspected them and was on their tail. Thanks to the secret GPS tracking units installed on all Farrington boats, the recovery feature would help him find them in the night.

Several hours before dawn, the ocean traffic held only a few boats going in the same direction. He had to get to the yacht before daylight.

Gaining on them, he spotted a yacht's running lights in the distance. The device on his console indicated the vessel was his grandfather's yacht.

Trent pushed the engines to a higher speed. "Roland, radio the Coast Guard and the police department and tell them we've arrived. I can't wait and I'm taking the dingy and going in." Trent released a deep breath. "Now I just have to hope I can surprise Marc and Eden and rescue Kate, which might not happen if the Coast Guard arrives first."

He was thankful for the light traffic on the water this morning. While he'd never get the speedboat near the yacht without being detected by the yacht's surveillance system, he might be able to get there undercover in the rubber dingy. He grabbed his weapons and a flare gun and put them in the pockets of his jacket.

* * *

At a knock on the stateroom door, Marc stopped humming 'Mary had a Little Lamb' and stopped sawing at the fabric of Kate's bra. She sagged with relief.

He opened the door and let Eden into the cabin.

"Why the hell do you have her hanging from the chandelier?" Eden planted her hands on her hips and threw him a nasty look. "Damn it. Are you losing your marbles? Throw her in the water before daylight as we agreed. We've got to get rid of her, and you have to drive. There are more boats out there, and something's going on with one of the engines."

The man headed out the door. "Queen Bee, I told you I'd take care of her. Now, get back to the helm and drive the boat, while I check the engine room."

Once the door closed behind them, Kate, who'd nearly been hyperventilating, caught her breath. She had to get loose. She stretched her fingers and managed to grip a metal part of the chandelier. She swung her legs, trying to rip the light fixture from the ceiling, but it held fast.

* * *

Trent motored the dingy alongside the yacht and cut the engine. Thankfully, it was still dark, but soon the sun would be coming up over the horizon. He had one chance at this. With the dingy line in one hand, he jumped onto the back diving platform of the yacht, then tied the dingy to the stern of the boat.

He climbed up the ladder and headed down the walkway on the port side. Marc Simpson and Eden came out of his grandfather's stateroom. Trent hid in the shadows as they continued walking in the opposite direction. They parted ways when Marc opened the door to the engine room and disappeared inside. His mother walked on toward the pilot house.

Where was Kate? His intuition bristling, he opened the door to his grandfather's stateroom. Tied by her wrists, Kate dangled from the chandelier in the middle of the room. Her shirt off, a tiny rivulet of blood stained her bra and ran down her stomach.

"Kate!"

"Trent!" she cried.

He rushed to her and clasped her in his arms, supporting her. "What the hell? Let me get you down. Wrap your legs around me to take some of your weight, and I'll cut the rope."

"Hurry, he might be back any minute."

"I'll do this as fast as I can." Trent began sawing through the rope around her neck.

She sagged against him. "Your mother...she wants to kill me! And *you!*"

"I know. Who else besides her and Marc is on the boat?"

"Just your mother and her assistant, I think."

Once the rope around her neck was cut lose, he began sawing at the rope binding her hands to the chandelier. "Are you all right? Did he hurt you?"

"No. I'm okay. But I didn't think you would come for me."

"Yes, and damn it, Kate, I didn't think I'd see you again. If you ever pull another stunt like that and go off to some place dangerous alone, my *brave* girl, I'll—"

"You'll do what, *Mr. Farrington*?" she said through chattering teeth.

"I'll reprimand you sternly and tell you to take me with you the next time," he said, finally cutting through the last of the bonds. "We're almost done." He blew out a breath of relief.

She chuckled through her tears, her face pressed against his chest. "I promise you I will."

Once he had finally freed her from the loosened ropes, he held her in a bear hug. "You sure, you're okay. He didn't hurt you?"

She shook her head. "Nothing serious, but he's crazy."

He nestled his face in her hair. "Let's get out of here." He slid her to the floor. "The dingy's at the back of the boat." She grabbed her discarded jacket and slipped it on.

Trent took the time to kiss her forehead. "Stay close behind me," he ordered as he opened the door. He kept her hand tightly in his.

The weather was serene, and the pink horizon indicated dawn was breaking. They crept down to the back of the boat and toward the dingy. "So far so good. You first, Kate," he whispered.

"Son of a bitch," Marc swore above them on the top deck. He raised his gun and fired. Shots whizzed by them. Trent and Kate ducked. Trent fired several rounds in Marc's direction and then his gun was out of ammunition. Marc fired and hit the dingy and it fizzled and slumped into a collapsed mushroom.

Trent took Kate's hand and they ran down the outside passage of the yacht on the starboard side. "We've got to find more weapons."

* * *

Minutes later, Marc was trampling down the stairs at the bow just as Trent located another gun. Kate's heart pounded ferociously.

"Put the gun down on the deck," he said waving his weapon toward Kate. "Or I'll shoot her, Farrington."

Trent gave Kate a pensive gaze, then laid the gun on the deck.

"To the helm." Marc marched them to the pilot house.

"Ship's on autopilot." Eden stepped onto the open decking. "Why, if isn't Trent? Didn't expect you." Hatred glittered in her eyes.

"You don't have time for long good-byes, Eden," Marc said in a cold voice. He reached into his jacket and handed her a gun. "You've been waiting. Take him out. He's all yours." He kept his arm tightly around Kate's shoulders and squeezed. "The girl is mine...for a while."

"Damn, Marc," Eden said. "I don't care how you get your thrills with women, but it's interfering with your business with me. Now, *you* shoot them both and get rid of them over the side. You were supposed to take care of this and not involve me."

"Trent, Eden hates you," Kate said, searching for words to distract them. "That's why she wanted me dead. It was to hurt you. Everything she's done—has been to hurt you. And she hired Marc to do it."

Trent eyed Kate for a second, then glanced at Eden. "My grandfather finally told me the truth. He coerced you into adopting me—and that made you hate me."

"You're right, you bastard, but you were too stupid to figure it out."

"Not too stupid that I didn't learn early on what a cold-hearted bitch you were."

Eden pursed her lips. "You've ruined everything, as usual. You were supposed to marry Cecilia."

"No, Eden, you've ruined everything for yourself. You don't want to go to prison for murder. Give it up. Roland is not far away in the speedboat. The Coast Guard will be here soon."

"You're lying," Eden snapped. "You take care of them both, Marc. That's what I'm paying you to do. I'll drive the boat."

Kate retrieved her keys with the pepper spray from her jacket pocket and aimed for Marc, but he slapped the device from her hands. "Puny. Doesn't work in the wind."

The pepper spray attempt was just enough of a distraction though. Trent jumped Marc. They rolled around on the deck, wrestling for the gun.

Her heart pounded at a rapid rate as Kate searched for a weapon. She opened a long white trunk and found fishing supplies. She grabbed a spear gun and a pole with a huge metal hook.

Marc wrestled the gun toward Trent's face. "You're going to die now, Farrington."

Afraid to use the spear gun because she might hit Trent, Kate set it aside and whacked the long, hooked end of the pole into Marc's back.

"Hell!" Blood spurted from Marc's wound and the device stayed implanted.

Trent forced the gun back toward Marc. A piercing shot rang in the morning air.

Marc struggled to his feet. A gunshot wound at his shoulder also bled profusely. He reached behind his back, trying to grasp the hook, but it was thoroughly lodged in his flesh. He gave up on trying to remove the hook. With anger etching his features, he pointed the gun toward Kate.

Fear ratcheted through Kate. She stared at the weapon and backed away.

A flare shot past her and rocketed into Marc's stomach. Marc's face gawked in surprise as he slammed back against the railing, then flipped over into the ocean below.

"Trent!" Kate cried. She looked and saw he had the flare gun in his hand. "You got him."

Eden stepped out of the helm room. "What the hell? *Marc?*" She aimed a gun at Trent and Kate. "Where is Marc?"

Weaponless now as the flare gun's one shot had been used, Trent and Kate backed away from Eden.

"Your grandfather manipulated me, just like the rest of you. Blake's been paid back for his treachery, and now you will be paid back, too. Your death will destroy James. I couldn't ask for anything more. Cecilia's pregnant with someone's child that I'll claim is yours, and we can keep this *bastard tradition* alive."

"Give it up. You'll never get away with killing us, Eden," Trent said. "The police know everything, and they're on the way."

The gun shook in her hand. "They can't prove anything."

"You have motive. You hated me and you hated Blake after he used you years ago to get company secrets. You tried to make him look like he sabotaged the company, when all along it was you and your assistant."

Eden shrugged. "I hoped you would kill each other. I'm glad Blake died at your hands."

"I didn't kill him," Trent blasted. "He fell on the scaffolding that Marc rigged because *you* hired him to sabotage the building. Now put down the gun, Eden. You don't even know how to use it."

Eden thrust the gun toward Trent's heart. "Pulling the trigger shouldn't be too hard. I didn't do all this to let you live and prosper, while I go to prison. I hate you. You, your grandfather, and your cheating father."

Eden cocked the gun. Her heart hammering, Kate rammed into Eden with all of her strength to block the gun's aim at Trent. The next thing Kate knew was excruciating, burning pain. So much, she fell to her knees.

Trent dropped beside her on the deck and put his arms around Kate. "Kate, no! Why did you do that?" She barely heard him through her anguish.

She clamped her hand over her upper arm. "I couldn't let her shoot you." she said, trembling all over.

He staunched the flow of blood.

"Enough of that nonsense," Eden snapped. She'd recovered and now pointed the gun at Trent.

Trent grasped the spear gun that lay nearby beside them on the deck and pointed it at Eden. "The Coast Guard is arriving. Put the gun down."

Eden glanced toward the horizon. The sun, coming up on the eastern horizon, sent fiery light across the water. The other Farrington boat was easily spotted on the ocean now. More boats were headed in their direction.

She shook the gun at them. "Not before you die—and I'll get away with it—or if I have to I'll launch one of the yacht's dingies. I'll say Marc was out to do us all in. That he worked for Blake. They'll believe me. That Mark killed my beloved son." She put the gun closer to Trent's head.

"Don't make me do this, Eden. I don't want to shoot you... I could have been your son—the son you wanted—but you just never loved me. In spite of everything and how you hated me, I loved you because you were my mother."

With a shaky hand, Eden pointed the gun at Trent. He aimed the spear gun at her as if equally determined.

Coast Guard's sirens blared. Their vessels roared toward the yacht and surrounded it. Bright lights flooded the yacht. Over a megaphone an officer yelled, "Drop your weapons. Put your hands over your head. Preparing to board."

Eden blew out a disgusted breath, "I can't go to prison... You wouldn't dare send me there."

She backed up and tripped. They watched her as if in slow motion as she soared backwards. She struck her head on the spike of the same anchor she and Marc had planned to use to drown Kate. Eden lay lifeless while blood pooled around her.

Kate trembled in relief as Trent encircled his arms around her and brought her face to his chest in a protective gesture to shield her from the horror.

CHAPTER TWENTY-EIGHT

An abundance of red roses abounded, and their sweet scent permeated Kate's living room in her little bungalow.

When the doorbell rang, Kate strode to the door. "Is he sending me more flowers?" she muttered to herself.

She opened the door. *Trent.* His Porsche was parked in the driveway.

"You're finished with the police already?" she asked shyly as she stepped outside onto the porch. It was a beautiful, tropical December day in South Florida.

"Yeah, and I'm looking for my wife."

"Trent, you don't have to do this. You can have the divorce or annulment. I'll sign the papers."

"I have other ideas of what I want to do with you." He pulled her down on his lap on the porch swing. "The Coast Guard couldn't find Marc Simpson's body. Although with all the blood he was losing, they think it's a sure thing the sharks got him."

Kate shuddered. "That's what he planned to do with me—feed me to the sharks."

"It's over, baby." He picked up her good hand and held it in his warm one. "You didn't have to risk your life for me by getting between a gun and a bullet, Kate. You could have been killed. Are you all right? Your arm, does it hurt?"

She lifted up her bandaged arm that was in a sling. "I'm okay. I didn't want to lose someone else that I... Uh, I didn't want anyone else to die."

"Say it, Kate? You didn't want to lose me. Say you love me, if you do...?"

Numbly, she nodded as tears rolled down her cheeks. "I love you, Trent. I couldn't bear it if something happened to you." She stared toward the road without seeing and raised her chin. "But I'm going to get on with my life, as I would have before I came here. I'm going back to school to become a psychologist. I want to help children. That's if you're not going to prosecute me for working at your company. You know I only practiced that one day with you—and you were in on it."

"I said that to scare you into staying with me—I couldn't let you go. Now look at me." When she did, he said, "Kate, *no divorce*—unless you really insist. I would have been here sooner, but I had to clear up everything with the police."

She frowned at him. "Can you forgive me for lying to get into the company?"

"Yeah, but forgive you? Forgive *me*. I should have listened to you earlier. I'm sorry, Kate. I was an idiot. And it an admirable thing you did, seeking justice for your brother, risking everything." He placed his arm around her, pulling her close. "And you found the killer, Kate—my own, so-called mother. She was never really a mother to me, and now I know why."

"How do you feel? Are you going to be all right?"

Trent nodded. "I only feel sorry for her, for the bitter life she led. My grandfather has asked for my forgiveness, too. And I said I'd give it to him. Partly, my covering up of how bad my relationship was with Eden, kept him from not really knowing all the details. He says he done with trying to manipulate others so he can have his way. Kate, he asks for your forgiveness as well."

"I'll give him mine gladly. Trent, I didn't expect she was the one sabotaging you." Kate laid her hand on his chest. "But I have to know that not only do you forgive me, but if you can trust me. If we don't have trust, we don't have anything, right? No future."

He cupped her cheek. "Kate, I trust you with my life—damn, you stepped into the path of a bullet for me, crazy woman. And I admit I was insanely jealous of Blake or anyone when it came to you."

"And your mother and my stepfather—wow. All I can say is that we didn't luck out in the parent department."

Trent nodded. "I'm just glad it's over. We're lucky." He pulled her close to him and lowered his lips to hers. Heat swirled through her. Moments later, he lifted his lips from hers with a groan. She gasped, not wanting their mouths to part.

"Kate, I love you. And as your husband, I want you to tell me everything your stepfather did to you, and then we'll forget it—or go to therapy. We can go spit on his grave every year if you'd like, but I'd rather you forget him."

"I'd like to let it go, too. You already know the worst. Most of my growing up was sheer neglect. I still remember being about five and standing on a chair cooking dinner over the stove, wearing a long robe. It's a wonder I didn't catch on fire. Mostly, Matt and I just tried to stay out of my stepfather's way, especially when things weren't going well for him. Then he was a monster."

"If I can help it, no one will ever hurt you again. You're my sweet, brave Kate. I want us to be happy and grow old together."

Tears misted in her eyes. "Let's do."

He blew out a deep breath and retrieved a folded paper from his pocket. "The prenuptial agreement."

When he started to tear it, she grabbed his hand. "You don't have to do that."

He continued to rip up the paper. "We are *not* going to start over in our very *real* marriage with something like this between us. I'll give the same amount that's mentioned in the prenuptial agreement to the Center as a wedding gift."

Kate gasped. "They'll be able to help more children."

He put his arm around her and squeezed. "I know how important that is to you, and I want to help children, too. You can make it your own project, if you want." His dark gaze lowered to her lips. All she wanted was to melt into his dark eyes. "However, there is something I want from you, Kate, in return. A proper honeymoon. A long luxurious one with just the two of us, with nothing to do but love each other."

She felt warm beneath his gaze. When he took her mouth in another searing kiss, she thought she would burn up in a blaze of desire. His fingers trailed up her arm and covered her breast. She moaned.

After some time, he lifted his lips from hers. "Why don't you pack for a month? Whatever else we need, we'll buy."

"As long as it's not on the yacht," she teased.

"Not for a long while." He rose from the swing. "It's Christmas time. Not much work gets done this time of the year, and I want to give Roland a chance to handle the company."

She stood beside him. "That's generous of you."

"He has to earn his way out of this for what he did. This is a first step. I think we all deserve a second chance and with Eden now dead, along with your stepfather, we have a chance to be a real family." He pulled her close and gazed down at her. "Now, why don't we get out of here before I take you into the bedroom, and we don't get any further?"

She reached up and pulled his face down for a kiss. "We'll get to our honeymoon trip, but let's start here, or I'm sure we won't get beyond the car—and it's kind of small."

"Let's begin all over again." He extended his hand to Kate. "Hello, I'm Trent Farrington. Architect, engineer."

She smiled at the absurdity. "All right. I'm Kate Meyers Farrington. I plan to one day be a psychologist and help abused children. It's so nice to meet you."

"I want a large family." He swung her up in his arms and carried her toward the door.

"Trent, what will the neighbors think?"

"They'll think we're in love. And we'd better get started. We need to have lots of kids so we don't have to force one of them to marry to continue *our* dynasty."

She smiled. "How about four…*or six*?"

He laughed. "Or a dozen? Whatever you want. No one would be any happier than my grandfather and me."

****

ABOUT THE AUTHOR

Debra Andrews writes **"Glitzy, Sexy, Romances with a Dangerous Twist,"** with strong, smart women and the handsome heroes who fall in love with them. Her books include romance, suspense, action-adventure, drama, humor, and always an emotional, knock-your-socks-off romance. Embark on their adventures, filled with danger and mystery, while each woman falls in love with the man of her dreams.

The standalone, romantic-suspense stories featured are part of the **ROMANCING WITH DANGER Series** and can be read in any order. The men are distant cousins bonded together by their uncle, and patriarch of the family, billionaire James Farrington.

****

MORE ABOUT DEBRA'S BOOKS

Thank you for reading *DISGUISED WITH THE MILLIONAIRE* (Romancing with Danger Series). I hope you enjoyed the story.

If you would like to help others find this book, leave a review on **Amazon.com**, **Goodreads.com**. Even a line or two makes a difference and is greatly appreciated by an author.

Stay connected and sign up for our newsletter.

http://www.debraandrewsauthor.com

BOOKS AVAILABLE BY DEBRA ANDREWS IN THE ROMANCING WITH DANGER SERIES:
(Books can be read in any order and are standalone stories)

WEEKEND WEDDING DECEPTION
DANGEROUS PARADISE
DISGUISED WITH THE MILLIONAIRE
HIS WYOMING LAIR (coming soon!)